GARDEN

OF

NAILS

Anne Biggs

PARADIGM
HALL PRESS

HBE PUBLISHING

Dedication

To Billy
I did it. I really did it,
but not without you.

One

On a chilly Boston evening, I left our marriage bed and slipped outside. My bare feet clung to the damp cement of the patio, as I gazed out over the backyard, and let the cold settle into my skin. The damp air awakened my senses.

Michael consumed my thoughts. There was a time I would have never left his arms; never left his warmth.

Times change.

I changed...

The rain began to fall, and I slipped back inside to sit at the hearth, watching as the fire dwindled to ashes.

Michael's face took shape in the coals, small flames danced in the embers, fixing my gaze with their intensity. The cut of his jaw exposed his anger. Through the heat of the fire, his eyes seared me.

Just past two, I slipped back to bed, pulling the sheets over my shoulders.

Late night awakenings were assumed seductions. I waited for Michael to reach for me and cringed as he pressed into the curve of my back. His hand clutching my breast.

My cell phone vibrated across the nightstand. I grabbed it to keep from disturbing Michael any more than I already had. I stumbled in to the hall, knowing how late-night calls always meant something terrible. My stomach tightened as I looked at the picture.

"Catherine, it's Claire, Francie asked me to call. Your mum's had a bit of an accident."

"What does Izzy want now?" Michael asked, calling from the bedroom.

"It's not Izzy. It's Claire, Mum's friend. Go back to sleep, I'll be right there."

I knew I wouldn't. Calls from Claire were never short.

"Call her back in the morning. Come back to bed."

"Michael, let me talk." My throat tightened. "Something happened to Mum. I'll be there in a minute."

I went downstairs as Claire gave me the details of Mum's accident. I could see her gestures, as she laid out the bits and pieces of the accident.

"Your Mum hasn't been doing well for a while. I don't know if your sisters have told you, but she's been confused. The day before yesterday, they found her in the park behind the house, walking around, crying uncontrollably."

"My God. Is she all right?"

"A jogger called the Guardia." Her voice softened as she continued. "He saw her walking in circles, calling out a girl's name, clutching at the arms of strangers, begging anyone for word of a girl named Finn. She fell, and hit her head on a bench. The Guardia called for an ambulance.

"I should have been there." Claire began to cry and I couldn't understand anything she said.

"Claire, slow down. I can't understand a word you're saying. Where is she now?"

"No one knew who she was—she was in emergency for almost six hours, before anyone called."

"Where is she now?"

"Still in hospital. Come home, Catherine. Your Mum needs you."

Stepping onto the patio, I listened as Claire continued through her tears. The rain had slowed to a drizzle.

"What are they doing for her?"

Claire regained her composure and I could hear her deep breaths. "They're keeping her for observation, with the fall and all."

"Why didn't Rose or Francie call?"

Then I heard the words again. "Catherine, come home. Francie hasn't left her side, and Rose is driving the doctors crazy. Your mum needs you here."

"How is she? Is she able to talk?" I nibbled on the jagged edge of my nail.

"She doesn't remember anything. She wants to go home, but the doctor is reluctant to release her. I'm guessing he has some concerns about her being home alone."

"Claire, you said she called out a name?"

"They said, Finn."

"Who is that?" I found myself at a loss.

"I don't know." Claire seemed hesitant. "When can you come?"

"I need to talk to Michael."

"Catherine, what is there to talk about? I'll send you money if you need it."

Claire's voice trailed to a jumble in my mind. I knew they'd keep Mum in the hospital long enough to check for a concussion or any internal injuries, but what would happen after the tests? Who would watch her? What if it's dementia? I needed to be with my sisters.

"Claire, listen. What did the doctor say?"

"He didn't say much, just that tests have been run. Rose is bossing everyone around. Poor Francie, she and Paddy are just sitting at her bedside, holding her hand, and trying not to cry. You need to come."

As the words spilled over the telephone, my heart ached, imagining Mum so helpless, "I don't know." I heard the reluctance in my voice.

"Michael won't let you?"

"It's not like that. There's a lot going on right now," I said, sitting in the lounge chair.

"Catherine, your mum needs you... so do your sisters."

"I'm just not sure when I can come."

"Don't wait too long."

I clicked off the phone, lay back in the chair and closed my eyes. I had to take this one step at a time. Mum wandering around the park, Rose driving the doctors crazy, and Francie trying to keep everything together.

I curled up in the chair and let my thoughts float back to when she took hold of my hand, squeezed it tight, and asked what brought me out on such a cold night.

"Michael wants to take me to Boston."

"And?" Mum brushed her hair back. "You're all grown up, but you sit in my garden as you did a wee girl."

"I'm afraid."

"When have you ever been afraid?

"They have attorneys, and houses, and children in Boston, don't they? Everything we have here?"

"It's not as simple as that— I'll be leaving home. I'll be leaving you."

"Maybe it is time to leave. I don't have the answer. You need to tell him what's in your heart. Don't deny him your truth because of fear."

"Would you have gone with Da?"

She wrapped her woolen collar up around her neck and pulled me close under her arm. "I'd have gone across the world with him."

"Maybe Michael doesn't love me enough, or maybe I don't love him enough?"

"Only you can answer that." She kissed the top of my head.

I found myself jarred back to my life when the dogs barked. Mum's garden held so many memories. As I looked out over the back yard, I realized I had tried to re-create them. Although I had everything I needed, I was missing something. I had no idea how to fill the hole in my soul. I needed to go home to mend my heart.

Two

I snuck back to bed and burrowed under the covers.

"What happened?" he asked, wrapping his arms around me, lacing our fingers together.

"Mum wandered away from the house and fell. They found her in the park. She's in the hospital." I whispered into the air.

He let go of my hands and brushed strands of hair from my face, then turned me toward him. I gathered my arms to my chest, he slipped his hand under my gown.

"Michael it's late."

"Come on, you're awake, aren't you?" His body inched closer. Even after so many years, I would have yielded to his touch. He drew me closer and ran his hands down the inside of my thighs. I wanted to be exhilarated. I wanted the sensation. I wanted to be hypnotized. But, too much had happened; too much we couldn't take back.

"What's wrong?" He asked, squeezing my breast to arouse me.

"Did you hear what I said about Mum? She wandered off. She's in a hospital."

"Well there is nothing you can do about it now. She's safe, right? Come on, baby."

"Michael, I can't do this. I can't just have sex, whenever. My mind is on my mother alone in some hospital. What's wrong with you?"

"OK, OK. Tell me what happened. Is she all right?"

"No, she isn't." I felt the rise in my voice. "She wandered off and got lost in the park. She was calling out for someone," I said, pulling myself up in bed.

"Who?"

"Finn."

"Who's that?"

"I don't know. Claire didn't either."

"Why did Claire call?" Michael questioned, pulling me back toward him.

"Michael, stop it."

"Isn't Claire your mother's friend? Why didn't your sisters call?"

"I don't know. It doesn't matter." I felt my frustration building. "She said Francie asked her to call because she didn't want to leave Mum alone. What does it matter?"

"You're giving me a pretty shabby excuse. What about Rose?"

I got up from the bed and turned toward him, only seeing his silhouette in the evening light. "Michael, it doesn't matter who called."

"It does. How can you be so stupid?"

"I'm not stupid. Claire's been family for as long as I can remember."

"But she isn't 'blood' family. You have an outsider calling about your sick mother."

"Why do you do that?" I pushed back my hair and sat on the edge of the bed.

"Do what? I'm not doing anything? I'm just pointing out the truth. Clearly, your family doesn't care enough to personally call."

"Do you realize how much your words hurt?" I dropped my head, not wanting to deal with him.

"All I asked, Cathy.... Why didn't your sisters call?" I recognized his tone. I'd heard it too many times.

Did he mean what he said? Did I mean so little that they made an outsider call? No— Claire was not an outsider. She'd always been family. I wouldn't let him fool me again.

"I have to go home."

"I thought here was home."

"You know what I mean, Michael. Don't do this."

He leaned over, pulling me toward him, trying to kiss me as if nothing had happened. He pulled on my arm to roll me toward him, but I jerked away.

"Come on, baby."

"Michael, stop." I pulled myself up on the bed. "She's my mother."

"And you went back a year ago. For Jonathan...."

I froze at the stinging tone of his voice. *How is it he could always cut me at the knees?*

"You knew what Jonathan meant to our family, and that's how you think of him?"

"I didn't mean it that way. Just, you were gone longer than you said."

I propped myself against the headboard, and flipped on the light. I stared into the cold blue eyes that had once mystified me.

"Tell me you're not that selfish or that jealous."

"I needed you here." He sat back as well.

"Jesus, Michael, you had to go to a fucking dinner party, alone. You said everyone understood."

"Do you hear yourself?"

"Yes. You're being ridiculous, trying to make me feel bad because I want—no, I need to go home."

He reached into the drawer and took out a cigarette. "Don't ever talk to me like that again."

"Why? I'm telling you the truth, Michael. I'm going home."

"Just tell me this. What can you do that your family can't? They're already there. Besides if she gets worse, or does something crazy, they'll put her away—that'll be the end of it."

"She's not crazy, Michael. How dare you say something like that? What is wrong with you? My mother is sick. She is not crazy. There's a big difference."

"That's even more of a reason why you don't need to go."

"That doesn't even make sense."

"What would you do?"

"Whatever she needed. I'd only be gone a while." I felt my throat tighten, struggling to remain calm. *I would not let my frustration slip out.* The smoke from his cigarette swirled above our heads. I had hated the smell when he started, but at that moment, I'd have sold my soul for one.

"This is not a good time, Cathy."

"It's never a good time. Give me one good reason."

"It's too expensive— for the flight and all."

"I don't need your money, Michael."

"Then how do you expect to buy a ticket?"

"I've been able to put quite a bit aside from working at the Center. Madeline paid me cash when I helped prepare court docs. I opened an account, and the money has added up."

"There is no way you have enough to buy an airline ticket."

"I have more than enough. I never spent any."

"You mean you had money, but you spent mine on all the crap you buy."

"No, I spent your money to pay our bills. I saved for emergencies, in case any of us needed it."

He didn't like the loss of control. His jaw tightened, his eyes narrowed, "You bitch."

"What? I didn't do anything. I never spent any of the money. I put it aside for whatever comes up. You knew I had it. I never hid anything from you."

"OK, fine. You have money. Look, she'll be in the hospital for a while, right? Just wait until they make a decision, then if you have to go, we'll go together."

"I'm not waiting, Michael. You're being ridiculous."

"No, I'm being realistic. Look, I didn't say you couldn't go, just wait until her condition is clearer."

"How is that realistic?"

"Don't blow it out of proportion, Cathy. I don't see why you have to jump the minute somebody calls."

"Good God, Michael. I'm not jumping for anyone." I turned back to him.

"Maybe Claire exaggerated her condition."

"It doesn't matter Michael. I'm going."

"No, you're not."

"I don't want to fight about this. Don't you think we should be thinking about my mother right now?

"I'm going home, Michael." I straightened the sheet and blanket, then took hold of the comforter.

Anne Biggs

"Your mother will be fine. She has family there."

"I'm her family, too." I turned toward him. He paused. There were tight lines in his face, his knuckles relaxed, and he pushed his fingers through his gray hair.

I sat down on the bed and watched as he moved toward my side.

"How long will you be gone?" He asked, calming his voice and taking a knee in front of me.

"I'll come home when she's better."

"What if...?" He took hold of my knees.

"This is not your decision. It's my family."

"Don't you think you should pay attention to the family you have here? I thought you loved me."

"This has nothing to do with my loving you."

It came so fast. I felt the sting before I even saw his hand. I touched the growing puffiness of my cheek, feeling heat beneath my fingers.

I got up from the bed, and shoved past him to the open window.

"Come on, Cathy." He grabbed hold of my arm. "You have to understand where I'm coming from."

The heat radiated from my face. I jerked free and moved from the window to the mirror and saw the red marks take shape.

"I told you," I said, unable to turn toward him because I couldn't hold back the tears. "If you ever hit me again..."

"You made me, Cathy. You know I didn't mean it."

"Yes, you did Michael," I said, still holding my burning cheek.

He went into the bathroom, slamming the door. I went

down stairs to the kitchen, took up a glass and the whiskey bottle, and thundered out the back door.

I sank down on the lounge and stared up at the clouds rolling over the stars. Alone, with my legs tucked under me, I sipped the whiskey slowly, hoping to become numb, to lose myself in its sweetness.

Before I heard his voice, I felt his hand on my thigh. I knew his touch, and for a moment I wanted him to take me in his arms, help me forget what he had said... and done. Instead, I pulled away.

"You all right?" He patted my leg, and I felt the weight of him as he sat on the lounge.

"How do you think I am?"

"I didn't mean it that way. God, how do you do that? You turn everything around." He tried to reach out again, but I pushed him away.

"I turn everything around?"

"You made me do it."

"Are you kidding? I told you if you ever hit me...."

"I just want you here," he said. "You get all messed up when you go to Ireland. Can't you just wait to see how she does?"

"You mean, wait until Francie calls to tell me Mum's dead?"

"I didn't mean that either." He turned away from me.

"Jesus, Michael, you keep saying things, then you tell me you don't mean them. Your words tear me apart. What the hell do you mean?" He got up from the chair and folded his hands across his chest.

"Look..."

"What, Michael?"

"Of course, you can go."

"You're giving me permission? Aren't you generous."

He threw up his hands. "I can't win, can I? If I say no, I'm a bastard, if I say yes, I'm overbearing. Do whatever you want, Cathy. I've never been able to stop you."

"You stop me every day. Regardless, I'm going home." In the distance, a horn blew, and the night air froze around me.

Without another word, Michael left me alone with the stars.

Three

The slamming of the front door announced Izzy's arrival. The scent of lavender, preceding her steps, echoing across the hardwood of the foyer.

"Where is everyone?"

"Kitchen—you're late."

"Only fifteen minutes. That's early for me."

Michael sat in the living room, reading the paper, vodka-seven on the end table. She swept in behind him, threw her arms around his neck, and scattered the paper across the floor. I watched from the kitchen doorway, and couldn't help but smile. Isabelle, our only child, had always been able to wrap her father around any finger she chose.

"Hey Dad," she whispered in his ear. "You miss me?"

"Always. What's the occasion? I haven't seen you in two weeks."

"Well, I have some news, and Mom mentioned a free dinner. So, here I am."

"So, what's your news?" He reached around, patting her arm.

"Nope, sorry, you'll have to wait until dinner, when I can tell you both."

"Well then, sit down. How've you been?"

"Just busy with work, and classes, of course. What are you up to?"

From the kitchen I heard their banter. Tonight, would focus on Izzy and her life. No repeat of the dramatics of last night.

Growing up, Izzy understood her father far better than I ever could, but she'd only tolerate just so much of his arrogance.

"Come on you two, dinner is ready. What do you want to drink, beer?"

"Sounds good."

"Mom, this is great. Been a while since I've had a home-cooked meal."

Izzy moved the plates around the table, as I filled them with roast, pilaf, and broccoli, her favorite. We paused, said Grace, then for a few minutes, ate in silence. I sipped white wine, Izzy and Michael drank their beer from identical mugs. She told him about selling her paintings at the gallery and he nodded his approval.

"All right, Izzy, we're well into dinner, what's going on? Do you need money?"

"Why do you do that?" Izzy asked, her voice rising, then she calmed when she heard the echo of her words.

"Why do I do what?"

"Always assume the worst."

"You sound like your mother," he said with a grimace.

She slammed her mug on the table, so hard the beer

spilled onto the tablecloth. "You make people feel small. No, that's not right. You make me feel small."

"No, I don't."

"Yes...you do." Pausing, she glanced at me. I grabbed her hand to stop her.

"Izzy, why don't you tell us your news?"

She looked at Michael waiting, her face firm with resolve.

"I'm sorry, Izzy, I didn't mean that," Michael added. "Tell us what's going on."

"OK, I don't want you to say anything until I'm done." I watched her take a deep breath. "I'm going back to Dublin. I finished my work at Emerson, and I've been accepted at The Institute of Art and Design on a scholarship."

Michael put his fork down and pushed his plate away. "Well, imagine that. When did all this come about?" Michael glared at me.

"I doubled up on my courses and applied to the institute last spring."

"Izzy, that's wonderful, but why didn't you tell us?" I asked, feeling an immense pride for my girl.

"I wanted to be sure everything worked out before I said anything."

"Did you get in some kind of trouble?" Michael asked, taking another bite.

"God, you're doing it again I try to tell you something good, and you turn it around, like I did something wrong."

"Well, excuse me for caring," he stated sarcastically. "I'm sorry." He acted like someone had brought him the wrong order at a restaurant, rather than talking about life-changing events.

"No, you're not. You do it all the time. You even do it to Mom...especially to Mom."

"What are you talking about?" Michael raised his eyes to my level, then almost squinted. His look of shock disappeared.

"I know what you've done. I can see the bruises. She tried to cover them with make-up."

Izzy moved from her chair and took my face in her hand. I got up and tried to smooth out the tablecloth, to deflect the direction of the conversation. Then it came.

"What happened, Dad? Look at her face, it's red." I pulled away from her touch, and put my hand to my cheek. "I know she didn't fall."

I stood there in a daze, trying to figure out how to deny it in front of Michael. "Oh no," I said, running my hand across my face. "It's just shadows."

"Mom, what happened?" She asked again. "I can see it. It's not shadows, it looks like you were hit."

I moved away from the table. Michael just sat there. Drinking his beer.

"You didn't do a very good job covering it."

"What happened?" She turned toward her father this time.

"It was nothing, Izzy."

"You did this, didn't you, Dad." She didn't wait for an answer. "God dammit, I knew it."

"Izzy, this has nothing to do with you." The look on his face changed, his jaw tightened, and he ran his hand across his mouth.

"Tell her, Cathy. It was an accident."

"What? She fell? You and I both know that's not true."

"You don't deserve this, Mom." Izzy wrapped her arm

around me, but I pulled away.

"You don't understand—"

"What's to understand?"

"I'm fine Izzy. I promise."

"How can you promise that?"

Michael slammed his fist on the table. "Look, you came to tell us some news, not to criticize our marriage. Now is there anything else you have to say?"

"This is not the time Izzy, please." I stared at Izzy hoping she would see the apprehension on my face.

"Yes, it is the time. There is no better time. He doesn't even feel bad about it."

"I'm not talking to you about this, and I suggest you drop it... now." Michael shoved his plate in front of him.

"You're supposed to protect her. She's your wife." Tears rolled down her cheeks.

"What goes on between us is none of your business."

"It is if you leave bruises."

"It was an accident. I didn't mean to hit her, she moved before I could stop my hand." He dropped his napkin on the table. "I'm done with this conversation. I've lost my appetite."

Michael got up from the table and gave me a hard stare. "Later, Cathy." He left the table without another word.

"Dad," Izzy called out. He turned toward her. "I don't want anything from you, and I don't need your money." She took a deep breath and sat back.

Michael left the room. I leaned into the table, pushed my hair from my face, then took hold of Izzy's arm. "You shouldn't have done that."

"Why not? Someone has to stop him."

Anne Biggs

"Do you think you stopped him? It wasn't your place. You just made it worse."

"Mom, if you can't protect yourself from him, someone has to. I won't let him treat you that way."

"You don't even know what he said." I got up and pushed my chair against the table. "I know you're trying to help, but—"

"You think I don't know, or remember things he's said?" Her whole body shook, as she stood up. There would be no stopping her. I motioned for her to follow her father.

"What do you want me to do? Tell him I'm sorry? That it's OK to beat you?"

"No. Tell him it wasn't your place to talk to him the way you did. The relationship your father and I have is different. Regardless of what you may think, it is not your place to change it."

"You're wrong, Mom. If he hits you and I know it, and do nothing...I'm just as guilty as he is."

"I understand what you're saying, but you need to mend your relationship with him. I'll take care of my own."

In the kitchen, I stared at the water, waiting for the sink to fill. She had to stand up for me. I wouldn't stand up for myself.

When I finished the last of the dishes, I hung the dish-rag across the towel bar, and moved out to the back yard for privacy. I ran the evening through my head, replayed everything that had been said. I knew how Michael would respond. It might be in an hour, or a day, but Michael would have the last word.

"Mom, I gotta go," she called from the kitchen.

I heard Michael's office door slam as he stomped up the

stairs. I knew his gait, how he moved across the room.

"No, Izzy, don't leave. Come out to the patio. Let's talk."

She walked through the kitchen, leaned against the doorway, and her eyes teared up. The look on her face spoke volumes. She went to the refrigerator and took another beer, then walked through the open French doors and let the cat slip between her legs as she took a seat in the chair.

"I'm sorry Mom. I made it worse, didn't I?"

"No, Izzy." I patted her leg.

"I should have never done that. He's going to take it out on you when I leave, isn't he?"

"No. I'll be fine. He'll go out for the rest of the night. He won't even come upstairs. He'll sleep in his office. Please, next time, watch what you say."

"There won't be a next time. The way he talks to you, is just wrong."

"I know, but your yelling at him isn't going to change anything. Did he say anything when you went into his office?"

"No. He just stared at me, like if he stared long enough, I'd apologize."

"Did you?"

"You're kidding, right?"

"No. Yes. Of course, you wouldn't apologize."

"Should I stay?" She drank from the beer as I pondered her question.

"No, I'm fine."

"I can stay the night, if you want?"

"You go home. But before you go, I have something to tell you. Your grandmother is in the hospital and I'm heading back to Ireland on Friday."

"What happened?"

"She fell in the park."

"Is she OK?"

"She's in the hospital, but Izzy, before you came over today, I bought a one-way ticket."

"Mom, that's great. I had planned to leave Sunday, but I can change my ticket. What airlines?"

"United. Flight 1998. 11:00, Friday."

"I'll make the change when I get home. This is great. You're leaving him."

"I'm not leaving anyone. I'm going home to be with my mother. We'll see what happens."

She put her beer on the table, reached and hugged me so tight, I lost my breath. I wrapped my arms around her as well, and felt a security I hadn't felt in a long time. We moved back inside through the kitchen to the foyer.

"Now, you go on, get your things ready. We'll be leaving in a few days remember?"

"I'm just worried about you. I think, in trying to defend you, I may have created a much bigger problem."

"Izzy, go home. I'll be fine."

"I'll be here Friday morning at seven."

"See you then." She kissed my cheek and picked up the portfolio she never had a chance to open.

Izzy walked back down the driveway as I closed the door. I looked up the stairs and knew how the night would turn out if I went upstairs. I went back into the kitchen.

I refilled my wine glass, and slipped out through the back door. If I waited long enough he'd be asleep, or too angry to approach me, or I'd be too drunk.

Garden of Nails

In about twenty minutes, I stood at the bottom of the stairway. Instead of going up, I took a seat on the bottom stair. I rubbed my cheek, wondering if tonight, words would be enough.

Four

The Final Act

When I decided he'd be the one, I let him have me one step at a time. He teased me, I teased back. I loved him, but not the way I had loved Dylan.

Dylan and I split, not because we weren't in love, but because we went in different directions. And we were too afraid to admit we had made a mistake.

Michael had been kind with his words, gentle in his touch, and had passion in his heart. Everything I wanted from someone I would spend my life with.

We lay in each other's arms, with the paper spread across the comforter, tea and biscuits on the tray, Sunday clothes draped on the chairs. He rolled me on top of him, caressed and kissed me, and in turn I smothered him with kisses. I laid my head against his chest and watched as the rain fell, his arms held every dream I ever had. I closed my eyes in bliss, sure we would last forever. He protected me, and loved me.

Years later, here we are in our forever, waiting for the other to fall asleep, or hoping one of us would be too angry or too drunk. How had it slipped away? I sat on the bottom stair, petting the cat resting at my feet. I ran my hands through my hair, dropped my head and tried my hardest to remember the good times, trying to push myself to his bed. To let him take me in his arms. Or would it be better to stay as far away as possible?

Why couldn't we keep those moments, so perfect, so innocent? Those moments when he stroked my cheek, when our worlds were one.

When he wrapped his arm around my shoulder as we strolled in the park, or he reached across the table for my hand. He had loved me. He had loved me in Ireland. In our home with Izzy, we had found happiness.

Would tonight be the night when everything changed?

Our relationship broke apart like a rose at the end of its prime—and I let it happen.

As we ate dinner, one night in Dublin, Michael stared into his plate, his eyes bulging, about to explode.

"What's wrong, why are you so angry?"

"We need to move to Boston."

"We can't. This is our home. It's all Izzy knows."

"I can't make a living here. It's the perfect time to start up in Boston."

"What's going on, Michael?"

"We can't make it here. Nobody trusts Americans."

"That's not true."

"Yes, it is. No one will use an American contractor. They think only the Irish can build anything. In Boston, I can

make it work. Here? Everyone's so cliquish, I can't even get a foot in the door. We have to move, before we have nothing left."

"Why didn't you tell me things were so bad?"

"Why, so you could fix them?"

"That's not what I meant."

"What did you mean, Cathy? What could you have done?"

"Michael, can't we start over? I'm sure one of my sister's husbands could help you out."

"You think I'd take anything from them?"

"I don't want to leave my family."

"I thought I was your family. Get ready, we're leaving in two weeks. Everything is settled."

"I won't hear of it. We can't take Izzy out of her life on a whim."

"You call it a whim?" You are stupider than I thought. You have no idea what it's like. I'm trying to keep our family from bankruptcy." He pushed his chair back and I got up at the same time. I went toward him, trying to soothe a rage I didn't understand.

"Michael, we can work something out."

He swung around, his knuckles catching the bridge of my nose. I hit the table and crumpled to the floor. I reached to stop the blood, but it gushed down my shirt onto the tile. He looked down at me, then turned and left the kitchen. I heard the front door slam.

After he left, I got up, cleaned the blood from the floor, and turned off the light. I went into the bathroom and stared at my face in the mirror. I splashed it with cold water, wiping away the blood, then I went to bed. Sleep would not come.

Two hours later, I heard the key in the front door and he made his way to our bed. I smelled the beer on his breath. I shrank from his touch.

"Why did you do that?" he said, his voice softer, almost transparent.

"Why did I do what? I don't understand."

"Cathy, you make me crazy. Come here. Let me make it up to you." He pulled my hips to his groin. "I promise, I won't hit you anymore. Just move to Boston with me."

The first time.

I slipped under the covers, trying to not even breathe. I lay still and felt the weight of him move closer.

"What's wrong?"

"Nothing. I'm just tired."

"Don't you owe me a little something, since you're leaving?"

"It's late, Michael."

"It's never been too late before. Come on." He took hold of my shoulder, pulling me close, stroking my hip.

"Please don't do this."

He leaned in, caressing my neck with his lips.

"Michael, please!" I tried to push him away, but he pulled me with him. I couldn't move.

"I've been thinking, Cathy. You don't need to go to Dublin at all."

"Of course, I need to go. How can you say that?"

"Well, since Izzy's going back, I mean. I assume, that was

what she came to tell us tonight. With her there, you don't have to go. She can take your place. Your sisters are perfectly capable of taking care of everything. Your uncle can handle the legal particulars, and there's always Claire who will do whatever is needed, if it should come to that. Izzy can be your eyes and ears."

"You sick fuck." I got out of bed, and turned to stare at him. I held the look until his eyes met mine."

Once again, I didn't see his hand, but was knocked to my knees by the force of the blow. He stood over me, his hand in a fist. Cheeks red, eyes wide open, his forehead tight. I had never seen such rage. He swung around again, and his fist squared me in the cheek. He missed my jaw, but I felt the assault just below my eye. I felt my head jerk back and tumbled to the floor. When I opened my eyes, he stood clenching his fists.

"Go ahead," I whispered, looking up at him, "hit me again. You're getting very good at it."

With the third hit, the room spun. I felt the blood trickle down and fold into my lips.

"Don't *ever* call me that again. Who do you think you are?"

He loomed over me. I knew if I got up he'd hit me again, but if I didn't, I'd never leave. I pulled myself to my feet, gripping the nightstand.

"That is the last time you'll ever hit me." I stood up, my hand against my face, burning from his rage.

I maintained my balance and walked past him, not caring what he would do. I went into the bathroom and waited for what seemed forever. Instead of coming to confront me, I heard the front door slam. I let out the breath that had been strangling me.

Anne Biggs

I opened the door and looked around the room, then-went to the hallway, peering downstairs to find any sight of him.

Michael had shown me the way. Maybe now I could find my strength, make my own decisions.

I reached up and felt my face, warm to my touch. I stared at myself in the vanity mirror. The marks were getting deeper, redder. By noon tomorrow, I'd be swollen and purple. I went back to the bathroom and splashed cold water on my face, still feeling heat radiate.

Tears came from the physical pain when I touched the corner of my eyes. The woman in me knew who to blame, but the child blamed herself...for every blow.

Five

In the last day and a half Michael had not returned home. I went about getting ready for our departure. He made it too easy, no calls, no confrontations. He hadn't left any messages. For whatever reason, he chose to stay away. Maybe, because of guilt, or maybe he moved on.

"What the hell?" Izzy said, as she slipped off my sunglasses.

Over the past two days, the red had turned to purple, I covered them with makeup; but she saw the marbled clouds leak through. She touched the tender, bruised skin, and pulled away as if she'd been burned.

"It's not that bad." I turned away, trying to cover the scars that had once been a relationship of love.

"Don't even try to say that," she scorned, reaching for my chin.

"I'm fine."

She barged past me, threw her purse on the table, then turned back around, and grabbed hold of my arm. I saw it in her face, that rage should have been mine. I twisted away from her, embarrassed I couldn't hide it, but ashamed I let it happen.

"When? After I left?" She asked, looking around the room as if she were waiting for her father to jump out from a corner." I knew I shouldn't have left. Dammit. How could he?"

"Izzy, it wouldn't have made any difference. You wouldn't have been able to stop it. I'm OK. I know what I have to do."

"Does he know what he did? Has he seen you?"

I walked to the suitcases by the base of the stairs. I moved the smaller bag onto the couch, opened it and began straightening the contents. I needed something to do. I couldn't look at her

"I haven't seen him for the last two days," I said, "I don't know where he is. He probably slept at the office. I'm grateful he didn't go to the bank. He could have been even more of an asshole."

"You're grateful? God, I can't believe it. You're grateful he didn't kill you, or take all your money? Jesus, Mom. What more does he have to do?"

It shattered me to think my daughter had to see the worst side of her father. She had seen the result of his rage. The man she had adored her whole life.

"Are you going to tell me what happened?"

"He didn't want me to go back to Dublin, and in the heat of the moment, I called him...."

"What did you call him?"

"I called him a sick fuck. I shouldn't have done that."

"God, Mom, you keep defending him. It doesn't matter what he thought. Look at yourself. Come here. Look in the mirror. He hurt you."

"I don't need to look. Believe me, I know what he did."

I rummaged through my purse, putting my passport and documents in accessible areas. I surveyed the room, hoping

I had left everything in order. I fingered my ring, debating about leaving it on the table, but I moved back to the luggage.

"Come on, let's just go," I said, not wanting to draw any attention to myself.

I placed an envelope on the table and walked away.

Izzy picked up her purse, but I saw her glance toward my shoulder. "Oh no. You can't be leaving him a letter. Dear God, you didn't apologize?" She held up the envelope.

"I need to let him know where he can reach me."

"Mom, you have a cell phone. He can reach you no matter where you are."

"I wasn't apologizing, just clearing things up." I continued, trying to free myself from the guilt. I fingered the envelope, then walked away from the table.

"You don't need to tell him shit, not after what he did," she said, motioning toward my face. She handed me the envelope. "Tear it up, throw it away. I don't care. Let him figure it out."

"That'll be my decision," I said, fiddling with the ring that hung on my finger.

"My God, what do you have in here?" Izzy asked, as she took hold of my suitcase, moving it toward the door.

"My life. I have everything I need, if I decide to stay."

I had left behind everything else, all the reminders of Michael. I stuffed the envelope inside my purse. I twirled the ring around my finger, then pulled it off and placed it on the entry table. I looked at Izzy.

"Now that will tell him where you are." She laughed and wrapped her arm around my shoulder. "Let's go home."

Izzy allowed me the few minutes I needed to say goodbye to the life I had been reluctant to face. There had been moments I thought I would never leave, but after his last attack, everything changed.

I looked around the room, then pulled the door tight, locked it and placed the key under the mat.

"Ma'am, is there anything else?" The mustached taxi driver asked as he closed the trunk.

"No, thank you. We're fine."

Just then, my cell rang and I saw Rose's face appear on the screen. I clicked on the speaker, so we could both enjoy Rose's rage.

"Hey Rose, what's going on?"

"Where are you?" She asked from across the ocean.

"In a cab heading to the airport. Claire called and told me about Mum. Izzy and I will be there in the morning."

"Why would Claire call you?"

"What do you mean? Francie asked her to call."

"It wasn't her place. She isn't family."

"How you can say that? She's always been family.

"If you're so upset about Claire, why didn't you call?"

"I was busy at the hospital. I thought Francie would call."

"I've talked to Francie. She knows we're coming." I heard the click of her phone and my screen went black.

I sent Francie a text informing her of our arrival and of Rose's call. Knowing Francie, she'd be jumping up and down at the gate, waving her arms all around. Anxious for details from Boston.

Six

"There she is, Mom. Aunt Francie!" Izzy called out, as we left the luggage area of the Dublin Airport. Francie waved to us, jumping up and down.

"Oh my God, look at you, Cate," Francie cried, as she threw her arms around the two of us. "Come on, let's get to the car."

I was home. Like a kid, I stuck out my tongue and felt the rain. I wanted to do my own little dance.

When Jean and Paddy saw us, Jean barreled up. Almost knocking me down, she wrapped her arms around me so tight she took my breath away.

"I'm so glad you're here." The rest of her words were muffled as she dug her face into my neck.

"How are you, my darling?" I asked, returning her hug.

"So much better, now that you're here."

Paddy took Izzy in his arms and kissed her on the forehead. How was your flight?" Paddy asked.

"Long, but good. I slept most of the time," I said.

Paddy and Jean each grabbed a suitcase and stuffed them in Paddy's trunk, then took mine and placed them in Francie's car. From the front seat, Francie watched in amusement at our forgetfulness of how everything reversed in an Irish car.

"I thought we'd go straight to the hospital. Mum's excited to see you. I hope you don't mind. The kids will meet us there."

"I hoped I could freshen up a little, but no, it's fine."

Once on the road, Francie turned to me. "It's good to see you, Cate. I used to think I'd never see you again, being so far away."

"Well, I'm here now. How are you doing?"

"I'm good, except for Mum of course, but no complaints." I smiled at my sister realizing, of us all, she had been the one to find the most happiness.

"Is she any better?" I asked, watching as the rain fell steady. *"A soft, Irish afternoon rain."* as Da would say. I realized I had even missed the rain.

"She's stable, but with the meds they're giving her, she sleeps a lot."

"Is that a problem?"

"She's just not herself. We don't know the details. Connor said the doctors plan to talk to us today about the test results. The nurses say she still gets confused. One of them found her wandering the hall, calling out for "Finn," like she did in the park."

"Who's Finn?" I asked, hoping Francie would have an answer.

"No one knows, even Uncle Connor said he had no idea. When she isn't babbling or sleeping, she seems to be fine. It's hard. When she's herself, we just want to take her home, but then she'll say something no one understands. Or she'll crumble into a fetal position from a headache."

I watched as her fingers turned white around the steering wheel. I had the sense there were things she wasn't telling me, but I also knew I would have to learn some of them on my own.

"A little heads up about Rose," Francie said, looking at me.

"Well, I'm assuming it's not good, by the look on your face. She hung up on me yesterday after I told her Claire called."

"I know," Francie, said, "she let me know Claire had no place calling anyone. I told her I asked Claire to make the call, but she didn't like that either."

"So how bad is Rose?" I asked.

"Beyond anything you could imagine. When Mum fell, she stormed through the hospital, ranting at anyone who got in her way. She demanded Connor bring Mum home, saying she should be the one taking care of her. She went a little crazy. Oh— and she doesn't much like the idea you're at the house."

"Where should I be? In a hotel?"

"No, of course not. Just letting you know she's having a tough time. Mum talks with Connor and Claire almost every day. I think she feels they understand her better. Rose thinks, because she's the eldest, she should have the final word on anything related to Mum, but Mum has her own ideas."

"What brought this on?" I asked, not surprised that Rose expected to be in charge.

"She's been having personal issues, and is taking it out on everyone, especially her family."

"What happened?" I adjusted my purse on my lap, preparing myself for anything Francie had to say.

"Charlie left Rose a few weeks ago and she's not taking it well. He just packed his bags and walked out. Got an apartment in the city. Sat down with the girls and told them nothing had changed between them, just he couldn't live with Rose anymore."

"How did they take it?"

"Well, Jean said it surprised her that he lasted so long. Marie became more upset. She stayed with her mother, but after three days, left. She couldn't handle her, either."

Francie didn't look at me as she spilled the beans about Rose. With Francie being so open about family details, I debated telling her what had happened with Michael, but after listening to everything going on in Dublin, I realized it was not the time to spill my woes.

Random cars dotted the parking lot. Francie pulled her car in a nearby space, turned off the engine, and stared at me.

"What is it? Why are you staring at me?" I asked.

"I just want you to be prepared. Mum has changed a great deal, Rose is out of her mind, and Claire has aged since you last saw her."

"We're all different— except for you, of course." I nudged her and we both laughed. "Don't worry, I understand."

"No. It is more than that. I don't know how to explain. She is different, more than just sick."

"We are all different, Francie. Time does that. It fools us because it slips away so fast and then when we look in the mirror, we go 'what the bloody hell.' I get it."

"OK, then let's do this."

Francie led me through the double doors and straight to the elevator. We stood in silence until it stopped at the fourth floor. Francie guided me out, and I followed her down the hall. I paused as we reached the door. I took a deep breath, knowing once we went through, everything would change.

The girls had already arrived. Uncle Connor wrapped his arms around me so tight I couldn't breathe. "I'm glad you're back, sweet girl."

"Me too." I buried my head in his chest.

"She'll be grand, honest she will," he whispered, staying by my side as we all huddled together.

Rose stood at the foot of the bed, stroking the edge of Mum's green and yellow afghan. It had begun to unravel from wear and tear. I hadn't seen Rose since Jonathan's funeral, but she didn't bother to acknowledge me. She just stood stroking the afghan.

It surprised me to see Rose so put together, after what Francie had said. But Rose never let anyone see her weaknesses. She wore small diamond studded earrings, a silk blouse and black tailored coat. She stood at the bed, her graying bob combed in place, with a hint of floral perfume.

"Good to see you, Izzy. You've grown quite a lot."

"Good to see you, too, Aunt Rose." Izzy looked at me. I just nodded, and moved toward the front of the bed.

"She looks tiny," I whispered to no one in particular. I couldn't take my eyes off the frail woman under the blankets. Francie had been right, the short time I had been gone had taken a toll. Her gray hair stuck to the side of the pillow, her cheeks pale, lips dried and chapped. I reached out and picked her hand up off the covers. A chill slid through my fingers. I held on to her wrist, turning it, and massaged it to bring back warmth. I stroked the red mark on her forehead that had healed since her fall.

I couldn't remember ever seeing her so fragile. Even after Da died, she had been a force to reckon with. Taking hold of her life, working her way through anything. But looking at her, the tears just came. I didn't want to talk to any doctors, I wanted it to be me, my voice to bring her back, but she didn't move. Nothing. Then I saw a flicker behind her eyelids.

Before long, the door opened and two men I had never

seen, walked in wearing white jackets and each holding manila folders. They stood in contrast. The older had a shiny, bald head, with a nametag, Dr. Redland. The other, a mass of chestnut hair, and faded freckles across his nose. His tag said Dr. Kelly.

"Thank you for coming," the older doctor said. "My name is Dr. Redland. I'm the Chief Liaison for the hospital's specialty clinics. This is Dr. Kelly, our neurologist. We have been working with your mother's doctor through all of this."

"Dr. Kelly has reviewed the results of your mother's tests."

We all stood together, our hands joined, except for Rose, who stood off to the side.

"Just for your information, your mother has signed power of attorney to Claire Steed and Connor Brennan. They will be making the decisions, when she cannot. But she has agreed, medical information will be shared with her entire family."

We nodded our heads, knowing how devoted Mum had been to her brother and Claire. From the side, I could see Rose having nothing of it, but she remained silent as Dr. Redland began to explain. By that time, Mum opened her eyes and pulled herself up. Dr. Redland took hold of her hand, squeezed it and nodded when their eyes met. She smiled at all of us.

"Go ahead, I know what needs to be said." She looked around the room, her eyes setting on Rose.

"I may as well be blunt," Dr. Redland said. "Your mother has a tumor at the base of her skull." I looked down and saw her squeeze his hand even tighter. "We can't get to it with surgery. We considered chemotherapy, but we can't guarantee it will shrink. Due to her age, and the intensity of chemo required, we are reluctant to begin any treatment until we can monitor her for a while."

"What will happen if you don't do anything?" Francie asked.

"She'll have episodes, like dementia. She'll forget where she is, who people are. The tumor will grow. In the next few months it will increase and cause additional concerns."

"We don't know how often her episodes will be, or how extensive, but we feel that's what caused her fall in the park. She went into an episode, forgot where she was, panicked and fell," Dr. Kelly added.

"We'd like to watch her for a while," his eyes, still on my mother. She squeezed his hand. He turned and stopped talking.

"I've made arrangements for myself to be transferred to St. Philomena's Center. I've been there, and it's where I need to be, for now."

"It's a multi-skilled nursing facility," Dr. Redland broke in. "She'll have her own room and as much freedom as she likes. A medical team will be available to her around the clock."

"It even has a green house," Mum interrupted, smiling.

Rose pushed herself to the front of the bed. "That is out of the question. I am her eldest. I know her better than anyone. Why can't she go home? I'll take care of her."

"With all due respect, Rose," Connor broke in. "None of this has anything to do with knowing her best. It's what's best for her, plain and simple."

"You need to let Dr. Redland finish. Connor is right, in the long run we have to do what is best for Mum." Francie shook the curls from her face, glaring at Rose.

"Being at home would be best for her. It is her surroundings. She knows where everything is, and I'll be there."

Rose's stern reply caused me to question her motives. The harshness in her voice showed a side of her I dreaded most of all.

"Rose," Dr. Kelly glanced at her. "I will be releasing your mother to the Center in the next few days. It is what is best for her. I understand your misgivings and I'll do everything I can to get her home as soon as possible, but you need to understand your mother is under my care, and I alone will make the decisions concerning her health. As long as Ms. Steed and Mr. Brennan agree, we will be sending her to St. Philomena's."

I sat stunned, staring at Dr. Kelly. I didn't know this young man, but I gained an immediate admiration for him. No one had ever put Rose in her place, not even Da. Rose turned away and moved toward the door. She gripped her diamond studs, and patted her gray bob.

Rose leaned against the wall and watched. I knew if she had her way, she'd have stormed out of the room, but she controlled herself and remained still, after Connor gave her a reprimanding look, like one does a child.

"If I may continue?" Dr. Kelly paused, then looked across the room at all of us. "We did cognitive memory tests. She struggled with them, but I know that symptom is related to the severe headaches. Those are caused by the tumor. We have her on some very strong meds to try to control the headaches, thereby controlling the episodes. I'm afraid it will be a while before your mother goes home."

Once again Rose lunged forward. "You can't do this."

"They aren't doing anything," Connor broke in. "She knows all about this. It's her choice."

"This is my choice. No one else's."

Dr. Redland looked around, patted Mum's hand, then let it go. "We have discussed this in detail with your mother and both Mr. Brennan and Ms. Steed. We aren't hiding anything. This meeting is at your mother's request. She waited for

Catherine to arrive, so she could have you all together."

"Does Mum have dementia?" Francie asked, pushing her curls from her face.

"No one said that, but she is showing signs of memory issues that could put her in danger if she is left alone," Connor spoke up.

"She won't be alone," Rose snapped back.

"I'm sick and I need the best care possible," Mum said, dropping her eyes on Rose. "I won't be going home until I'm ready. I've been forgetting things, putting things in the wrong places, and talking about people who are long gone. I know what that means."

"Please, I understand how stressful something like this can be on a family. We'll do everything we can to ease the transition," he said.

"Dr. Redland is right. It's important we support each other... for her," I blurted out before Rose could say anything.

"I'm in good care. Please don't worry. Just come and see me." She looked around the room and a soft smile spread across her face, her eyes gentle, and soothing.

"What are you doing here?" Rose yelled.

"Where the hell did that come from?" Connor asked.

"This is not about anyone, except Mum. We need to work together," Francie said.

Silence filled the room, Izzy moved behind me, away from Rose. She grabbed hold of my hand while Dr. Redland continued to detail Mum's care and treatment options.

"There were times when your mother couldn't remember things like addresses, or lists, but then there were times she remembered everything like names and dates. Some of her memory lapses were due to her headaches."

"So, she gets mixed up. That doesn't prove anything," Rose said, now being outright defiant.

"How she answers the questions and what she remembers, tells us a great deal about her prognosis," Dr. Kelly said.

Before anyone could say anything, Rose stormed out of the room, slamming the door. We fell silent, and Dr. Redland put his pen into his jacket pocket.

"Shit. Why does she do this?" I said beneath my breath, sheepishly looking around to see who heard me.

Seven

Dr. Redland and Dr. Kelly nodded to us and left the room. We stood like school children, not knowing what to do or say. Mum cleared her throat as best she could to gain our attention. It worked.

"Go home. I have good doctors who know what I need. I don't need anyone feuding over me. Get some rest. Come and see me, bring me things from the house that will make me comfortable."

We stood even more helpless than before. "I'm a bit tired. All of you go on now. Treat Catherine and Izzy to a fine dinner, then let them rest and settle in at the house."

She looked around at us, as if wondering what we were waiting for. "Go on now."

One by one we filed out, like obedient children. In the hallway, we clustered in groups. The cousins huddled around Izzy, surely making plans for their time together. Connor and Claire whispered to each other and Francie stood next to me, maybe waiting for our world to go back to normal.

"We have to find Rose," I said, nudging Francie's shoulder.

"No, we don't. I don't care where she went."

"Wait in the car. I think I should talk to her."

"About what? Tell her what an ass she is?"

"No, Francie. She's upset, we've barely said hello to each other. I need to find her. Maybe she went to the cafeteria, or she's in the lobby. I hope she didn't leave."

"No telling when she gets riled up."

"Meet me outside. Tell Izzy if you see her. I'm heading to the cafeteria."

"Do you think she'll listen, after everything the doctors said?" Francie asked. "You know how she gets."

"I don't know, but I have to try." I surveyed the empty hallway.

I stepped into the elevator, and rode it down to the cafeteria. No luck. I went back up to Mum's room. As I rounded the corner I saw Rose open Mum's door. I stood back, so she wouldn't see me.

I moved behind the door, pulled it open slightly, just enough to leave it ajar. I had to know what she was going to say. I knew it betrayed Rose and Mum both. I kept telling myself I was not an eavesdropper, by nature. It was evil. But I could live with being evil, for Mum.

Rose drew the chair away from the window and pulled it close to Mum's side. She adjusted her slacks, and laid her jacket on the chair. By the look of things, she was prepared for a lengthy conversation with no assurance Mum would participate in any part of it.

I had a perfect view. I could see Rose's movements, her hands reaching for Mum's, and the expression on her face as it would change if things went awry. I could see Mum if she moved, or slumped, or even tried to get up. I couldn't have planned it better. Mum's eyes were closed, but at the simple touch of Rose's hand, she opened them.

"There you are, my dear girl."

"It's Rose."

"I know. You startled me. I thought everyone had left."

So tiny, lying there. The bed over-powered her. I watched Mum pull herself upright, tug at her gown, then fluff her hair. She seemed stronger talking on her own behalf with the doctors, but here alone, she was fragile. It shattered me to see her so helpless.

I continued to hold the door ajar with my foot and leaned against the wall to listen. A stillness filled the room, the smell of disinfectant seeped through the crack in the door, and an air of uncertainty dangled like the vines in Mum's garden.

"How could you do this? You know I could take care of you so much better. In no time, you'll be right as rain."

"You heard the doctors, and I've made my decision," Mum said, adjusting her blankets.

"Why did you choose Uncle Connor and Claire?"

"Because I trust them. They understand me. I am sick, and I'm not getting better. I have to know people will listen," she said in a faint whisper.

"Why would you agree to live some place without asking us?"

"Now I have to ask permission?"

"No—I'm not saying that, but why didn't you tell me. I felt like a fool hearing it for the first time in front of everyone." I heard the rise in Rose's voice, and sensed judgment would be coming.

"I don't need to get approval from you or anyone, dear. It was never anyone's decision, but mine."

I clenched my fist, and wanted to applaud—to jump through the door and cheer, but I stayed still. So far things were not going well for Rose.

"No, Mum," Rose continued, "you should have at least told me."

"Why would I do that?" Mum said, her words filling the air.

"Because I'm your oldest daughter. I'm the one you need to turn to. Your brother is too old to know what is best for you, and Claire, she isn't even family."

"Understand this, girl, before you question my life again. I do as I please, though I will always love all of you, Claire has been in my life longer than anyone. I trust her with everything. As for your uncle, he'll always be my guiding light. In time you will understand." Her voice sounded like a lullaby, soothing, gentle. Her muscles didn't tense, she folded her hands across the afghan.

"Why aren't you listening?" Rose raised her voice, struggling to remain calm.

"Don't be a maggot, Rose," Mum said, her voice steady, as she pulled herself up.

"How can you say that? I am your eldest daughter, I'm supposed to take care of you."

"Rose, I don't need you to take care of me. You have your own life to worry about. Your girls need you. You have a husband."

"I don't need you reminding me about my life."

"Rose, I'm being taken care of. You see where I am, don't you?" Mum asked with a smile across her face.

"Why are you doing this?" Rose almost screamed, then stood back and caught her breath.

Mum lay back on the pillow, showing a sigh of relief on her face, her jaw relaxed. I couldn't begin to imagine what she must have been thinking, after being silent for so long. Though she may have appeared frail, she spoke volumes.

I had known and cherished the relationship between my mother and uncle and I knew he would damn near die for her, devoted to every part of her life, as she to him. And Claire...

Mum adored Claire for as long as I could remember. They had an unshakeable bond that shone like a star in her life.

On the other hand, Rose never did have a clear idea of the value of friendship. She never trusted anyone enough. She never believed people liked her or valued her existence. I saw how she treated people.

"Dear," Mum began, in a yielding voice. "I love you as I do all my daughters, but you have no say in my decisions, it is that simple. I am sick, and I have to do what is best for me. I may never get out of here, so I came up with the best plan for me. You have to trust it. There is nothing more to be said."

"No." Then she stopped. No words vibrated across the room. I peered through the slit, but couldn't see any movement, then the words tumbled out. Rose may as well have had a gun, and shot it in the air. "If you don't let me take charge, I'll tell."

"What? What would you tell?"

"I know all about it, and you know I do."

Mum's jaw clenched. She took hold of the sheet, her hand forming a fist. Then everything relaxed. I watched her reclaim her calm.

"Now that you brought it up, I've been thinking, I need to talk with all of you. There are some things I need to explain."

"You can't tell them," Rose blurted out. "You said. You told me it would destroy everything if they knew."

For the first time since going into Mum's room, Rose's cheeks flushed. She moved toward the window and leaned against the sill. But through the slit I watched Mum, her face became even more tranquil and she folded her hands on the blanket.

"It's time I take charge of my life," Mum said, still in a whisper.

"I'll tell. I'll tell your precious Claire, and I bet Uncle Connor would love to know."

I leaned in close, almost falling through the door, but caught myself. *What secret did she know that none of us did? Why would she even consider betraying Mum in such a way?* I wanted to burst through, but something held me back. There was much more to be said.

"You must know by now, I have no secrets from Connor and Claire. Even if you think you know, there is nothing you could say that would change things." Mum remained calm, but I saw defiance in her eyes. In this moment, she knew she had won.

"I know about the pictures," Rose blurted.

"I'm clear-headed now, girl. You can say whatever you want and it will change nothing. I make my own decisions now. Even if there is a secret, it will be mine to do with as I please. But I have to ask, Rose? Why? Why would you do this to me? If you know what you think you know, why would you try to hurt me? I don't understand. Is this how I raised you?"

She moved to the foot of the bed, tried to calm herself, and then spoke in the softest voice I had heard. "I know who Finn is."

Who's Finn?

"I've seen her pictures and read her letters."

Pictures and letters? What the hell was she talking about?

"She does not belong to our family. She is nothing to us."

"Let me be very clear here, Rose. I have four daughters. I love them all. Should you ever attempt to shame *any* of your sisters, as you have just done, you will never be welcome again. Mark me, girl, I will always remember this day."

Rose moved toward the windowsill, looked around the

room, then back at Mum. After a few minutes, she grabbed her coat from the chair, tugged her arms through the sleeves, and fumbled with the buttons.

"She's a second thought, nothing. She's not even blood."

"Rose, I'll say this once. You are my daughter. Now, leave me be, before you say something you can never take back. And as far as my secret, do as you will. I have decided."

Rose grabbed her purse, draped it across her shoulder, gave Mum one last glance, and stormed from the door. She didn't see me, but as she went down the hall, I followed her, watching as she switched her purse from one side to the other.

When I caught up, I touched her arm. She stopped, and turned. "What do you want?" She looked up at me, straight-faced, a familiar bitterness in her eyes.

"To talk. I'm worried about you."

"Since when?"

"Since forever. Don't you know?"

"What do you want?"

"Rose, I heard what you said to Mum."

"You eavesdropped?"

"Why would you try to shame her?"

"It's none of your business what I say to her or anyone."

"Jesus, Rose, you blindsided her, then threatened her. What is wrong with you?"

"I tried to help her."

"Oh, that's what you call it?"

"I get it. Everyone thinks she's sick, so fine. Let her stay in the hospital. She'll wither away and die, then no one will have to worry about her, then I can say I told you so."

"Oh my God." I reached for her hand, but she pulled it back. "Is that all you want from this? To be right?"

"Is that what you think?" Rose shrieked at me.

"You've always had to be right, always the last word. Why do you think everyone leaves you, Rose?"

"Because I'm a bitch—or because I'm right."

"Maybe this one time, you're wrong. Did you ever think about that?"

"What's the point, Catherine? I have nothing to say to you—to any of you. You have your mind made."

"It seems like you have yours made up, as well."

"What do you know?" Rose said, walking away.

"Enough with the drama, Rose. We have to get through this together."

She jerked away from my grasp as I caught up to her. I felt like we were little kids in the play yard fighting for a toy.

"Rose, stop this now. Come on. Come to the cafeteria. Let's sit down and talk."

I heard the pleading in my voice, but she surely saw it as an attack. Maybe I could contain her wrath at least for a while.

"I don't know why." She looked at her watch. "You have ten minutes." I stood there with my mouth gaping. *I had ten minutes? Was she going to time us?* "Well? Are you coming or not?" Rose turned and walked to the elevator.

So, Catherine, why should I listen? You seem to know everything. Enlighten me."

"Rose, don't be a bitch."

"I'll be who I am. You're only here for the time being. What do you know about Mum? You moved to Boston, Francie moved to Cork. I was the one who stayed here. I'm the one who really knows her. Neither of you cared about Mum or me. You never thought about what I was giving up." Rose's hands twitched, and her eyes darted around the room.

"You mean because we moved away and lived our lives? You think we didn't care about Mum? You, selfish bitch."

"I know the truth."

"Both of us did what we could. We're a family, I don't understand why you are trying to tear us apart."

In the middle of our 'discussion', I realized there was no point in continuing. I was talking to a wall, or the rain. No, I was scolding a child who was never going to be wrong.

"Look, we're all here now. Can't we put our differences to the side for Mum? She needs our help to get through this."

I sat back watching, as the cafeteria filled with doctors and nurses, the smell of blood sausage, steamed vegetables, and sweet apple pie, blended with the scent of wintergreen hand wash and disinfectant.

"Rose, she wandered out of the house. She fell and hurt herself. She didn't know where she was, and then she started going in circles, searching for someone named Finn. Who's Finn, Rose?"

She smiled, leaning back in her chair. "I have no idea."

"I don't believe you."

"Of course, you don't," Rose said, her voice almost raspy. She held her finger to her lips, "shhhh…it's a secret."

"Mum didn't keep secrets."

"Oh, you're such a stupid girl. We all have secrets. I bet you have a secret right now you would love to tell, but you're too scared. I can see it in your eyes. You don't trust anyone, do you?"

"You have no idea what you're talking about."

"Catherine, I don't care what's going on in your life. That is not my point."

"Then, what is your point?"

"My point is, Mum has secrets she never told anyone but me. I'm trying to protect her...and her secrets."

"You think Mum needs protecting? And blackmail is going to bring her to her senses?"

I looked around the room at the other tables, still full, but muted conversations dropped like parachutes over the room.

"Would you like to order a late lunch?"

"No," she blurted. 'We didn't come in here as friends to have lunch. I said you had ten minutes, and it's about up. You were spying on me. I will never forgive you."

"No, I wasn't. I wanted to talk to you. We should have it done years ago."

"So, let's talk. What else do you want to know?"

"Why are you so angry, Rose?"

"I'm angry," she paused, "because no one listens. No one hears me."

"Rose, you have to admit you try to bully everyone into believing you."

"Because I know I'm right."

Rose was not going to budge. The more we argued the more she dug in.

"You probably are." I conceded, hoping that would soften her edges a bit. "You're the oldest and outside of Connor and Claire, you have known her the longest, but can't we decide together what might be best for her?"

"Go back to Boston, Catherine. I mean, I'm glad you

came. Even stay in the house for a few days, see the city, be a tourist...then go home."

Rose stood up, grabbed her coat, and pushed her way past my chair, not even turning around. She smoothed her sprayed hair in place as she hurried out.

I stayed seated for a while, trying to figure out my next move. Rose was right. We all had secrets.

I left the cafeteria and walked through the lobby and out the double doors. *Rain.* I ran to Francie's car, plopped into the passenger seat and took in the calm.

"Are you OK?" she asked.

"You mean did I make heads or tails with Rose?"

"OK, that too."

"I failed miserably."

"Are you ready to go? We can head to the house."

"Yes." I laid my head back and closed my eyes. I could feel the car turn and swerve, then steadied as it moved down the thoroughfare.

"You OK?" Francie asked again. I felt the weight of her hand patting my knee, as if I were a child.

"What was I trying to do? I knew in my heart she wasn't going to listen to anyone, least of all me."

"I'm guessing it didn't go too good?"

"Oh God, it was awful." I opened my eyes and looked around. "I don't remember her being so...."

"Then you haven't been paying attention."

"She wants me to go back to Boston."

"Of course, she does." Francie stopped at the light and looked at me.

"I'm not going home."

"Now, you got it. Come on, let's get you settled in, before Rose has the locks changed."

We drove out of Dublin Center with rain pounding against the windshield. When we turned onto Mum's street, I wondered what memories I'd find that would make Rose's fear a reality.

Francie placed her phone on the console, and as she pulled into the driveway, it vibrated. Rose's face flashed up.

"You better answer it," I said, trying to hide my smile.

"I'll call her later. I can't deal with her antics right now."

"I know why she's calling."

"Catherine, she calls all the time."

After Francie stopped the car and pulled the key from the ignition, I didn't get out. I felt an eerie presence, the kind that made my neck itch, that made it hard to swallow. Rose wasn't going away. Her accusations struck a chord.

"She said I'm the reason Mum got lost and fell. My moving to Boston broke her. This isn't my fault," I whispered, rubbing my elbow, trying to ease the tension crawling up my arm.

"No one's blaming you, Cate," patting my leg again.

"You didn't hear what she said. She was vicious."

"You know Rose, she always tries to make something out of nothing."

Eight

Francie opened the door to Mum's cottage and walked in. I stood in the doorway, emotions flooding my senses. I steadied my breathing, and tried not to cry. It should have happened when I saw Francie, or seeing Mum in the hospital. Instead it was here, at my childhood home. Memories of scraped knees and pillow fights; Christmas' and Sunday suppers after church. Da's smoking on the porch and Mum's garden. It all came back. Reminding me where I came from, who I was. I felt the muscles in my throat relax. This was the place I felt safe. The same floral couch sat against the wall. The glass coffee table took center stage and her roses, not yet wilted, sat in a vase on the dining table. Everything was in order.

"Mum kept up with her flowers, but when the weather turned bad, Claire or I dropped by with a bouquet," Francie said, noticing my gaze at the roses. "They always put a smile on her face."

I smiled when I saw Mittens sitting in the window. "She's still here? Oh my gosh." I went to the window and picked up the overweight cat that had far exceeded nine lives. There were times I swore Mum just replaced her with a look-a-like, but hearing her purr; I knew Mittens. I placed her on the edge of the sofa and waited for her to nudge me for attention.

"Not much has changed," I said, letting my purse drop onto the cushion as I continued to look around the room.

"Let me fix some tea. It's been a tough afternoon, I need to relax," Francie said, pulling off her coat

I followed her to the kitchen, trying to see everything at once. I ran my hand across the chipped tile of the kitchen counter, remembering our times here, standing over the sink, wet towels in hand, singing along with the latest heart throb on the radio. It was a time we were whole.

"Those were the old days, Cate," Francie said watching my face, knowing somehow I'd been taken back.

She came and put her arms around me. I leaned into her, feeling safe. I kissed my sister on the cheek.

"I just got lost for a moment."

"I know it's hard. Seeing her like that. It's been hard for all of us."

"It's not that." I found myself at a loss for words. "It just... everything, I guess."

"After Mum went to hospital, Rose came in and cleaned everything up. Washed the dishes, replaced the flowers, made everything good as new. She hates to see anything out of order, like everything needs to be perfect."

"That was nice of her," I said, looking at the yellow roses.

"Rose wasn't being nice. It terrified her, people would say Mum had gone looney."

After overhearing Rose's conversation with Mum, then trying to talk to her myself, the things Francie said made sense. "Kind of makes you wonder who's looney," Francie added.

"You're terrible."

"Hey, if the shoe fits." Francie snorted as she took a sip of tea.

"When did Mum do a Power of Attorney? Whose idea was it?" I asked.

"Late last spring, but I think she'd been planning it for a long time. She was determined to stay in control. She had it worked out so she could make her own decisions."

"What was she so worried about?" I asked.

"I don't know, but keep in mind, when she set it up, you were in Boston, I was in Cork, and well, you've met Rose, right?"

I raised my eyebrows and nodded. "It just hurts she didn't feel safe with us. I know she has every right to choose the care she wants."

"I can't blame her," Francie said. "Her whole life, people controlled her. As much as Da loved her, he still had the last say. I think she just wanted to have things her way. It makes sense to me."

Francie turned toward the window, as if she wanted to say something more, but couldn't find the nerve.

"Are you sure she made good choices? The best care possible?"

Francie nodded. "I have to believe that. Just because she wants to do it her way. I'm pretty sure she did tons of research before any final decisions were made."

"Do you think she'll ever come home?" I asked, moving the teacup in front of me.

"I hope so. She loves this house. Da gave her everything, but to answer your question...I don't know."

"How are you doing?"

"Me? Hey, I'm resilient. I always bounce back—really, I'm good. My kid is happy, my husband is good," she said, wiggling her eyebrows. "What more could I ask for?"

"Again, you're terrible."

"But, you love me anyway."

"Of course, dear baby sister." I patted her hand. "You know, you're probably the only one...of all of us, that can say that."

"What, I'm the only baby sister in the family?

"Seriously Cate, Mum has missed you. She talks about you a lot." Francie pulled her phone from her pocket. Rose's picture popped up on the screen again.

"She'll be asking about you," she said, covering her grin.

"Why do you say that?"

"You're here, and she's not. I have to tell you, she can't stand that you'll be staying here."

"What the hell did I do to her?" I looked at Francie, but she just laughed.

"You left, she didn't."

"She blames me for everything, doesn't she?"

"When something goes wrong, Rose blames anybody she can. If it makes you feel better, it's not just you, she blames all of us."

"Now, you're just trying to make me feel better."

"Of course. Now, tell me everything. I want gossip."

"How about I tell you that I'm just grand, and after Mum is better, I'll be going back to Boston."

"How about you try telling me the truth."

"You don't buy it?"

"Come on Cate. I can read you like a book. Something is up. It's written all over your face. You've always worn your sorrow on your sleeve. So—are you going to tell me?"

"Michael didn't like that I came to Ireland."

"Can't say that I blame him, a man shouldn't be OK with his wife being a world away."

"You're not helping."

Francie laughed as she brought the cup to her lips. "Look if you aren't ready to talk... fine. I get it." She reached across and took my hand. "Cate, I want you to know I'm here for you, no matter what. You have a home here as long as you need."

"I know." I grasped her hand in mine. "I'll tell you everything when the time is right."

"Don't wait too long, OK?"

"I promise. You'll be the first."

"Do you miss work?" She asked, taking another sip of tea.

"More than I thought I would, but I've been volunteering at a women's shelter."

"Do you like it?"

"I love it. My heart aches for these women, so I do whatever I can."

"What are you doing?"

"You know, filing paperwork for restraining orders, medical forms, even simple things, like address changes."

"That's good."

I touched the petals of the flowers on the table. "I miss the real work though," I said.

"So, start over, nothing's stopping you." Francie's phone rang again. Rose's picture appeared like magic...again. She flicked the phone and it spun on the table.

"OK, I think you better answer it now," I said, reaching for the sugar bowl. "Go ahead and answer."

I ran the spoon around the inside of the cup, waiting. Hoping for a change of topic. I didn't want to talk about why I quit work. Too many open wounds.

"I don't need to be talking to her. I'm talking to you."

Just then I felt the vibration in my pocket. I slipped out my phone and saw Michael's picture and set it on the table.

"So?"

"I don't need to be talking to him. I'm talking to you."

She cocked her head and laughed. "Fair enough."

Francie got up and took her cup to the sink. "I want to ask you something," I said.

"Ask me anything," she said, turning away from the window.

"Who's Finn?"

"Who?" She turned toward me, the color drained from her cheeks.

"Finn. Claire said Mum called out the name, in the park, and again at the hospital."

"I know. She told me that, too. I've never heard the name before."

"Do you think Connor knows?"

"If anyone would, it would be Claire and Connor." She turned back to the window. Something changed. Francie seemed suddenly distracted.

"Hey, if you need to go, it's OK. I'm fine here."

"No, I'll stay. You shouldn't be alone."

"Francie, I grew up here. I'm exhausted and I need to unpack. Connor said something about dinner. I'd love to take a nap."

"Yeah, he said we had reservations at The Fresca for six-thirty. I need to pick up something for Colin, before we go. Are you sure you don't mind?"

"Yes. Go do what you need to. I'm fine."

"OK. Call if you need anything. Text me if Connor calls."

"Of course, I will. Go on now."

I walked Francie to the door and kissed her good-bye. I stood in the doorway, waving as she drove away. I closed the door and plopped on the couch, time to reflect, to breathe, no one questioning my every move. Quiet.

Mittens jumped up and twirled in my lap, settling in the curve of my folded leg. I dug my fingertips deep into her plush fur, looking around the room, oddly hoping to find something out of place. But everything remained, just as Mum had left it.

On the table, her magazines laid out in a row. The fireplace mantel sparkled in the sunlight peeking through the windows. Her cell phone, sat alone on the coffee table, calling out for attention. I fingered it in my hand, remembering the day Izzy took Mum to get it for the first time.

"You never know when you'll need one," Izzy said, grabbing her coat as she took her grandmother's arm and led her toward the door.

"You just want to keep track of me," Mum grumbled, as she followed behind her.

"That too," Izzy laughed, as she squeezed her hand, and helped her to the car.

I fingered it, then flipped it open. The battery had run down, so I took it into the kitchen to find the charger. Sure enough, it sat under the towels in the top drawer, right where it was supposed to be. I connected it, set it on the counter to charge. I felt like an intruder, staring at the dark screen. As if I were spying, trying to learn more of my mother. After hearing Rose in the hospital, there seemed to be a great deal Mum was hiding, at least from her daughters.

As the charge slowly returned, I watched as the phone lit up. I clicked on the call log, and found nothing unusual.

The calls and texts on Mum's phone told a great deal about her life. How she stayed connected. In the last few weeks Connor, Claire, Rose, Francie, and Paddy had all called, even a call from Izzy. Seeing the names, I felt guilty. My name wasn't on the list. Had I been so wrapped up in my broken life that I hadn't bothered to at least, check on her? Her text messages were the same. *"Checking to see how you are?"* *"Do you want to do lunch?"* Just as I was about to flip it closed, I saw the name Finn, caught between texts from Connor and Francie. I pressed the icon.

"Just want you to know I'm thinking about you today."
Love Finn.

She was real, Someone Mum knew well enough to attach her name to the number. But who was this Finn? Somehow, she had connected herself to Mum's life, enough for Mum to open her phone and see her name. Was Finn a friend, like Claire, someone from her life before us? Maybe someone she had helped a lifetime ago?

I closed the phone and put it back on the counter. The cat had followed me into the kitchen and jumped on the counter. I scratched and rubbed her neck, trying to figure out who Finn was. Had that been just a random message after an afternoon lunch?

I flipped it open, and pushed the button for her messages.

"May you find happiness." Finn (28 Sept)

"Thinking of you." Finn (28 Aug)

"Hope you are doing well." Finn (28 July)

"I think of you every day." Finn (28 June)

They went on for months, always on the 28th, for almost a year. There was never a return message. I closed the phone and laid it down, realizing Mum hadn't lost her mind at all. I turned on the faucet, and let the cold water run over my hands, then splashed it against my face to clear my head. Maybe her deliberate ramblings weren't a part of the illness, but something very real, very heartbreaking.

I took my suitcase upstairs, and went straight to Mum's room. I set it in the corner and let the scent of roses overtake me. I had to laugh, not only did she have roses downstairs, but a small vase stood on her dresser, though wilted, I imagined Francie or Rose must have placed them there. I'd remind myself to take them downstairs and replace them.

It had been at least eight years, since I'd left. A few random visits, but her room hadn't changed, not a bit, not the smell, not the furniture, not even the sense of her presence. I choked back tears, but they fell, as I walked around the room touching everything familiar. I opened the window and welcomed the afternoon breeze.

The dusted maple dresser stood against the wall, a glass tray of perfume bottles sat on top, along with her brush and comb set in the middle. Her tiny pearl earrings reflected in the light. It looked so normal, as if Mum were in another room. She'd come back, dress, comb her hair, and start her day.

I opened the top drawer of her dresser and saw everything folded and in order. I flipped through her garments, careful not to disturb anything. Inside, leaning against the side, were old cards, birthdays and holidays from a time past. They dated back long before I'd left for Boston. A birthday card from Paddy, an anniversary card from Da, small scraps of paper, filled with words of endearment. I placed them back in their secret cache, remembering how much she loved celebrations. She'd bake cakes, sing songs, and toss out her love to all of us. A chill fell as I closed the drawer and stepped back, embarrassed that I had invaded her privacy.

I wondered if Izzy had ever done the same in my room, found things she had no reason to find. Touched pieces of me that didn't belong to her. Why, when someone becomes sick, does it give family a right to search, to find dark, hidden secrets, that could change everything? If she carried a secret, it was not mine to find, at least not now.

For a reason I couldn't explain, I continued my search. I opened another drawer on the other side of the dresser; her belongings still neatly folded, hosiery, camisoles, and scarfs. Next to it, a jewelry box, flat and wooden with a carved swan on the lid, Da had given to her one Christmas. I opened it and saw the remnants of her jewelry. A pendant with purple violets, a simple gold bracelet lay on top. As I fingered through the jewelry, memories of Mum dressed for different occasions came to mind.

More cards and letters lay at the bottom of the drawer, in their place. I held the card and again inhaled the scent of roses. Then I saw a postcard from America, Oregon to be exact, but no return address.

Alice,

Just wanted to wish you a happy birthday. I think of you every day.

Finn

Holding it close, I again smelled the roses. I put it back, closed the drawer, and sat down on the bed, running my hand across Mum's worn quilt. The one she made when we were just girls. I clenched the bed cover tight, as I curled myself up in it, staring at the patches; remembering the memory of each patch. Da's flannel nightshirt, Mum's silk blouse, Rose's

Garden of Nails

Sunday skirt, they were all together, the memories sewn into this minute. I lay in the stillness for a short time.

I don't know how long I slept. I opened my eyes and looked at the room my mother may never see again.

I went into her closet and flipped through her clothes. Most looked familiar, but there were new slacks and shirts of bright colors. Between the old and new sat a memory she cherished, Da's sweater, the one she had wrapped herself in on the day she came home from the hospital alone. She had refused to give it away. I pulled it down and clutched it close. It no longer held Da's smell. Now it was her I smelled. I returned it to the closet and straightened the clothes.

I looked around for other memories. This seemed the place she kept them, memories of Da, memories of us girls, even Finn. I peeked up on the top shelf of the closet, but saw nothing unusual, boxes of all sizes and shapes covered the shelves, but there in the corner was something dark, maybe navy blue, but I couldn't tell. I reached up and my fingertips grabbed hold. I pushed the two white boxes on top of it back and it fell into my hands, a leather-bound album.

I flipped through the clear-coated pages that enclosed the pictures.

The first photo resembled a passport picture, but one from a long time ago. I took it from its holder and turned it over. 1953, was written on the back. The little girl had a big white bow that covered most of her short bob, and flopped on her face. Her eyes, like slits, were set deep in her wide forehead. They drooped a bit, but she stared straight ahead. Her rounded jaw almost tucked behind her neck. There was such sadness in her face. The puffy cheeks, the pouty lips... I couldn't look away.

Why was the first picture so sad? Who could this little girl be?

I felt like an intruder rummaging through the private moments of Mum's life. I slipped the picture back and continued flipping through more pages. I couldn't help it, I was transfixed. Not even an hour in Mum's home and I was pilfering through her privacy, sifting through her things, as if they were set out for auction.

I laid the album out on the bed, flipping through the pages. I slid out a wedding picture and read the back. *1973, St. Helen's. The little girl? It couldn't be. This girl had bright blue eyes with freckles splashed across her face.* I put the picture back and flipped to the last page. This woman resembled the one in the wedding dress, but older now, streaks of gray in her hair, wrinkles at the corners of eyes. On the back, *Finn 2004.*

This was Finn. Her life unfolding in the album

How did it relate to Mum?

Still holding the picture and staring at the album on the bed, I pulled the afghan off the footboard, and rolled myself in it. Laying my head on the pillow, I waited to drift off to sleep, but it didn't come. I turned to my side and flipped back through the pictures. Another set of wedding pictures, no name on the back, just a date—2000. The same woman appeared animated, almost jumping off the page in front of me. What the hell? *Who were these people? Why were they in an album hidden in my mother's closet?*

I closed my eyes and tried to connect the dots. The messages, the photos...a faint memory finally made the connection.

"Mum, we're here," I called out.

There she stood in the dining room on the phone. Her jaw tight, her fingers grasping the counter.

"No. It can't be possible," I heard her say, turning away from me.

I held Izzy back from running into her grandmother's arms, as she always did. Something was wrong. I saw the fear in her eyes when she looked up at me.

"Please don't call again. I can't help you with this matter."

She replaced the receiver and came back into the living room. Her face ashen, her fingers red, still clenched tight. At the sight of Izzy, she lightened.

"How is my sweet girl?" she called, her arms stretched out.

"Can I stay?" Izzy cried.

"Of course, you can. We'll have a grand time. Going to bake a cake, we are."

"Mum, who was that?" I asked, taking hold of her arm.

"No one. Don't be bothered."

"You told them not to call again. Is someone disturbing you?"

"No. I'm fine."

"Come on, Mum. Is there a problem you can't tell me about?"

"Catherine, leave it be," Mum brushed the curls from Izzy's face.

The opening of the door jarred me from the memory, and I awoke with a start, as Izzy burst into the bedroom.

"Mom, what are you doing? Whose pictures are those?" She asked, hopping on the bed and grabbing up the album.

"What are you doing here?"

"We came to pick you up for dinner."

"Izzy, leave those pictures alone."

"You're looking at them. Who are they?" She continued to flip through the pages, until I grabbed them from her hands.

"I don't know."

"Why are you going through her stuff?"

"I wasn't. I was trying to make room in the closet to put my things away, but I must have jarred it, because it fell off the shelf in the closet."

"You were snooping."

"Please Izzy, I wasn't snooping. I'm putting these away," embarrassed that I had been caught.

"Well hurry up," Izzy said, still staring down at me. "Uncle Connor said he has reservations for six-thirty."

"What time is it? How long was I asleep?"

"A little before six. We just got here. He told me to come up and get you."

"Dear Lord, I need to get ready. Why didn't you call?"

"I did, you didn't answer. Left messages."

"Give me a minute, I need to take a shower and change. Go down stairs, I'll be as quick as I can."

"OK, but hurry up. We don't want to be late."

"Are you ready?" I heard Connor call from the bottom step.

"Almost," Izzy called back. "She's putting on lipstick, she'll be done in a few minutes," she said, heading toward the stairs.

I put the photo album back on the top shelf and opened my suitcase to dig through my clothes. Hopefully they weren't too wrinkled. I picked out a pair of dark slacks and a light sweater. Something to help keep off the rain.

As I dressed, I debated about asking Connor about Finn. He had to know. There was too much here, the text messages, the postcards, the picture album? He knew.

Maybe everyone knew. All the blank looks, the change of subject whenever Finn was mentioned. Maybe Boston had distracted me from my real world.

"Connor, can you come up here a minute?" I asked.

"Aren't you ready yet?" I smiled at the minor irritation in his voice.

"Yes, I just need to ask you about something."

"Well, let's get on with it." I heard the tapping of his shoes on the stairs.

"You know what, never mind. I'm not feeling well; would you mind going without me?"

"But the dinner is for you and me, you have to go." Izzy whined from the foot of the stairs.

"Fine." I shook my head in exasperation. I could make it through a couple of hours.

Nine

Just past ten o'clock, Francie pulled into the driveway. She hugged me as we walked to the house. I flipped on the foyer light and she went directly to the kitchen. On a mission it seemed.

She opened the cabinet next to the refrigerator. "You want a glass?" I watched her take a bottle of whiskey from the top shelf.

"No. I'm good," setting my purse on the table.

"Well, I'll pour you one anyway. In case you change your mind."

"I'm sure I won't, but thanks."

"I'm glad they talked me into going. It was exactly what I needed. I had forgotten how well the kids get along. Of course, they're not really kids anymore. Getting old is hell." I shook my head with a smile.

"Speak for yourself. I'm never getting old. Paddy will be an old codger before I give up my title of baby girl. And Colin calls me sexy mama. I'm never giving that up."

"I don't blame you."

She poured the whiskey until it brimmed right to the edge of both glasses. We sat together. I watched while Francie sipped her whiskey.

"Jenny is amazing, isn't she?"

Francie laughed. "She runs circles around me. Poor Connor just swings from her coat tails."

"That's what I want to do." I took a sip of whiskey from the overflowing glass.

"I thought you didn't want any."

"What can I say? You're a bad influence."

"Why thank you, Catherine. I do try." Francie raised her glass to acknowledge the compliment.

"So, what is it you want to do?"

"Have a passion for something. At her age, Jenny carries herself like a true professional. I did that once." Francie smiled back but didn't say anything. "Did you see how she was dressed, classy flats, a tailored suit, with a tucked in silk blouse?"

"Are you jealous?"

"Yes. I am. Jenny and Rose are both elegant, but Jenny... Jenny is something special. Rose wears her elegance. Jenny is elegance. The real deal."

"I know what you mean."

"She is an absolute joy to watch move across the room, where Rose is quite terrifying. You don't know who she's going to attack next," I said with a chuckle.

"So be Jenny, and tell Rose to feck off." Francie suddenly erupted in laughter. "Oh my, I can't believe I said that." We laughed. "I'm sorry that was mean. I didn't mean it."

"You might well be sorry, but you meant it, and it is OK. I'm so tired of holding everything in." I drank from the glass again.

"Connor has missed you," Francie said.

"No, he's missed Izzy. He was the one who arranged almost everything. He loves her like his own."

"Did you hear him tonight, going on how Izzy couldn't have done so much without your support? He was tumbling all about himself."

"He loves us all."

"You're right. He's helped all the kids. He's been a pretty amazing uncle."

"Your Izzy is quite amazing. What a feat for her to get an internship with Jenny. You did well, Sis."

"I have a question for you. Why would Rose call Izzy and ask about our flight and the house?"

"Because she is nosy? Because she doesn't want you here? Do you want me to keep going?"

I got up from the table and opened the French doors, and flipped on the light. I stared out into Mum's garden. It was the first time I had really looked at it since my arrival. It was breathtaking, even with winter coming on.

"Let's go sit in the garden. I have to tell you about something I did, in the hospital, today." I stepped out and took a seat on the bench, watched as Francie followed.

"Whenever I'm around Rose, I'm ten again. No matter what I do, it's not good enough. God forbid something happen to Mum—I leave a door unlocked, or forget something. How would I deal with it if something happened on my watch?"

"Where's this coming from?"

"I don't know. It's been simmering for a while," I said. I felt the heat of a blush move up my face and took a deep breath.

"If you don't want to be here, go home. I can handle Rose," Francie said with a frown.

"God no, that's not what I meant. I need some time on my

own; I need to be here." I looked around and felt a sense of who I was.

"OK, so tell me about the terrible thing that's eating you up."

"I spied on Rose."

"OK, that sounds like you are ten."

"After we talked to the doctors and everyone left, Rose went back. She threatened Mum with a secret she knew."

"I'm sure Rose knows a lot of secrets."

"She was so cruel. Mum was so helpless."

"What did Mum say?"

I got up from the bench, then turned toward Francie. "She told her to go ahead and tell us. She was going to do it anyway."

"Go Mum."

"That's not the worst of it. She knows who Finn is."

"Who is Finn?"

I looked back at Francie, brushing her curls from her face. "Finn, remember that was the name Mum called when she was in the park."

"You know what? This is not the time. I'm a little drunk, and tired, and I'm going to go upstairs and go to bed."

"Francie this is important. We need to know what Rose knows."

"You do. It's not important to me. Let Mum keep her secrets and let Rose feel important, for a while. I'm going to bed."

I was drunk as well. Two drinks at the restaurant, and now almost a full glass of whiskey, but I didn't' want to sleep. I needed to talk.

"No, don't go to bed not yet. I need you."

"Now who's being a bit selfish?"

I stared as if she had insulted me. "What?"

"You might be more like Rose than you think."

"So, you think I'm a bitch?"

"No, not exactly, but look who's calling the kettle black?"

"I can't believe you just said that."

"Rose isn't the only one who can get testy."

"OK, spit it out. What are you implying?"

"Nothing. I need to go to bed. Let's finish this when we are both clear headed."

"I'm not really like her, am I?" I wiped my cheek before Francie noticed the tears.

"No, Cate, you're not. It's late. It's raining...do what you want. I'm going to bed." She wrapped her arms around me, then gently kissed my cheek. "I love you Cate." She turned and walked away.

Since my arrival in Dublin, I felt trapped. Any moment my emotions would overwhelm me. Now was not the time.

Part of me wondered how Francie could have talked to me in such a way. But she was probably more right than I could ever imagine. Francie's realization embarrassed me as much as it shocked me.

I didn't respond when I felt the first vibration of my phone, but when the second came through, I placed it on the bench face up, staring at the picture.

I went back to the kitchen, took the bottle from the counter, refilled my glass, and walked back out on the patio, into the half-lit night. This place had been my mother's joy.

Outdoor lights hung from the eaves. Connor must have added those, so she could see out into her yard. For years she had planted, pruned, and spent hours out among the trailing vines and white roses. I often wondered what drew her. Was it the silence or the sense of pride in what she had created?

I was drawn to it as well. I caught the delicate petals between my fingers that felt like velvet. I caressed the life around me that my mother had created. Everything here was representative of the woman I thought I knew. But here in her garden, with her away, the magic was diminished. I saw it as it really was. I bent down and touched the swans that had weathered. Did they know her secrets? Were her demons contained here, safe from prying eyes?

In the garden, caressed by the roses and the swans, away from the fears of a middle-aged woman, I no longer worried about where I stood in the line of succession. Succession had lost importance. The sister I had loved from the day I was born, always wondered where she stood, always pressing Da for his undying attention.

"Da, you will always love me more, right?"

"Of course, I will," he had said, *"but I will love her equally as well."*

"But I will always be your first, right?"

"Yes Rose, you will always be my first."

Years later, she'd remind me again and again, of the power she held.

My phone vibrated once more. I pulled it from my pocket and saw Rose's face. *God not here, not again.* I slipped it back in my pocket, and took a sip of the whiskey; mild going down, soothing, like the petals. The phone rang again, and I hit the green button.

She didn't wait for me to say anything. "I'm outside. I have a key, but I expect you'll let me in." The line went dead.

I didn't run to greet her. I waited for her to ring the bell, show a curtsey to my privacy. She let herself in, calling through the house. I took the last gulp of whiskey and sat on the bench. I'd wait her out. If she had to see me, she'd have to come find me.

"Where are you?" she called out. I heard the door slam as she stomped through the living room.

"Enjoying Mum's garden, Rose,"

"I always hated this garden," she said, standing in the doorway. "I never understood why she loved it so much."

"She was free here. She didn't have to be anybody, but who she wanted to be."

"She's our Mum, who else would she want to be?"

"Rose, tell me you are not so provincial, to think we were all she had in her life."

"I didn't say that. I just never understood her passion for this place."

"Then I guess you never really understood Mum, did you?"

"Just because I don't like the garden, doesn't mean I don't understand her."

I stared at my sister as she moved across the patio. Her stylish bob bounced in place. "It's awfully late, what do you want?" I asked. I watched her finger her diamond-studded earrings.

"I tried to call you," she said, brushing the bench off before she sat down.

"Yes, I know. Can this wait? I'm getting ready for bed."

"No, we need to talk." She checked her phone and then set

her purse on the ground in front of her.

"Are you drinking?" Pointing at the glass my hand.

"Why yes, I am. And it looks like my glass is empty, but not for long." I said. "Would you like one of your own?"

"No."

"Too bad. I'll have another. You want to wait here, or go inside?"

"I'll go in."

She followed me into the kitchen. Sliding the coat from her shoulders, she took a seat at the table. I reached for the bottle, and filled both glasses three quarters full.

"OK, Rose what is this all about? It's past eleven. Why are you here?"

"I know why you came," she blurted.

"Of course, you do. Claire called. Mum wants us all here."

"No. I mean why you came home. It wasn't about Mum."

"Good God, Rose what are you getting at?"

"I know about Michael."

I took a drink and leaned back in the chair. "Of course, you do. I'm married to him."

"I know you left him." She got up and moved behind the chair, resting her hands on the back. Her knuckles white with the grip.

"Why would I leave him?" Swirling the whiskey in the glass.

"God, you just don't want to face the truth."

"What the hell are you talking about?"

"I know why you got on the plane without him."

"What are you taking about?" Rose had a habit of taking

things, about which she knew very little, and twisting them to fit what she wanted. Sometimes she didn't even need details. She took assumptions and made them fact.

"I'm being realistic." She smiled a crooked little smirk.

"No, Rose, you aren't." I wanted to slap the smug grin off her face. "You have no idea what my life is. If that's what you think, sorry, you win the consolation prize."

"Go home, Catherine. Patch things up with your husband. I think that is more important than taking care of Mum. We are all here for her."

I took my glass from the table and placed it on the counter. "You don't know anything about Michael."

"I know he cheated on you."

"Wow." I had to keep a straight face. "And how do you know that?" I wasn't about to tell her the truth. I imagined it would be so much easier to believe he cheated on me, or had a one-night-stand. That would have been much easier to forgive, but how would someone forgive being beaten by the person you loved. I would never give her the thrill of knowing my truth.

"You're not denying it?" She persisted. She moved her hand up to her earring, swirled it between her fingers. She did that the way Francie bit her lip.

"You always have to be in everybody's business? I don't get it. What good does it do?"

"That's not true." Rose straightened the pendant on her silk blouse.

"I asked you a question. What good does it do you?"

"I don't know what you're talking about."

"Good God, Rose, you know exactly what I'm talking about. No one does anything better than you." I walked away from her, but turned back and stood in front of her. "And for the record, you have no idea what the hell you're talking about. I won't even dignify your assumptions."

"I know it's hard to admit, when your husband cheats, but you need to go home and work things out." She fiddled with a cuticle on one of her painted nails, and stared back at me.

"God, you've got nerve Rose, I'll give you that."

"I know he cheated on you. You must just feel awful."

"Get out of here, Rose. Go home."

"You can't kick me out."

"I just did. Get the hell out of here before I say or do something I'll regret."

"You just can't face the truth." She smoothed her hair, and her jaw tightened.

"I face the truth every day, I don't need to hear lies from someone who knows shit about my life."

"You need to leave, Catherine. Go back to your marriage, what's left of it. Mum doesn't need you looking after her house," Rose said.

"Look who's calling the kettle black. Be careful where you throw your stones, big sister. For the record, I'll stay here as long as I think I'm needed." I tucked my hands into my coat pockets; one, so I wouldn't hit her, and the other, so she wouldn't see the tremors.

"I know what you're doing, and you have no right." She ran her finger across her lips, I imagine checking to see if her eight-hour lipstick was still in place.

"What are you talking about?"

"You've been rummaging through Mum's private things."

Suddenly it all came together. She knew, but why would

it bother her with what I found? She already knew, or so she said. It didn't matter.

"Don't deny it. Izzy told me about the picture album." Rose picked up her purse, and adjusted it on her shoulder.

"Why would you call my daughter to see what I was doing?"

"I was being a caring auntie."

"You were being a conniving bitch."

"How dare you call me that."

"Fine." I took a breath. "I found some pictures. I don't know who anybody was, except that there was a woman whose name was Finn, and she seems pretty important to Mum."

"What did you do with them?" Rose asked.

"What do you think?" I looked straight at her. "I put them back where I found them.

"What's really going on, Rose? Wait. Let me see if I can figure it out. You think it's your duty to take care of everything: Mum's health, my marriage, Francie's career. The rest of us couldn't possibly be as good as you."

"I never said that."

"You didn't have too." I leaned against the counter.

She opened her purse, pulled out her keys, then snapped it closed. She moved toward the dining room. "I just know what is best." She straightened the flowers on the table, picking at the petals that had dropped, without even looking up.

"You're a fucking bitch Rose, you always have been."

Petals blurred as they flew off the table. I ducked, though her aim had been off. Shards of glass fell across the floor. Water dripped off the table.

We stood frozen in the moment. Rose turned toward the door.

"I want you out of here by Sunday, and if you tell anyone, you'll be sorry."

Was I ten?

I didn't pick up the broken glass, or the rose petals strewn about. Instead, I took a glass of whiskey up to the room I had shared with my sisters. I stood in the doorway, observing the pieces of our lives we had left behind. Rose's dolls sat on top of the dresser, Francie's U2 posters still hung from the wall. My books, from the poetry of Sylvia Plath, the literature of Bronte and Lawrence to Segal's, *Love Story*, were piled onto two over-stuffed bookcases.

Dolls, posters, and books defined our lives. It felt odd. My head whirled from the whiskey. I had not forgotten the evening. The conversation with Francie, the solace of Mum's garden, then Rose, digging at my skin, filled with good intentions.

I showered and dressed for bed. I opened the window, relishing the cool, damp air.

I pulled the covers tight, realizing my childhood had disappeared.

I ached to be loved. I had a hole and didn't know how to fill it.

Ten

Ilooked at the clock on the nightstand. 2:30 am. Sleep would not come. I slipped out of bed, closed the bedroom door and sat the top of the stairs.

I tapped his picture and waited. It rang once, twice...

"Hello." His voice crisp and strong.

Why did I do this?

"Cathy, I know it's you."

"..."

"Are you all right?"

"..."

"If you're not going to talk, why did you call?"

What could I say? I let the phone drop to the floor. A few seconds later, it rang. When I saw his picture, the ache dug deep.

"Michael."

"Come home. Cathy. I've changed. I'm not the same person."

"It's been three days. You haven't changed. You can't change."

"Give me a chance..."

"No. I don't know why I called."

"Cathy..."

No Michael, I've got to figure things out for myself. I'm staying here."

"Let me come there, then."

"No. I shouldn't have called." I disconnected the call before he could say another word. Twenty-five years of marriage finished with the press of a button.

Memories crept through my mind. Laughter...Loving.... Shattered by the loss of control.

I told myself I wouldn't cry.

Everything was as I left it. I cleaned up the glass scattered in the dining room, put the whiskey back in the cupboard and turned on the burner to heat water for tea. I put the glasses in the sink and wiped down the counter. I gazed out the kitchen window at the morning sky. The sun just breaking through, the ground wet with dew.

The doorbell rang as I poured the steaming water into my cup. Standing beyond the glass panels of the door, a familiar figure fidgeted with her hair. It had been years since I'd seen Mum's best friend. I smiled as Claire adjusted the scarf draped over her shoulders.

There she stood, just as I remembered. Her deep green eyes shining with tears. Her smile was my true welcome home. I pulled her into a hug.

"Oh Love, did I wake you? I know I should've called, but my errands got the better of me." She blushed in the morning sun, and tugged at the gold cross on her neck.

"No, no. I've been up for a while. I'm so glad you're here. I've missed you so much."

"Would you like some tea?" I asked.

"Oh, that would be grand. I'm a sight." She slipped out of her coat, and pulled off the flowered scarf. As she walked into the dining room, she looked around. "Catherine I've spent a lot of time in this house, and I've never seen the table without roses."

"There was a bit of an accident last night."

"You dropped the vase?"

"No." I paused unsure I should say anything. "Rose threw it at me."

"What? Who on earth would throw a Waterford vase?" Claire looked at the table.

"We got into a fight. We swore at each other, she threw the vase—I threw her out."

"What could have been so bad?"

"Everything, or maybe simple jealousy. We've battled for years. Last night it came to a head."

"I'm sorry that it came to this." I saw true sympathy in her eyes. She must have thought we had more control than we displayed. "One of you must replace it."

"I know. I will as soon as I can."

"Shame on you both. When will you get past all this nonsense?"

"I've missed you."

"You're changing the subject."

"I know. I've gotten quite good at that."

"Very well. How are you?"

"The truth?"

"What else should you tell me?"

"I'm a mess."

"Tell me something I can't see written all over your face."
She laughed and held my hand. "It will get better."

"I saw your Mum, last night."

"Now who's changing the subject?" She smiled and cocked
her head. "How was she?" I asked.

"Just grand, she smiled, even called me by name. We
talked, had tea and shared a tart, I smuggled in." Claire raised
her eyebrows.

"So, she was coherent?"

"Oh, yes, I wanted to wrap her up and bring her home."

"That's good. I'm glad." The whistle of the kettle brought
me back to reality.

"Let me help with the tea." Claire opened the cabinet and
paused. She reached and pulled out a hairbrush from behind
the cups and set it on the counter.

"How did that get there?"

"I imagine your Mum thought she was putting it away."

"Oh my gosh. I found a bracelet hanging from the key
holder, but I didn't think anything of it. I just put it back on
her dresser."

"She doesn't really have dementia, you know."

"Dr. Redland told us about the tumor, but how bad will
things get?

"This is just the beginning," she said, pointing at the brush.

"You were with her when no one else was. What did you
notice?"

"About a year ago the headaches started, and I noticed
things, little things at first. Forgetting she said something,
or that she bought something at the store. One day I found

her standing in the hall staring at a picture of your Da. She handed me the frame...." She paused again.

"What did she ask?"

"She pointed to your Da and asked why that picture was in the frame. When I told her, she pulled it close. She said she had never met him."

"Why didn't you tell us?"

"I did. Everyone here knew."

"And no one thought it was important to call me?"

"We didn't want to worry you, Rose came almost every day, practically smothered the poor woman, Francie and Paddy came, too. Your mum was well taken care of. Someone was always with her, we made sure of it.

"After a while, it was your mum who asked us to take her to Dr. Murphy. He ran tests and found the tumor. She made us promise not to tell you girls about the tumor."

"And you agreed?"

"You know your mum."

"No, obviously I don't."

"Let's go get breakfast," Claire said, taking the cup from my hand. "Change your clothes, I'll wait for you here." She set the cup on the sink

"Francie is here. She's upstairs sleeping."

"Let her sleep, I want you to myself. She can join us later."

Once upstairs, I looked in on Francie, snuggled deep in the covers.

"Hey are you awake?"

"No," She said inaudible, turning away from me.

"I'm going to have breakfast with Claire, do you want to come?"

"No. Colin is coming soon. I'll sleep a little longer."

I slipped into a tailored blouse and black slacks, dabbed on make-up, with a touch of Mum's perfume.

As I came back down, Claire sat on the bottom step, talking to Mittens in whispers. The cat leaned into her shoulder.

"I'm coming down in case you have any more secrets to tell," I called out.

"Nope, all done," Claire said, "everything is secure with Mittens."

We stepped out the front door, the rain had stopped, and the clouds had opened to let the sun through. The sidewalks were puddled, and the wind blew leaves across the street. Arm in arm we headed down the lane.

"Claire?" I asked, "where does she go?"

"Your Mum?"

"Yes. Do you think she knows? Does she suddenly forget? You know, like the hairbrush in the cupboard?"

"I don't know Catherine. I'm sure if she knew beforehand, she wouldn't do it."

"I just wonder what it's like...for her."

"I don't think it is something she thinks about until someone mentions it."

"It's hard to imagine. She always prided herself on being on top of everything."

"If it's hard for you to understand, imagine how she must feel."

At the end of the street, Claire pointed to the left toward the town center. "There's a great little café just around the corner."

Garden of Nails

"I remember this place," I said staring at the store front next to the cafe."

"It's open, do you want to go in?" Claire asked.

"No. We would stop here on our way to and from school. Da slipped coins in our pockets each morning, so we wouldn't have to do without treats. Rose always told us what to buy, but every now and then, Francie and I would buy something different, just to spite her."

"And?" Claire looked up.

"And she won most of the time," I said, opening the door to the café.

"I remember once, when you girls were little. I came to pick your mum up for something. A church meeting, I think. You and Rose were running through the house, screaming about a doll. You both were in quite a rage."

"I remember that doll."

"Your da gave it to Francie." Claire smiled. "From then on, every time I came by, that doll was wrapped up in her arms. She cherished that thing for the longest time." Claire laughed, lost in the memory.

"I guess things haven't changed much," I said.

Inside the Costa Café, almost all the tables were full. Men ate biscuits and blood sausage. Women, wrapped in coats and scarfs, drank their mochas and lattes, with toast.

"It used to be an Italian restaurant," Claire said, "but the owner died, and his daughter decided to move into the 21st century."

We found an empty table in the corner. Next to us, a man hovered over books piled high on his table.

"I'll be right back," Claire said, "the toilet."

I put my coat on the chair, took a seat and glanced at the

titles of the books *Irish Law Legal Research Methods, and The Modern Family: Relationships and the Law.* I remembered pouring over these same titles in the Trinity Library, struggling with briefs, creating profiles of make-believe clients.

The man looked up and tipped his cap back. "You know the law?" He asked.

I touched the bindings, then pulled away, as if burned. "It just reminded me when I threw myself head first into those exact books."

"Did you have a favorite?" He asked, looking at me with a familiar smile.

"Dylan?"

"Oh my God. Cat? Is that you?

"Well, look at you. How long has it been? How are you?"

He stood up, bunching his hat in his hands. "Yes, it has been a long time. I'm good."

"I can't believe you're here. I heard you moved to Boston." Dylan ran his hands through his hair, gave a broad grin, and laid his cap on the stack of books.

"I did, but Mum took a spill. I've come back to help with things." I couldn't take me eyes off his face, the angle of his jaw, everything I remembered about him, and loved. "Wait, didn't your family live here?"

"Yes. I split my time between here and Trinity. My parents passed away and well, left me the house. I'm usually here on the weekends. Would you like to join me?" He asked, moving a chair closer to the table and motioning for me to sit down.

"I'm here with a friend. She went..." I paused, looking around for Claire. "She'll be right back."

Dylan had a trimmed beard and moustache, along with

the palest of green eyes. He tapped his pen on his yellow legal tablet.

"Wow—you look great." I felt like a school-girl meeting her crush. I could feel the blush burn my face. "Are you still practicing law?" He asked.

I bowed my head and stepped out of the way as a waitress came down the crowded aisle. "I gave it up when we moved to Boston."

"We?"

"After you left for Oxford, I finished my degree and got married. We moved to Boston about twelve years ago."

"That's too bad."

"Excuse me?"

"No, I just meant, you were a great debater. If I remember, you kicked my butt every time." Dylan stepped away from the table and helped me settle in my seat.

Suddenly I found myself back at Trinity pouring over law reviews. He was as handsome as ever, but now he was...more distinguished. He had a certain presence...Oh, hell...I didn't know what to think. I had loved him. For some reason I felt the heat burn deeper into my cheeks.

"You were pretty good yourself, I mean, I remember when you took on some of those experienced lawyers one-on-one." I ran my finger across my lips, realizing it had faded since we left the house, maybe faded, or licked away. "What are you doing now?" I asked, feeling my face almost explode.

"I teach law at Trinity," he smiled. "Who would have thought?"

"Everyone," I said, "you were destined for it." Claire returned to the table and immediately grabbed my arm and nudged me. "Claire, this is Dylan Nolan. We were law students at Trinity. We were just ran into each other."

They shook hands, and Dylan pulled up another chair. As we sat down, Claire looked at me with a devilish grin. I kicked her under the table, which only caused her to laugh.

As the waitress took our order, and I stared at Dylan, still fiddling with his cap, I slipped back to a memory of him, a memory that had stayed with me after all those years.

"Come on, let's call it a night. The library is closing pretty soon," Dylan said.

"I need one more source. Can you help?"

"What's the source?" Dylan asked.

"I need a quote for socialized government."

"OK, I'll look ten minutes then you're on your own. Got it?"

"Thanks."

I watched as he pulled six books from the shelves, sat down on the floor, and began going through them one by one.

"There. Found it. Always in the last one."

I pulled him from the floor, he took me in his arms, and our lips touched, just barely, then he kissed me.

"What do you want?" Claire asked, jarring me back to the café.

"Just coffee and muffin."

"Their breakfast sandwich is really good. If you're hungry."

"That sounds great."

Claire kept looking back and forth between Dylan and me. "Well... I'll go up and order. You two try to remember to breathe, OK?" Claire moved toward the counter, shaking her head.

Dylan's eyes were laughing. "If you aren't practicing

anymore, what are you doing?" he asked, leaning in on the table.

"Well in Boston, I... I mean we, raised our daughter. I volunteered for some social service programs, and helped with legal documents, not a lot, but I kept my fingers in the pie. I really enjoyed it." I folded my hands on the table, just a few inches from his. "But like I said, my mum is sick, so I came home."

"What happened, if you don't mind my asking?"

"She took a fall, and she's in the hospital."

"I remember your mum. I hope she feels better soon. Give her my regards, won't you?"

"I will, thank you. How's your family?"

"They're both gone. That's why I have the house." He blushed and dropped his head. "My wife passed on a few years ago."

"You got married?" My tongue got tied up.

"Yes. You seem shocked."

"No. I just...Well, I..."

"Here you go. Got your breakfast," Claire cried out, causing us to look over at her. Dylan even stood to help her place everything on the table.

"Did I come back too soon? You are blushing and..." she looked at Dylan, "so are you, come to think of it. My, my, did I break up a reunion here?"

"No, don't be silly." I brushed random strands of hair away from my face, and for a moment I wished I had taken more time with myself before leaving the house.

"You are flirting." Claire whispered into my hair, looking back at Dylan.

"No."

"Yes, you are. I know flirting when I see it."

"It was nice to see you," Dylan said, getting up from his chair. "You look grand, really, but I'm afraid I need to go, I have a class this afternoon."

"Always late, are you?"

"Oh, you remember?" He ran his fingers through his beard and gave me a shy smile.

"Yes, I think I still have the bruises." I didn't look away this time, but stared straight into the green eyes I once loved.

We laughed, and I knew we had both recalled that same memory of our first meeting--a head-on collision around a corridor of the halls of Trinity College. Our eyes met. Dylan reached for his coat, and handed me a card.

"While you're here, call my cell. I'd love to catch up."

I took the card, and looked over at him. He continued to stare. We shook hands and the warmth of his skin sent a chill I remembered all too well. I grinned, almost embarrassed, but didn't let go.

"It has been nice to meet you, Dylan," Claire called from her chair.

I watched as he gathered his books, and moved toward the door. While balancing the books, he pulled his jacket around his shoulders, then turned back with a smile and waved.

"A very handsome gentleman," Claire said, still staring at the door. "You went to law school with him?"

"Yes. We debated together. He was at the top of the class."

"You had a crush on him?"

"A little more than that."

"You loved him?"

"Yes. I did."

"I'm refilling my coffee, you have some things to tell me, girl."

Claire got up and went to the counter. In a few minutes she returned with two steaming cups. She set them on the table, and sat down. "Tell me everything."

"Are you sure you want to know?"

"Is this the first time you've seen him since Trinity?" Claire asked, still staring back at the door.

"After he went to Oxford, I never saw him, until right now."

"Is he the reason you married Michael?"

"He was everything to me, but I chose something else."

"Catherine, you did what you thought was best at the time."

"No. I was foolish. I lost a wonderful man, but I have Izzy, so life turned out just right."

"Are you going to call him?"

"I don't know." I looked down at the card, and the tiny numbers in the corner. I stared at it for a few moments, then slipped it into my pocket.

"Are you going to tell me the rest?"

"I did." I drank the last of my coffee and looked around, still dazed.

"That isn't what your face is saying. Have you seen yourself? You're crimson, and I'm being nice."

"He was my first." I could feel a rush of heat move up my body.

"First, what?" She looked over at me, "oh, that...." She grinned. "Spill. I may be an old lady, but I do love a mushy love story."

"No. Really Claire, it would be like telling Mum about the first time I had sex. Can't do that. Come on, we have to get back."

"Tell me what he meant to you. I won't leave until you do."

"Seeing Dylan put my head into a tailspin, and I can't get the image of him out of my mind. Things would have been different, had I made another choice, perhaps the right choice. I told myself that for years," looking up at Claire. "But it did me little good. I let him slip away, and it changed everything."

Claire didn't respond. She took my hand, and we walked back in silence. Claire always knew when it was not the time to talk. She slipped out of her coat and sat down.

"OK, let's get started, but before we do, let me tell you up-front, there will be nothing about Dylan. Are we clear?" I asked, almost staring her down.

Claire stuck out her upper lip, looking like a child. "Fine."

"Now what do you want to talk about?" I asked.

"You and Rose."

"Why do we need to talk about Rose? She gets under my skin."

"Tell me what happened last night."

"I'm going to give you the simplified version. She came over and said I should go back to Boston, that I had no right to violate Mum's house."

"What does that mean?"

"Hell, I don't know. We had an argument at the hospital."

"About?"

"I overheard a conversation with Mum. She threatened her with a secret."

"What secret?"

"It had something to do with Finn, the person Mum called for in the park."

"Why would she threaten Alice?"

"Hell, if I know, but Finn is real. I found her pictures."

Suddenly everything about Claire changed. She straightened up, brushed her hand through her curls, then licked her lips, as if it was time for me to pay more attention.

"You know something," I said, staring at Claire. "I can tell. You always do that, you lick your lips. You're an awful liar."

"It's not my place, Catherine."

"Jesus, that's what Connor said."

"Believe me, you'll know everything, when the time is right. Rose believes it's her job to protect your mum. Being the eldest, she always felt responsible. How did you not know that?"

"Maybe I was too busy being a kid."

"Rose and your mum, in Rose's eyes, they were much more than mother and daughter. She thought she should know every aspect of her life, and they were more like best friends. She hated for anyone to get in the way of their relationship."

"What does that have to do with my being here?"

"She's afraid you'll take her place." She walked over to the kitchen counter. "Don't you realize, in Rose's eyes, your mum doesn't belong to her children?"

"Can we stop talking about Rose? I get it. I'll back off."

I wiped my mouth, and looked up at Claire. "I'm done talking. Can we get out of here? I need some air."

Eleven

Connor drove to St. Philomena's Care Facility which had become Mum's new temporary home, at least that's what I kept telling myself. Connor hummed to a song on the radio.

After a while, I broke the silence. "How do you think she'll be?" I asked, feeling anxious. My fingers twitched, and I fiddled with my hair.

"I don't know. I called earlier this morning and Mrs. Moore said she was fine. Let's hope she's still fine."

From the driveway, it looked nothing like a healthcare facility, except the sign at the drive. Just a few blocks from Trinity, the three-story building sprawled across a beautiful landscape. Even with its lush outside beauty, I imagined every door bolted, with patients hidden from the world they once knew. The tears came.

"You can't be doing that now. You got to buck up, girl, be strong for your mum. You can cry all you want when you get home."

I brushed the tears away and waited for him to park the car. I could feel the heat in my face.

"No one is to blame for this." He brushed my nose, like he did when I was a little girl.

Anne Biggs

He said what I was afraid to. I tried to blame someone, so I wouldn't feel so guilty. Connor turned back toward me, and patted my hand.

"You're not alone in this. We all tried to find someone to blame, but it just happened. It's nobody's fault. It's what we do now, that counts."

We walked in through the double doors, hand in hand. The receptionist greeted us with a nod, telling us that Mrs. Moore would be out straight away, and that we should take a seat. We sat in the brightly colored lobby, country scenes of Ireland hung from the walls. Connor picked up a brochure and flipped through, nudging me now and again to show me the pictures. We both heard the door open and looked up. A tall woman in a blue suit walked toward us with her arm outstretched.

"I'm Mrs. Moore. Good to see you again, Mr. Brennan. You must be Catherine?"

"Yes, hello."

"I'd like to start with a tour of our facility. It is really very lovely, and your mother has settled in well."

The main floor had all the attractions, the rec room, the dining room, even the infirmary. The second floor held the bedrooms of the patients who were still mobile and could utilize the amenities on their own.

Though the rooms were not overly done, they did have a touch of old Irish charm. Everything looked comfortable and welcoming. I could feel myself relax as we moved through the facility.

"Right now, your mother is on the second floor, eventually, she'll need to be moved, but so far, she's doing amazingly well. The third floor is for those needing extensive care."

"Can we see her?" I asked, almost dreading the answer.

"We've been watching her closely. After meeting with the

team, we think a visit would be a good idea."

She led the way down the corridor to the elevator, and Connor continued to hold my hand until we reached a door midway down the hall.

Mum sat in a rocker with her afghan across her lap. Her head lay to the side, dozing, as she held a picture frame to her chest.

She looked fresh, sitting up in her chair in a mint green sweater and a hint of blush to her cheeks.

The room looked like any bedroom, almost like home. But it wasn't her home.

There were books on the shelves, that Connor and Claire must have picked out, hoping to make her feel more comfortable. A bottle of her perfume sat on the dresser, along with her brush and comb set.

She had a window with sheer curtains, dotted with flowers. On the second floor she could look out on the rooftops of the neighboring buildings, and the grounds of the college, with the students hurrying to their classes.

A clock and several magazines were on the night table.

On the dresser was a picture of her and Da at the beach, and another in a gilded frame with all her grandchildren gathered around her, hugging her and laughing. I couldn't see the picture she held to her breast.

The room looked better than I had imagined, warmer, friendlier, and the soft blue paint was soothing.

I saw the smile I remembered. I knew that, at least for now, she was here, in the room with us.

Mrs. Moore tapped her shoulder very softly. "Alice, are you awake, dear?" She paused for just a moment, then touched her again. "Alice, how are you feeling?"

I watched from the corner, afraid to move. Here I stood in mum's room, watching her sleep. Mrs. Moore tapped her a third time, rocking the chair ever so gently. She moved over to the bed, so that Mum could see her when she opened her eyes. I felt like an intruder.

Mum opened her eyes, then closed them a few more seconds. Finally, she looked around the room, slowly focusing on Mrs. Moore who stood in front of her. Her expression changed, her muscles tightened. She looked back and forth between Mrs. Moore and the bed. I could tell she didn't know who Mrs. Moore was. She sat up, but held her hand to her head and grimaced in pain. She looked over at the male assistant who had a tag on that read, Eric. "Aidan is that you?"

Eric looked over at Mrs. Moore, and she nodded her head. "Yes, Alice, it is." He bent down and patted her arm.

"Are we going out?" she asked, staring at him.

"No. I'm going to fix lunch and we'll eat at home, on the patio. It's a lovely day."

"Who are you? She asked, reaching out her hand to Mrs. Moore, letting the frame fall to the floor.

"I'm..." she paused and looked over at Eric, who still had hold of her hand. She nodded and pulled herself up from her knees. "I'm a friend, Alice."

"Do I know you?"

"Yes. I come to see you every day."

She looked up at Eric with even more confusion. I realized that she had no idea who anyone was, but I also saw the pain in her eyes from the headache.

"Do you like my room?" She asked, looking around.

"Yes, it is lovely," Mrs. Moore, said.

"I like it much better than I thought. The room is smaller

than I had hoped, but I have my things." She glanced around with a look of contentment. "Eric helps me every day," she said, grabbing hold of Eric's hand, and patting it. Something changed in her eyes. The pain had disappeared, and she was back.

"Claire came to see me last night," she said. "She wanted to take me to the city, but I was busy." She got up from the chair and moved over to the dresser and looked in the mirror. She ran her fingers through her cropped hair, then dabbed a bit of perfume behind her ears.

"Did you enjoy your visit?" Eric asked. He moved close and reached for her hand. She looked up, her eyes narrowed, and she stepped back. She was gone without even blinking her eyes.

"Oh Aidan, you're here."

Mrs. Moore looked at him. "Yes."

Mum took Eric's hand. "I have a bit of a headache. I miss my garden. Do you think someone could bring some flowers?" She leaned in and whispered, "And maybe some whiskey."

"No whiskey tonight, Alice," Mrs. Moore said.

She laughed and took a seat on the bed. "So how long can you stay, Aidan?" Mum looked at him so lovingly, so tender.

Eric knew his work, and picked up Mum's moods right away. "I'll be here all afternoon. I'll try to bring you some fresh flowers tomorrow. How would that be?" Smiling warmly.

I immediately fell in love with this young man who understood Mum better than anyone. He made her feel safe.

"Have a seat Aidan. They'll be ringing us for lunch, pretty soon. You'll stay, won't you?" Eric nodded slowly and patted her hand.

Twelve

After we left the facility, Connor weaved through the lanes of traffic, his attention fixed on the hectic patterns of the city.

For me, everything blurred. The pedestrians, the shops, the other autos, all merged into momentary flashes. Images mixed and obscure.

I lost myself in the moments of the day. I tried to isolate each one. Prioritizing and placing them in queues. But each was just as important as the next. Much too important to be layered. None could stand above the other.

We took the final turn in to Mum's drive. He turned off the ignition, he sat back and took a breath.

"She's never coming home, is she?" I asked, wanting the question to be rhetorical.

"I can't answer that, girl."

"I don't want an answer. I just said it out loud, so I could hear how the words sounded."

"We just have to let things play out. I'll call you later and set something up for tomorrow. Try to get some rest tonight, OK?" I squeezed his hand and got out of the car.

As I moved to the house, I noticed Francie's car parked at the curb. Finding her on the couch didn't surprise me. The glass of wine and the cigarette in her hand, did.

"It's not even four o'clock, how long have you been here?"

"About a half hour. I poured you a glass," she said, motioning to the coffee table. "Where did you and Connor go?"

"How did you know it was Connor?"

"I know the sound of his car."

"We went to see Mum."

"And?" She propped her legs on the edge of the table. I watched her casualness and envied her spirit, her sense of herself, as she fiddled with her massive red curls. She had been the youngest, the shortest, but the strongest of us all.

She spoke her mind and accepted every consequence. I never understood where she learned those habits. There never seemed to be a question of direction. Even as a child, she was an old soul in a baby's body.

"I need to talk to you," I said. "About something serious."

"I have to tell you something, also." Francie took a sip from her glass, then took her feet off the table and sat up.

"Me first," I said, picking up the glass of wine and sitting in Da's chair.

"No, I better go first because you might not ever talk to me after I tell you this."

"You're scaring me." I picked up Mittens and wrapped her in my arms, rubbing my fingers between her ears as she purred.

"OK, here goes. Let me get it all out and promise you won't hate me," Francie said.

"I could never hate you."

"Really? Promise?"

"OK. I promise I won't hate you. So, what is it?" Mittens jumped from my lap to Francie's and started rubbing against her chin.

"Stop," she said, pushing the cat away and scratching her chin.

I thought it might be a good time to tell Francie I had seen Dylan, and how it made me feel. Then I thought I'd tell her about the pictures, the album that told a lifetime, but I waited. She seemed pressed with her own agenda.

"Michael called me last night."

I froze in the moment. "Did you hang up on him? Did you tell him to rot in hell? Did you tell him to go fuck himself? OK, that was mean. I'm sorry. What did he say?"

"Well, first he asked how you were. Then he asked for a chance to explain." She looked up and took a sip from her glass. "So, I listened, as I would to anyone."

"Aren't you the sweet one?" I looked away.

"Why didn't you tell me? All the times I called and you just bullshitted about everything and nothing. Why did I have to hear it from him?"

"Because I was embarrassed. Because I thought I could make him stop. Because I thought I could work it out. Take your pick." I took a sip of wine.

"He said everything was his fault. He said he was sorry."

"How considerate. He said the same thing to me."

"Cate, what did he do?"

"He beat me." I couldn't meet her dumbfounded stare.

"He didn't mention that. Just said he was mean to you and it was all his fault."

I gave the details of my marriage to my baby sister. "When I didn't say what he wanted to hear, or I questioned him, he unleashed his rage. He was unhappy and he took it out on me."

"I'm sorry. He should never have hit you. You were right for leaving."

"But, you still talked to him?" I moved from the chair to the ledge of the bay window.

"I didn't know it happened." I heard the frustration in her voice.

"I should have told you. If it's any consolation, I never told anyone. I was too embarrassed."

"Look, this isn't about you not telling me." Francie bit her lip.

"I'm sorry. You're right, but it seemed silly to say anything. What could you do? What would I say, 'guess what, Francie, my husband is beating me?'"

"Yes, that's exactly what you should have said. Did you tell Mum?"

"If you were the safest person in the world, how could I tell the one woman who had the best husband in the world?"

"Don't be too quick to put Da on a pedestal. He was human."

Just then, I realized what Francie said. In that moment she put Michael into a different light. Not one of forgiveness, but of humanness, of making mistakes. It's just that Michael had made the mistake too many times.

"Did you believe him?" I turned toward the couch and wrapped my arms around myself and held on as tight as I could.

"Yes. I believed he was sorry, but it didn't make it right.

Actually, you should have left him sooner." She came over and tried to take hold of my hand, but I pulled back.

"Don't try to tell me what he did was OK."

"I'd never say that. Cate, give me more credit than that. Listen to me. I'm not taking his side. I swear. I just want to figure it out, so when I talked to you, I could understand better."

"What is there to understand? I was there. Remember, it happened to me."

"I know it did. I support you one hundred percent."

"Well, I hope you told him he was an asshole."

"Cate, I'll never take his side. You are my sister, but no I didn't call him that."

"Then promise me you'll never talk to him again." I knew I was being unreasonable as the words came out of my mouth.

"He told me how he thought your marriage came apart. Do you want to hear his side?"

"No, I don't want to hear anything he had to say. I know when things began to unravel just as well as he does. Do you want to hear them? I can tell you right now."

I took a healthy drink of wine and decided to tell her things I had barely been able to say out loud. She reached over and cupped my face in her hands.

"You don't have to do this." Her voice so soft, I was sure that if I closed my eyes I'd see Mum standing in front of me.

"You want to know what broke us apart, so you'll understand better. Right?" I removed my sister's hands from my face and went back to the couch. "What one thing changed everything?"

"Cate, you don't have to," Francie said.

"I know, but I think I should." I took a deep breath.

"You're my sister. If I expect you to support me, you need to know."

"Cate?"

"It started after I gave birth to Izzy. He wanted me to get pregnant again, as soon as possible. He wanted a boy."

The words slid out and I sat back on the couch, rubbing my hands down my jeans. Even saying it out loud didn't make me feel better. It sounded archaic, even for Michael. I pulled away when Francie reached for me.

"Michael loved you."

"Of course, he did, once upon a time, but after Izzy, it got worse. He wanted a son more than anything in the world. He told me that over and over. When Izzy was seven months old he brought home a shirt that had "Gabriel" written on it, the name he had chosen for his son. I wasn't even pregnant. She wasn't even a year old."

"But he loves Izzy. I know he does. I saw him with her. I saw how he treated her. She was his princess."

"Oh God yes, but it didn't take away his need for a son."

"Did he ever hit you when you were pregnant with Izzy?"

"No, and he never touched Izzy. If anything, I was safer when she was around."

"Did you ever tell Mum?"

"No."

I got up from the couch and moved back to the window, watching the rain, as it came down in a soft mist.

"Why couldn't you come to us?"

"Because I thought I could change him."

"My God, what is wrong with this family? We collect

secrets like people collect coins. This is ridiculous." Francie didn't even try to hide her rage.

"You had a secret once."

"Yes. Colin and I went to Mum and Da as soon as we were sure about the pregnancy."

"See, how can I tell you about my problems? You face your problems head-on. You're... Why are you so perfect?"

"That's what you thought all those years?" Francie covered her mouth trying to hide her laugh. "Far from perfect. I wasn't very good at burying my problems. I always had to find a way to talk them out. I got help. It wasn't always the help I wanted, but it kinda kept me from going crazy."

"So now, you're condemning me?"

"Jesus, Cate. No. Where did that come from?"

I couldn't hold back the tears. I felt the tightness come up from deep inside. I brushed my hair from my eyes.

"You've been married over twenty-five years. Would you consider going back to him?"

"So it could start all over again. No. I told him that last night."

"He's heartbroken.

"Yeah, right. I just wished you hadn't talked to him."

"I wouldn't if I had known. I didn't mean to hurt you."

"You know what, Francie, I can't talk about this anymore. I appreciate you telling me and even though I don't sound like it, I get it. I'm not mad and I don't hate you."

I had either just been socked in the stomach, or more loved than I could ever have imagined. For the first time I no longer had second thoughts about anything.

"I'm sorry. I didn't think talking to him would be a problem."

Her face grew sad as the words came out. I saw the sorrow in her eyes, the way her hands came up to her face. My younger sister had no idea about my experiences. She had a husband who adored her, a son who trusted her every move and a place she called home. On the other hand, I had none of those, living in someone else's house, a world away from the life I had so desperately wanted.

"Please don't talk to him anymore. Can you promise me?"

"Yes, I can."

"OK, done. No more about Michael."

"I'll stay with you tonight, if you want."

"No. I'll be better tomorrow."

"Hey, you never told me what you wanted to talk about."

"It's nothing that can't wait. I'll see you in a few days."

As we went to the door, Francie put on her coat, leaned in and kissed me good-bye. "Call me tomorrow. Promise?" Francie said, wrapping her scarf tight.

"Yes. I'm just tired. Forgive me?"

"Of course."

Thirteen

I didn't call Francie as I had promised. I didn't know what to say. I found myself consumed with thoughts of Dylan, and how life could have been different, of Michael and how we could have been if he hadn't hit me.

It stormed for two days. Thunder and lightning filled the sky, rain flooded the streets. I didn't call anyone during that time, nor did I answer Mum's random calls, or listen to her messages. Instead, I hid under the covers, stared at pictures of some family in Oregon. In the end, it made no sense.

Mum had kept pictures, postcards, even text messages from someone who had no connection to us. Why would she keep pictures of a family no one knew? She had found a connection, but for the life of me, I couldn't connect the dots.

Michael called three times. I listened to his rantings, telling me enough time had passed, that I needed to come home. I didn't return them, only cowered under the covers replaying them, like a lovesick teenager. Rose left vicious messages, reminding me that perhaps it was time to go back home. Why did everyone want me to leave?

On the third day, when the skies cleared for a few hours, I walked around Mum's garden, grabbing hold of wisps of branches as they floated in the wind, trying to contemplate my next move.

The pictures kept flashing through my mind. In the last year, Mum had received more from the woman, than I had ever given her. She had no letters or messages from me for her to linger over.

I went back upstairs promising myself it would be the last time I would intrude in Mum's secrets. I flipped through the pictures and read the letters. I put everything back where I found them, except for one picture, the little girl with the white floppy bow. I left it on the dresser. I took a quick shower, and in fifteen minutes, I was ready.

Traffic on the thoroughfare piled up, but the driver took to the side-streets, by-passing most of the congestion. In less time than it had taken me to get ready, he was dropping me off at Trinity. I handed him my money, and nodded to keep the change. The grounds of Trinity still felt familiar. Memories as a student, rambled through my mind. I crossed them now as an observer. Instead of a young woman, my observations strayed to thoughts of Dylan and times we shared.

I walked the four blocks from college and stood in front of the double doors of St. Philomena's Care Facility.

I slipped my hand in my pocket and rubbed the picture between my fingers. I'd ask her about the little girl with the floppy bow. I promised myself to accept whatever the answer was.

The receptionist insisted I should have called and rang Mrs. Moore's office in a moment of defiance. I waited in the lobby, still stroking the picture.

"Catherine, I wasn't expecting you. I do wish you would have called."

"I didn't come to see you. I came to see my mum. May I?"

"Of course, she is in the rec room. You're lucky, she's having a good day."

"Could someone show me? We didn't get there on the tour."

"Yes, I'll have the receptionist guide you. I am late for a meeting."

"Of course, you are," I said under my breath. I caught my rudeness, bowed my head, and moved to where the receptionist waited.

I followed her down the main corridor past the elevator, and entered through the double doors, across from the dining room.

She pointed toward the window. "She's over...."

"I know my mother, thank you." My rudeness continued, even as I bit my tongue.

She sat staring into the garden, while others sat at tables, playing cards and putting puzzles together. She looked lovely, serene almost. Mrs. Moore was right, she was clearly having a grand day. They had combed her hair and dressed her in one of her favorite slack outfits, olive green flowered shirt, with matching olive slacks.

I touched her arm, not wanting to startle her. "Mum, it's me, Catherine."

She jumped with a start, at first, not seeming to recognize me. I bent down next to her chair, then she turned toward me. "Yes, my dear," she said, patting my hand. "Catherine, so good to see you. How are you?" She squeezed my hand and smiled.

"How are you today?"

"Oh Catherine, I thought I'd never see you again." Her eyes narrowed and she gripped hold of my fingers.

"I know. I should have come sooner. I'm sorry, but with the

storm and all, for the last few days."

"I'm just glad you're here now. Can you stay awhile?"

"Of course. How are you feeling?"

"Today is good, no headaches, no episodes." She smiled and turned back to the window.

I pulled a chair next to her. "The rain has stopped, would you like to go for a walk?"

"No. Can we just sit here? I like the view." She looked out over the vast lawn of Trinity College, even being able to see as far as O'Connell Bridge and the Liffy River.

"Sure, that's fine."

"How are things going here?" I asked, looking around at the variety of tables filed with canasta players, puzzle keepers, and quiet conversationalists huddled together.

"It has been lovely, Connor and Claire have been ever so gracious to see that I have everything I need, and Francie, dear girl, has come almost every day, but I miss my house, and Mittens. How is she?"

"She's good. She sleeps a lot."

"And Rose?" She looked at me when she said the name.

I smiled and held the gaze. "Rose is Rose."

"Yes, she is." Mum broke into a smile, but tried to hide it. "She doesn't like me here. She's angry that I didn't include her in my decision. Are you?"

"Let's say I was surprised, but no Mum, I'm not mad."

"The doctors told me that Rose walked out of the meeting."

I nodded. "She did, but she'll come around, don't worry."

"I just knew that Claire and Connor would be the best to see to my wishes. I never meant to hurt anyone."

"Mum, you have every right to do what you think is best.

I think we're just disappointed that you didn't allow us to be a part of the decision. I've talked to Claire and Connor, I understand."

She nodded, adjusted her glasses, and smiled as she looked up at me. "You know, Catherine, Rose always felt responsible, especially after your Da passed. I spent my life having people make decisions that they thought were best, but they were never quite what I wanted. I had to take charge. Does that make sense?"

Listening to Mum defend her choice, filled me with remorse. I had questioned her right to a life as she saw fit. I brushed the tears away, so she wouldn't see. I hadn't realized it before, but being with her now, I realized how my ignorance had betrayed her. The guilt ate at me.

Again, I fingered the picture in my pocket, debating whether it was the right time to bring it up. Maybe better if we kept it a friendly visit, so she wouldn't feel betrayed.

"Did you know there's greenhouse here?" She asked. "You know, for flowers and plants."

"Yes, Mrs. Moore told me. Do you go there?"

"As often as I can. Eric works with me and we re-pot flowers and herb shoots. The patio is full of flower pots that I've planted with Eric's help." When she talked about the garden and patio, her face lit up.

"That's great Mum." I moved my chair so I could be directly in front of her and it happened. Without moving, she changed. Suddenly, she was no longer my mum sitting there chatting. Her head arched, she stood up, looking away from me.

"Sara, we have to go downstairs now," Mum said, looking down, not seeing me. Wringing her hands.

I glanced around to see if anyone stood behind me, but no one was there.

Mum had known a Sara, but she had died the same year as Jonathan.

"Mum, Sara isn't here. It's me, Catherine. We were talking about the plants and the gardens."

I looked around the dining room and felt helpless. I didn't know how to bring her back... I didn't know where she had gone. I took a deep breath and stepped back.

"Now Sara, if we go upstairs, we'll have time to collect the laundry and take it to the folding room. We must find Marie as well, before anyone finds out where she's hiding. Sister Helen will be so angry, we must hurry."

"Mum, it's me, Catherine. We are here at St. Philomena's. I don't know who you're talking about."

She stared out the window, watching the rain. *"Tomorrow, when the rain stops, I'll go outside and get fresh vegetables, maybe even pick some wildflowers. I know Jonathan won't mind."*

She fell silent and sat back down at the table, her head slumped, and her arms dropped in her lap. Eric came toward us, and I motioned to him.

"It's OK, tell her you'll take her downstairs. If you try to tell her she isn't there, she'll get mad and run off. Just reassure her that everything will be OK. Whoever she is asking for, tell her they will be with her soon."

"I don't understand. Shouldn't I tell her where she is?"

"No, she'll come back on her own. In a few minutes, she'll forget she had the conversation. It's OK, Catherine. She goes back to what she remembers. In a few minutes she'll want to take a walk and she'll have forgotten that she fell into the past."

"It breaks my heart. I don't know how to handle it."

"Alice," Eric called out, touching her hand with just the slightest motions, "we're going to the nursery, would you like to go?" He took hold of her hand and looked back at me. "It's very difficult for the families. We are with them all day, so it's easier. We know what her triggers are, and how to bring them out. She'll be fine."

Mum looked up at him, the twinkle back in her eye. "Yes, perhaps you could help me cut a bouquet for my room."

"I'd love to. Let's do that."

Eric stepped aside, and I took hold of her hand. He motioned toward the door to the nursery. Mum and I walked through arm in arm, while Eric pointed to a second door.

"Go right in there. There is a place she can sit down, or she can plant if she likes. Talk to her about the flowers. She loves that, tell her the roses are hers. She gets very agitated about roses."

Eric waited at the door and watched as I interacted with my mother. I kept looking back at him. Eric nodded, and motioned for me to continue. "Mum, your roses are beautiful."

"Yes, even during the winter, they still bloom. Can you imagine that?"

"You've done a very good job. Should we cut a bouquet and take it to your room?"

"Oh, that would be lovely, dear."

Eric moved over to the workbench and took the shears, handing them to me. I cut each rose carefully, still looking to Eric for approval. I could see him hiding his smile, but when I smiled back, he broke out into a wide grin. We both knew she was back.

"How's this, Mum?" Showing her the buds that I had cut.

"They're lovely, Catherine. How is Michael? Is he coming to see me soon?" Eric took the buds and wrapped them in newspaper.

"No, Mum, he had to stay in Boston."

I fingered the picture again, debating if I should show it to her. Maybe I could just lay it on the table and see if she noticed. I should have asked Eric, I thought to myself.

I decided to approach her first. "I have something I'd like to show you Mum. Can you come sit down?"

"You have a present?" Her face lit up and she took a seat in the corner.

"Not exactly. It's a picture I found. Would you like to see it?"

"Yes, is it of Izzy?"

"No, it isn't. Look," I said, taking the picture from my pocket, and placing it in front of her.

After staring at it for a few moments, she looked at me. "Oh, such a wee one. I didn't know her then." In a few moments, her eyes teared. "I can't bear to look at her."

She got up from the chair and started walking toward the door, still holding the wrapped flowers. I saw the nervousness in her hands as she clenched her fists. She turned around and went back in the nursery, toward the rows of plants.

"Please take it away. I've never seen that picture before. I don't know who that poor baby is."

"It's gone, Mum," I said, slipping it back into my pocket. I guided her to the table where she could dig her hands into the rich brown soil. "Do you want to plant something Mum?"

"Yes, let's repot the ivy." She scooped soil into the small pots next to her, then broke apart the trailing ivy and placed a cutting in each in a pot. She had not lost her ability to plant or her love of flowers. She moved slower now, but I could see the love ingrained in her actions. I watched her fingers moving in the moist earth. Then she stopped, like she'd been pinched. I looked at her face, tears streaked down her cheeks.

"I need a little towel," she said, suddenly, moving her hands again, but not wiping the tears away.

She pushed my hands out of the way, telling me she didn't need my help. She took the towel and wiped the pot clean.

"Can you write my name on it, so no one will take it?"

"Yes, of course," Eric said, moving over to the table.

We finished cleaning up, she managed most all the details. She swept the leftover soil into a small bag on the table, put the tools away, and declared she was hungry for lunch.

Eric walked us back through the main hall. He looked at me with smile. "You're worried."

"That's an understatement." I shook my head.

"She'll be OK." He said. "She cries a lot, without any reason, but she always comes back."

"Thank you…. I'm not sure how to handle it." I was embarrassed that I had to reach out to a stranger to learn how to deal with my mother. He had only known her for a few weeks, yet she trusted him beyond measure.

"You'll do fine. Just remember she isn't doing anything on purpose. She can only see the world through her eyes." He took hold of her hand and wrapped his fingers around hers, bringing her wrinkled hand up to his lips, kissing it ever so gently. She smiled back at him so tenderly, I felt embarrassed, like I had invaded a private moment.

"It's sad to think she's losing pieces of her world. I'm afraid she may never get them back."

"That day may well come, but until then, she needs you to

keep that sliver of light open." Eric guided her down the hall, motioning me to stay by her side.

"I did something I probably shouldn't have. I showed her a picture I thought she'd recognize, but she got so sad. I put it away, but I think she's still thinking about it."

"She'll be OK. You have to remember she just sees things differently now."

"I guess I just have to get used to it."

"Give yourself time. Maybe you can show it to her again when you come next time. If the response is the same, then don't do it anymore."

When we arrived at the door. Eric patted Mum's arm, then went off toward the recreation room, while we went to the cafeteria. I didn't bring out the picture for the rest of my visit, and she didn't go into an episode. After lunch Eric came back to the cafeteria.

"Are you having a nice visit with Catherine, Alice?"

"Yes, we were in the nursery and did some potting, then had some lunch, but I'm getting a little tired."

"Would you like me to escort you back to your room?" Eric asked looking back at me with a wink.

She still held my hand. "Would you mind Catherine?"

"No, Mum, you go on and rest. I'll see you in a day or two." I kissed her good-bye, and squeezed her hand. I watched as Eric took her back down the hall toward the elevator.

I stepped out through the double doors of the facility and meandered down the street. I pulled the hood to my jacket up to cover my head from the rain. I thought about the picture tucked away in my pocket.

Since it was still early, I decided to explore the grounds of Trinity. Wandering through the gardens and trees, I remembered my days as a student. It felt so foreign, yet familiar. The architecture still mesmerized me. I ran my hands across the ancient stone. The rain picked up as I found myself in front of the massive oak doors of the library. Memories of days spent buried in books, came flooding back as I walked into the Long Room. The smell of centuries-old leather and paper. I felt my soul settle. Here, among the greatest minds the world has ever known; the writers, the philosophers, the religious and legal minds, I was safe. I could face any problem; there was always an answer.

I wandered the stacks, my fingers grazing the gilt letters. Caressing the tooled leather and raised bands.

I felt my stomach growl. A young woman seated at one of the tables looked up and smiled. I checked my watch. I had been in the library for three hours. Time to head back to the real world.

After a few blocks, I found a pub just past the college. I ran across the street and decided I'd grab a cup of coffee before getting a taxi to Mum's house.

I sat at a small table near the window, where I watched the students walking from the campus. As a couple strolled by, arm-in-arm, I couldn't help but notice the look of joy on the young woman's face. Her beau leaned in and whispered in her ear, she laughed and pushed him away. He grabbed her by the waist and pulled her into his arms for a quick kiss.

As they walked by, I heard a familiar voice entering the pub. I felt the blush the second I looked up.

Fourteen

"**W**ell, look who's here. This is grand." Dylan walked away from the other man and came toward my table. He wrapped his arms around my neck.

"Good to see you," Dylan said, standing back, looking at me in the darkened pub with a wide grin.

I took a deep breath. In that moment, he looked more handsome than the day I saw him with Claire. I laughed in my embarrassment. "What are you doing here?"

"We come here all the time. You don't remember this place? Think back about twenty-five years."

I looked around, then back at Dylan. "Is this the same place?"

"Yep, they remolded it and have different owners, but this is it."

It was in the far corner, next to the telephone booth, that Dylan kissed me for the first time. My back arched against the paneled wall, my face in his hands. I could have stayed in that moment forever. After the kiss, he looked at me as if I was the only person in the room.

The crowd surged, reminding us we were not alone. After he let go of my lips, he took hold of my hand.

"Let me get you something. What would you like?"

"I was just going to grab a light supper, then take a cab back to Finglas."

"Perfect, you'll join us for supper?"

"No, I shouldn't." I looked around as the pub began to fill up.

"Why not?"

"You're with someone, I'd be a bother."

"No, not at all," he said. "Come join us, I'll introduce you, and you won't be strangers. We'll have supper and I can give you a ride home. I was going back there anyway. It'll save you getting a cab. And look it's still pouring." He motioned toward the window.

"OK." I smiled as he turned and moved toward the table, pulling out a chair for me. His friend stood back, seeming a little shy.

"This is Henry. He works with me at the college."

Henry seemed older than Dylan, hunched a bit in the shoulders, and wrapped snuggly in an overcoat, with a woolen cap, clean-shaven, with a square jaw, and deep-set eyes.

"This is Cat," Dylan said.

I blushed at his familiarity. Henry took my hand in both of his. "Any friend of Dylan's..." He pulled out a chair and sat down.

"What do you want, Cat? I'll go up and order, it'll be faster."

"A chicken sandwich on sourdough, with coffee. No cheese."

"Henry? Anything to eat, or just the pint?"

"Actually, make it a coffee it to go. I just remembered I promised to stop by my daughters this afternoon."

When Dylan went to the counter, I looked around at all the different people deep in conversations, some with bowed heads, some gesturing in heated discussions. In a few minutes Dylan returned to the table with a pint and the coffees. He placed a few napkins on the table, then took a seat next to me.

"Thanks for the coffee, Dylan. I gotta go. I'll call you later." He grabbed up his satchel.

"I'm sorry. I should be the one going, not you."

"No, no, stay put. Monday, Dylan? Meeting is at nine, sharp. Nice to meet you Cat. See you again sometime soon."

"Nice to meet you as well."

Dylan got up and moved toward Henry and they shook hands.

"You OK?" Dylan asked as he sat back down.

"I should have been the one to leave."

"No, we were just going to hang out for a while, then go home."

"So, what are you doing in the city?"

"I came to see Mum."

"How is she doing?"

"She was good today." I found myself pausing. "Yes, overall it was good."

"It must be hard for you to watch this happen. I remember your Mum. She was grand, always in the garden, she was."

"Yes. She loved her garden. We were in the greenhouse today. She spends a lot of time there, repotting flowers, and ivy, almost anything she can get her hands on."

"Are they taking good care of her?"

"Yes. St. Philomena's has been wonderful. She has this young man, Eric. Oh my gosh, he is devoted to her. He knows exactly how to be with her, how to calm her down, stop her from crying, but more importantly, he keeps her safe, and she trusts him."

"I've heard very good things about them. I'm glad she is safe."

"It does take a load off, I mean what if she were being abused or something?"

"You'd never let that happen."

"Funny you say that, she picked this place. She actually did the research. She knew time was getting short.

"It wasn't until the doctors sat us down, that we found out the plans had already been made. Rose, went ballistic. She stormed out in the middle of the meeting. I never saw anyone so angry, but it was Mum's decision."

"Your mum is smart. Many people wait until it's too late, then they get terrible care and are miserable."

The waiter brought the sandwiches and for a while, we didn't say anything. I watched Dylan as we ate. He was at ease, comfortable in his skin. I remembered that about him.

"How long will you be staying in Dublin?" He asked, taking a drink of his pint and watching me fix my coffee.

"It all depends on how Mum gets along. We're actually hoping she'll be able to come home soon, but the doctors aren't too convinced."

"How would it be if she came home?"

"Well, we'd have to get her full-time help, and someone would stay at the house with her. It would probably be me, because everyone else has their own home here," I said.

Dylan was being too nice. The more questions he asked, the more I wanted to tell him everything. Mum...Michael....

"So, how's it going for you?" Dylan asked, taking a drink from his pint, wiping his mouth with his napkin then smiling down at me with such tenderness I could feel myself melting into the table. My reserve dissolved.

"You know, I wish I could be sitting here telling you how great things were, and that I was getting ready to head home to my wonderful life and my great job, but to be honest everything's a mess." I took a deep breath. I wasn't going to let him see me broken. He hadn't earned that right yet, but he had earned the right to a bit of the truth.

"So, what else is it, beside your Mum?"

Looking at Dylan, and his kind face, I decided I couldn't tell him anything about my private life, not yet.

"She's not in St. Philomena's for dementia. She has a brain tumor, but they can't get to it. The tumor has been causing headaches and memory lapses. Episodes where she goes back in time and thinks we're people from her past."

"So, it is worse than dementia, not saying that dementia isn't bad."

I felt a schoolgirl blush take over. I should have just taken a cab from the facility.

"I do hope your mum gets better."

"I keep waiting for the day that this will be behind us."

"Cat, I wish I could say something to make you feel better."

"It's hard seeing her so helpless. She should be home, with her cat in the garden, having a whiskey."

He hid his laugh behind his hand, his eyes softened and I let myself relax. "I remember her."

"Was it the cat or the whiskey?"

"The whiskey. I came to the house to pick you up, and I found her in the garden on the bench. She had a glass of whiskey. She greeted me as if we were old friends. She asked me if I wanted a glass. I declined. She was lovely." I watched him recalling her in his memory.

"It's not that bad. I just need to get used to seeing her at St. Philomena's."

"You sure?"

"People get used to it every day."

When a waitress came around, Dylan raised his glass for another pint. "You sure you don't want a pint or glass of wine?"

"No, I shouldn't."

"What are your plans for the evening? Do you have to be somewhere?"

"No."

"Then come on, have just one."

"OK. I'll have a glass of white wine."

The waitress grinned and told us she'd bring it right over.

"Do you miss practicing law?"

"More than anything."

"So, why'd you give it up?" he asked with true sincerity.

"Well, after Izzy, Michael thought I should stay home with her. We were hoping to have more children, but that never happened. After a while, it just fell into a routine."

I felt my shoulders relax and allowed myself into a simple conversation about the past. Dylan drank from his glass, then took a bite from his sandwich. He had relaxed long before he even took a drink from his pint.

I took a sip of my wine and studied everything about him;

the turn of his head, the lift of his brow, as he glanced around the pub. It didn't take long to remember everything that had made me fall in love with him. I wondered if he saw the same in me?

"So, tell me about this Michael?"

"He's in Boston. Working."

"Is everything OK with you guys?"

"Sure." I paused. What the hell was I doing? "No, not really. He didn't like the idea of me coming home, but I had no choice."

"Of course, you didn't. He should have known better than that. Will you be going back to Boston?"

"I don't know. Things weren't going as we had hoped. I thought I'd stay here for a while, make sure that Mum was OK, and… well, we'll see."

"Cat, what are you not telling me?"

"This isn't the time or place."

I drank the last of my wine and Dylan went to the counter to order another.

"You know what, let's stop talking about me. I haven't even asked how you are. How are things with Dylan?" I smiled at him and watched as he ran his fingers across his beard.

"Well, with winter break almost two months away, I've been pretty busy, meeting with interns, doing research, plus I have an academic book coming out next fall."

"I'll say you're busy. Will you be doing any traveling?"

"No. I'm staying put until next year, this time. We're sponsoring a new program for eligible seniors. The pilot goes through next fall."

"Congratulations on everything. I miss that."

"I imagine you would. You were very good with the law."

"I did some pro bono in Boston, but Michael didn't like it, so I gradually gave it up little by little."

The Pub began to fill up for the dinner hour. There were college students, professors, and working Dubliners. The wind blew in through the open double doors. Candles glowed from each table and behind the bar.

"What did you do?"

"I helped women coming in for assistance. They had no idea how to file documents for restraining orders, or separations, or even report their abuse."

"You must have been a great help."

"I had my moments." I laughed, taking a sip of my wine.

"If you stay in Dublin, would you go back to work?" He asked.

"I've thought about it, but you know I've been out of it for a long time. Much is different now."

"You'd probably have to take some professional development, but it wouldn't be hard to renew your license, if you think you might be staying."

"Nothing is final yet. So much is going on."

"Well, I have some connections if you're interested."

"It would be like starting over. I don't know if I could do that."

"No, your degree never expires. You've got the basics, the laws never really change, they just make new laws."

I pushed my hair behind my ear and lowered my head. He embarrassed me with his compliments. How did he know I could succeed?

"I better get through all the family stuff, but thank you. I'll get back to you if I change my mind."

"You know it will always be there." He picked up his glass, drinking the last his of beer.

"I need to go. It's getting late, I'll get a cab."

"No, let me give you a ride home."

"I've already interrupted your evening. You completely abandoned your friend and whatever plans you had."

"Oh no, we're fine. There are times he's done the same to me. We're almost like brothers."

"When you see him again, please apologize."

"Absolutely, but there is no reason. He's fine."

Dylan held the door as we walked out of the pub. He gestured to the left and we walked to the parking lot.

"Your chariot awaits, M'Lady," as he opened the passenger door. Books and papers occupied the seat. "Oh, sorry," he said, moving them to the back

The leather of the seats held the faint scent of his cologne. Not overbearing like the Old Spice Michael wore, just a hint of something I can't describe. Something comfortable. I found myself smiling as the clouds continued to break.

Everything about him was different from Michael—his thick brown hair, almost a whole head taller. He had a bit of a pouch and small lines around his eyes. He had weathered well.

We drove out of Dublin Center in silence, except for the music from the radio. We glanced at each other periodically, and I sensed he had more questions. When he pulled into the driveway, he finally turned to me. "Would you like to go out for a real dinner?" He smiled, and I think I saw a blush, in the dim light of the dash.

"Yes, I'd love to, but you know I'm still married?"

"I'm not looking to break up any marriage, but we both need to eat...."

He paused, and adjusted his hands on the steering wheel. "Besides, we go way back. Haven't we been friends for a very long time? And don't we have a lot to catch up on? I promise I'll be a gentleman the entire time. I won't even try to kiss you."

"Well that would be a disappointment." I smiled and squeezed his hand.

We walked to the door and just as I put the key in, he pulled me to him. Our lips met. I pulled away and looked at him. "I thought you weren't going to kiss me?"

"I lied. Sorry."

"And I thought you were an honest man," I said, smiling.

His fingers touched my cheek and he moved to kiss me again. I didn't pull away. I wrapped my arms around him and kissed him back, feeling myself melt in his arms.

Fifteen

I watched as he drove into the darkness. Standing on the porch, I felt recharged. Dylan wanted me. He hadn't said it, but I knew it was there. He gave me back my sense of value.

I felt giddy, not from just the kiss, but also from the idea that he believed in me.

I tossed my purse on the couch and took the picture out of my coat pocket, staring at the white bow. I went upstairs and put it back in the album.

I ran my fingers across the plastic that covered the pages. I stared at young children. Hugging grandparents, laughing at parties, living happy lives.

This album held the chronicle of someone's life—like a movie, if I turned the pages fast enough, I'd see their life pass by. This woman had to be someone very important, or Mum wouldn't have hidden them.

Had Finn been an orphan?

We all knew when the orphanage kids arrived at school. They sat in the back of the room, separated, but watching our every move. They weren't allowed a book or pencil. They had to just sit and listen.

If we misbehaved, our punishment was to sit in their row. I

remember the smell, like vinegar and lye, and all of them with terrible breath. It was nauseous. It lingered like a cloud over them. Their clothes hung from their shoulders. Sometimes their shoes had holes, or they were too big, or too small.

It all came back. For a moment I could smell the lye and see their ragged jumpers. I had told Mum how bad I felt. She sat us all down and told us to be kind. She said I could invite one home to lunch, but I never did. Often, she put an extra apple, or treats in our lunch bags. They refused, but stared at us from their corner, while we ate.

One girl, named Evelyn, was smart. She could answer the math problems in her head. She didn't even need a pencil. Her hair was long, bunched in tangled knots. Her brown eyes drooped, hiding what seemed this incredible sadness, but she sat quietly, listening to the Bible stories. I watched her dreaming, or so I thought.

She looked out the window, never at the teacher. She knew the stories, and spoke them silently with the Sister. Then, one day, Evelyn was gone. I never saw her again.

"She's been sent away," Sister Margaret said, when I asked. "Say a prayer for her. She's not as blessed as the rest of you." Then Sister Margaret walked away, and never spoke of her again. I lingered in that memory of Evelyn, wondering what happened, where she was now.

Had Finn not been blessed?

I flipped through the album again. I saw the little girl on a tricycle, standing by a rocking horse, in a Holy Communion outfit. Were these Finn?

Had she been bought by one of those rich families in America, never to be seen again? Were the rumors true?

I closed the album and brought it downstairs. I placed it on the bureau, picked up my cell, and rang Francie. Her face appeared on my screen, but I went blank.

How would I tell her that I had figured out Mum's secret?

If this was Finn, she had a right to know us as well. She'd want to meet us.

"Francie, can you come to the house? Now."

"What's wrong?"

I held back tears and I took a deep breath. "I found something you and Rose should see. I think it will answer some questions." I stared at the picture of the woman, with brown shoulder length hair, and a burgundy sweater. Her blue eyes stared back at me. What would she say, if she could?

"Can you, Francie?"

"I was heading out to run some errands, but yes, OK. I'm on my way." Her tone softened.

"I'm calling Rose as well. The three of us need to talk."

"Good luck, getting Rose there. She hates to talk about anything unless she's in charge of it."

"We're sisters. We need to come together. Make peace... for Mum." I found myself begging my sisters to come together, because of a hunch about these pictures.

"Rose doesn't want to make peace. She thrives on discord. I think she knows more than she's willing to say, but heaven forbid, she go out of her way to share."

"You're probably right, but we have to bring Rose in on this, Francie. We're all she has." I outlined the face of the woman in the picture I held in my hand, as Francie reminded me that basically we weren't anywhere near a sisterhood.

"Let me ask you this while I have you on the phone," Francie said, "why the hell is Rose so angry, anyway?"

"I confronted her at the hospital. Izzy told her about some

pictures, and me staying in Mum's house. Does that cover it? She wants me to go home."

"That would be, Rose. She gets pissed really easily, especially if she thinks someone is after her." I heard another laugh come across the line. "OK, another question. You keep talking about pictures. What pictures?"

"Francie, just come, OK?" The pleading in my voice embarrassed me.

"OK, OK, I'm on my way."

I set my phone on the table and walked around the living room, going back and forth between the couch and the window, with everything still running through the maze in my mind.

So much had happened, finding the pictures, visiting Mum, seeing Dylan, Francie's insight into Rose. And Michael.

Staring out the bay window, I watched the rain, it was slight, almost a mist. It settled against the window, almost invisible.

I went back to the kitchen and took the wine from the refrigerator and a glass from the cupboard. Suddenly, the rain fell harder. I could hear it on the roof, exploding as it beat down on my world.

I leaned against the wall, gazing at Mum's garden. *Well, let's get it over with.* I dialed the number and listened to the ringing on the other end of the line. Rose's voice came on, but it was only to leave a message. "Rose, please call me, right away. This is important. It's Catherine."

I thought that maybe dinner would be enticing, but niceties did not impact Rose. A few seconds later, Rose's face popped up on my phone.

"Thank God, you called back," I said.

"What is it, Catherine? I'm busy."

"Can you just listen?"

"I have an appointment, and I'm late."

"This is important." I heard myself pleading.

"I have to meet with the decorator."

"Rose, this is more important than your stupid decorator."

"It's very hard to get an appointment."

"Jesus, Rose, can you just come over? I'll have dinner brought in..."

"I don't think we have anything to talk about. You know how I feel and I don't want to have dinner with you." There was a pause. "Just tell me what you want so I don't have to make the trip."

"Francie will be here." Somehow, I felt like I was playing a trump card.

"And that is supposed to change things?"

"Jesus, Rose, why do you have to be this way?"

"What am I being, exactly? A bitch?"

"I didn't say that." Rose was at it again. God, she was a nightmare.

"But you were thinking it. I know."

"Just stop, Rose. Please come."

"First tell me what's so important that I need to be there."

"I found some things that belong to Mum. Just come."

"I know what you found, and you had no right."

"OK, I'll admit that I should not have gone through Mum's things. Does that make you happy?"

"No. Nothing about you makes me happy. I will not allow you to ridicule me."

"What are you talking about? Why would you say that?" I could tell by her tone that she had chosen her battle, but we had to find a way to get back together. This had to be a start.

"Fine, I'll come. But if you think you can get away with treating me like shit, you have another thing coming."

After I hung up from Rose, I cut some wild vines, made a small bouquet of green climbers, wild roses, heather, and daisies. I put the flowers in a vase, and set them in the center of the table. I took a quick sip of wine, just before the doorbell rang. I grabbed my wallet, and paid for the meal. Just as I closed the door, I saw Francie pull in the drive.

Francie tossed her coat and purse on the couch. Her hair loosely pulled up, her red ringlets tumbled all around. Copper hoop earrings hung to her chin, she came through to the dining room with an awkward smile.

"Great. Thanks," Francie said, taking the glass from my hand.

She looked relaxed, wearing baggy jeans and Bohemian shirt, with a hint of lipstick, a pink blush from the cold, colored her cheeks.

"Is Rose coming?" She asked, brushing a ringlet from her face.

"Well, she said she would, but would refuse to stay if we talked bad about her."

"Oh my God, does she ever think about anyone but herself? Why would she think that we would talk bad about her?"

"Should I pour a glass for Rose?" I asked, as we clicked glasses.

"Let's just see if she shows up." We both laughed, but

there was an eeriness to our laughter. We both realized the possibilities.

While we waited, I had more wine than I should have. I told her about meeting up with Dylan, and that he wanted to take me to dinner.

"I remember him. Is he still as handsome?"

"Yes, just older. He wears a cap now and carries a satchel."

"We've all aged." She laughed with a pure sweetness.

We fell into easy conversation. Francie talked about volunteering in the nursery at the hospital on Wednesday afternoons. We laughed, drank more wine and finally, after a while, I got up and brought the album from the bureau to the table.

"OK, I don't think she's coming. So here they are. Have you ever seen these?" I asked, moving the open album closer in front of her.

Francie flipped through the pictures, randomly looking up at me. "Who are these people?"

"I think they're Finn and her family."

"Who is that?" Francie asked, looking back at the pictures. "Oh wait, that's the name that Mum called out when they found her in the park."

"I think this album belongs to her," I said grasping hold of the wedding picture. "I'm pretty sure she's been keeping in contact with Mum, letters, text messages, and obviously pictures. I found messages on Mum's phone that dated back almost a year."

Francie walked around the table, and I saw her jaw tighten. "Do you think Mum ever met her?" Francie looked up at me.

"I don't think so, maybe that's why there are so many text

messages, and post cards," I said.

"Cat, do you think she could be our sister, I mean older than Rose?"

"She would have to be older, look at the dates. Rose was born in '59. These pictures are in chronological order. Someone took a lot of time putting them together. The passport one starts at '53. Mum wasn't even married then. I think she was in London going to school, or at least that's what she said. Mum went out of her way to hide them. I found them on the top shelf of her closet. Remember when we helped her clean out dad's clothes? We would have seen them then. We almost emptied out the closet, so they came after Da died."

"Look at her," Francie said, taking the wedding picture from my hand. "She's beautiful. She has Mum's hands—and look at her eyes."

Francie was right. She had pieces of us. This had to be part of the secret, but there must be more. Who was Finn's father? Was it Da?

I couldn't even begin to imagine.

I rummaged through the drawer and pulled up a picture of Mum and Da on the beach in Howth. I took it to the table, picked up the wedding picture and held them together in the light for both of us to see.

"Look, they both have creases in their cheeks that start at the nose and run down to the mouth."

"They could be related," Francie said, again taking the picture and looking closer.

The front door slammed. "OK, I'm here. What's so important?" Rose interrupted. Her manicured hands held her keys tight.

"Would you like some wine?" Francie asked.

"I'm not staying." She stood next to the dining table, her hands clenched tight. "You have fifteen minutes. Say what you have to, then I'm leaving."

"Come on, relax, Rose, have some wine," I said, going back into the kitchen.

"Just get to it. What's so important that I...." She noticed the picture album. "What is this? Where did you get these?" She asked, flipping through the pictures.

After a few moments, she finally sat down, tapping her manicured nails on the table, totally ignoring the picture album.

I took a deep breath. "These are the pictures I found in Mum's room. I moved it over in front of her but after only a few pages, she shoved it to the center of the table.

"So?"

"Rose, don't you think it's odd that Mum has these pictures?"

Rose sat quiet and finally took a drink from the glass. "It's not a big deal. I know who they are."

"What? How do you know?" A chill ran through me. I looked at Francie. She bowed her head, and turned away, and walked around the table.

"How do you know about these?" Francie sat down in the chair next to Rose.

"I just do," Rose said.

"Stop the bullshit, Rose," Francie said. "I think if this woman has the slightest chance of being our sister, we have the right to know."

"Well, if you have the right to know, then why didn't Mum tell you?" Rose took a sip of wine.

I tried to stay calm. "OK, fine, Mum told you. Can you tell us what it's all about?"

"I learned about it years ago."

"And you didn't think we needed to know?"

"It wasn't my place." She looked away, as if examining the room for redecoration.

"OK," Francie said, trying to remain calm. "Can you tell us who she is, and what she has to do with Mum?"

"Her birth name is Finnouala Claire Brennan, but her name now is Claire Fisher.

Rose walked toward the window, then turned back around and faced us. "Mum got pregnant and her family made her sign the baby away. She never told anyone, not even Da."

She said it so calmly, like she was having a conversation about the weather.

"How do you know all of this?" Francie asked?

I was beyond angered and confused. Sitting here with my sisters, I felt helpless. How was it that Francie and I had no idea? The more questions we asked, the worse it became.

"OK wait a minute," I said, "you're going to sit here and pretend it's no big deal, we might have a sister?"

"I can't believe you didn't say anything." Francie took a drink, then folded her arms across her chest.

"I told you it wasn't my place, and obviously Mum didn't want you to know. Let it go." Rose ran her fingers across her lips, and adjusted her jacket. "Are we done? I'm missing my appointment."

"No, we're not done. How can you take this so lightly?" The confusion dissipated, but the anger rose.

"I'm not taking anything lightly."

"Fine, start at the beginning. When did you find out? How?"

"It was years ago. You and Michael were living in Dublin and Francie you had moved to Cork. I brought the girls to the house, one day and a nun was here. I thought she was from Mum's parrish, but Mum was very upset. The nun handed her an envelope, which Mum immediately hid."

"What made her tell you?" Francie asked, "if she was that upset."

"I wouldn't leave." Rose took a drink, opened her purse, then snapped it shut. "Francie, do you have a cigarette?"

"Yeah," Francie said, walking back to the couch. "If she didn't want to tell you, why did you push her?"

I got up and went into the kitchen to get an ashtray. For the first time since as long as I could remember, we weren't fighting. Rose had let her guard down. I didn't care anymore how she got the information. I just wanted to know.

Francie placed the cigarettes on the table along with a lighter and one by one we all three lit up. It had been awhile, so I coughed and spurted. Rose and Francie had no problems.

"OK, Rose, go on."

"Mum tried to tell me it was nothing, but I could see it in her eyes. She looked scared. I don't know how to explain it. She took the girls into the living room and turned on the tele, which she never did, when they were there. She took me into the kitchen, and started talking."

Francie and I looked at each other. "What did she say?"

Rose began in a calm voice. "She said she'd never talk about this again and asked me to never talk of it, either. Then she told me not to interrupt," Rose said.

"Mum said she had had a baby when she was just a girl.

Before Da. Grandpa made her give it away. It was shameful, her to be pregnant and not married. That's all there was. Mum didn't say any more about it."

"You're kidding," Francie said. "That doesn't sound right. What about the nun?"

"Sister Eleanor came to the house and told Mum, that the girl had searched the old records and wanted to meet, but Mum told her she didn't know this woman and there was no point in digging up the past. She never spoke of it again."

"What do you mean gave her away?" I picked up the passport picture and looked for something that connected them.

"Just what I said. Are you stupid, or just don't listen. What Mum did was shameful. The family would never live it down, if she was allowed to keep the baby."

We sat there in silence, our cigarettes burned down to the tip in the ashtray. Francie took her glass of wine and walked to the bureau, leaned against it, while I stayed seated at the table. Rose kept looking back and forth between us.

"Do you think Mum ever met her?" Francie asked, staring at Rose.

"I don't know. I never asked."

"Weren't you curious? Why the hell didn't you tell us?" I heard my voice, embarrassed that it had risen in anger.

"I kept it to myself, like she asked me to."

"Did you ever think of saying anything?" Francie asked.

"No, I told you, Catherine was gone, and Francie, you'd already moved to Cork, and I didn't see either of you, so I kinda forgot about it."

"How do you forget about something like that?"

"I don't know, Catherine. I didn't think about it every day.

My life wasn't picture perfect itself. I had my own problems to deal with."

"OK, how did you know about these pictures, and how did you find out her name?"

"I was helping Mum take some of her clothes to give to church. I don't know why, but I opened the drawer of her nightstand and I saw the album, so I picked it up, and flipped through it. All those pictures were there," Rose said, pointing to the album. "She walked in on me and I couldn't very well deny it. So, I asked her if this was her daughter."

"What did she say?"

"She started to cry. She took the album from my hands and wrapped her arms around it. She handed me a letter."

"Jesus, Rose, what did it say?"

"It was a letter from Finn asking if this was Alice Brennan. The letter went on, telling Mum about her life. I don't remember most of it. Mum took it back before I could finish and put it in another drawer. I never saw it again and she never talked about it."

"Did you know about the text messages?"

"No. I didn't know she was texting."

I went into the kitchen and pulled out Mum's phone.

"Here they are. They go on for almost a year, same date each month."

"Wow, she doesn't give up. How stupid is she?"

"Why would you say that? She isn't stupid. She's determined."

"The point is, Mum doesn't want to see her. She needs to stop." Rose walked away from the phone and picked up the glass from the table and took a sip of wine.

My head pounded as I tried to comprehend everything Rose had said. I watched Francie and could only imagine what ran through her head.

"Look, I'm sorry. OK? I should have told you."

I never heard my sister apologize to anybody for anything. It allowed me to see her in a different light. Maybe this would change things, after all. Maybe we could finally come together as a family and be there for Mum as we should have been for years.

"OK, now that we know, what are we going to do?

"Nothing." Rose blurted out. "There's nothing to do."

Francie's jaw dropped. "You've got to be kidding. We need to be there for Mum. All of us. Wherever it takes us."

"You have no idea what you're saying." Rose crossed her hands and leaned back in the chair. I saw her jaw tighten. Her calm demeanor was an act. Francie had hit a nerve. She was very good at that. She could catch a lie like the wind would catch up leaves.

"Are you saying we shouldn't support Mum in this?"

"Not at all. Of course, we should support her, but we don't need to make matters worse. Look at her. She's sick, as you have both constantly reminded me. She doesn't need the added stress. All we'd be doing is causing more turmoil. Let it go."

"You can say what you want, Rose, but I know our Mum. I know how much she loves us," Francie said, almost in tears. "And if this was a daughter she had to give up, I imagine she loves her just as much. If Mum is as bad as you say, she just might want to see her one last time."

"I don't believe you either," I said. "Francie is right. Mum has been there for us since day one. If she had to give up her daughter and could never tell anyone? My God, her heart must have broken every day."

"I have a responsibility to protect Mum from anyone who bothers her." Rose stroked her hair and adjusted her pearl earring.

"Protect? Bother? If this Finn, or Claire, or whatever her name is, is looking for her mum, I don't call that bothering. I call it desperation. I would hope, if I lost a daughter, she would do everything she could to find me. And how do we not know that Mum didn't search for her?"

"You don't understand any of this, and I have nothing else to say. To either one of you."

I hated that words coming out of Rose's mouth. I hated her inability to recognize anyone's emotions, and I hated her need to say whatever came into her head, without thinking how it would hurt someone.

Francie went back to the table and took a seat. She shook her head in disgust. Rose returned to the table and wrapped her fingers around the wine glass. I could see by the look on her face, we had angered her. Gone was the compassionate woman who sat at the table earlier.

"I think we need to talk to Mum. Let's tell her we know about Finn. What do you think?" I stared at my two very different sisters.

"I think that is a great idea," Francie said. "Mum needs a lot of support right now. Maybe we could even bring Finn here, if they haven't met."

"No. She is not a part of our family. She doesn't need to come here."

"Rose, whether you like it or not, she's our sister. She's as much a part of Mum as we are."

"But she isn't a part of Da, so she's not part of the family."

I wanted to scream, but it wouldn't do any good. She couldn't hear it. I imagined what Finn must have been going through. Her pictures showed she had a life, but it was incomplete. We were worlds apart.

"Don't you even want to meet her, Rose?" I asked.

"Look at these pictures, look her jaw line...." Francie picked up a picture and almost shoved it in front of Rose, before I could even finish.

"And her hands... they're Mum's," I said.

Rose began to fidget in her chair, primping her hair, fingering the backs of her earrings. "She doesn't look like any of us. Why are you saying this?"

"Oh my God, I finally get it," Francie said. "How could it take me so long? You don't want to meet this woman because she'll take your place. She'll be the oldest. You think you'll lose your place in the family."

"You're being stupid," Rose said.

"No, you're jealous. She's our sister, whether you like it or not."

"I'd never be that way, but just for the record, she's not my sister and never will be."

"We need to talk to Mum. She needs to know we support her and that she can give up the burden of keeping secrets," Francie said.

"You can't say anything to Mum," Rose said.

"I think it would be a relief," I said.

"No one is going to talk to Mum about this, do you hear me?"

"You can't tell us that," Francie said, "we can do whatever the hell we want. Maybe it's time Mum is given the chance to let go of this. Let her decide."

"Don't you dare tell her you know anything about this. I'm warning you." With those words, silence filled the room. I sat down and poured another glass of wine.

"You can't intimidate us," Francie said.

"We're not children. You won't stop us from doing anything," I said. "I just hoped you would come with us, so Mum knew all her daughters were there to support her."

Rose stood up, grabbed her purse from the table, and headed toward the door. Watching, I realized Francie was right. It wasn't because it might hurt Mum, it was because she would lose control.

"How can you leave? You're a part of this." Francie raised her arms in what seemed like absolute disgust.

She turned back toward us: "I'm warning you, don't do this." The front door slammed as Rose left the house.

Sixteen

"God, I need a cigarette." Francie rubbed her hands through her hair. "So, what now?" Francie inhaled and slowly let the smoke creep from her mouth.

"I'm taking the pictures to Mum. She needs to know we support her. Do you want to come?"

"Of course, but what do we say? How do we tell her we know about..." she waved her hand over the album."

"We tell her the truth and promise we'll do whatever she wants."

My heart ached. If this were true, maybe instead of bringing pictures, we needed to find a way to bring Finn.

Francie sat in silence. I gathered the pictures and set the album on the bureau. My rage simmered as I cleared the table.

"How can Rose be such an ass?" Francie asked. "Can't she see what Mum must have gone through? Geeze...."

"I don't think so." Francie was right. Rose had no idea what Mum had been through. "She didn't know, but even worse, she didn't care." I heard the realization in my voice. It broke me in two.

"We have to do this. We need to find Finn and bring her here."

"Your right, but where do we start?" Francie asked, showing a ray of hope in her face.

"Mum's the only one who knows everything," I said. "We start there."

"Maybe we start upstairs. What else is there? Letters?"

"Just post cards, really. Nothing that could give us a way to contact her.

"Wait, maybe Rose is right. How could I be so dense?"

"What?"

Her cell phone; the text messages. There is a phone number.

I opened Mum's phone and scanned the messages. "Ok, I have it. Look there are over ten messages here. All from the same number.

"God Francie, look at these."

"They've met. These aren't messages from a stranger." I read the numbers out loud so Francie could write them down. "It doesn't matter what Rose thinks, Finn needs to come home."

"OK, should we call her now?" Francie asked.

"No, look at the time. She is in Oregon, right. So, it's ten here, and there's a five hour difference to Boston... it must be about one or two there. We should wait until later in the day."

"So, if it is about five in the afternoon here, then it would be nine in the morning then. Then let's call her tomorrow at six. That will give us time to figure out what we want to say."

"Oh my God how did it get this easy?"

"Well we're not positive it's still her number."

"Look," I said. "She called just two weeks ago. I don't think she would have changed her number since then."

"Your right."

"OK, I'm going home. I'll call you tomorrow and we'll call her tomorrow afternoon.

I closed the door and leaned back, taking in everything that had happened. I stepped out onto the patio and wondered what we would say to Finn, what she would say to us. I closed my eyes and envisioned the woman I had seen in the pictures, brown hair, blue eyes, and a splash of freckles, educated as her letter had said.

"Is this Finn?"

"Yes, who am I speaking to?"

"This is your sister in Dublin."

"Oh my gosh, you found me."

"You have to come home."

"I'll be there tomorrow."

I opened my eyes, staring into Mum's garden. I broke into a smile, realizing it had only been a fantasy. The rain had stopped. For a short time, the night sky lay still. I inhaled the cold air as it blew across my face. Day by day, living in Mum's home, I came to learn how she found peace in the garden.

I thought I had known Mum so well, yet outside of her love for Da, her children and her cat, I knew little.

Of course, she was there for us, she threw birthday parties, set curfews, curled up under a blanket to watch movies with us. She told us of her childhood antics and about the beaches in Howth.

Nothing about a little girl with a white, floppy bow.

I took a seat in the garden and waited for the sky to split apart.

I pulled my phone from my pocket and tapped Dylan's number. I watched the blank screen blink through four rings, but no answer. Just when I decided not to leave a message, his voice came on.

"Cat, is that you?"

"Oh gosh, it's late. I don't even know why I called. I just wanted to…. I'm sorry."

"No, don't hang up. It isn't late, just past ten. How are you?"

His voice, so soft, so easy to listen to. I fancied him reading one of his law books, sitting back, with a glass of whiskey.

"I'm fine, just relaxing in the garden, waiting for the rain."

"Well, you won't be waiting too long. You know storms are expected."

"When are there not storms in Ireland?"

"Are you OK? I can come by, if you want."

"I'm doing good. I know it's silly, I just wanted to tell you how good it was to see you, and to thank you for supper."

"You're welcome. When can I see you again? Maybe having a real date?"

"I'm not sure I'm ready for that."

"Then let's just call it dinner. I have meetings tomorrow night, but how's Thursday? Say seven-thirty?"

"That'd be grand. How should I dress?"

"Wear whatever you like. It'll be casual. How about Italian?"

"I'd love that."

"I'll see you Thursday."

"Remember Dylan, it's not a date."

"No worries. You've made that very clear."

Even though the wind had picked up, I wasn't cold. I felt giddy.

I have a date!

It excited me to have something to look forward to, something to think about besides all the drama. I had one more thing to do before I turned in.

Claire's soft voice came over the line, with instructions to leave a message. I asked her to call as soon as she could. Claire would be the one to guide us through this maze with Mum and Rose. I refused to follow Rose's advice, no matter how much she tried to intimidate us.

Just past ten-thirty, my cell rang. I expected to see Claire's face, but my heart sunk. Though I didn't want to talk to him, I knew the longer I waited, the harder it would be. I had to free myself. I had to stand up to whatever he had to throw at me.

"Hello, Michael."

"How's your mother?" His voice, barely audible sounded concerned.

"She's doing OK. I saw her today." I held back from telling him about her condition. "She seems to like where she's at," I said, determined to limit our conversation. He had no right to grieve for her.

"She's in a home?"

"Yes, she's not ready to come home. They want to monitor her episodes for a while."

"Catherine, I'm sorry," he said, his voice still calm and concerned. "I didn't realize she was so sick."

"She has good days and bad days."

He paused, I heard a deep breath.

"What do you want Michael?"

"I want to know when you're coming home. I miss you."

"No, you miss taking everything out on me." I stopped. "I'm sorry that is not what I meant. I need to be away from you. I can't let you hurt me."

"I won't do that again. You just make me crazy sometimes..."His voice became deeper, just as it did when he felt he had the right to make demands.

"I know you won't. I'm not coming back. I've decided to stay here permanently."

"We're still married. You're my wife."

"I won't be a punching bag."

"I never hit you that much."

"So that makes it OK?"

"I didn't say that either."

"What are you saying?" I ran my hand across my cheek, remembering the times he hit me; how the humiliation paralyzed me.

Being away from him had given me insights, a chance at a new beginning. If I didn't take it I would be a fool.

"You need..." he paused. "To come home." I could hear the anger in his voice. He was not used to being stood up to—by anybody.

"No. I'm done." A new voice took over me.

A silence filled the air and then it came, the abuse that even he didn't recognize.

"What can you do there? Nothing. You have obligations here." His voice turned bitter.

"Michael, we have nothing more to say."

I moved the phone from my ear and looked at the picture in front of me. He had taken it all.

"Cathy..."

"I'm hanging up now." I clicked off the phone and sat staring into the garden. The dark softly hid my tears.

I shook my head to steel my emotions and headed upstairs to the shower.

Slipping out of my clothes, I stared at the woman in the fogging mirror. She looked determined, in control.

Looks can be deceiving.

I stepped into the shower, letting the water steam away any reservations that were clinging to my tears. Michael couldn't hold me.

I braced myself against the shower wall, pushing away the day. My thoughts swirled in the flow. Mum...Rose and Francie...Michael.... The most surprising, Dylan. In his tenderness, I found something I'd been neglecting.

With the water cooling, I turned off the spigots and wrung the water from my hair. Mom's thick robe felt heavenly. Plush and warm.

I sat down on the bed, for a reason I couldn't explain, I opened the nightstand drawer, thumbing through the envelopes. At the bottom of the drawer, I found a small, flat box, one that might hold a necklace or bracelet. I expected to find a treasure from Da or one of us girls. What I found was a small pendent hanging from a stained string. I looked closely at the Miraculous Mary medal. I took it out and wrapped it in my fingers and held it up to the light. Why would she have a medal attached to a string?

I placed the box back in the drawer, but I held onto the necklace. I pulled back the covers and crawled into bed, feeling a drunk-rush as I closed my eyes.

"Do you want to come in?" I asked. His jaw softened, his eyes dropped as I watched him flirt.

"I'd love to, but it's late. I have a meeting... and you have an exam in the morning," he said teasingly.

"Thanks for the help, and the pint." I leaned against the wall to the entrance of my building. He kissed me again. As he did, his hands slipped under my sweater. They were warm, but I still shivered at his touch. I wrapped my arms around his neck and pulled him closer. His lips were wet, and I hungered for him even more.

If I let him go any further, he would consider me easy. We stopped, he looked in to my eyes, stroked my face, and kissed me again.

I wanted him.

"If we are going to do this, we better go inside, my neighbors will talk."

He pushed open the door, and we shuffled our way inside, fumbling with our clothes.

"You know what's going to happen, right?"

"Yes," I said, barely able to catch my breath.

My skin felt like fire wherever he kissed me, and when his tongue traced my ear, I melted. We made love without thought, pure instinct took over, his touch searing pleasure into my skin. I wanted him to keep touching me, to fondle me. At that moment, having him was all that mattered.

Garden of Nails

We found our way to the second-hand couch in the corner. He began to peel my clothes off, first the sweater over my head, then my jeans. We lay on the couch, arms and legs entangled.

In the morning, I awoke in my bed. A note sat on the nightstand.

"See you in court."

Seventeen

I woke with a start. My mind fuzzy, mixed with lying in bed with Dylan, and visions of an infant wearing the necklace. Looking down I noticed that I still had the necklace wrapped in my fingers. I put the necklace back in the drawer and tried to clear my head.

I threw on a pair of sweats and made my way downstairs for coffee. The dreams fading to fragments, I felt a blush creep across my cheeks at the thought of Dylan, I started to giggle. I hadn't dreamt of sex in years.

It was a very good dream.

A knocking at the front door interrupted my memories. Setting my coffee on the table, I moved to see Claire through the glass of the front door. Even through the frosted panel, I could see her anxiety.

"Good morning. Is everything OK?" I asked as I opened the door.

"Just grand," she said with a sour look. "You're the one that called. What do you need?" She flipped her keys back and forth and ran her fingers through her short, grey bob.

"You don't look grand. You look worried, anxious, and nervous. How am I doing?"

Claire set her purse on the couch. "It's your sister, she just called."

"Let's see, that must have been dear sweet, Rose."

"How'd you guess? I swear, that girl has more quills than a hedgehog."

I couldn't help but laugh. "She blasted out of here last night, swearing we were out to destroy Mum."

"I love all of you, but sometimes that girl is just a little off-kilter."

"I know what you mean. Want some coffee?"

"Sure, but give me a hug first," she said, as she reached around me, and squeezed me tight. "Thank you. A little bit of sanity."

Though not officially related, Claire had always been so important to me. As a girl, I used to think we looked alike, that her brown waves were mine and we shared the same tiny fold in our chin. Even now with her graying hair, and worry lines, I still found a resemblance.

She had lost a daughter in an accident that almost broke her right in two. Mum held her up, until the day came when she could stand on her own. I bonded to her, thinking I could replace her beloved. I figured Mum had Francie and Rose, but Claire had no one. It made sense to me.

The album still sat on the side-board. When we walked into the kitchen, she glanced, but didn't touch it. She took a seat at the table, and straightened the lace tablecloth.

"OK, I'm either blind or stupid. What's going on?"

"What do you mean?" I asked.

"The album. You left it there on purpose."

"OK, I'm not very good at being a sleuth. That's why I called you last night. I didn't want to say anything on the phone. I found them in Mum's closet. There are postcards and a letter as well."

"Did they just accidentally fall into your lap? Doing a little snooping, were we?" She smiled, but I saw the disappointment in her eyes.

"No, you're right. I'm sorry." I brought the coffee and the mugs to the table, to distract from my confession.

"I know all of this. Rose called telling me the same thing, but the pictures didn't worry her."

"Don't tell me, she ranted that I would tell Mum, and she'd lose her royal crown in the family?"

"For whatever reason, she worries about confronting your mother."

Claire picked up the passport picture and ran her thumb over the surface. "Sweet looking girl, isn't she?" She said, gazing at it with a tender expression.

"No, I think she looks very sad."

"Why would a little thing like this be sad?"

"I hoped you could tell me." I took a sip of coffee.

Claire watched me. "A part of me wants to tell you to put those pictures away and never tell your mother you found them."

"And?" I watched Claire rummage through the loose pictures that had fallen out.

"The other part of me wants to tell you to run into her arms with them, so she can finally be free."

"OK, now that I've heard from both sides, what should I do?"

I knew Claire well enough to know that she would advise me from her heart, but provide a touch of warning from her head. Those words right there, were from her heart. She had loved Mum and protected her for as long as I could remember, as Mum had done for her. They had loved each other as sisters.

"Claire, don't we have the right to know about our sister, if that is what she is?"

"It's so much more than that. So much you need to understand."

"Who is she? If Rose knows, then I'm sure you know, too."

"Yes, I do. I've seen her, I've even held her in my arms."

"Geeze, Claire, can someone just for once in their Goddamn life tell me the truth? Just tell me what happened to Mum. Can you at least do that one thing?"

"OK, don't get so dramatic, you're making me feel bad." Claire took off her coat and laid it over the chair, then unwound the scarf from her neck, as if she were allowing herself time to prepare for her next statement.

"Your mother never told anyone what happened to her when she was a girl, not her sisters, or Connor, not even your Da."

"But you know, right, and Connor knows?"

She nodded her head. "Connor knows, now. But when it happened, your grandfather said she was away at school. They wouldn't tell him where she was. Just at school."

"Catherine, there is so much more than your mum having a baby. She's lived with this secret so long—I thought she'd take it to her grave. I guess I was wrong."

"Rose knows about the baby, but she seems to be lacking details. She told us never to ask Mum about it. Francie and I think we should. If she is that sick, don't you think she would want to see her daughter?"

"She has seen her, met her, and talked with her. She loves her very much. She's afraid what people will think, so she never told your Da. She never told anyone. She didn't find out until after he died that he had known almost the whole time they were together."

"Oh my God." I plopped back in the chair. I knew if I tried to stand, I'd collapse. I took a deep breath and picked up the passport picture. "Whoever this is, is Mum's daughter, correct? And for whatever reason Mum had to give her away. Then this Finn/Claire spent years looking for her mother, and found her. And she sent Mum an album of her family. At least tell me that part is true."

"Yes, that's all true."

"Wait a minute. Her birth name was Finn, but Rose said her name had been changed to Claire. You were there. Mum named her after you."

I didn't expect it to hit me like that, but the tears came down, and nothing I could do stopped them. I wiped them away as I looked and saw that Claire had them as well. I couldn't decide if I was more moved by Claire's devotion to Mum, or Mum's devotion to Claire. I knew they had been friends, but I had no idea they were so intertwined.

I flipped through the album, studying the pages as if I'd never seen them before. Here was Finn's life. She graduated from high school, married, and had children, even grandchildren. She fell in love, had dreams and faced life as we all did, but she knew nothing about us. It struck me, we had her life here, in front of us.

I picked up the picture again and realized something I had not thought of. The girl in that picture looked to be three or four. If that was true, where had she been for those years? Did Mum keep her somewhere? Did someone put her in an orphanage?

"I want to meet her. I want to bring her home"

"No.... I don't think that's a good idea." Claire's words stumbled over each other, as she picked up her mug. I followed her back into the kitchen, almost tripping on the heels of her shoes.

"My God, Claire." I grabbed hold of her arm and turned her toward me. "Why can't you just tell me?" She twisted, turning her head away. "Look at me. You promised her, didn't you? You know everything that happened, but you made some crazy promise, that you would never tell."

"I love you Catherine, but my devotion to your mother goes way beyond what I have with you. You have to know—"

"That's the point. I don't know shit about any of this. I'm sorry, but I'm so frustrated. Seems like, in a matter of days, I move home to Dublin, I find out my mother has a tumor and is dying. She had a daughter she gave away, and everyone in my family has been lying to me—forever."

"Please tell me you understand more about your mother than that."

I paused and looked up at Claire. I realized she would do everything in her power to protect Mum, even from her daughters.

"No. I don't. Help me understand Claire. I don't mean to be judgmental toward my mother—or you, but if she is our sister, don't we have the right to know who she is? Shouldn't we be allowed to let her into our lives? Can Mum keep her from us?"

"Who else knows about the pictures?"

I almost laughed out loud. "I'm not running out in the

streets telling people, just Francie and Rose.

"Francie and I think we should try to find her and bring her to Mum, before it's too late. We have her cell number. She's been leaving texts, at least once a month."

"I know. Your Mum would wait for those days, like expecting to get a post."

"Why didn't she answer?"

"Why do we not do a lot of things? Fear? I don't know, she never said. But she showed them to me each time they came."

I didn't know what to say. I didn't know how to be. "Claire, I want to call her."

"Oh Jesus. I knew this day would come."

"Then it is true? You aren't denying it?"

"I told you, it's not my place. Your mother will have to tell you."

"What if she dies, or doesn't remember. You know the tumor is causing her to lose chunks of time. What if...."

"Your mother is a smart woman. She noticed when things started going wrong and did something about it. She called us—"

"Meaning you and Connor?"

She nodded. "We helped her make some decisions. She asked opinions, but they were her decisions."

"But—"

"No BUTs, Catherine.

"When your mother realized she was sick, she asked Dr. Redland about her options. She read articles he gave her, to learn more. He advised her on possible symptoms; he told her about the other things to look out for. She knew what to expect. She knew what she needed to do. After visiting St.

Philomena's, she did the paperwork and signed the papers. She often met with Mrs. Moore and they had long talks. She visited a few other places, but didn't like them as well."

In Claire's words, I saw my mother through different eyes. She wasn't helpless. She had taken steps to determine her own future.

"Why didn't she tell any of us? Francie, or even Rose? All this time, Rose has been acting like her protector, and she didn't know anything."

"That's exactly why. You were in Boston and from what Izzy told her in their letters, she knew your plate was full."

"Wait a minute." I didn't know if I should throw something or remain calm. "My daughter told her about my marriage."

"Not exactly. She just said you and Michael were having problems. She never gave any details. I don't think she knew. You know what it's like, gut reactions when you see someone you love being hurt.

"Jesus, is nothing sacred in this family?"

"Wow. You're digging into your mother's life, but you don't want yours shared?

"This is not about you, Catherine. It's about your mother."

"I'm sorry." I started to cry again, embarrassed by my selfishness. "I'm just trying to get from point A to point B, and have it make sense."

Claire wrapped her arms around me. I resisted, then melted into her. I was angry at everything. I pulled away and looked up at her face, as she wiped the tears from my eyes. "OK, I'm ready to listen," I said.

"She asked that Connor and I tell her whenever she did things that might be a sign it was getting worse. We did. We noticed when she began to talk like she was in the past, or call out to a stranger on the street. It didn't happen that often, but one day I came by the house, and she had no idea who I was. I've told you this already. I don't need to go on and on about it."

"We're her girls."

"Yes, you are. And she's your mum. Give her the respect she deserves. She raised you to make your own decisions. She gave you the confidence to live your lives, and she didn't question your choices.

"You girls need to offer her the same curtesy. She is a very capable woman.

"I don't have any more to say. I can't tell you about your mum. Not about Finn, and not about her choices. You need to understand that she didn't want you girls to be saddled with her illness."

"It's our job. I mean we're her daughters. She spent her life worrying about us. Now it's our turn to take care of her."

"Not if she's able to do it herself."

"Why can't we just go talk to her?"

"You can talk to her any time you like, but she won't tell you. She won't tell anyone until she's ready."

"We'd never judge her."

"You know that, and I know that, but your Mum can't understand that. She has lived with this secret her entire life. She is a proud Irish woman. She won't let it go so easy."

"I just can't understand any of this. What am I missing?"

"What part?"

I watched Claire, the relaxed free-spirited woman I once knew, was replaced by a saddened woman, whose complexion had gone pale. She slumped onto the table, wrapping her fingers around her mug.

"All of it," I said.

"You need to know how important this is to her, Catherine. She's afraid you'll think she's crazy. She's afraid that her episodes will get worse and she'll mix things up. She's doesn't want to be remembered a crazy old lady."

"I'd never think that."

"I know it doesn't make any sense, but it can't come from me. You have to understand." She reached out and took hold of my hand, pulled it up to her lips, and kissed my knuckles. In that one moment, she broke me in two.

"You have her perfume on."

"I put it on this morning, I don't know why. I think about her every day."

"So, what are you going to do?" Claire asked.

"I don't know."

"I do. I want you to see something before you make any decisions. Be ready tomorrow at one o'clock, and have Rose and Francie here, as well."

"Francie and I wanted to call Finn, this afternoon. Would that be OK?"

"Can you wait until tomorrow evening?"

Eighteen

Just past one-thirty, I checked my phone for messages. "What time did she say?" Francie asked.

"She said to have everyone here by one. I don't know what the hang-up is."

"She's usually pretty punctual. Hope everything is OK. Did you talk to Rose?"

"I called her earlier, but she was adamant that she'd go nowhere with Claire. She's convinced Claire is trying to split the family apart."

"I'm not surprised. What do you think Claire has in mind?" Francie asked, petting Mittens.

"I don't know. I think she knows some things about Mum that she's been keeping to herself."

"Where does she want to take us?" Francie asked again

"Really, I don't know."

"Do you ever think about what happened to Mum? I mean how do you think she got pregnant?"

I gave Francie a sly grin. "I think we're old enough to know how it happened," I said.

"No. I don't mean that, I mean the circumstances. Do you think she fell in love with someone, but Grandpa wouldn't let her get married? Or he just left one day. Or...?" Francie paused. "No, it couldn't be that. She must have loved someone and her father sent him away."

"I can't imagine Mum loving anyone but Da," I said, trying my hardest to disregard what Francie had said.

"Why not, Mum was pretty, and I bet tons of boys gave her a second look," Francie said.

"I don't mean they didn't, I just meant.... I just think it was always Da."

"Don't be so provincial," Francie said. "I bet Mum and Claire had a lot of dates together."

"You think so?"

"Sure. They've known each other forever. Teenagers, weren't they? I bet they had a grand time, as young girls," Francie persisted.

"Did she ever tell you how they met?" I asked.

"No. I always thought they had gone to school together, or met in Dublin when Mum was there for school."

"Come to think of it, Mum never told us anything about Claire. Ever. She's just always been there." As we waited, I realized that Mum had never told us much about any of her past. She told stories of her and Connor, when they were kids. And about Howth, when she met Da, but nothing else.

"Sorry, I'm late," Claire cried, as she hurried through the door. "Traffic.... Anyway, I'm here."

"OK, where are we going?" Francie asked, taking up her coat and moving toward the door.

"You'll see when we get there."

"No," I said, "I'm not going anywhere until you tell us where, and explain why."

"I've made a decision and it may be the worst decision I've ever made, but I'm taking you and Francie to Meadows Glen, where your mum grew up. So you can see for yourself. You need to learn her story before you see her, and I'm... I'm going to do what I can for you. And Francie you're going to drive."

"None of this makes any sense," Francie said.

"You need to see where she came from, to learn your mum's past. So you can better understand."

"The only time we've ever been there, was for our grandmother's funeral. I have'nt thought about that day in a very long time. We whisked in and out, in a matter of minutes, not talking to anyone."

When we reached the roundabout, Francie turned the wheel toward the freeway, following Claire's instructions. I stared out from the back seat, as Francie slipped in and out of the lanes. Well over an hour later, when we pulled in to an empty schoolyard, and Claire opened her door.

"Come on, let's go for a walk. I want to show you something," Claire said.

"Whose school is this?" I asked, looking around, taking in the warm breeze that filled the afternoon air.

"It's the school your Mum and Connor went to."

"I'm confused, Claire, why did you bring us here?"

"It is beautiful," Francie said. "Look at the trees. Is this school still open?"

"No, I don't believe so. Come on, I want you to follow me."

Claire took a deep breath and started heading down the lane.

"Something happened here that changed your mum's life, forever."

"What happened?" I asked, following behind her.

"Your mum was raped here, on her way home from school. She was fourteen"

I stopped, and let Claire's words wrap around. I didn't know which words hurt more, the rape, or that she was fourteen, or that it was Mum. I didn't know how to give the words meaning. It was hard to imagine, that this idyllic setting, was the scene of such violence. Violence against my mother. The trees swayed in the afternoon sky. I could smell the wild jasmine and heather that grew along the lane. The greens and the lushness of the foliage, were a perfect Irish countryside. But it wasn't beautiful, it was tarnished.

I continued to walk down the lane, touched the branches, while I kicked the gravel beneath my feet. I reached down and gathered tiny rocks in my hand, felt the cool wetness against my skin. Was that what she felt? Small rocks digging into her back.

Did it happen on the gravel?" I don't know why it made a difference, but holding them in my hand gave me a sense of reality.

Francie reached for the pebbles as well, rolling them over in her hand, looking up at me, with tears in her eyes.

"Yes, from what she said, it happened here." Claire pointed to the ground.

"How do you know this?" Francie asked.

"Your mum brought me here one time, when she thought of telling your Da. She had never told anyone. I guess she had to know she could say it out loud."

"I feel so guilty," Francie said, "an hour ago we were wondering how she may have loved. She hadn't loved anyone."

"At fourteen, she didn't know what love was," Claire said. "She didn't even know his name."

I tried to imagine what that must have been like. My mother, just fourteen, her whole life ahead of her. In a single moment, everything changed.

I kept along the lane, brushing away branches, kicking and disrupting the gravel. Just then, the rain began to fall. First in a soft mist, dropping to the leaves, dripping down to the ground. In a few minutes, the skies opened up and the rain pounded the gravel. I pulled my coat tight and looked up to the heavens. Today, everything changed. I understood why Claire had the need to tell us. I ached that Rose would not allow herself to learn the truth. It was Mum's truth. It was our truth, who our family was. It changed everything I had ever known.

"Catherine?" Francie called out, catching up with me. "I know why she kept it a secret."

"What are you talking about?" I turned toward her, the gravel clinched in my hand.

"When I became pregnant with Paddy, Da was going to send me away, but Mum stood up to him. I understand now."

I walked on for a while, still lost in what I had learned about my mother's life. I dug my hands into my pocket, letting the rain pummel me.

Maybe that explained the sadness in her eyes every now and then. As children, we were too young to notice.

"What did her father do?" I asked Claire.

"When your grandfather found out, he sent her away."

"Why?"

"He blamed her."

"What about grandmother?"

"She was helpless. He demanded that the parish priest come for her, and she was gone the next day. Without a word to Connor or her sisters."

"What do you mean helpless?"

"Your grandfather believed that it was more important to protect himself, his image in the community, than it was to believe his daughter. He knew, for a fact, your mum was the cause of the shame. It didn't matter if it was rape."

I stood on the lane dumbfounded. Looking behind me, I tried to imagine what that moment must have been like. Did he hit her from behind? Did he push her down? Did she see his face?

Were those the memories she saw every time she closed her eyes? How did someone get past that?

I thought about the pictures, the woman Mum had kept hidden. Finn was the product of that vicious attack.

Claire came up behind me, and took hold of my hand. "Come on, let's go for a drive. I think you guys have seen enough. Francie came up on the other side of me and put her arm around me. We turned and walked back toward the car, arm-in-arm. Francie, still following Claire's directions, pulled out from the school driveway and drove down the same lane we had just walked.

As she drove through, we saw the small houses set back from the road, surrounded by fields. The countryside was rugged; rock fences enclosed the pastures where horses, sheep, and cows roamed.

Claire instructed Francie to take a small dirt road on the right. We drove for another half mile, passing a freshly painted house with a black wrought-iron gate. The mowed yard displayed roses and wisteria that draped the garden fence, along with small white jasmine flowers.

A woman with an unleashed black and white collie came through the gate. She waved, but only Claire waved back. Francie slowed down, then pulled into the overlapping vines and ivy covering the lane, still following Claire's directions.

"Why are we stopping here?"

"Do you remember this house?" Claire asked, pointing back to the whitewashed house we had just passed.

"No, I don't think I've ever seen it before. Do you recognize it, Catherine?"

"I think this is grandma's house. The gate looks familiar and I remember the flowers in the garden," I said, looking back at the woman with the black and white dog.

"Claire is this part of your plan?"

"It's your Mum's house. Do you want to go inside?"

"No," Francie said, before I even realized what Claire had asked. "I can understand why she never brought us back here."

"What about you, Catherine?"

"No. Francie's right. I don't want to see it, either."

Francie pulled out onto the road and in a short time we were back on the turn-way. Claire didn't say anything. I had no idea where Francie's mind was. I was trying to wrap my head around everything we had learned.

Raped.

Nineteen

I paused before getting out of the car in front of St. Philomena's. At four o'clock, there would be time to talk to Mum before we sat down for dinner.

"Come on Cate. You can do this. We agreed," Francie said.

"I know, but it feels different now. It feels real."

"I know what you mean."

"I think I want to throw up. I'm afraid, Francie."

"It'll be OK."

"No, it won't. What if this causes her to go into one of her episodes? What if she never comes out? We may never learn the truth. I know what Claire said, but that's not everything. There are still secrets. What if we lose her before we even have a chance to be there for her? And why can't Rose see this? We need to be a family. We're sisters. What does she think she's doing?"

"I wish Rose were here, too. But, I think it's best that it's just us. Mum doesn't need any more drama. Come on, let's get it over with." Francie grabbed my arm and walked me to the door.

I stopped before we entered the building. "What if there is more to it? More than Mum being raped?

"How can there be any more than that? I think Mum has pretty much experienced the worst there is.

As we came through the double doors, we saw Mrs. Moore hurrying down the hall, clasping her hands together. The halls had their usual hum, even the TV could be heard from the lobby, but Mrs. Moore looked terrified.

"What's wrong? I can see it on your face." I held my gaze with Mrs. Moore.

"Don't worry, we have it under control," Mrs. Moore said. She pulled at her rumpled jacket, and licked over a slight stain of lipstick across her teeth. I heard the edge in her voice.

"What are you talking about? You look terrified," Francie said, doing her best to keep her composure.

"Mrs. Moore, what's wrong? Is it our mother?" I asked.

"One of the other patients snuck into her room and took her statue. Eric's been the only one able to keep her calm."

"Can't someone just go get it for her?"

"She hid it."

"Who?" I wanted to lash out, but I knew I needed to remain calm.

"Can we see her? Maybe we can help," Francie said, stepping toward Mrs. Moore.

"Please, come into my office." She pointed toward the door.

"We don't want to sit and discuss this, we want to see her and make sure she's OK. Don't you understand?"

"We'd like to see her. Now, please," Francie said in defiance.

"She's hasn't been able to stop crying."

"We understand that. That's why we would like to go to her room and try to help." Francie took my hand and moved past Mrs. Moore.

I nudged Francie as Mrs. Moore followed behind us. "We need to get into the room," I said.

I saw the tension in Francie's eyes turn to fear.

When we reached the elevator, Mrs. Moore pushed the button and we waited in silence. We left Mrs. Moore behind as we bolted from the opening door. We could hear the cries as we rounded the corner. Francie pushed the door open. Da's picture, from the nightstand lay, toppled to the floor. The flowers had been overturned and water dripped down the face of the dresser. Everything that had once been on the vanity, lay sprawled on the floor.

"My God," Francie said, putting her hand up to her mouth. "What the hell happened here?"

Two of the statues Connor had brought to Mum, lay in pieces on the floor. It was the one we couldn't find that caused Mum such heartache. She sat huddled in her chair, rocking back and forth, uttering a grieving moan.

"My baby, you have to get my baby back," she whimpered, grabbing her knees.

Eric came over from the side of the dresser. His thick hands clutched the shards of porcelain, he had gathered from the floor.

"I'm so sorry, Miss," Eric looked up at Mum, his spiked pink hair fell over his forehead.

"What happened?" I asked.

"Alice and I were enjoying some reading time. Mrs. Jennings snuck in, knocked everything to the floor and grabbed the statue from the dresser. She ran out the door, screaming the statue was hers. Of course, I knew it didn't belong to her, I was here when your uncle brought it in."

"Eric," Mrs. Moore motioned to him. "Go down to Mrs. Jennings room. Don't comeback until you have the statue."

"Yes, ma'am, but you know how she gets."

"I don't care, just get it," Mrs. Moore said.

"How you could let something like this happen?" I stood the lamp upright on the nightstand.

Francie ran her hands across the top of the wooden rocker while I walked around to the other side. I knelt in front of Mum. Her eyes were vacant. She hadn't returned from whatever world she had slipped into. I touched her shoulder, and ran my hand along her arm for her to feel the warmth of my skin.

"Mum? It's Francie and Catherine? Can you hear me?"

She sat in the chair, leaning forward, clutching her knees. I grasped her hands, her fingers cool to the touch.

"My baby's gone. They took her." She looked up, tears streaming down her cheeks.

"Mum, who took her?" Francie asked, rubbing her shoulder.

Her body stiffened as she sat up straight. "Don't touch me. Get my baby, I need to see her before Reverend Mother comes. She's going to take her and I'll never see her again."

"Mum, it's me, Catherine. Let me help you."

Mrs. Moore stood in the corner. "She doesn't know what you're saying."

I felt Mum push me away.

"Please." Her cries turned into wails. "Bring my baby back, I must say good-bye."

"Alice, we're doing everything we can," Mrs. Moore motioned for me to step back.

"No. Get away. You took her. It's your fault." Mum pulled away as Mrs. Moore moved closer.

The door swung open and Eric came through with the statue clutched tightly. He moved in front of Mum and knelt, placing the Virgin Mary statue in her grasping arms.

"There you are. You've come, Sara. Look and see. I have her in my arms. She is safe now."

"Who is Sara?" Mrs. Moore asked, looking over at us.

"No worries ma'am," Eric said. "She often calls me that. I'll be whoever she needs me to be."

Mum held the statue, cradling it in her arms. She motioned for Mrs. Moore to see. It didn't take long to realize that it wasn't the statue that brought her contentment. In her mind's eye, she held her baby. Mum held the baby she could never speak of.

Eric took on the role of Sara and soothed her as she rocked.

"Sara, can we hide away my dear one, so no one will find her?" She asked, clutching *the baby* to her breast.

"Yes, Alice, we'll hide her, she'll be safe," Eric's eyes welled up.

"We need to talk, Mrs. Moore," I said.

"We'll adjust her meds to help her settle down."

"I don't mean her meds, I mean about the situation with the other residents. About this." I pointed to my mother, rocking back and forth with a statue in her hand, and an orderly soothing her fears.

"We'll keep Mrs. Jennings away from her, I promise."

"They'll come for her," Mum suddenly cried out, "but I won't sign. I won't let them take her."

Francie and I moved toward her. She smiled at us, trying to speak, but not finding the words. "Mum we're going to help you to bed where you can lay with your baby."

"No, let Sara. She knows how. Please Sara, help me put Finn to bed, so no one will come for her."

"I'll watch over her, don't worry." Eric stepped between us and took hold of her arm. I pulled the covers back and Francie adjusted her pillow.

"Thank you. You'll stay with me for a while, Sara?"

"Don't worry, Alice, I won't leave you." Eric took hold of Mum's hands. She was totally engrossed in the scenario of Sara and the baby.

"Thank you," Francie said, watching Eric guide Mum to her bed. He pulled up the covers and adjusted the statue, then sat on the edge softly singing a lullaby.

Mrs. Moore turned to leave, meeting Connor at the door.

I motioned for him to back out. He stepped back into the hall and watched. We all stepped away, except Eric. He sat with her, holding her hand, waiting for her to drift off to sleep.

"She had a bit of an incident, but everything is fine now," Francie said, as we entered the hallway.

"Connor, we need to talk," I said.

"What's going on?" He asked, still peering over us to see what he had missed.

"It's over."

"I didn't ask that. Look at her. She's cradling a statue like a baby. The orderly is holding her hand and everybody has a look on their face that they just survived a fecking earthquake. Is someone going to tell me?"

"Not here." Francie shoved her way past him. "The Corner Pub is just down the street."

"Then I think we should go there straight away. Someone is going to start talking."

We walked the two blocks in silence. Once inside the crowded pub, we found a table in the back corner. Connor took our coats, and hung them on the coat rack, and took his seat at the table. The waiter brought our drinks.

"OK, I'll start," I said, taking a deep breath. We know, as a teenager, she had a baby. We know about the rape. We know Grandpa sent her away. She had to give the baby up. To who… we don't know. How am I doing so far, Connor?"

"You'd be doing grand, but none of us knew what happened. After I returned from University, I found out. After that, I went looking for her."

"Help me with this, so I can understand," Francie said, in a pleading tone. "When I got pregnant with Paddy, and Da mentioned sending me away, Mum stood up and said she would have nothing of it. She refused to allow him to do anything of the sort. Why didn't someone do that for Mum?"

"It was different back then. A different time. Our Da saw himself as shamed. In his mind, he had no choice."

"So, she paid the price for his shame?" Francie asked, barely looking up.

"I couldn't help your Mum until I knew about it." He dropped his head. "I tried my best to find her." He took a drink and wiped his forehead.

"I found your Mum in Howth. Jonathan and Marie gave her a place to start over."

"So that's how Jonathan knew her. She never said. I always thought he was a relative," Francie said.

"He was the world to me. It's good to know that someone took care of her. I always knew he adored her," I said, recalling times we had all been together.

"Your Mum kept so much private. She feared that people would think less of her. Did you ever wonder why you never met your grandparents? Your aunts? She never went back home, and after everything, she refused to talk to her sisters again."

"So why did she talk to you?"

"Because I came after her. No one else did. I don't blame them, they never knew, but she never got over it."

"And you expected her to?" I asked.

"I didn't mean it that way. She surprised all of us, that she did as well as she did." Connor took another sip of his pint, and tugged at his jacket.

Everything finally made sense. I had to wonder if Rose knew these details, would she be so angry? If she knew what Mum had gone through, would she be so bitter?

"Are there any more surprises?" Francie asked.

"We never meant to surprise anyone," Connor said, looking around the darkened pub.

"Have you seen her episodes like this before?" I asked.

"Yes, and it breaks my heart. Do you have any idea what it's like to see your sister so broken, she doesn't know who she is?

"I'm sorry for you girls, as well."

"We're all losing her. Piece-by-piece. What makes it harder, is knowing someone is out there who could make a difference." I said.

"I need to go. I'm sorry you girls had to find out this way, but at least you know," Connor said.

"Connor, none of us wanted to learn about it this way, but I have to ask you, and you need to be honest. Is Finn the baby she gave away?"

Connor bowed his head and looked away. "Not tonight."

Francie grabbed hold of his hand, grasping with both of hers. Connor stared at her, saying nothing.

"You've already said it without saying a word. You knew all this time and you didn't tell us. Did you meet her?"

Connor let go of Francie's hand. "I can't do this now."

I nodded as I watched him leave.

"Are you ready to go home?" I asked, looking over at Francie.

"I'm exhausted. I hoped you'd say that."

We paid our tab, and headed out into the rain. Francie took hold of my arm and we walked along in silence. We had nothing to say. Our tears fell like the rain. Soft, a mist surrounding us.

I thought about Mum, Claire and Connor, and the secrets they guarded well.

I held tight to Francie, holding the only thing from my history that was true. I pulled my coat tight against the chill as we arrived back at Francie's car.

As the defroster cleared the windows, Francie looked over at me. "Do we forget about asking Mum about the pictures?"

I shook my head. "No, we need her to tell us her story. I want to know her heart, what she went through. In her own words, not from Connor or Claire. I want to know what it was like to give up Finn, and to go on without her."

Francie pulled out into the street. I stared out the window as we moved through the town. We pulled into the driveway and sat in silence.

"Thank you," I said, "for going with me." Francie leaned over to pull me close. I could feel the wetness on her cheek.

"I want to go back and see her, but I don't know if I can handle seeing her like that," Francie whispered, and held me tighter.

I raised my hand, cupping her face. "I think the episodes are going to happen more."

"It breaks my heart to see her like that."

"As mine, but we'll get through it. We have to." I hugged her, once more and stepped out of the car. I watched as she drove away.

As I went inside my cell vibrated in my pocket. I saw Rose's picture.

"Are you home?"

"Yes, I just came in from seeing Mum."

"How was she?"

"It was bad. She had an episode and it broke my heart."

There was a long silence.

"Are you there?"

"Yes, of course I'm here."

"Then why aren't you talking?"

"I'm sorry about Mum. I don't know what to say. It's been a while since I've seen her. I don't know what to say to her."

"Rose, Mum needs us."

"No, she needs you—I should never have called. I have nothing to say to you." I heard the click and her face faded to black.

Twenty

I fell onto Mum's bed and pulled the afghan over my head. I closed my eyes, but couldn't stop seeing her huddled in the corner in her chair. I felt helpless. Eric seemed to be able to care for her better than any of us.

I imagined Mum holding Finn, her first born in her arms, then she's ripped away. Now, Finn, the adult, learning her history of childhood abandonment. The visions lingered, but in time I became lost in a deep sleep, free from everything that pulled at my emotions.

I awoke to my cell vibrating off Mum's night table. Dylan's name appeared.

"Hey, you're calling early."

"No, not really, it's past ten, in the morning."

"Oh my gosh." I grabbed my watch and realized I had slept for almost twelve hours.

"You OK?"

"Yes, I'm fine. I didn't realize it was so late."

"The reason I called, I wanted to ask if it was OK if we made a bit of a change for dinner tonight?

Tonight? Oh, it's Thursday! "Can you tell me where we're going?"

"That's the change. I know I said informal, but I thought maybe The Clarence?"

"Really? That would be wonderful. I've never been there."

"Great, I'll pick you up at seven-thirty."

I suddenly realized I had nothing to wear, especially not to The Clarence. I made two calls.

Francie came through the door at two o'clock announcing herself, as she always did. Her red curls pulled up, baggy jeans slung low on her hips. I laughed at the sight of her. I planned on taking fashion advice from this train-wreck of a sister?

"You look a little ragged," I said to Francie, shocked that her disarray didn't bother her. "What have you been doing?"

"A lot. I did some work for Colin this morning, gardening..."

"In the winter?" I interrupted.

"Yeah, the storm really made a mess of the yard, so I needed to clean it up. I didn't have time to do my hair after my shower. So, I agree, I look a little ragged. Hey, I don't have to explain to anyone. You want these clothes or not?"

"Oh no, I'm very grateful, just not used to seeing you... what can I say? Not so put together?"

"I'm as put together as I can be today." Francie laughed out loud, hearty and happy.

Behind her, Izzy came bouncing in. "I'm here, I brought my make-up."

"And I have the clothes your highness requested. Let's have a fashion show," Francie said, her arms as wide as her grin. Izzy came up behind her with a big hug.

"This is going to be so much fun. I've never dressed you for a date, Mom. Who is this guy?"

"Dylan was her college sweetheart," Francie continued,

"they almost got married, but your Mum refused to follow him to London. Being her own woman, she stayed in Dublin to finish her law degree."

I listened as Francie and Izzy gossiped of my college days. Every now and then, my daughter raised her eyebrows, giving a look of shock. She listened very intently, as if hoping there would be some tidbit Francie would accidently reveal.

"Wow, Mom, I never saw you as a rebel."

We all laughed. "I had my moments."

"That she did," Francie laughed.

"So, more details about this Dylan. I don't remember you talking about anyone from Trinity."

As my entourage followed me upstairs, Francie began to spill all the *Dylan* secrets. "They met in her second year of law school. Oh my God, *he* was the love of her life, for what? A year?" Francie teased, tugging at my sweater. They were inseparable. It was always, Dylan this, Dylan that."

"Yes, we had a year together. Now that's enough, OK? Francie let's see what you brought."

"I brought something for every event, except an evening gown. Don't have one of those." Izzy looked over and laughed, and she seemed happier than she had been in a long time.

"Listen, you guys don't make a big deal of this. It's dinner. We're old friends having a night out."

"I get it, dinner, but if I remember correctly, Dylan was one of your better choices...." Francie paused, "that got away."

"That got away? So more than a just a boyfriend?" Izzy looked at me, with such softness in her eyes, like she suddenly understood something that she had never realized before.

"I loved Michael," I said, looking over at Izzy for moral support.

"That would be the operative word, *loved* him," Francie said.

"Don't play semantics with me."

"Mom, it's OK for you to be going on a date. You and dad are splitting up. You have a right to go on with your life."

"You bet you do." Francie broke in. "No sister of mine is going to go back to a man who beats her."

I didn't say anything to her response at first, but looking back and forth between the two people who cared for me the most, I took a deep breath. "You're right."

I had fought it, long enough. I kept telling myself I'd make a decision when the time was right. I didn't understand why it took so long to realize the decision was made long ago.

"Come on, let's just make this as simple as possible. Which do you think would work the best?" I asked, taking one of the sweaters from her and stepping in front of the mirror.

Since we were almost the same size she had just the right thing for a night on the town. A free spirit, she had also developed a sense of style in my absence, not as strict as Rose's, or as casual as mine, but one that clearly defined her.

"Colin likes this outfit best," she said, flashing a short black dress. "But hey, try on everything, then you decide."

"You wear these?"

"Mom, these are great clothes. I have to admit Aunt Francie, I've never seen you in these before. They're sassy. I'm impressed."

"Well thanks, Izzy, and yes, I wear these clothes, in fact Colin and I have regular date nights. It keeps the spice alive, you know." She winked, then broke out laughing.

"Well at least someone has some spice," Izzy said, watching me hold the dress up in front of me.

"OK, let's see what you have here, but not the black dress."

"Chicken." Hearing Francie laugh, it comforted me to be with my sister and daughter, to laugh and not think about anything but girly stuff.

Izzy flopped on the bed, falling on the clothes and giggled like a schoolgirl. Watching her made me giddy. Francie brought three dresses, four tops, and two dress slacks with shoes to match. My staying in Dublin, would mean I had to go shopping—soon.

Besides the very short black dress, she also brought a royal blue dress that fell just below my knees. It had a boat neck collar that draped almost to my elbow, and a sliver of a belt. I loved the color, but didn't feel comfortable showing that much.

"I like the belt, just the perfect accent," Francie said, walking around me, looking at every angle.

Izzy got up and walked around the bed, staring at me, at first like a stranger, then with a smile. Without words, she approved. We caught eyes and both smiled. I wanted to wrap my arms around her, but we held our gaze.

The second, a cocktail dress, was too fancy for my taste, so I didn't bother to try it on. I could tell with the tag still dangling, that Francie hadn't worn it either.

The black slacks fit perfect, and the gold and silver shell with a matching sweater had just enough sparkle to be casual fancy, but comfortable.

"That will be perfect," Francie said, still twirling around me. "Just enough glitz, but subdued. What do you think, Izzy?"

"I love it. You look, romantic, sophisticated, and well, you look good Mom. Sexy."

"You sure about this?"

"Absolutely. Not too fancy, not too plain. Just enough sparkle," Francie said.

"Don't know that I like 'sexy'. Maybe I should wear that sweater instead," I said, pointing to the forest green one she had tossed on the bed.

"I brought a scarf that would be perfect with that."

I slipped the sweater over my head and watched how it fell on my shoulders, how it rested on my hips, not too tight, not too loose. The scarf added the perfect color, the elegance I needed.

"Awe, Cate, you look grand. Really, you do."

"I agree, Mom. This is more you, at least for your first grown-up date."

"Did you bring any earrings?" I asked Francie.

"Yes, I'm sure I have something that matches."

"You really think I look all right?"

"Yes, if we say it again, you'll get a big head," Francie said.

"It's just been a long time."

I looked at myself in the mirror and smiled. I wondered what Dylan was going through to prepare himself for our evening. Then I thought he didn't need to do too much. He could dress in cords and a sweater and look amazing. He could wear sweats and I'd think he'd be grand. *I had to raise my standards, no sweats.*

"I suggest you hang on to the other outfits for a while, just in case there's a second date, or a third." Izzy laughed, then caught herself, bringing her hand up to her mouth."

"Cate, just for the record, you need to go shopping if you plan on sticking around. I want my clothes back." My sister gave me a grin of acceptance, and I hugged her tight.

"What about my hair?" I looked into the mirror, but didn't feel too attractive with the lopsided top notch.

"How about a French twist, again just a little bit of style. Come on sit down. I'll do it now and you won't have to worry about it later."

She brushed the tangles from my hair, gave me a few wisps that curled at my ears. She wrapped the remainder around her fingers, and inserted pins that were hidden as she lightly sprayed my hair all over. She added a silver beaded comb from Mum's dresser for the finishing touch.

"You only need a tiny bit of makeup, just to bring out some color," Izzy said, opening her purse and pulling out a makeup bag.

"You wear this?"

"Sure, every day."

"It doesn't look like it. You look so natural."

"That's my secret." Izzy added a taupe shade of eye shadow, amber blush, and a berry lipstick. "Just before you go, add just a touch of each, not too much."

I looked into the mirror and for a few moments, forgot about everything. I had never been so full of color. I could honestly say I looked appealing, attractive even.

"Look at you, all dressed up, Cate."

"What would I do without you guys," I said, winking at them in the mirror.

"You'd be looking like me tonight, if you had your way."

"You really do look pretty, Mom." Izzy paused with a long look.

"I missed this," I said, moving toward the closet for hangers. "We should have more times like this."

"Cate, I'm so glad you came home I don't like what has happened to Mum, but we are getting a better understanding—and we're getting back what we lost."

Izzy looked back and forth, first Francie, then me. "Since you brought it up, I need to ask you guys something, and you have to promise to answer honestly."

"OK, we promise. What is it?"

"Something is going on with Grandma. Are you keeping something from us kids?"

I looked over at Francie and then back at my daughter.

"If something is wrong," she continued, "you need to tell us. She is our grandmother, and we love her."

"You're right. There is something, but we don't have all the details. We've been hoping they would reveal themselves."

"What are you talking about?" Izzy asked.

"When your grandmother was fourteen, she was raped." Francie started it, but looking in Izzy's eyes, I knew Izzy wouldn't let her stop until she had the truth.

"After the rape her family sent her to a 'home', after the baby was born, she was given away. Your grandmother never told anyone, not us, not your grandfather, no one."

"And so, we have Finn. We think she is the baby. She has sent your grandmother pictures and letters, but they're vague.

"We tried to show Mum her picture, to ask about it, but she had an episode and we couldn't."

"Can't we just bring her here and let her see Grandma?"

"Well that's our plan, but it is going to take some time," Francie said.

"Have you told Paddy or Jean and Marie?"

"I told Paddy everything we have just told you, but we haven't seen the girls. I doubt if Rose has said anything."

"Does she know what's going on?" Izzy asked.

"She doesn't want to believe any of it." I paused after saying it, feeling a betrayal toward my sister, but I also knew my daughter deserved the truth.

"I wish Rose would be more willing to be a part of this," Francie said.

"Rose is Rose." I turned away. It sounded cruel.

"That's not good enough. We need to get them back together. What can we do?" The excitement in Izzy's voice heightened.

"We're thinking of calling her, telling her that we know who she is...."

"And bringing her home," Francie broke in.

"When are you going to call her? I want to be here, and I bet Paddy would, too."

"In the next few days. Don't worry, we'll let you know."

I leaned over and kissed Izzy on the cheek, and hugged Francie.

"OK, you guys, go. Get out of here. I have to prepare myself. I only have a few hours."

"Call me when you get home. Don't do anything I wouldn't do. No wait," she turned around. "Do exactly everything I would do." This time she winked.

"Text me if you need a ride home." Izzy laughed, then reached over and hugged me. "No, have a great time. I mean it."

With still a few hours before Dylan would arrive, I took

off my new outfit and laid it on the bed. In an hour, Francie and Izzy had done everything I thought would have taken the entire afternoon.

I threw on some sweats and went down stairs. Now that the clothes were done, I just had to figure out what I would say to him, especially after we kissed.

Restless, I moved from room to room. I picked up a book, read for a while, sitting upright, to make sure I didn't mess my hair.

I couldn't get into the book, so I flipped on the tele and watched a talk show. I meandered upstairs, downstairs and in the garden, taking my time. I found myself laughing because I hadn't been on a date in over twenty years.

The rain had stopped. The weatherman said, though it would be cold and cloudy, the rain would hold off, at least for the evening. Ireland never listened to the weather forecast.

I checked to be sure Francie's up-do stayed in place. I couldn't help but be surprised at how much my little sister knew about fashion, for someone who always described herself as a "free-spirited hippy-child."

I followed Izzy's directions, added a touch more of blush, re-applied the lipstick along with her taupe shadow to offset my eyes. I slipped on the black slacks, adjusted the sweater, and stepped into the flats. It still shocked me, looking a second time into the mirror, I adjusted strands of hair around my ears.

I went into the kitchen and set out two wine glasses. I'd be prepared to invite him in before we left, or they'd be all set when he dropped me off.

I jumped when I heard the doorbell.

Twenty-one

I lingered the necessary few seconds before going to the door.

"Wow, you look amazing," Dylan said, his gaze settling on my face.

"Not too much? It's been a long time. Francie and Izzy helped."

"Not at all. You look captivating."

"Thank you."

"Izzy? I know who Francie is."

"My daughter, remember? I told you."

"Oh yes. I'm sorry."

I felt a blush rush across my face. "You're striking as well. Please come in."

In a tweed sport coat and scarf around his neck, he looked handsome. He didn't wear a cap, so I saw his thick course hair, black and white like his beard. His tie had splashes of blue and green, over a background of deep brown. There were gentle creases in the corner of his eyes.

"Would you like a glass of wine before we go?" I asked.

"I would love one, but we have reservations for seven-forty-five."

"Maybe when we come back?" I suggested.

"That would be grand."

I walked over to the couch, grabbed my coat and purse. Once in the car, Dylan leaned over and kissed my cheek.

"What was that for?"

"Because I wanted to do that for a long time—I know, a little childish. You do look lovely."

Dylan slipped in and out of the traffic, as we chatted. We talked about his projects, the weather, and news topics on the radio.

After pulling into the lot, Dylan parked the car and guided me to the front of the restaurant.

"Wait," I said, as I stopped and stared at the lights. "I've forgotten how the lights of the city shine from this side of O'Connell Bridge."

Dylan took hold of my hand. "Ever wonder why you left?"

I stopped to catch my breath, then looked at him. "More than you know."

We walked through the glass double-doors; bright lights from the chandeliers glistened from all corners. Once inside, I took a seat in the lobby while he gave the hostess his name. In a few minutes, the waitress waved for us to follow, as she zigzagged through the tables. We were seated in the cove of a bay window, looking out over the lights of the city.

"Did you request this table? The view is breath-taking."

"Yes. I had to grovel and beg for this exact spot, but they still wouldn't guarantee it. This must be our lucky night." He laughed as he held my chair out.

I hooked my purse over the back of the chair, and took off my coat. I stared out at the Irish lights, shimmering off the Liffy.

The waiter brought wine to the table. "Sir, would you like to check your order?"

Dylan looked over at the bottle, and nodded. "That's perfect." He looked over. "I ordered white, I hope that's OK."

"Yes, it will be fine." I couldn't believe he remembered what wine I preferred. In the candlelight, his green eyes matched the pastel of his shirt.

As Dylan poured the wine, he looked over with a mischievous smile. "So, what do we talk about?" he asked.

"How about the weather, or what's playing at the movies?"

"Didn't we already talk about those things in the car?" He asked.

"We could talk about world peace. Wait, I know, how about the political situation at the college?"

"I would like you to be awake for the appetizer," he laughed. "How's your Mum doing? Can I start with that?"

I looked deep into his face. Such an honest calm overtook him. I found it hard to believe that he actually cared.

"Yesterday was bad. Mrs. Moore called and said she had a restful night, but she still refuses to socialize. I'll probably go see her over the weekend."

"That's good. I imagine she'll be excited to see you," he said.

"Is it OK if we don't talk about Mum?"

"Why don't we talk about us, then?" Dylan asked, taking a sip of wine.

"I didn't know there was an *us*." I watched as his eyes held my glance. I couldn't look away.

"There used to be—a long time ago."

I laughed and took a sip of wine. "There used to be a lot

of things," I looked down at the utensils. "I guess London changed things. Speaking of London, how was it?"

"I loved everything about it." His face broke into an easy grin. "I could have lived there forever. It had my soul."

"Why did you leave?"

A waitress with a mass of blonde hair piled high came to the table, handing each of us a menu. "Take your time. Let me know when you're ready," she said.

He nodded his thanks and continued, "I practiced law, and got married," he said, looking away.

"You got married?" I looked over at his hand. "So," I paused. "What happened? Why did you leave London?"

He took another drink, and watched the wine swirl in the glass. "It isn't that simple. I lost everything—So I came home."

"If you loved it... I don't understand."

"In my first year of practice, I met Lena. She came from Cork, and had a two-year internship in London. We met at a social and everything just clicked."

"The job you always wanted... you found love. That's great."

He gave me a questioning look.

"Really, I mean it. So, Lena—your wife?"

"Yes. We lived in London Center for fifteen years."

"Did you have any children? I'm sorry. I'm asking way too many questions." I opened the menu to distract myself. *All I could think was why not me?*

"No. It's OK. We couldn't, but we were happy. We traveled, did all the things that couples with children can't do. We had our careers. We had each other, our dogs. We lived the lives we had hoped."

"Where is she now?" I asked.

"Gone."

He stopped. The blonde waitress came back to our table.

"Have you decided yet?" She asked.

"Yes. Cat, what would you like?

"I'll have the chicken pasta."

"I'll have the corned beef."

I smiled when I heard his order.

"What?"

"Corned Beef?"

"It's always been my favorite." He blushed.

He took a deep breath, as the waitress walked away, adjusting his silverware, and taking a sip of his wine.

"What brought you back here?" I asked.

"We were coming home from a weekend in the country. A car pulled out of nowhere, on a roundabout. The doctor said she died on impact."

I was overwhelmed with guilt and sadness. "How long ago?" I kept asking questions. I couldn't stop myself.

"Seven years, March."

I couldn't look up. How could someone cope with such a loss ?

"I've said too much. I'm sorry."

"No, no, it's OK. I can't imagine what it must have been like for you."

"I don't talk about it much. Well, I've told you my sad story, now tell me yours."

"You want to know about Michael." I smoothed the napkin on my lap. "The truth?"

"Always."

"I loved him, I guess. . ... That's not right. I did love him. Still do. I believed we belonged together." Suddenly, I closed my eyes and Michael was standing in front of me.

We stood in the corner of The Pub, a drink in his hand, stroking my hair, caressing my face. Handsome, athletic, and gentle, like no Irishman I had ever known.

"I met Michael through some friends, a year after you left. We started slow. He listened. I found him appealing."

"Different from me?"

"Yes, you were intellectual, he was athletic, more care-free. He didn't think too hard about things. He just reacted, without thinking it through. While you...." I looked at Dylan through my lashes.

He started to laugh. "So, I'm the deep thinker. That's a compliment, I hope?"

"Compared to Michael? Oh yes. You have no idea. I'll take a deep thinker any day."

"So, I don't have to change my ways?"

"No. Stay just the way you are."

"So, what happened, Cat?"

"With Michael?"

"Are we talking about anyone else?"

"He was kind while we were in Dublin. We were happy, but when we moved to Boston everything changed."

Our waitress set the steaming plates on the table. She had come at a perfect time. It gave me a chance to take a break from spilling my story.

"I have to tell you this, before I lose my nerve." I laid my hands in my lap, entwining my fingers.

"Before you left for London, I loved you so much," I said.

"I loved you as well," he said. As he looked into my eyes, I saw a sadness I had never seen before.

"I'm sorry," I said.

"For what?"

"For not having enough faith in you.... In me, in what we had."

"Where did this come from?" he asked.

"I think I realized it a long time ago, but we had gone on with our lives. It didn't seem right to call you and say 'Hey Dylan, I know we haven't seen each other in fifteen years and I'm married, but I changed my mind and I'm still in love with you. Why don't we both jump on a plane and meet some place tropical?'"

He spurted the wine he was drinking onto the table. "Excuse me," he said, wiping his lips with a napkin. "You caught me off-guard."

"I see," I said, smiling, raising my eyebrows.

"So, what happened with Michael?"

"After you left for London, I threw myself into work. A year later I met Michael. It excited me that he came from Boston and that he had lived in exotic places. Can you imagine Boston as an exotic place? It was to a small-town Irish girl. And he knew things other than the law. We were married a year later and then had Izzy. I decided to stay home with her. It worked for a while."

"You told me that already. You're repeating yourself."

"I'm sorry. It's all pretty fresh in my mind."

"Is Michael still in Boston?"

"Yes. I told him I had to come home."

"Why did you leave him?"

Anne Biggs

"I should have left a long time ago."

"That doesn't answer my question. Why did you leave him?"

The waitress returned to the table. "Is everything good?" she asked. She replenished the water and took the wine from the bucket and filled our glasses.

"We're fine. Thank you."

"He hit me."

"I'm sorry."

"I could have lived with it if it had been an accident, or only happened once, but after a while, it was happening more and more." I stared out the bay window to the city lights, unsure how I would say the rest out loud. "His words did far more damage."

Dylan dropped his fork and reached his hand across the table. I started to pull back, but I took hold of him and held on tight. "I'm sorry. It's hard to imagine you being hit by anyone. You were so strong. You kicked butt all the time."

"Somehow." I bowed my head, embarrassed to admit that I had seen it coming long before I did anything about it. "He took everything I said and turned them around to suit his needs. When that didn't work, he lashed out at anything close, usually me."

I said way more than I planned. Maybe the wine? Maybe being with Dylan? Or I just had to say it out loud?

"This is really a lovely restaurant. Izzy said they remodeled?" I said, attempting to distract from the current topic.

"Yes, that's what I hear. I'm glad you like it. I always wanted to come here. Tonight, makes the perfect occasion."

"I really want to thank you for tonight. It's given me a chance to just relax."

"I don't know if you were really able to relax. You've looked a bit tense at times. I am sorry about Michael. No one deserves to be treated that way."

"I'm sorry you lost Lena. She must have been perfect for you."

"I loved her, but it's been seven years. I'm ready to move on."

As we finished our meal I began to regret that I had said too much, but Dylan made it easy. I felt comfortable with him.

I couldn't help but wonder about Lena, what made him fall in love with her, what she looked like. How she won him over in a year, when I couldn't.

"Don't do that," he said, his eyes fixed on my every move.

"What, I'm not doing anything."

"You're wondering, why not us?"

"A little I guess. What was she like?"

"The exact opposite of you. Blonde hair, blue eyes, in looks, I mean. I couldn't be reminded of you every day. But like you, I found her smart, determined, and strong."

"Well that certainly isn't me."

"Why would you say that?"

The waitress returned to our table. "Your check, Sir. You can pay whenever you're ready."

"Thank you." Dylan reached for his wallet and handed her a card. He didn't look at the bill, just turned back toward me. "There's music, would you like to dance?"

"No. I can't dance."

"Come on. It's slow. Listen, remember this song, *Never Gonna Give You Up*. This is perfect for us."

He took my hand and guided me through the tables until

we hit the empty dance floor. He pulled me close, wrapping his arms around me. I laid my head against his chest. He didn't whisper anything in my ear, just held me tight and before I knew it, tears were streaming down my face. I wiped them away, but they kept coming. We moved across the floor, not paying attention to anyone, wrapped in each other's arms even as the music stopped.

Dylan stepped back and looked down at me. "Well, look at you. You're smiling."

"It's been a long time since I have actually been happy."

"I'm glad, it has been wonderful."

He took hold of my hand and we returned to the table. I grabbed my coat and purse and he led me out the door. We both felt the gush of wind coming from the river. He pulled me close as we walked to the car.

We drove down the thoroughfare to classical music gently flowing from the radio.

When we reached the driveway, he turned off the motor and looked me. "Cat, do you think we could try it again?"

"What do you mean? Go out?" I asked, looking over at him.

"No. I mean us."

I didn't know how to react. Instead of relishing in his affection, it brought tears.

"Why are you crying? Did I say something?"

"Yes, you definitely said something."

"Cat, I never wanted to leave you."

"Let's not do that. Our lives happened. You asked me if we could try this again. Yes, a hundred times, yes. But you know I'm still married, at least legally, but I will never go back to him. There is nothing there for me."

"Good, then how do we do this?" He asked.

"Slowly."

Twenty-Two

The next morning, I came downstairs and started coffee. I was famished. I stirred up eggs to scramble and started to fry the bacon. My cell rang. *Of course.* I stared at the phone from across the room. I had a choice, either I answered it and the smoke from the burning bacon would stink up the house all day, or I let it ring.

In a few minutes it rang again. With everything under control, I reached over and picked up my cell without even looking.

"Hi, how are you?" I reached for the fork and began to flip the bacon.

"I'm good. Just fixing some breakfast."

"I just wanted to say, well, I'd like to do it again."

"Do what again?"

"Dinner. If you would like to?"

"Yes, of course, I'd love to," I heard myself whispering.

"When would you like to go?"

"First off, I want to say thank you."

"For what?"

"For last night. For believing in me, for believing that this could all be real. There are days I just don't know what to think."

Anne Biggs

"I'm afraid I am quite a mess right now. I shouldn't have been such a.... You know."

"What?"

"An infatuated school girl?"

"Really. Did I miss an opportunity?"

"You make me laugh," I chuckled. "You probably did." I felt my face flush.

"I'd have jumped at the chance, if I had only known," he said with a languishing sigh.

"Don't tease."

"I'm not teasing. I would have taken you to bed last night if you'd have given me even the simplest signs. But it wouldn't have been right. You're hurting. I won't take advantage like that."

"I always knew you were a gentleman."

"Don't go spreading rumors."

"I just didn't want to hate myself come the morning, Dylan."

"I wouldn't have let that happen.

"Cat, your life is not a mess. You just have some tough things you're going through."

"Thank you for being kind. I'd love to go to dinner. And about the gentleman thing? I won't tell a soul." I laughed.

"Well, it's Friday, how about Sunday? Can you wait that long? There's a cute little place on Stephen's Green. I'll pick you up about six. Dress casual, jeans are fine."

"Can I call you tomorrow? I need to check about Mum."

"You can call me any time. I'm staying at the house, so if you need anything, I'm close by."

"I think I'm good. Going to stay in today. Maybe do laundry."

"My, you do lead an exciting life," he laughed. Talk to you soon, luv."

"Bye."

I clicked off the phone and poured the coffee, adding my usual brown sugar, then stepped to the French doors. The garden looked cold and blustery, no surprise for mid-November. A typical Irish winter. I pulled my sweater tight and moved back to the kitchen table.

Mittens twirled around my feet, wanting attention. When I sat at the table, she immediately jumped into my lap. Wet from the dew, she curled up to take her morning bath. Her black and white mittens rested on my knees as she dug into my skin, kneading and purring at the same time, all while cleaning her luxurious fur.

I felt the vibration from my pocket and for a second, thought I'd just let it ring, but after the third ring, I took it out and saw his face. The serenity I had been feeling was gone.

"What do you want Michael?"

"I'm at the corner, in a taxi. Can I come in?"

"Are you kidding? Why?"

"I told you. I want to work things out. You have to let me fix things."

"It's not a toaster, Michael. You can't fix it. You should've let me know you were coming to Dublin. Why didn't you call?"

"You'd have told me not to come."

"Damn straight.

"Michael, I don't want to see you. I'm not ready."

"Look, either let me in, or meet me at the Café."

I rubbed my temple with my fingers. "I really don't need this, Michael. Why can't you leave me alone?"

"We need to get over this. I need you, Cathy."

"Don't give me that crap. You never needed me."

"That's not true. I've always needed you. You just set me off, sometimes."

"Fine. I'll meet you at the café on Gaylord Street. I'll be there in twenty minutes. Don't come to the house."

"Five minutes, Cathy, that's all I'm asking. If we can't do it, I'm gone. I'll go back to Boston."

"God, I wish I could believe you."

"You can. I promise."

I knew Michael's promises meant nothing, not to me, not to him. "Fine, twenty minutes."

I walked in to the café with purpose. I needed to put on a show of strength. I might not of felt it, but he needed to see it. With my back straight, I opened the door to the eatery, ready to counter anything he would throw at me.

The only problem, he wasn't there. Six of the small tables were occupied. From the two vacant, I chose one in the middle of the room, thinking the more public the better. I ordered a cup of coffee as the server made her rounds.

Michael opened the door of the café and came directly to my table. Standing there, he looked fragile, crumpling his coat in his hands. His hair was disheveled, and he appeared to have lost weight. *My God, it had only been a few weeks.*

"Is it OK if I sit down, or do you have a problem with that, too?"

"I don't have a problem, Michael." *I could tell where this was going.*

"I'm sorry, Cathy. I don't mean to—"

"Don't worry about it. By all means, sit." He tossed his jacket over the back of the extra chair. "What do you want?" His eyes narrowed, before looking down.

"I told you on the phone, we need to work this out. I need you, you're all I want—all I can think about." I rolled my eyes at his remarks. "Don't be that way, Cathy. I know I hurt you, but that was before." He leaned over the table. "I told you, I'm different. I stopped drinking. I swear to you."

I kept my mouth shut. Anything I had to say was better left unsaid. After a few silent moments, his hand began to shake.

"How's your mum?"

"She's been better."

"And you?" He asked, looking around the room.

"Busy with Mum, going to see her as much as I can."

"When are you planning to come home?"

"I'm not."

"You're kidding, right?"

"What's there to come home to?"

He put his hand across the table and grabbed hold of my wrist. "How many times do I have to say I'm sorry?" I saw the rage in his eyes. Still holding my wrist, he pulled me toward him.

"Let go." I pulled my arm back, barely able to get out of his hold.

"You bitch." He raised his voice, then brought his hand toward me again. "You said you'd come back."

I jumped out of the chair, disrupting the table behind me.

"You haven't changed at all. Look at you. The minute I say no, you raise your hand. Is that how you treat someone you love?"

"I didn't mean that." He withdrew his hand and sat back down.

"I never said I'd come back. I told you I'd never let you hit me again, and I meant it." People watched, but with embarrassed stares, like caught in something they were helpless to turn away from.

"I told you I was sorry." It came out soft, with a tone that he really may have meant, but I saw it in his eyes. He couldn't control the rage. "What does it take?" He slammed his hand on the table, and again people turned. He clenched his fist and put it under the table.

"It's not about being sorry. Michael, you need to understand that." I sat back down, leaning away from him.

People had returned their stares to their tables and lattes. Michael unclenched his fist. "Then what's it about?"

"Michael, you hurt me. What does it take for you to understand that?"

"I never meant for it to go that far."

"It's not just about you hitting me. It's about who you think I am." I paused and stared at him, he wouldn't look up. I could almost see the steam rising from his brow.

"I don't understand, you're my wife. My lover...What do I need to do to get you back?" He asked in an eerily calm voice.

"I'll make it simple. Nothing."

"What the hell did I do to you that was so bad?"

"You made me believe I was worthless."

Our words became whispers. I leaned in to be sure he heard. "Every day, you took the best part of me, my dignity.

And the worst thing about it; I let you do it. Every time you belittled me, or hit me, I let you take a bit from me. I got smaller every day and you never saw it.

"Plain and simple, just so there's no doubt, I'm not letting you do it anymore."

"I want to make it up to you. That is why I'm here. Can't you find a way to forgive me?"

"No, not now."

"Can you ever?"

I hadn't even asked myself that question, so I had no answer for him. I watched as he groveled, so unlike anything he had ever done before. It didn't fit him. It made him seem less than a man. I also realized it wasn't real. He would do whatever it took to get his way, then revert to his old ways.

He sat back, then waved toward a waitress. "Do you want something to eat?"

"No, I need to go. I just came here to get things settled."

"How is Izzy?"

"I wondered if you'd ask about her."

"I thought we should work our things out first."

"Your daughter is doing fine, actually better than fine. I'm supposed to meet her in the city at one."

"Can I come with you?"

"No. If you want to see her, call her on your own."

"Cathy, you're giving up too soon. I made some mistakes, I'll admit that. But I said I was sorry, we have a life together. We had a child."

"Yes, you're right, we did, but she's grown. I have nothing left to keep me there."

"You belong in Boston... with me."

"I belong, Michael?"

"You know what I mean." His voice raised and a woman in front turned and looked over. I saw the concern in her eyes, but I shook my head to let her know I was fine.

I stared at my husband, a man I didn't recognize. It had barely been any time at all. He hadn't changed, I doubt he could. He had no clue how to even go about it. He didn't understand what it meant to love someone.

"I know you came here to make things better, but I don't think it's possible. It took me a few days to figure it out, but I'm not going back. I'm not going to lie to myself anymore. You hurt me. I won't let you do that again. Go home Michael." I looked at him and continued, feeling braver than I had in a long time. "Do what you need to do. Find a girlfriend, whatever. Just leave me out of it. I don't care anymore. I need nothing from you. I'm starting over."

"What the hell are you talking about?" The control he had tried to maintain left him. People turned toward us, either out of curiosity or concern.

"I'm telling you, do whatever the hell you want to do. I don't care. I won't be a part of it."

"I'll ruin you."

"There's nothing to ruin. Go home Michael."

He stood up, and slammed his hand on the table. He didn't notice the man standing behind him.

"I'd never raise my hand to a woman, ever." Dylan walked up to the table. "Are you all right Cat?"

"Who the hell are you?" Michael whirled around and faced the stubbled professor.

"If you leave now, no one needs to know you were here, it's over and done. And I won't have to call the Guardia." I sat with my chin held high, staring straight at Michael, I didn't need to pull back in fear.

"Who is this?"

"I'm a man who doesn't like to see someone make a fool of himself."

I continued to hold my stare on Michael. "Let me be, Michael. I won't tell anyone what you've done. I'll just say our lives went in different directions."

I knew even as the words came out, they were a lie, but it didn't matter. I didn't care about any of it.

"Cat, good to see you again. How are you?"

I smiled and looked up at Michael, as Dylan stepped forward from the shadow. "Michael, this is Dylan." Before I could finish the introduction, Michael grabbed his coat and rammed his way through the crowd.

"You'll regret this." In his rage, he knocked people to the side on his way out the door.

"I thought I'd better come over when he stood up. It looked like he might hit you," Dylan said, wearing a look of concern.

"No. He'd never do that in public, but he showed his true colors."

"He's getting into a taxi now," Dylan said, pointing toward the window.

"He was my lie," I said, wiping the tears that had fallen unknowingly.

"The husband?"

"Wow, you're smart."

We laughed, but I looked past him to see Michael settling

in the taxi. The cab headed off down the road. I took a deep breath as it disappeared around the corner. Did this mean I was free?

"Are you all right?" He asked, placing his hands across the table on to mine.

"I will be." I took a deep breath, and let out a laugh. "I stood up to him."

"You did," he said shaking his head. "I'm proud of you."

My hands were shaking, I was crying and laughing at the same time. "You know what? So am I."

"You are a wonder, girl. Can I get you anything? Coffee, sandwich, pint?" He motioned to the waitress.

"No." I squeezed his hands. "Thank you for your chivalry."

"Anytime, Cat. Anytime."

We both half chuckled and for a minute I felt relieved. Patrons had settled back into their conversations. Michael and his rage had bolted, leaving everything to settle in place. Dylan took off his coat and took the seat where Michael had been.

"We came here because I didn't want him at the house."

"That was smart."

"I don't think I would have been quite so..."

"Strong? Cat, you are one of the strongest women I know."

"I was going to say harsh."

"Harsh? When were you harsh? You were civil. That's more than I can say for him. He's an ass." Dylan's eyes flared, matching the passion in his voice. I smiled and squeezed his hand.

"Well, I'm glad you didn't let him in."

"Do you want to know what it was all about?"

"He was quite vocal. I think I know." He rubbed my wrist with his thumb, making my thoughts stray. The light friction across the back of my hand was disruptive, to say the least.

"Again, thank you for being my knight in shining armor."

"Are you sure you don't want something?"

"What time is it?" I suddenly remembered I had an appointment in the city.

"Just past twelve."

"I'm supposed to meet Izzy. We were supposed to have lunch. I need to call her and let her know I'll be late."

"Would you like me to drive you in? I'd love to meet her."

I had thought about Izzy meeting Dylan, but I wanted more time with him. I needed to feel more comfortable. "Let me call her first, then...I need to call her."

"Go ahead and call. I don't have to stay, but I can drive you into the city if you like."

I stepped away from the table, going through the single door.

It rang twice. "Mom, are you on your way?"

"No, I'm running late. I'll explain later. I'm caught up at the university." *At least with a professor.*

"Did you get my message? Something came up, I have to cancel."

"No, I've been busy, too. That's OK we can make it another time."

"Are you sure?"

"Yes. It's fine. Do what you need to. I'll call you tonight."

I stepped back inside the café. Dylan's elbows were perched on the table. He stood up when he saw me coming. "Everything OK?"

"Yes, Izzy couldn't make it either, so here I am."

"How do you feel now?"

"For the first time in a very long while, I feel free. I know I'm really not. But for right now—for this moment," I paused. "I am free."

"You are what you want to be, Cat."

We sat over coffee laughing and reminiscing. We discussed everything under the sun, except politics and religion. Neither of us wanted to test those waters. I told him about Izzy and her art, he told me more about Lena, her quirky ways, and how he had fallen in love with her.

"I think you two would have gotten along; just enough differences to complement each other." He stared past me as if he was holding her in his memories.

"Well, I can tell you and Michael wouldn't have gotten along at all."

"Why, thank you. I take that as a compliment."

"Tell me about your work. What's on the docket these days?"

For the next hour, we talked about Trinity and the new exciting ways they were teaming with the city to help people. I watched as his arms lifted as if he were ready to take off. I sat back and took in the show.

"Am I that boring?"

"You're not boring at all. It's a delight to watch you. You really believe in what you do. It's exciting." Glancing at my watch, I noticed it was almost three o'clock. "Oh my, I need to go.

We stood outside, and he helped me with my jacket, then pulled me close. "Can I kiss you?"

Twenty-Three

Over the weeks, I had gotten comfortable in Mum's house, remembering the nooks and crannies, the special places where I found peace.

Today, I could find no peace. My world was on a collision course, no matter where I turned, explosions rocked my course.

Michael...Dylan....Both had my stomach lurching. One in a good way, one in a twisted sense of entitlement.

I went into Mum's garden, and took a seat on the bench. The mystic beauty of the late afternoon took over my senses. Droplets of rain clung to the leaves, rose petals glistened, even the grass sparkled as the sun broke free from the clouds. Every inch of her garden was magic.

This was why Mum loved her garden. The roses, the vines, every inch spoke to her passions. Even the swans. I wondered what memories her garden held as I watched the heather and honeysuckle floating in the afternoon air.

For no particular reason, I went upstairs and began to prowl through Mum's belongings. On the vanity, stood her jewelry box. It was made of polished rosewood, with an enameled shamrock glued to the top and carved rose trellises spanning the corners. Da had given it to her the year Rose was born. I adored it as a child.

Anne Biggs

Looking at it now, I could see how inexpensive it was. The emerald-green clover had flaked from Mum's touch and her caress had worn the stain from the roses. She cherished the box as if it was made of the finest rock crystal. In truth, it was more precious than gold.

I sat on the bed and slowly opened it. There were her pearls that she had worn for each of our weddings.

Each piece told her story. Most of them I knew, like the random sets of earrings we girls had gifted her. But some, like the little medal on a string, she had kept hidden

Tangled in the necklaces and chains at the bottom of the box, was an emerald cross strung on a small gold chain. I held it up in the light and allowed a smile to cross my face. My mother had done a good job of keeping her secrets. I had never seen it.

I laid the box on the bed and held the cross to the light, so tiny, so fragile.

I reached for the medal lying in the tray of the vanity. Somehow, I knew they were both from Finn. I could almost feel her wound in the tangles of chain.

I slipped the medal and the cross into the pocket of my jeans and put the box away. I went down stairs and grabbed my coat from the couch. I didn't call anyone, didn't ask anyone's opinion. I just slipped out the door knowing exactly what I needed to do.

Across the street a taxi was parked at the curb. I tapped on the window, and asked if he might be heading into Dublin Center. He told me it was my lucky day. He had just dropped a passenger off and was waiting for another.

"Well here I am," I said. I hopped in and gave him the address for St. Philomena's. In a few minutes, we were on the thoroughfare. It seemed everything had come into focus.

It was just past five when I came through the double doors. I hadn't called Mrs. Moore, but we had been told to come any time. I felt the medal, warm in my pocket, and debated how I would ask. I wondered if it would trigger something. As I squeezed it in my hand, guilt overcame me. My hand became clammy. I took it out and rubbed it against my thigh.

I waited until the doors closed before stepping into the lobby. The reception desk was empty. Past the lobby, in the recreation room, tables were arranged with picture puzzles, magazines, and books. Lots of books. Children's storybooks, romance novels, thrillers, that could be read in a few days.

The room stood empty, puzzle pieces scattered across the table tops, magazines opened at random. It must be suppertime.

I went back to the lobby, turned left and tapped on Mrs. Moore's door. She seemed surprised to see me as she opened the door. "Hello, Catherine. I wasn't expecting you."

"I guess I should have called."

"No, no. You're fine. Family is welcome anytime."

"How is she doing?" I asked.

"She's been sleeping a great deal. We changed her meds and she seems to be responding well, I think she is doing much better."

"Can I see her?"

"Of course. You could have supper with her, if you plan to stay that long. I believe she is still in her room."

"I'd love that."

"I think she'd like it as well."

"Can I go there now?"

"Yes. Would you like me to come with you?"

"No, I'll be fine. Thank you."

I nodded and went out the door. Coming out, I heard the television and light conversation, now coming from the recreation room. I waited for the elevator to open, then stepped inside. It only took a second and the door opened. I stepped out and walked the two doors to her room. I tapped once, and walked in.

"Catherine, I'm so glad you're here." Her whole face lit up as she peered at me from her rocking chair. "I've been having a bit of a time, lately."

"Yes, Mum, I know. Mrs. Moore said they changed your meds. How are you feeling?" I came over and stood by her chair, taking hold of her hand.

"Just tired. Not sleeping at night, then tired all day."

"I've been coming to see you every day."

"You're a sweet girl."

"Mum, I worry about you."

"I'm fine. Sit down and talk. Tell me how things are."

"That would be nice, I'd love to talk with you."

She looked regal sitting in her rocker. She knew who I was. She seemed alert. I took a seat on the bed and decided to approach her about the medal, hoping it wouldn't take her away from me.

"So, what would you like to talk about?" She asked, grabbing hold of my hands, squeezing tight.

I slipped my hand inside the pocket of my jacket and grasped hold of the medal, letting the string wrap around my finger. I pulled it out, but kept it tucked in my hand, out of sight.

"Mum," I held my breath, "I found this." I placed it on her lap, then pulled my hand back.

She picked it up and wrapped her fingers around it, then looked up at me. "Do you know what this is?"

"Yes, it's a Miraculous Mary medal."

"Do you know what it means?"

"Yes, anyone who wears it will get special graces from the Virgin Mary."

"She saved me you know." She held up her hand and opened it in the light of the window. "I won this as a little girl in a contest, but I gave it to someone very special."

"Why did you give it away?"

"Because it was important."

Mum looked out the window, then back at me. "Where did you find it?"

"In your jewelry box."

"What were you looking for, dear?"

"I'm sorry, Mum, nothing," I paused. "Everything." I stuttered, like a child caught in a lie. "I found the secret flap. I pulled it down and it fell out."

She looked over at me and patted my hand. I knelt down next to her, bowing my head, feeling so guilty that she might have thought I violated her.

"This is very special to me, but it is not the time to talk about it. When I am ready, I promise I will."

"Do you want to keep it with you?"

"No. Please put it back, and when the time is right, I'll ask you to bring it to me."

"I'm sorry I took it."

"Oh no, dear, don't be sorry. I might have done the same thing. It'll be fine. Put it back and I'll claim it when I'm ready. Can we go to the dining room and have supper?"

"Of course." I opened the door, then went back and helped her from the chair. She pulled herself up and moved toward the door. "Do you know what they're serving today?"

"No."

I shut the door as we walked out into the hallway and down to the elevator. Once inside, she took hold of my hand and looked over at me.

"Rose once asked about that medal, but I wouldn't tell her, either."

So, Rose had not been innocent after all. She too, had gone through Mum's things. For the moment I felt relieved, knowing that I was not the only daughter to have sinned.

"Oh, don't worry sweet girl. There are just things that are meant to be kept secret, and that is one of them, for now." She smiled contentedly, and we walked out the elevator toward the dining room.

"Mum what if I told you I might know who it belonged to?"

"I'd tell you that you were wrong, and you had no idea. You might know a half-truth, but you don't know the whole thing. No one does." She patted my hand and we took a seat at a table by the window, with a vase of roses in the center. Mum smoothed out the white tablecloth and sat quietly. We were late, most of the tables were empty.

"Would you like beef or chicken?" Asked the young girl with sparkles in her long blonde hair.

"I'll have chicken and tea. Thank you," Mum said, looking up at the young girl. "Look at her nails, Catherine. That color is spectacular." The iridescence of the nail polish glittered in the sunlight.

"Thank you," she said. "And you, ma'am? Chicken or beef?"

"I'll have chicken, as well."

We sat in silence. Mum stared out the window, then abruptly turned toward me. "How long have you known?"

"Known what?"

"Don't play shy with me, girl. I am clear-headed, and I know what this means. If you found the medal, you found other things. You may not know it all, but you know some. What do you know?"

"Are you surprised?"

"Answer my question."

I took a sip of water the girl had left at the table. "I know about Finn."

"What else did you find?" She asked, not showing any signs of shock or dismay.

"I found pictures, and postcards."

"Did you put them back?"

"Yes, I put everything back, except the medal, but I promise I'll return it."

"Catherine, let's just have dinner and talk about the weather, my grandchildren, and gardening. I don't want to talk about the past for today."

Just as I was about to answer her, the same blonde with sparkles, brought out two plates, along with our tea and some bread. Mum immediately grabbed hold of the bread and scooped the butter onto her plate. I took a sip of the tea, and watched as Mum ignored my every move, too busy gathering her food together. I watched her move the gravy and potatoes around on her plate, mixing them together.

"Eric has been very kind, you know. He has been with me in the green house. We have one you know."

"Yes, I've seen it," I added.

"We are repotting shoots of lavender and jasmine. If they take hold I can have a few pots in my room. I'd love that. I've always loved the smell. Even as a girl, we grew lavender by the fences. It grew wild, you know."

"No, Mum, I never saw the garden at your house."

"But I grew it at home. You remember it, in the pots in the back yard, in the garden?"

"Yes, I remember them, but not the house you grew up in. The only time you took us back there was to bury Grandma. We never knew anyone."

"We went there, often. You used to play in the field with your sisters."

"No, we never did. We played in the park behind out house." Mum's eyes seemed to have a glazed appearance. A tear welled in her right eye.

"I'm done now. I want to go back to my room. Will you call Eric?"

"I don't know where he is. I can take you back. Don't you want to finish your supper?"

"No, I need to take a nap. Could you go find him please?"

I looked around the room, beginning to feel anxious. Something happened in the last few minutes, I wasn't sure what it was. I hoped I hadn't triggered something. Looking in her eyes, I felt something was coming on, but she seemed relaxed. She knew where she was, even asked me to find Eric.

I left the table and went down the long hallway away from the dining room. Eric came around the corner carrying a bundle of towels, and seemed in a hurry.

"Eric, I'm sorry to bother you, but my mother would like you to help her back to her room."

"I thought she was having supper."

"She was, she was doing grand, then suddenly she stopped and asked me to come find you."

"Let me put the towels away, then I'll come to the dining room. Is your visit over?"

"I guess so. I don't know, she suddenly said she was tired and she's not acknowledging me anymore."

Eric had whittled a way into her heart. He had a place in her life now and even when she went back in time, there was something about him, maybe his kind green eyes, or the pink strand of hair that constantly fell across his forehead. His hands were gentle, and he never startled her.

I went back to the dining room. She was gone. The plates were still on the table and her tea had barely been touched. I went into the recreation room, going from table to table, but I couldn't find her. I went back down the hall, looking into every open door. It seemed impossible that she could have disappeared.

Just as I was about to open Mrs. Moore's door, I heard it. At first I didn't know where it came from. Then I recognized the voice I had heard this cry only one time before, on the day that she said good-bye to Da at the hospital. We left her alone in his room, while we waited outside. I stood there and saw Mum in the corner, Eric sitting by her side holding her hand.

"Why won't you bring her to me?"

"Alice, she isn't here."

"Why did they take her? You promised." She screamed in a broken voice." Eric grabbed hold of her hand, patting it in a soft stroking motion. "You said you'd take care of her. I believed you. Why is she gone?"

By the time I got to her side she was inconsolable.

Thrashing around, then slumping back to the floor in sobs. I ached to see her like this. Her whole body shaking, pounding her fists on the floor.

"Catherine, this is not a good time," Mrs. Moore said, pulling back on my arm.

"I was just with her. She was fine. What happened? I went to get Eric, but when I came back she was gone."

"I didn't realize you were still with her," Mrs. Moore said.

"What happened?"

"I don't know. She fell into Eric's arms, then started crying."

"This doesn't make sense. Eric, I was just talking to you."

People began to gather in the hallway, but Mrs. Moore shooed them away, giving Eric room to gather Mum back together.

"She's in an episode, she can't see anything that is real. If she does, she doesn't recognize it. All we can do is wait for it to pass."

"No. You have to do something. We can't leave her on the floor."

"You can try." Mrs. Moore stepped to the side. I moved toward her, reaching out my arms, then slumping to the floor to gather her up. I pulled her close to me and held her, pressing her face to my chest. She was so tiny in my arms, so fragile, like holding a child. I had to steady myself.

"Mum, it's me, Catherine."

"Oh, Claire you've come back. Where's my Finn? Can you fetch her?"

I realized no matter what I said she would not know I was her daughter. All she could see and feel was Claire. So, to soothe her, I lied.

"Alice, it's me, Claire. I'm here, you'll be all right." About that time, Mrs. Moore came up behind me and nudged me. I turned away from my mother and she handed me a baby doll wrapped in a blanket. It felt real in size, but if you looked at the face, you knew immediately it was a doll. She motioned for me to pull the blanket up, then to rock it, and talk to it. And so, I rocked and coddled it.

"Alice, I'm here. I have your Finn. I swayed my body, holding the doll, hiding it within the blanket. When she saw the blanket, she calmed down, but she wasn't there. Once she had the bundle in her arms, she was back in the infirmary at Castlepollard. She didn't even open it, just held it close to her, rocking back and forth.

"Oh my baby, I'm so sorry," she lamented. I nudged closer to her, holding her as tight as possible. She reached her hand up to my face, brushing my hair from my eyes, with tears on her cheeks. I thought she was back, but then she looked straight into my eyes.

"She's beautiful, isn't she Claire? Just perfect in every way."

"Yes, Alice she is. Here let me help you get up so you can be more comfortable." Eric and I lifted her off the floor and sat her on a chair. I didn't try to take the doll. Even if I had, she wouldn't have let me. I brushed her hair back, and wiped the tears from her cheeks.

"She is beautiful, Alice," I said, petting her shoulder.

"I'm so tired," she said in almost a whisper.

"Here, let me take her and put her in the crib, so you can sleep. You'll need your rest to take care of her."

"You'll bring her back to me?"

"Yes, as soon as you wake, I promise."

She handed me the yellow bundle and closed her eyes.

Then Eric swooped her into his arms and without a word, moved to the elevator.

"She needs to be in her room."

I looked back at Mrs. Moore, still standing behind me. She too, had tears in her eyes. A nurse stood next to her and took the doll from my arms.

"What the hell just happened?" I asked.

"Something must have triggered while you were having supper. Something must have been said, or triggered by a memory."

"How did you know about the doll?"

"When I first started my career, I watched a nurse do this, and it was miraculous, so since then I have always had a life-size baby-doll wrapped in a blanket. Whenever they cried for their baby I would use the doll. It has never failed."

"I've never seen anything like that."

"The one memory that so many women go back to, is holding their babies. Did your mother lose a child?"

"Yes. She had a stillbirth," I said, realizing I'd lied. "She didn't even know me," I said, still staring at Eric, stepping into the elevator with a tiny woman in his arms.

"When she wakes up she won't remember. She'll be thrilled to see you and will have no idea what happened." Mrs. Moore straightened herself and seemed to have control of the situation.

"What should I do now? Should I stay here?"

"Eric will take her to her room and the nurses will tend to her. She'll probably sleep through the night. We'll keep someone close by, so when she wakes up, she won't be scared. I'd come back tomorrow. She'll be much better."

Garden of Nails

I left Mrs. Moore behind as I went out the double doors. I didn't know where I was going or what I would do. I thought about going back in to call for a taxi, but I kept walking.

Twenty-Four

I stood outside the gate and rang Dylan. He answered immediately.

"Can we meet somewhere? I really need to talk."

"Where are you?"

"St. Philomena's."

"Wait for me there. I'll pick you up"

I hung up and began to pace, not able to focus on anything substantial. Back and forth, with the rain falling all around me. I fell into a haze with the hissing of traffic. Images of Mum and her baby, Rose trying to forbid any of us from visiting; Michael thinking he had a right to make demands; and Dylan with that sweet, calming voice.

"Cat, are you all right?"

I turned and saw Dylan coming from across the street. Once on the curb, I let myself fall into his arms, sobbing uncontrollably. He held me, taking off his coat and wrapping it around my shoulders.

"Come on, you're soaked. You need to get out of the rain."

I let him guide me to the car, wrapped securely in his arms. I didn't say anything as he pulled into Dublin traffic, I didn't even try to hide my tears. After a few blocks, he pulled to the curb and stopped the car.

"Cat, what happened?"

I pushed strands of wet hair from my face, and stared out at the blurring lights.

"Cat, talk to me."

"I don't know what to say. I had never seen Mum like this. I didn't know who she was, or what she was talking about. She went somewhere."

"What happened. Where did she go?"

"Back to the moment she had to give her baby up. Dylan, my mother was raped and had a child."

"What are you talking about?"

I looked around, for the first time actually seeing Dylan. He wore an expression of confusion and fear. I hadn't even realized that we were sitting in his car. I started to cry again. "I am so sorry. Look at me, I'm a mess."

"What do you want to do?"

"I don't know. A part of me wants to be with my mother, but then, I want to get as far away as possible."

"Why don't I take you to the cottage? We can have dinner and you can pull yourself together. Then I'll take you home."

I looked around, still feeling confused, then nodded. I had no clue how to deal with anything at that moment. "Are you sure?"

"I'm positive. I'll get a chance to show off my culinary expertise, or we can order in. I'm really not that good of a cook, if truth be told."

I laughed for the first time in a long time. "Thank you," I said.

"For what?"

"For not making me feel like a fool."

We drove in silence and before long, we turned on to Evergreen Street. I stared out the window and watched as the sun made its final attempt to break through. As he drove, I slowly pulled myself together, wiped away the tears, readjusted my hair and tried to look normal. In a few minutes, he pulled in to a quiet neighborhood. Lights glowed from behind curtains.

After pulling into the driveway, Dylan immediately came around to open the door. I grabbed my purse and waited while he unlocked it. A leather couch stood against the far wall, with an afghan thrown over it. Books were everywhere.

"Welcome."

"So this is how a professor lives? I haven't seen this many books in one room since my last visit to the library."

"I'm sorry, they're one of my passions."

"No. I love it."

"Can I get you a glass of wine?"

"Thanks."

I sat on the couch, inspecting the room where, I assumed, Dylan did his work. A large desk in the corner overflowed with books, yellow tablets, and an open laptop. He came from the kitchen holding two glasses, placing them on the coffee table. He picked up a box of matches, and lit all the candles in the room. A warm glow filled the house and calmed my heart.

"This is your parent's house?"

"It was. It's mine now. I have an apartment near the university where I stay if I need to be in the city for a couple of days. I grew up here. After my parent's passed, I decided to keep it—kind of a getaway, besides I couldn't bear to get rid of my father's belongings. I have no room in Dublin, so as you can see..." He gave me a broad childlike smile. "I am usually here every weekend. Would you like to see the rest of the house?"

"No, not right now. Later, maybe? If that's OK?"

"I'm sure you'll have plenty of opportunities. Why don't I call for takeaway? How about Chinese?"

"I thought you were going to cook?"

"Maybe another time. I don't want to impress you, too much."

I laughed out loud. "You've impressed me enough, as it is."

"I don't want to put you on overload."

I shook my head. "I feel much better. I just lost it for a while. Chinese would be perfect."

Dylan flipped out his phone and in a few minutes ordered two dinner plates.

"That was fast."

"Now we can enjoy our wine, and wait," he said, refilling my glass half full.

We both took a seat on the couch, and I continued to look around the room for anything I might have missed. I took a deep breath, for the first time since leaving Mum, I felt every part of me let go. Maybe it was the wine, the rain, or maybe, just maybe, it was Dylan.

"Can you talk about it?"

"I couldn't do anything. I had to leave her with Eric. I felt so helpless and useless."

"What happened?"

"It was awful. Dylan, it was like watching her die. Like I was losing parts of her, I'd never get back." I took a sip of the wine, it tingled going down. I leaned back and ran my fingers through my hair, fiddling with the curls that had fallen. "I don't know how to explain it."

"Take your time. We've got all night."

"It breaks my heart to see her like that." I felt the warmth of his hand when he reached for me. I leaned into his shoulder. "She was so vibrant, feisty and energetic. When she was with Da, she was reserved, but when she was with us, she was magic. She made us laugh, work hard, and she taught us how to be strong. Now she's... helpless."

"It's hard to watch our parents go through the process of aging."

I pulled away from him and sat up straight.

"No, this isn't natural. Her life is being stolen and there is nothing she can do about it."

"It comes for everyone."

"Not like this. Not for everyone. Da was in his right mind. He remembered everything and everyone. For God sake, he collapsed at church setting up for a Novena.

"I don't know how to handle this."

"I don't have an answer. I lost my parents way too soon, as well. I lost both within six months. My Da died of a heart attack, and Mum—I think she died of a broken heart. Six months later, almost to the day."

"I'm sorry. I had no idea. I feel like a fool. I still have my mum."

"No, I think I had it better. I didn't have to watch. Both went rather suddenly. I didn't have my heart broken a little bit at a time."

"Well, Mum did have a hard time the last few months. That's why I think it was a broken heart, She just folded into herself."

"That must have been hard."

"Yes. They were such a loving couple. I'd be embarrassed to tell you what they called each other."

"What? It can't be that bad."

"He would call her a rúnsearc."

I sputtered my wine. "His secret love? Why was that embarrassing?"

"I think it had something to do with the look in his eyes. It gave me an entirely different connotation.

"When he died, you could see her light fade."

"I wish I could have met them."

"Anyway, tell me what happened."

"We were having such a good time, eating dinner, and suddenly everything changed. She wanted to go back to her room. She asked me to find Eric. When I came back she was gone from the dining hall. I found her on the floor of the hall in Eric's arms."

"Does it bother you that she seems to trust Eric more than you?" Dylan asked.

I looked up at him. "No, that's not it. I'm not jealous. I understand he's just doing his job."

"Then what is it? You go there almost every day and you talk about her good days and bad days, but today, something's different. You've fallen apart."

"I know. I feel so foolish."

I pulled the necklace out and laid it on the coffee table, waiting for Dylan to say something.

"It's beautiful," Dylan said, picking it up off the table.

"I found it in her jewelry box. I've never seen it before, it is not something she would have bought."

"Who do you think bought it for her?"

"Her daughter, the one she had to give up. She had another that I had never seen before. It was a Miraculous Mary medal on a stained, white string. I brought it to her. She told me I didn't understand anything. She told me to put it away."

"What did you say?"

"Nothing. She asked me to put it away, so I did. Then she started talking about going to the greenhouse and how much she loved it. Everything changed after that. She seemed to go into a panic attack, but her body was relaxed. She didn't actually tell me to leave, but I think that was what she was saying." I took a sip of the wine, suddenly feeling anxious. My throat tightened. I took another sip, and rubbed my hands down the legs of my jeans.

"You OK?" Dylan stood, taking the glass from my hands.

"I'm sorry, I sound like a spoiled child."

"No, but I am worried."

"Me too, but for tonight I have you. I need to let it go. There is nothing I can do, anyway."

"Looks like you need more wine. I'm going to refill these. Why don't you call and see how she's doing?"

"Good idea." As I pulled my phone from my pocket, Dylan went back to the kitchen.

"Mrs. Moore, this is Catherine, Alice Leary's daughter. I was calling to see how she was doing." I waited. "Really?"

I paused and listened to the monotone voice coming over the line. "Is there anything I should do?" I watched Dylan refilling the two glasses. "Yes, I understand. Thank you. Yes, I will."

"What did she say?" He asked, setting the glasses on the table.

"She's sleeping, and doing fine, and there's no need to

come, that I should call again in the morning."

"Do you feel better?"

"I guess. Hopefully she's dreaming of better times," I said, laying my head back.

"Since you talked about the medal, I've been thinking. You said there is a chance that she met Finn. Maybe she gave the necklace to her, as a birthday present?"

"I never thought about that. I remember one time after we got into a fight, I bought her some earrings, to tell her I was sorry."

"Does she still have the earrings?"

"Yes. They were in her jewelry box."

I took the necklace out of my pocket and handed it to him. Dylan stared at it, turning it over in his hands, then looked up at me.

"It is beautiful. I have a feeling it was a very important present."

I suddenly became too sad to even think about the connection between my mother and the necklaces. I wiped the tears away, and looked at Dylan. "She must have thought of her every day."

"Your Mum as well."

I got up and walked around the room, touching the books overflowing his desk, then came back to the couch, as the doorbell rang. Dylan immediately went to the door. I watched as he traded his euros for the bag of takeaway.

"What can I do?"

"Plates in the cupboard, over the sink, silverware in the first drawer."

I took plates and silverware to the dining room table. Dylan walked over and pulled out the chair and I took a seat. He set our glasses of white wine, along with the bottle, on the table.

He scooped noodles onto my plate. I smiled as I watched him. Then he did the same to his plate and took a seat.

"A waiter as well as a scholar. Wow."

"Will wonders never cease? I'm sorry, next time I promise, a gourmet meal."

"No problem, this is perfect. You don't have to wine and dine me."

"It looks like I have."

We both laughed, then began to eat. The sandalwood scent mixed with the evergreen candles flowed in from the living room. As I wound the noodles around my fork, I watched him. He seemed lost in the moment. I didn't realize noodles could be so mesmerizing.

After we started eating, I decided to take the conversation in a different direction. "Tell me about your family. You had two sisters I believe, one older than you, one much younger, but I never met her."

"My sister..." He paused and looked at me, "I'm embarrassed telling you this. I should have told you sooner, but well, I'll tell you now.

"My older sister spent time in a home, in Roscrea, Sean Ross."

My hand came to my mouth automatically, but I didn't have any words to say.

"My parents paid her fees and she returned to us right after the birth of her daughter."

"And the baby? What happened to her?"

"They brought her home and pretended she was theirs. Amy, my youngest sister, was actually my niece. No one ever told her. She died not knowing her sister was really her mother."

"Why didn't anyone tell her?"

"For the same reason your Mum couldn't tell anyone about her past. The only difference—Amy grew up with family, loved by everyone."

"And Finn was sent away as a disgrace?"

"Yes, I'm afraid so."

"How did you find out about her, if they didn't tell anyone?

"My sister told me. She asked me to watch out for her, and so I did. She was very dear to me."

"You said she died? I don't remember you ever talking about this in school."

"I didn't. They were both killed in a car accident my first year at Trinity. I left for school that fall and we never talked about her again. We all have our secrets."

I sat back in my chair, overwhelmed. I watched Dylan take a drink. I remembered his tender nature, but now, I saw a whole new side. His reflection glowed in the candlelight. I realized that Michael would never have done what Dylan did. It would have been too tedious, too time consuming.

"Your sister, what was her name?"

"Catherine. Named after my grandmother. You know, the old Irish way."

"Katherine?"

"With a K. We called her Kathy."

"And you never told me?"

"I never told anyone, until now. I'm as good as any Irishman with his secrets."

I suddenly saw my selfishness in my response. "I'm sorry. I took it personal and it had nothing to do with me."

"Don't be sorry. Ever since you talked about your mum, in my mind, I saw my sister. She had your curls, and so did her daughter."

"What was your sister's name?"

"God, don't hate me, please."

"What?"

"Alice."

"Holy shit." I sat motionless, staring into space. "You've got to be kidding. It never dawned on you to tell me?"

"No. You weren't connected to my sister. There was no reason to."

I realized then that something had brought us together, some divine intervention caused our paths to cross. On that day, I dropped my books and thought he caused it.

"I didn't know your Mum then. I never met her," I said.

"Don't be silly. Don't you see? It was meant to be. Everything."

"You mean us?" I asked.

"Yes, all of it."

"Until I left you."

"But you came back." He got up and came to the other end of the table. He stroked my cheek, and kissed my forehead. "I never stopped loving you Cat. I just had to move on."

"I know."

We didn't talk about Katherine or Alice for the rest of the evening. We took a seat on the couch with our wine, lost in the moment.

"I should be going. It's getting late." I stood and moved over to pick up my coat.

"Don't go."

"I wrapped my arms around him. "What are we going to do?"

"You can stay"

"But what will happen to my reputation? What will the neighbors say?"

Dylan pulled me up from the couch and wrapped his arms around me. I took his face in my hands, and kissed him, then stepped back. His eyes were warm and kind. He stroked my face and the gentleness of him brought me to tears. His kisses took me back to an easier time.

Twenty-Five

A few days later, Mrs. Moore called to make arrangements for Mum to come home for a visit. There had not been another episode for three days and she felt it might do Mum some good to be in the real world for a few hours.

Francie and I decided a family afternoon would be just the thing. Plus, it would be impossible for Rose to ignore. Everyone would be at the house, including Connor, Claire, Francie, all the kids, and of course Rose, if she decided to make an appearance. Rose refused to return anyone's call. We went on with our plans without her.

Izzy spent the night and helped plan supper. We had everything in its place. I had replaced the Waterford vase and made sure the yellow roses looked no different than the day Mum had left. We stocked the refrigerator, and even replaced the whiskey on the chance she asked for a sip.

I was in the dining room when Rose came through the front door. She didn't acknowledge anyone, but immediately came to the table, digging through her purse.

"I owe you money."

"For what?"

"The vase, of course."

I looked over at the new vase, then back at Rose.

"No. It was as much my fault as yours."

"Did you tell Mum?" Rose asked.

I shook my head. "We aren't teenagers anymore. We need to solve our own battles. We need to make peace, if not for each other, at least for her."

"I'll be civil as need be, but I will never make peace."

"What did I ever do to you?"

"You came home."

I wanted to slap her. "Of all the stupid, selfish—" I could feel my blood pressure skyrocket. "Fine. Let's just leave it at that." I immediately felt guilty agreeing to be civil. I should have taken her outside and had a knock-down-drag-out battle of sisterly love.

"Does anyone know?" She asked, looking around the room.

"About your outburst?" I thought about lying, but at this stage I saw no point.

"Yes, everyone. Rose, we've fought over everything our whole lives. What do you expect? I've told Claire and Connor. There you have it. I'm done with the lies."

Rose turned toward me and whispered. "Let's just keep our distance."

Just then, Claire burst through the front door. She looked as elegant as always, her gray bob in place, and her cross necklace resting against her crepe blouse.

"Greetings all," she called out.

Rose turned toward the kitchen. Claire and I hugged.

"You two all right?"

"Not in this lifetime," I said, "but we promised to be civil, so I don't think there'll be any vase throwing tonight."

"What time is Connor coming?" Claire asked.

"He and Francie went to pick up Mum. They should be back any time. I'm a little anxious."

"She's your Mum—she's coming home—enjoy the moment," Claire said going into the kitchen.

"That sounds too easy."

"Don't worry, it will be a great evening. You'll—"

"You know what, I'm not doing this," Rose interrupted. "I can't stay. She won't even know we are here." She grabbed her purse and moved toward the door.

"What are you talking about? You need to be here," Claire said grabbing her arm.

"It's a joke, Let me go. " Rose pulled away from Claire with such force that she fell to the couch.

"Don't do this, Rose," I heard myself begging.

"The day Mum shut me out, she made her decision."

"What the hell are you talking about?" I asked as she adjusted her purse.

"Stop this now," Marie called out, coming over, blocking her mother's way. "You're being ridiculous. Grandma needs this visit, and we need to support her."

I couldn't believe Rose could be so childish.

Suddenly, Marie stepped away from the door. "You know what, Mom? Leave. If this is the way you're going to be, we don't need you here. Grandma doesn't need to know that you want to make the one day she gets to come home, all about you."

"No, Marie, she needs to be here." Jean said, moving toward her mother.

"No, she needs to go home and stew in her own juices.

Grandma doesn't need the drama."

I didn't know if Rose expected a fight, or just glad that her daughter told her to leave. She turned and bolted out the door.

Shaken by Rose's sudden departure, everyone milled about the living room. No one knew what to say. None expected such childish behavior, yet it seemed to fit Rose. Why should we expect her to act as a rational human being?

"Izzy, can you help with the table?" I asked.

"Sure. Do we need salad forks?"

A few minutes later, we heard Connor's car. Everyone crowded at the front door.

Connor came up the steps with Mum on his arm. She was dressed in her favorite yellow jogging suit. The ones with the applique of kittens on the jacket.

Her hair was neatly combed, soft around her cheeks. Once through the front door, Connor let go and Mum walked about on her own.

"It's seems like forever," she said, looking around the living room.

"It's been a few months," I said. I watched her eyes, looking for any sign of an episode.

"Oh Alice, you look just grand, you do," Claire said, reaching out for Alice's hand. Paddy went to her other side and escorted her to the living room. "I always loved those kittens."

"Thank you, me too.

"Why is everyone looking at me? I'm fine, just give me some room—Oh, the roses," Mum beamed as she moved to the dining table and reached to touch the petals. "You remembered, the roses."

We watched Mum move through her house, as if she'd never been gone. Seeing the joy in her face, was the best thing ever. Francie and I looked at each other and nodded...we could make things come together even if only for just the day.

"Do you mind if I sit down for a while. I'm a bit tired?" Mum asked, grabbing hold of the edge of the couch, then coming around to take a seat.

Connor and Claire sat next to her. Jean took her purse while Marie adjusted the afghan that had fallen onto the cushions. We all hovered, each trying in our own way to be sure she was comfortable. Her eyes were clear and she smiled.

"You've got to quit hovering. You're going to smother me." She laughed, eyes glowing as she looked around the room. "Everything is so nice."

"Grandma is there anything you need?" Paddy asked, taking a knee next to her.

"Where's Rose?"

"She was here, but she left," Claire said, turning and looking at me.

"What bee got in her bonnet?" Mum asked, still looking around.

We all smiled. I tried, unsuccessfully, not to laugh. When Da was angry, she would ask the same thing. Da would clinch his lips: she would touch him on the tip of his nose. No one could keep a straight face. Da couldn't stay mad when she bopped him on the nose.

"At the last minute, she decided she had some place to be," I looked over at Claire who nodded.

"I imagine she did," Mum said, still staring at the roses. It must have become clear to her that Rose had taken a stand.

Suddenly, she stood and walked around the room, weaving her way between us, as if we weren't there. She ran her fingertips over the doily on the back of Da's easy chair, then across the back of the couch. The sun came through the windows in slivers, flickering off the floor. She turned around repeatedly, staring, as if she were memorizing every nuance.

"Can everyone come sit down?" she said, guiding herself back to the couch. "I have some things I'd like to say before I forget where I am."

We all gathered around, surrounding her. Paddy stood next to the door, almost unnoticed, until Mum called him over. The look on his face saddened me. He seemed to see something, maybe in her movements or in her words.

"Well, first off, I thought I'd never see my house again. I am glad to be home, even if it's just for the evening. Thank you for doing this.

"Please, don't tiptoe around me. I'm not going to shatter, like some vase," she said, looking directly at me. "By the way, Catherine, the old vase had a chip on the lip."

I rolled my eyes. "I can't get away with anything." Everyone laughed and the tension eased just a little.

"I know I'm sick, and I'm not going to get better. There'll be episodes and they'll get worse. I'll forget the things I love most. I'll forget your names, your birthdays," she shrugged her shoulders. "Maybe even who you are. I know some of you have seen the episodes and I'm sorry for what I've put you through."

"What can we do to make you comfortable?" Izzy asked, moving over toward Paddy, taking hold of his hand."

"You can treat me as normal as possible. I hate that this

is happening, and I know it affects all of you. I don't mean to hurt you, so I'm apologizing now."

I looked over at Jean and Marie who had settled in at their grandmother's knee. They struggled to hold in their emotions. I knew how Mum's condition influenced me, but watching my nieces, I realized what her loss meant to them.

"Mum, you don't have to apologize for anything. We understand," Francie said.

"No, my dear Frances," she continued, "you have no idea what it is like to lose the things you cherish most. To wonder when it will slip away and you will do or say something so foolish, no one understands."

We laughed and realized that Mum had attempted to joke about it, but I saw the pain in her eyes. Walking into the dining room, she turned and began looking in all directions.

"Where is Mittens?"

"In the garden. See, over there." Izzy pointed toward the door.

With Francie's help, Mum moved to the French doors and gazed out onto the patio.

"I remember the day I bought the swans," she said, pointing to the far corner. I wanted to decorate my garden with scents and color, so I went looking for sweet smelling flowers. It was raining." Her eyes seemed to lose focus. "I found roses, jasmine and honeysuckle, but as I left, I looked over under a bench, and there was a dirty statue."

I couldn't tell if she was even with us. She pressed on, even as she stepped into the garden, touching the branches that overhung onto the walkway, caressing the vines.

"I asked about it, and Mr. Simpson just gave it to me. I brought it home and washed it off. It survived a lot of winters, even the blizzard from a few years ago.

"You know, I remember burying a box, but I can't remember why. I put the swan over it, so no one would find it. I wonder what it was." She turned to us and shook her head. "I don't remember."

I looked at Francie and Claire. It saddened me to think it had only taken a moment for her to drift away. Back to when a young mother felt the need to bury a secret.

"Grandma, what do you think you buried?" Paddy asked, stepping up behind her.

"I put it all in the box, every bit of it. I couldn't tell. I never did." She grabbed Izzy's arm. "I never told," she repeated.

Between one breath and the next, something changed. She looked up and patted Izzy's hand. "It's going to rain dear. What are we doing outside?"

"You wanted to look for Mittens," she said, still holding on to her grandmother, but looking over her shoulder at the rest of us, as if asking for help. Francie came and helped Izzy guide Mum back toward the house.

"Are you ready for supper Mum?"

"No. I had a late breakfast. There is something though."

"Anything. What can we do?" I asked, as she stepped through the French doors.

"I'd like to walk in the park with my daughters, before the rain comes. It's been so long. I miss it. I never get to go outside much anymore."

"When do you want to go?"

"Now. If it's all right," she said, moving over toward the door.

There was sense of urgency in her voice. I looked over at Francie and we immediately grabbed our coats. Paddy got Mum's, and helped her put it on.

I looked at Connor. He winked and nodded. Claire stood up and I saw a relieved look, her face relaxed. They knew something.

"That will be great. We'll get everything ready while you're gone," Izzy said.

"Mum laughed, then hugged Paddy before stepping out the door.

"I'd like a glass of whiskey when we get back," Mum said.

"Done," Connor said. "I think I'll join you," hiding his smile.

We started out the door, Mum between us, wrapping her scarf around her neck. Francie and I each had an arm. She held tight, as we walked down the driveway. We negotiated the narrow corner and found the park crowded, even with the weather. Mum held tight, as we walked in silence. She would nod to the people strolling by with her shoulders arched just enough to stand tall.

The cold air splashed my face, and the scent of wild jasmine engulfed the air. I had walked with Mum so many times before, along this lane. I looked at Francie. I could see the memories written on her face, also.

"Girls can we sit for a bit?" Her step had slowed, and her breath came with deep sighs. Her cheeks had reddened from the cold.

"Sure, the bench up there is empty." Mum let go of our grip, and walked ahead of us, taking a seat. "Are you all right?" Francie asked.

"Of course, sitting will make it easier to talk."

She took a deep breath, looked around the park, drizzled with dew. In that moment, people seemed to disappear. It was just us. Boys ran off, tossing their balls out in front of them. A couple kissed intimately, then continued down the path, huddling close.

"Girls, I know I've been having a tough time lately, but right now I'm feeling good. I need to tell you what is on my mind, while I'm clear-headed, with no one to question or stop me. I need to get this out."

She took hold of our hands, as she had done when we were little, about to tell us something special. Glad for the undivided attention, I still wished Rose had been there.

"Mum, would you like me to call Rose?" She shook her head. "She could meet us here."

"No, she made her choice. I wouldn't force this on anyone," Mum said.

"You don't have to do this," Francie said.

"You do whatever you need." I had a feeling she was going to tell us about Finn.

"I've been keeping something from you," she said, not looking at either of us. "I'm going to tell you now, before I forget who you are." She laughed. Francie and I remained straight-faced, seeing no humor in her attempt.

"Mum, we know," Francie said.

"You don't have to do this." Even as the words came out, I knew I wanted to hear them from her, her version of what happened.

"You say you know—You think you know—You know nothing. You must let me tell you, while I can. If it had only been the baby, I think I could have told everyone. Long before it consumed me, but it was so much more."

"Mum…"

"Please girls, I need to do this." She sat up taller and let go of our hands. "At first, after the rape, I wanted nothing to do with the baby growing inside of me. But as the months went on, I could feel her, like I felt all of you. I wanted to keep her, but my Da wouldn't see it. After nine days he demanded that I sign her away. I never saw her again. I had just turned fifteen. It had nothing to do with love. He said I had shamed him. I never went home after that. They sent me to the Laundries to help me forget, but I didn't. Not ever."

"Mum, we know all this," I said, taking hold of her hand.

"No, you don't," she said, gripping tighter. "It happened to me. Someone else told you my story. It was mine to tell. I've waited too long."

"After they took Finn, he let me be locked away." I looked in her eyes, she was gone. "I washed and cleaned every minute of every day." She began running her hands back and forth on her lap. She was back in the Laundries. "I couldn't question anything, or they'd beat me. They cut my hair." She combed her fingers through her flimsy curls. "See, it's all gone. She cut it all off. She took my name. They took it all. They called us sinners and told us every day how we had to repent. Then he raped me, again and again."

It was everything Claire had told us about the baby. What Claire said about it not being hers to tell, made more sense.

"I worked in the garden, with Jonathan," Mum continued. She got up from the bench and moved toward the bushes. "He came for me. He made me do things. I begged him not to. I told him I was a good girl."

Francie came up behind her and touched her arm. Mum turned. I could see by her movements that she was back, but the look in her eyes was pure rage. "He raped me again, and again, and again. I couldn't do anything. There was no one to tell."

"Who raped you?" Francie asked, braver than I at the moment.

"Father Matthew. He was the priest who took me to

Castlepollard. He knew there was nothing I could do. My only escape was the garden."

Claire had not told us that. Had she not known? Now it made sense, all the years, though she had gone to church, she never once said a prayer out loud, or greeted the priest after services.

Now I understood why she never went home. What was there for her to go home to?

"In the garden, I found Jonathan. He taught me everything. He gave me my love of plants." She lifted her hand to the hanging vines of ivy.

It made sense that Jonathan had been the one. We all knew how much he and Marie adored her. Had he been the one to rescue her? Bring her to Howth? Would this be the time to ask?

"Mum, who was Jonathan?" Francie asked, still wearing the same look of confusion we both had.

"Jonathan? Hurry he said, we must be very quiet." She turned and put her finger up to her lips. "Don't move until I tell you, he said. Sara and I, we kept our head down in the truck, so she wouldn't see."

"Who wouldn't see?" Francie asked.

"Reverend Mother. She was perched high in the front seat. Shush, I told Sara. I was so afraid she'd give us away. We bounced around in the truck. We huddled through it all, the bumpy roads, the noise, the waiting. The moment we peeked out, knowing we were free."

I knew she was recalling a memory. I could tell by her words.

"We need to go back now. Do you know where you are?" Francie asked.

Mum looked around, still holding on to the branches. She was alone even though we stood right by her. She brushed the tears from her eyes, then turned around. "Yes, I know exactly where I am."

I reached for her hand. Francie put her arm around her waist.

"I know who I am. I know where I am. So, now you know what happened, why I couldn't tell. If you don't understand, then you never knew me as well as you thought you did."

We walked along in silence. The picture was very clear. I didn't need for her to tell me more. I wouldn't have told anyone either. I understood, my heart felt as if it had cracked in two. There was an ache that would never go away.

"You know, it was here where I first saw her. In this very park, walking with her own daughter," Mum said, still looking straight ahead.

"You saw who?" Francie asked, looking confused, not sure where Mum was at this moment.

"I've kept our secret over fifty years." Mum talked like no one was there. She stopped and pulled away from our grips, looked out into field as if she were speaking to Finn right now. "You searched me out, and found your way home." She bowed her head with a smile.

She walked on. The gray clouds hung down as if waiting for permission to open their hearts and gush down over the earth. She had no more words about her life. When we came round the park for the second time, she blurted out. "I'm ready to go. Take me home please."

Twenty-Six

Connor met us at the front door with a small glass of whiskey. "Just a wee sip, Alice. Supper's on the table."

Mum took the glass and downed the entire shot. "Thank you, I've been missing that."

Supper was spent with Mum asking the grandchildren about their lives. I could see the pride in Mum's eyes as Izzy went into great detail about her internship and upcoming gallery showings.

Supper finished and coffee sipped, Connor took Mum back to St. Philomena's without incident. The kids left the house with promises to call in a few days and it wasn't long before Claire grabbed her coat, brushed our cheeks, and promised to call, as well.

Francie and I cleared the table, the silence spoke volumes.

I couldn't find the words to explain what I was thinking, and I felt she was having the same dilemma. Mum's conversation in the park had driven our thoughts inward. Even arranging the pots and pans in the dishwasher was disquieting.

I looked at Francie wiping down the counter. "I'm calling Finn today," I said, matter-of-factly.

"I don't think we're ready for that, we need to talk about it more."

"We've talked about it too long. There's nothing more we need to know.

"We need to bring Finn home."

"Let's dig up the box in the garden, first."

"What do you think she buried?" I asked, turning back toward the table.

"I don't know. Documents? Letters? Pictures?"

"Well, whatever it is, it must have been important."

"Cate, she knew exactly what she was doing, but now, she can't keep things straight; things get mixed up. We need to find out what she buried. It might help us understand."

"OK, let's do this," I said, looking out the kitchen window.

"Right now? You do know it's raining?"

"Let's get it settled, once and for all. Besides if it's wet, it'll make the ground soft, easier digging. Besides, when have we ever let a little rain stop us?"

Francie took the shed key from the drawer, while I got an umbrella from the hall-stand by the front door. We grabbed our coats and went to the far corner of the garden. Francie dug through the shed for a shovel, as I tried to shift the swan from its place under the trellis.

Francie plunged the shovel into the muddied ground. It only took a few seconds to hear the clink of metal on metal.

I knelt on the wet grass and finished uncovering the box with my fingers. A painted swan appeared, as I wiped away the mud. At the touch of painting, I felt a tingle move up my spine. *It's still here, I felt Mum say.*

"Let's go in to the kitchen and wash it off," Francie said, helping me stand.

Setting it on the counter, she wet a towel and wiped away the years of dirt. The swan jumped from the top, as she worked through the grooves.

I moved it over to the table and ran my fingers along the edges. Francie slowly lifted the lid, taking out a stack of folded papers. I laid them out separately on the table. There were two birth certificates, a letter from her mum, one from Connor, and two others, both yellowed with age. The was also quite a large sum of pound notes. Folded bills spilled out everywhere. I unfolded the first letter, and slowly read it out loud.

Dearest Alice,

Connor told me, in bits and pieces, what they did to you. I can understand if you never want to hear from me. If it is any consolation, I know how much I wronged you. I knew it the minute I saw you into the car, but I could do nothing about it. Your Da felt you shamed him, and he couldn't bear to live with it. It didn't matter how it happened..

I loved you as much as any Mum would love her daughter, but I couldn't defy him. He is my husband. I couldn't go against his wishes. I had to try to keep our family together. I understand if you can't forgive me. I can't forgive myself.

Connor told me you married a fine man, I hope he treats you right. He told me of your babies. First there was Rose. I was disappointed you didn't name her Marie, but I understood you couldn't have the reminder. Then came Catherine. Connor said she has chestnut waves. And Francie, red ringlets tumbling around her cheeks. He shared pictures of them. They are beautiful. I imagine I will never see them, but at least you have your girls and won't feel so lost. I hope you never have to make a decision like I did. Be a good wife and mother.

I imagine if you have this letter you have also found the letter from Reverend Mother, and you know the truth. I could only hope you will find a way to forgive me.

Love your babies.

Mum

A second letter on faded parchment was more formal than the first. The words were written in clear and firm hand.

Mr. and Mrs. Brennan,

We need to make arrangements for her transfer as she is due any day now. As we told you upon her arrival, the fee is £90. We will need the money before she can be released. If you are unable, or refuse to pay, she will be transferred to Dublin to a Magdalene convent, where she will work off her debt. The work will be strenuous, but she will be provided social skills and a basic education. When we feel the time is right, and her debt has been paid, she will be released. Please note, she can only be released to an adult male relative or her parish priest.

Everything we do, is in her best interest. She must learn the consequences of her actions. With due penance and atonement, I'm sure God will forgive her of her transgressions.

We will notify you of the birth. After that, you may come on the ninth day with the £90, or sign papers for her transfer. We expect to hear from you soon.

May God be with you.

Reverend Mother

Castlepollard

Another, more of a note than an actual letter.

Dear Alice,

I just wanted you to know we took care of all the details of Da's estate. Thank you for your help. I am sorry we were not able to come together. We were hoping to get to the City, but time got away from us. I have enclosed your share of the estate money. Should you have any questions, call me.

I wish you and your family the best.

Margaret

Another letter signed by Connor, explained his loyalty.

Dearest Alice,

I have looked everywhere for you. I left Meadows Glen two months after they took you. I attended university in Dublin and have a job in London now. I wrote Mum to ask where they sent you, but she never answered. I never really expected her to, not with Da there. He wouldn't even let us mention your name, so I'm sure he wouldn't let her write. I have been looking for you forever. I heard rumors about Castlepollard, but they told me you were gone. I found a convent in Dublin where someone finally talked to me. I showed a picture and asked if you had been here. He asked me why I was looking for you. I told him I was your brother. He said to write you a note, and he would try to get it to you. If you're reading this, I guess he found you.

I'm sorry about everything that happened. I'm sorry that I wasn't there. But I'm here now. Whatever I can do, just let me know. I hope this finds you.

Connor

Francie unfolded the last paper—a list of vital statistics for one Finnouala Claire Brennan.

Birth Name: Finnouala Claire Brennan

Adoptive Name: Claire Grace Fischer

DOB: 20-11-49

Transported to Oregon September 1953

Graduated Westwood College December 1973

Married Name: Claire Hamilton

Date of Marriage: April 4, 1973

Daughter born 4-4-78 Devon Hamilton

Son born 23-7-79 Adam Hamilton

DOD: 15-1-84 St. Patrick's Hospital, complications from surgery.

I held the faded yellow papers that had come from the family that disowned her. I didn't know where the others had come from. I looked up at Francie, who had read every word along with me. We stared at the letters. Francie dropped them on the table, as if on fire and the flames had singed her fingers.

Each letter added a piece to the details of Mum's life.

"Cate, do you know what this is?" She asked, holding up the last paper.

"This says she is dead. D.O.D., that means date of death."

Francie flipped the paper back and forth. "Who's it from?"

"I have no idea. There's no notation."

"It says she died in 1984. We know she's not dead, we have cards after that, and the texts."

"Just saying..."

"Something's wrong, here."

While Francie continued to try and figure out the puzzle, I went out to the yard and shoveled the dirt back into place. A small mound remained, but it would settle with the weight of the planter and the rain. I replaced the swan, and draped ivy over and around the statue. As I returned the shovel to the shed, I looked across the garden. There was no sign we had dug up her past, just a small white swan, nestled under a trellis of ivy.

Our lives had been changed forever.

Francie looked up as I entered through the French doors. "There's a lot of money, here," she said, holding up the pound notes. "Why would she bury something that she could have used?"

"It looks like it came from her inheritance. From the letter there had been a check. She must have cashed it, and put the money with the letters. But why?"

"I'm not a money hound, but why wouldn't she spend it, or at least put it in the bank?" Francie said, gathering it together, separating each color.

"I have a feeling that she decided she wasn't going to have anything to do with their blood money. In her eyes, it was poison, so she buried it." I wiped away a tear.

"Do you realize how much is here?" Francie asked, almost blushing.

"No. I'm embarrassed to even touch it."

"She could have used it for something to make her life easier."

"But she didn't. That's the whole point. I think that's pretty amazing."

"But she did without because of them," Francie said.

"They took everything from her. Using their money would condone what they did. I'm proud of her, we're not going to use it either."

"Then let's just put it back. Pretend we never knew anything about it.

"Wait, I have a better idea," Francie said. "Let's use it for something good."

"What are you talking about?"

Francie picked up the bills and one by one counted them out loud, laying each down on the table. I counted to myself as she went along. There was over a thousand pounds. "I think we should use the money to bring Finn home. There's enough."

"Are you serious?"

"Yes. We've talked about calling Finn, so let's do it. Let's use the money to pay for her ticket. If we're serious about helping Mum, let's bring Finn home."

I took Mum's phone from the kitchen drawer and sat at the table next to Francie. I retrieved Finn's text messages and tapped the call button. "Here goes," I said. turning on the speaker. It rang, twice, three, four times. I looked at Francie, then I heard a voice.

"This is Claire. I can't come to the phone right now. Please leave a message."

I pushed the red button and watched the phone go black. "She didn't answer."

"Why didn't you leave a message?"

I looked up sheepishly. "I don't know. I panicked."

"Cate, you never panic. Call her back."

"I just got scared." My emotions were so mixed, I didn't know what to do.

"When you call someone, and they don't answer, you usually leave a message don't you?"

"OK, OK I get it. I didn't leave a message. What should I have said? Hey, I'm Catherine. One of the sisters you've never met. Our mum never told us about you, until now. By the way, I found your history buried in the garden. My God, Francie, she'll think I'm crazy!"

"Come on, Cate. You don't think she's been waiting for this call...like forever?"

"Maybe we should call Rose. Make one last-ditch effort to make her a part of this?" I asked.

"If you call Rose, then you truly have gone daffy. Haven't you been listening? I thought she made it very clear that she doesn't want anything to do with Finn.

"What are you waiting for?"

"I'm waiting to stop feeling like I want to throw up."

"You are never going to stop feeling that way."

I knew everything Francie said was true. I picked up the phone and slowly pushed the button, then waited. Four rings, nothing.

"This is Claire. I can't come to the phone right now. Please leave a message."

"My name is Catherine, I'm calling from Dublin. Our mother is Alice Leary. I believe we are sisters." I took a deep breath. "Please call this number at your convenience."

I clicked off the phone and looked at Francie. "Now we wait."

Twenty-Seven

Finn didn't return the call, and for reasons I couldn't explain, I was not surprised. After the chaos, things calmed down. There were no unexpected visits, no craziness. It was nice.

Dylan and I took a break from the world. We went to the city for a movie. After the drive home, we sat in the car in front of the house and made out like teenagers. My cell remained silent. Dylan ignored any calls that came through, even one from the university. We smothered each other with kisses, then blushed at our antics.

"Do you want to come in?" I asked.

"No, I better go home, otherwise we both know what will happen."

"You must hate me."

"No, I get it, can't say I like it, but I get it. Go to bed and dream of me."

"I will. I promise."

"I'll call you tomorrow." I kissed him and left his arms at the doorstep.

The call came in about five-thirty the next evening. Francie and I were sitting down to dinner, discussing why we hadn't heard from Finn. When I heard the ring, I felt my heart jump, and looked at Francie.

It was an unknown caller, but it was an Irish number.

"Catherine?"

"Connor, what is it?"

"Your mum fell. She hit her head and they've taken her to Mercy Hospital. You and Francie need to get there, right away. I'll meet you as soon as I can. Claire already called Rose."

"We'll be in, straight away."

Francie placed her fork upside down on the plate, and sat patiently watching me. "What happened?"

"Mum fell. They're taking her to Mercy."

"Oh, my God. We gotta go."

Francie started to clean the table, then just dropped the silverware. "What am I doing? This doesn't matter."

"It's OK."

"No, it isn't. This is it. This is what we've been waiting for, without saying we've been waiting. And she hasn't called back, yet."

"It's a fall. Don't make it any bigger than it is. They're probably just taking precautions."

"Are you trying to convince me or you?"

"Stop it."

"Call her again. Do it now."

"We have to get to the hospital."

"Good God, Cate, it will take two minutes. Do it, or I will."

"OK, fine."

I took the phone from the table and moved toward the

window. I tapped her name and waited. It rang like it did before, then the same message came on. I held it out for Francie to hear.

"Leave a message. Tell her how important it is that she calls you back. Do it."

"Finn, this is Catherine again. I know you might be afraid, but please call back, it's really important. I know we are sisters, and we need to talk. Alice is in the hospital."

"Good, that was better. OK, let's go. I need to call Colin."

"I'll call Dylan."

I took my coat from the rack and Francie opened the door.

In the car, neither of us spoke. My fear of losing Mum was balanced at the edge of my senses. I kept silent, staring at the darkening clouds, telling myself she'd be fine. If she wasn't, I'd blame Rose for the rest of my life.

The minute we hit the lobby, I went to the Information Desk. "Alice Leary?"

"She's in the third door to the right, but you can't go in. She's with her doctors."

"What do we do?" I asked, trying to catch my breath.

"There's a waiting room at the end of the hall. The doctors will come out when they're done."

"Thank you."

Connor stood, as we entered the waiting room. "She'll be fine, you'll see." He wrapped his arms around both of us.

"What happened?" Francie asked.

"Eric was with her in the green house. He said she was repotting some ivy and just collapsed. She hit her head against the edge of the table. There was no way Eric could have caught her."

"Have you been able to talk to anyone?" I asked?

"They think she's hemorrhaging. She hasn't woken up yet. The nurse said the doctor would be out to speak with us, once they knew more. They're doing all they can."

"Did you call everyone?" Francie asked.

"Yes, they should be here shortly."

"And Rose?"

Connor took a seat in the chair and dropped his head in his hands.

"Claire did. I think she just left a message."

"We should call her again. She needs to be here."

"You can try," Connor said.

Francie pulled her phone from her pocket. After the fourth ring it went to voice mail.

"I'm out. Leave a message."

"You need to come to Mercy Hospital. Mum fell. We need you here."

Just at that moment, Dylan came in through the double doors. "I was at the university when I got your message." He wrapped his arms around me and kissed my forehead. "What happened?"

"She fell. They won't let us see her, yet. The doctors are with her."

"I just called Rose," Francie said, "but she didn't answer, must be getting her hair done. God knows, we wouldn't want to interrupt that," Francie remarked.

We both looked at her, I was surprised by her sarcasm. Dylan took my hand. "This is different. She'll come."

I hated this hospital. Every memory was bad. Mum always bragged that we were born here, but Da took his last breath here. It was here, I lost the baby. It was here, we sat waiting for Jonathan to wake. He never did.

Before long, Claire, Izzy and Paddy arrived, and a few minutes later, Marie and Jean.

Two hours later, still no sign of Rose.

Connor walked the halls, looking for the doctors. Finally, escorted back by a nurse, promising they would be out as soon as they knew anything.

After another half hour, two doctors came into the waiting room. "Leary family?"

"Over here," Paddy said. The taller of the two stepped up as we gathered together.

"I'm Dr. Simpson, and this is Dr. Carter. We've examined your mother, and ran some initial tests. "Are you her daughters?"

"Yes, but one sister isn't here."

"I'm Francie and she's Catherine," she blurted.

"I'm sorry, we can't wait for your sister. Your mother's fall has created a brain hemorrhage. We've put her in an induced coma to stabilize her.

From her scans we know there's extensive damage to the right frontal lobe. The situation is critical, and the prognosis is not good. She will, most likely, not recover."

I was stunned by the doctor's bluntness. Dylan pulled me close. I noticed tears in Connor's eyes as he hugged Claire. The kids stood in a group holding hands. "We've transferred her to ICU where she will be closely monitored.

"Can we see her?" Francie asked.

"Unfortunately, we cannot allow visitors. Not tonight,

anyway. Her condition is too unstable. Maybe in the morning. You all need to go home. Get some rest. The next few days will be very intense."

"I'm not going anywhere," Connor and Claire said in unison.

"Yes, you are," Dr. Carter said. "All of you need to go home. There is nothing you can do and waiting rooms are no place to get rest. Please do not make this any tougher than it is."

"Go home," Dr. Simpson chimed in. "Get some rest and come back in the morning. If there is any change, I promise, I'll call. I'll have the nurse call you first thing in the morning to let you know her progress."

Just as the doctors left the waiting room, Rose burst down the hall, clutching her purse tight.

Claire and Connor walked over and brought her into the small circle, that we called family. Her smug look was gone, replaced with a somber face of concern.

"What the hell happened?"

"She fell in the greenhouse at the facility."

"Who was watching her?"

"Eric was right there with her."

"Who the hell is Eric?"

"Well, if you ever went to visit her, you'd know," Francie said, standing back, her words caustic.

"Stop preaching, just tell me what happened."

"She fell," Francie said, holding her stare.

"Yes, it was an accident. Eric said she just went down before he could catch her," Connor added.

"They put her into an induced coma," I said. "There's some bleeding at her right frontal lobe. It doesn't look good. They said the next few days are going to be touch and go."

"What are they doing for her?" She pulled her purse to her chest.

"Everything," Connor said. "We can't see her until tomorrow. You just missed the doctors."

"Well, call them back."

"No," Connor said. "We can't do that."

"I need to talk to them."

"They've already talked to us," Francie said. "They've already given a briefing, and we just told you everything."

"Then I'll go find them."

"Jesus, Rose, just stop. You can't come in here and take over whenever you decide to. It is not about you, anymore. Take your petty shit and pedal it someplace else," Claire said. "We're going home and coming back in the morning. You can do whatever the hell you want."

"I agree," Connor said matter-of-factly. "We should take the doctors' advice, and go home. We can be back in the morning, in shifts if we need to."

"There's enough of us to go around. We can take turns," Francie said, "she'll never be alone."

I looked around the room. Here was my family. They were blood, and we had trusted each other through everything. But things had changed. Now we had Finn.

She should be here. She was us. More importantly, she was Mum.

I saw Connor gather his coat and cap, and help Claire with her scarf.

"We're leaving," Connor said taking hold of Claire's hand. "I'm taking her home."

"You knew all of this about Mum, didn't you? Like Claire."

"It wasn't my place, Catherine." He got up and moved down the hall with Claire's arm wrapped in his.

"Connor, please," I said grabbing hold of his jacket.

"Your Mum could never tell your Da, but he knew, and he loved her anyway. Your Mum did nothing, but love you girls. I hope you can understand," Claire said, holding tight to Connor.

"Don't you think you should be giving this lecture to Rose? You know Connor, there is nothing Mum could ever do that would change my love for her. She's my Mum."

Dylan took hold of my hand and we followed Connor and Claire out the door, Francie followed with her arms wrapped around Colin, the kids right behind. We stood outside the door in silence. The smoke from Connor's cigarette swirled in the late evening.

"I called Finn again, after the doctors came out, but she didn't answer," I turned and said to Francie.

"Let's call her back, get her here as soon as possible. We don't know how long Mum will last. She has a right to see her oldest daughter," Francie said.

"You can't call her," Rose said, coming up behind us.

"A little late for that. I already have."

"We've actually left her a couple of messages," Francie said.

"She won't come," Rose said.

"Why not. I think she'd come if she knew Mum was sick," Francie said.

"She won't come, because I wrote her. I called her, as well. I didn't think a letter would be enough. I wanted to be sure. I told her to leave Mum alone, leave all of us alone. None of us wanted to hear from her."

"Why the hell did you do that?" I screamed. The words echoed off the sidewalk.

"You had no right," Francie said, tears welling in her eyes. "What the hell...?"

"Why are you upset? I did it for Mum. I had every right to. Finn doesn't belong here. She's not one of us."

"I don't even have words for you, Rose. All I want to do is slap you," Claire said. Connor grabbed hold of her arm.

"All this time, you knew. You had been in contact with her, and you kept it from us. How could you do that?" Francie asked, her rage, boiling to the surface.

"I'm calling her, again. You can't say a word, not ever." I said.

I walked away and headed back to where Dylan stood. Francie and Connor called my name, but I didn't stop.

"Cate. Stop, wait."

I turned toward Francie, wiping my cheeks with my sleeve. "How could she?

"I'm calling her. Now."

"What time is it there?"

"I don't care. We need to call. We can apologize for the inconvenience later."

"It's ringing."

I took a deep breath, staring at Francie, then over at Dylan. After the third ring there was no answer. Finally I heard a voice.

"Hello."

"Is this Finn, I mean Claire Hamilton?"

"Yes. Oh, my God. Catherine, is that you?"

Just hearing her voice made my eyes well up. "Thank God, you answered. Yes, it's me. Francie is right here, too." I put it on speaker.

"Hello?" There was a long pause.

"Please don't hang up."

"No, I'm not. I just don't know what to say."

"We found your number in our mother's phone. We found your texts."

"Oh my, you must think me a crazy lady."

"No, not at all. She got them all, she just, well I guess she couldn't answer them."

I heard her voice choke up over the line. "Are you all right?

"No, I'm not. I never thought I'd hear from anyone. Rose made it very clear."

"That doesn't matter. Mum is sick. We're hoping you'll come to Dublin."

"Catherine...,"

There was a long pause. I looked over at Francie. She motioned for me to continue. "Rose was wrong. She had no right to speak for us. We want you to come. It's important."

"Are you sure?"

"Very sure. If Rose doesn't like it, she can shove it up—"

"Francie, stop.

"Finn—Claire, Please come. Can you make arrangements?"

"I guess so. I'll have to take care of some things. Can I call you?"

"We'll pay for your ticket. I am serious about this."

"Can I bring my daughter? They've met and she's become

very attached. We'll pay our own way."

"Of course. She has to." I couldn't imagine leaving Izzy home. "There's plenty of money for both of you. We'll take care of it."

"I can't let you do that."

"It's done. Mum had money set aside. What better way to use it than this." I paused, "You'll come?"

"Yes. Let me check my calendar. I'll text the information."

"Perfect, then I'll take care of the payment. You have my number, right?"

"Yes. I don't know what to say."

"There is nothing to say, just come as soon as you can."

"How long should I plan to stay?"

"I don't know. Why don't you just make it one way? We can figure out a return flight after you're here. Is that OK?"

"I'll call you in a day or two."

"Please hurry, we're not sure how long she has."

"Yes, of course."

I clicked off the phone and brushed hair from my face. Suddenly, I felt flushed. Looking over at Francie, I smiled. "We did it."

"What do you think?" Francie asked.

"You heard her. I think she sounded lovely. I think I caught her off guard—I think I terrified her—But, I imagine, Rose terrifies her more."

"What do you think Rose will say?"

"I don't really give a shit. We tell her she is coming. Plain and simple."

"I agree." Looking over at Dylan, Francie said, "I'll be at my car, when you're ready, Cate."

"What do you want to do, Cat?" Dylan asked.

"I want to go home with you and hide for a few days, but I can't do that. Can I stay at your apartment tonight, so I can be in the city if they call?"

"Of course. I'll bring you back, in the morning.

"Wait, we have to do something first."

"What?" Francie asked.

"We have to go see Rose."

Looking at my sister, I could see the doubt in her eyes, but I knew we had to make one last attempt.

"I don't know what good it will do, but, if we have to, let's get it over with. I'll drop Cate at your place. Rose doesn't live far, I'm pretty sure she went home."

"Call me when you are on your way. Francie, I'm at 34 Grafton Street."

"I know where that is. Don't worry. We'll be fine."

I kissed Dylan good-bye and watched his car pull out of the parking lot. It was just past ten and the city was bright, lights came from all directions. Francie weaved in and out of traffic, and before long, she pulled into the driveway of a two-story brick house, with a blue door.

There was a light in one of the upstairs widows. Downstairs, the windows were dark. Francie picked up her cell and in a moment Rose's face appeared.

"We're outside. Open the door."

Francie clicked off her phone and we moved toward the landing.

Rose opened the door slightly, but Francie rammed her way in. "You're going to listen to what we have to say, whether you like it or not."

I stepped in behind Francie, "We talked to her."

"To who?"

"You know God damn well who she's talking about. Stop acting so innocent," Francie said

"I don't believe you."

"Believe what you like, she'll be here by the end of the week," I fibbed.

"She's nothing to us," Rose said, slurring her words.

"She's our sister."

"Not my sister. Never will be," Rose said, trying to walk from the room.

I looked over at Francie questioning what was going on. Rose seemed disoriented. She stumbled to the couch.

"What's wrong?" I asked.

"Nothing. You force your way into my house, yelling at me about someone I don't even know. How would you feel?"

"She's coming and she's bringing her daughter," Francie interrupted.

"Are you kidding? You're letting strangers into Mum's house."

"Jesus, Rose," Francie said. "She's no stranger. Why are you making this so hard?"

"You need to leave...now."

"Fine, we're leaving. We just wanted you to know."

"Get out now, and don't be telling me what to do. I don't want to ever talk to her." She pushed us out the door, slamming it behind us.

We stood on the doorstep looking at the blue door. "Are you fucking kidding me?" I looked over at Francie in shock. I hadn't heard her talk like that since we were teenagers. "I'm sorry, but I'm just so pissed I can barely breathe!"

"Come on, let's go. I'll drop you off at Dylan's. Call him, so he can meet you downstairs. Have you ever been to his place?"

"No, just his house in Finglas."

"Did you spend the night?"

"No. We got close, but it wasn't right. He took me back to Mum's."

I called as we got back to the car. Dylan stood at the curb and held the car door. We walked inside the gate just past ten-thirty.

Twenty-Eight

O n the fourth of November, I sat with Mittens curled up in my lap, reading the latest Patterson thriller, when my cell rang.

"Catherine, this is Claire." Her voice had a sense of excitement. "I thought it was better to call then text."

"That's great. When can you come?"

"The eighth. I just want to be sure that it's still all good. I don't want to come in the middle of anything."

"You're going to be in the middle of something, but you need to be here. Mum thinks about you every day."

"The first time I met Alice she gave me a set of journals that explained a great deal. Would you like me bring them?"

"I'd be lying if I said no. We don't know anything about that time of her life."

"Good. I'll bring them. There's a United flight #311 on the eighth. It arrives in Dublin at ten o'clock in the morning. Would that be all right?"

"Wonderful. Let me take a look. I see it. I can book it right now, two seats, one for you and one for your daughter. I need your information to book the flight."

In a few minutes everything was done. Claire Hamilton

and her daughter Devon would be in Dublin November eighth. I laid my phone on the couch and sat back. It was done. They would be here in three days, and Rose could do nothing about it.

We continued to make short visits to the hospital. The doctors had brought her out of the coma, but she was only semi-conscious, most of the time. We didn't leave her alone. We were like clockwork. When one was ready to leave, there was someone coming in the door. Even Rose participated, but made it a point to steer clear of Francie and me. I was just fine with that. I didn't need to see her. It was more important that she just be there.

On the morning of the eighth, I straightened the house, even picked some flowers for the dining room table, but not roses, not this time. I brought her picture album down stairs with the intention of taking it to the hospital, but at the last minute, decided to leave it at home. I let Mittens out on the patio, taking one last look at the swan. It had settled nicely. There was no way of knowing that the ground had been dug up.

I came back inside and latched the door, then chuckled at my foolishness, thinking how the house looked would make a difference for Finn. I couldn't begin to imagine what she must be feeling, coming here when she had been rejected for so long.

Claire and Francie arrived at the house simultaneously. Connor had called, deciding not to come. He thought it best not to overwhelm them. I reminded him he was her uncle, but he said it was sister time. He'd wait until supper. Francie and I asked all the kids about meeting Finn at the airport. They agreed, unanimously with Connor, not to overwhelm. There would be plenty of time later. Though notified, Rose didn't leave any word about her interest in meeting Finn.

"Do I look all right?"

"You both look fine," Claire said, pulling us in for a hug. Remember, you all have something in common. You're sisters. It just took a lifetime to get to this day."

"Yeah, almost half a century." Francie looked over and laughed, but there was a sadness there, we all heard it.

"It'll be something for me as well," Claire said. "I haven't seen her since she was a babe. I held her in my arms and kept her as safe as I could."

It was Claire who teared up first. I put my arm around her, realizing it was as big of a deal for her, as for us. She was here representing Mum, and who wouldn't want to meet the nurse who was there for the delivery.

Once, in the car, Claire began a nervous chatter, as Francie crisscrossed the lanes, getting through the traffic. Francie and I both nodded and responded but, at the moment, we didn't have much to say. We were too engrossed with thoughts of Finn.

Even though I had pictures, I wondered if I would know her. The pictures were two years old, could she have changed, in some way?

Almost fifteen years older. I wondered if we would have been friends, or would she have been more worried about taking care of me? Too many questions, and none of them mattered. I had to shut off my mind.

"Claire, what if she doesn't like us?" Francie suddenly asked.

"Good God, Francie, you're not ten. She's your sister. She'll love you," Claire replied.

"I know what you're doing. Stop it. Everything that

happened had nothing to do with you. You girls had no control over it." Claire reached back and patted my knee, as she had done when we were girls. I grabbed hold and squeezed tight, and drawing her knuckles up for a kiss.

"Thank you," I said.

We stood at the gate, and watched as the passengers disembarked, waiting like school children, anxious for what was to come.

"I wish Rose were here," Francie said. Melancholy had taken her smile, and there was the same familiar sadness I had seen in Claire's eyes.

"Do you really? Finn's first day here and she faces Rose's wrath. No one deserves that."

"I just thought this might have changed things."

"Why don't we worry about her later," I said, looking around the holding area as families began to gather.

Suddenly, Claire nudged me. There she was, coming down the runway, a full head of brown hair, white scarf over a red sweater, a black jacket, and tennis shoes. She looked exactly like her picture. There was nothing pretentious about her. No fancy clothes, and just a tired stare. The young lady walking with her, must be Devon. Same brown hair, but with a look of excitement in her eyes.

I loved this girl already.

Claire stepped forward and called out. "Finn."

She turned toward us and stopped in her path. A smile slowly came to her lips. "Catherine?"

"I'm Catherine," I said. "This is Claire."

"So, I'm your namesake?"

They wrapped their arms around each other. Tears streamed down their cheeks.

"I'm Claire."

"As am I. I held you when you were a newborn. Look at you... I thought about everything I would say to you if I ever saw you again. I promised her I.... You look grand."

We all smiled.

"This is Catherine and Francie, your sisters." Finn broke down when she heard those words. She embraced the two of us, and I could feel her muffled sobs.

"I thought I'd never meet you. She was so afraid."

"Well, there was a lot to be afraid of, but not anymore. We're all here," Francie said.

"This is my daughter, Devon." She came forward and shook each of our hands. Francie pulled her close. A handshake was not enough.

"I never thought this day would come. We've waited so long. I just hope it's not too late," Devon said.

"She's been having a time, but seeing you, will surely help," Francie said.

Finn looked up. "I never called her mum, or mother, or anything like that. It seemed wrong. When we met, I called her Alice, out of respect."

"Call her whatever makes you comfortable. You belong, regardless of what you call her," Claire said, taking hold of her hand.

"Thank you. I've worried about offending anyone, calling her something I had no right to, or being some place I wasn't wanted. How will Rose be?"

"We called you, remember? Believe me, you're wanted," I said.

I had so many questions. So much I wanted to know. I wanted to hear about her work, her hobbies, what she did to relax. What made her happy, what made her mad. What buttons to push and which to avoid. All the little things sisters should know.

I wanted her past and her future. Her history and her dreams. I wanted to know her life.

Everything jumbled in my head. I needed to talk, but I didn't know what to say, where to start.

"We are so glad you came, both of you," Francie said, hugging Devon. "We didn't know that you actually existed until a few weeks ago."

"I know. I'm sorry for that," Finn said shyly. "I've known about all of you for...I guess it's been nearly ten years. Alice gave me pictures."

I took hold of Finn's hand and we walked toward the baggage area. "Rose didn't come?" Finn asked.

"Rose is having problems with this," I said.

"I'm not surprised. Her letter spoke volumes. There was so much anger."

"She's been very protective, and to be honest, she doesn't believe you're real." As fast as I said it, I came back with, "I'm sorry."

I saw her expression change. I saw the concern, the same tightness in her jaw. She reminded me of Mum.

"Come on," I said, pointing toward the escalator. "We'll go this way. It will take a while for them to bring the luggage down."

"How is she doing?" Finn asked.

"It's been touch and go. All we can hope for, is a good day," I said.

"I called the hospital this morning and they said she was awake and doing good," Francie broke in.

As we waited, we answered Finn's questions, as best we could. Most of them were about Mum. Claire explained the tumor, Francie told her about the episodes.

"They were all about you, you know. She was afraid of losing you," I said.

"They were all about me? What do you mean?"

"Her episodes," Claire said. "She goes back to the home—when she had to give you up.

"She never forgot you," Francie added.

"I know, she told me that the first time we met."

Francie reached over and took Devon's hand while we waited for their luggage to appear on the carousel.

We walked through the doors together. Claire linked her arm around Finn. We went up the elevator, but were stopped at the nurse's desk.

"You can't all go in at once."

"We won't. We promise. We just have someone she is real anxious to see," I said.

The nurse glanced at us all, then moved in close. "Your Mum is still very fragile. We can't have anything upsetting her."

"Her daughter and granddaughter are here from the States. She hasn't seen them for a very long time."

"Just two at a time."

"I understand. Thank you."

I looked through the window in the door, and saw Paddy

and Izzy inside. I waved to them and they stepped out.

"Paddy, Izzy, this is Finn."

"So, nice to meet you. My mother is Francie," Paddy said.

"And this is my daughter, Izzy."

"You look so much like your mother." Finn said.

"We're going to visit Mum, for a few minutes. Devon is with Claire in the waiting room. Go get acquainted."

"I'll wait here," Francie added.

Inside the room, a nurse adjusted her pillow and raised her bed just enough, so Mum could see us. Her head lay to the side.

"Mum, are you awake?"

"Yes, of course dear. Oh, Catherine, it's you." She reached out and took hold of my hand.

"Mum, we have someone here to see you." I moved to the side, letting go of her hand, so Finn could step forward.

"Alice, it's me, Finn. I'm back."

Mum pulled herself up to see the woman who stood in front of her. She looked over at me, I nodded.

"You're really here."

Mum held her hand. There were no words needed. It was as if nothing had kept them apart. I pulled a chair from the far wall for Finn to be closer.

"I'm going to step outside."

"No, stay please. You belong. Can you bring Francie in, just for a few minutes?"

I stepped outside and motioned for Francie, who immediately knew my message.

"Come sit here, dear one. So, I can see you." Her voice was soft, almost a whisper, as she patted the bed.

Francie and I stood back while Finn sat. They grasped each other. Mum couldn't pull her eyes away.

"How are you?" Finn asked, as she brushed the tears from her eyes.

"Oh, don't cry, child. I'm so glad you're here."

"I am, too."

Mum looked up and waved her arm. "Come closer." Francie and I moved to the bed. "Here are my girls." Then she looked around, confused. I thought, for a minute, we had lost her, but it wasn't an episode.

"She wouldn't come," I said, realizing who she was looking for. We tried, but it was too much for her. It will take some time."

"I don't have time."

Finn held her hand, Mum's eyes watered. Her head dropped to the side. I felt the pain I could see in her eyes.

I didn't need to know what Finn thought; I could see it. I wished Rose could see that moment, even though she wouldn't have seen it for what it was.

A nurse stepped in, closing the door behind her. "I'm sorry, she needs to rest, now." She stood by the door, dropping her hands to the pockets of her smock.

In the time it took for the nurse to escort us out, Mum had fallen asleep. I watched through the window. A peacefulness fell over her and I finally knew what she had missed.

Francie took Finn in her arms.

We made our way to the waiting room. Devon stood and moved toward her mother, "I'd like to see Grandmother, if it's all right?"

"She's asleep, but go ahead," I said. "I am sure the nurses will let you in."

I would have loved to be there, to hear the words she had for her "grandmother" in private.

Devon seemed much like Izzy, standing up for herself and her mother. She had made this trip, just as Izzy would have.

But Finn stood tall, almost regal. This woman was not going anywhere.

Claire pulled Finn to sit and began asking questions: *What was she doing? How was life in Oregon? Was she happy? Would she ever consider staying in Dublin?* Questions she would be asked a thousand time over.

Finn responded in a friendly, casual manner. I sensed nothing was held back. There would be no secrets—nothing off-limits.

After a few minutes Devon came back to the waiting room. "I didn't stay long, she was sleeping, but she woke up a couple of times."

"Did she remember you?" Finn asked.

A smile broke across Devon's face. "Yes, she even called me by name."

"Did you get to talk at all?"

"She asked how I was, but I mainly just held her hand. That was enough. I was just glad to see her." I couldn't help but smile.

"I'm sure she was, too." Franie said.

"We have reservations at six at a quiet little Italian place," Francie said. "We'll have just enough time to stop by the house and drop off your bags.

"Are you sure you're up for this? You must be exhausted from the flight," I asked.

"I wouldn't want to miss a minute," Finn said.

Twenty-Nine

The four of us walked into the restaurant and I immediately saw Connor and Jenny in the corner. Izzy sat next to him, along with Rose's girls. Francie and Colin sat with Paddy across the table.

I took a deep breath. I knew this would be a long night and extremely emotional.

We introduced everyone, before taking a seat. Claire took Finn and Devon to the head of the table, while Connor ordered wine. I took the chair next to Izzy.

As drinks were served, the questions started flowing in both directions. It was amazing to see the familiarity from people who had never met. I guess common threads say a lot. I felt a sense of happiness I didn't know I had been missing.

She began by telling us about her life after the adoption. They told her Mum had died. I sat back taking it in. It was hard to imagine. She had spent her life believing she was an orphan, while we were living our lives, knowing nothing of the secret buried deep, in Mum's heart.

She talked about the Sisters at the Home, how they treated

her as she searched for Mum. It reminded me of what Francie and I experienced. But her, being the bastard daughter, was the spawn of sin, rejected and abandoned, again and again.

"I've waited such a long time to meet you. I had hoped she would have been able to tell you about me. I have been longing for this moment..." Finn said. "I just wish we could have met before she got sick."

"Alice was terrified to tell anyone," Claire said.

"I know. The year I met her she wouldn't allow us in the house, and she forbid me from contacting you," Finn said, nodding toward us.

"We didn't know about you, at all. As we started putting the pieces together, we realized that she was afraid we'd stop loving her, if we knew" I said.

"I never meant to hurt anyone. I needed to learn about my heritage, especially after I found out that she hadn't died."

"Why? Weren't you satisfied with your life the way it was?" Jean asked, taking a sip of wine.

"Jean, why would you ask such a thing?" Marie asked, elbowing her sister. Jean didn't break the stare.

"No, that's OK. I was happy. I had my children, a career." She reached over and took hold of Devon's hand.

"My mother has searched for you, for as long as I can remember. It consumed her life. I knew who I was, when I looked in the mirror, but she didn't. I think that was what drove her," Devon said.

"I needed to fill a hole in my heart," Finn said, looking around. "Something was missing."

"Mum kept her secrets well. We never knew about you. There was Da, the three of us, and Mum. We were a family," Francie said.

"I began my search in 1985. I found her in 1990, but she told the Sisters that she wouldn't see me."

"I was still at home then," Francie chimed in.

"That's the conversation Rose overhead when she brought the girls to the house," I broke in, remembering Rose's reaction to the pictures.

"The Sisters said she never wanted her family to know. So, I stopped, but I continued to write hoping they might try to contact her again.

"I left a letter for her, but it wasn't until twenty years later, that I learned they never sent it. I went back to my life, raised my family and continued my career, but I never forgot her. I just tried not to of her as much."

"I wish my mother would have known these things," Marie, Rose's youngest daughter, said. "She'd have understood. I'm sorry she isn't here."

"Rose did know about me. She called and told me to leave your grandmother alone. She told me I was bothering the family."

"My mother wouldn't do that." Marie said. She didn't know you. She didn't understand."

"To put it bluntly," Jean chimed in, "she doesn't believe you exist. She was very protective of Grandma. She told me a long time ago about a letter from a woman in the States. She made me believe you wanted to hurt our family."

"I know. She sent a letter, telling me to stop. So, I did."

There was silence around the table.

"You should have told us," Francie said, her eyes hard.

"I promised her, I wouldn't."

"God, this family and their fucking secrets," Francie said.

I looked over at Paddy and Izzy, sitting in silence, watching Devon and Finn.

"Maybe before I leave, Rose will see me," Finn said, looking around, settling her look on her daughter. "I want to meet her. I don't want anything. I'm not here to hurt your grandmother or your family. I hope you understand that."

Finn was believable. There was no reason to question the motives of this woman, with Mum's blue-green eyes and cheekbones. Devon had our smile. She could easily be called a Leary.

I stood pulled the worn medal from my pocket and laid it on the table. Connor looked at it, then up at me.

"I gave that to her when we met, the first time. She was surprised that I had kept it," Finn said.

"Why?" Paddy asked, becoming part of the conversation.

"I can answer that," Claire said. "I promised your mum that I would make sure it stayed with you," Claire said, reaching over to touch the string.

"She said she wanted her daughter to have something she could remember her by."

"I held you as your mother put it around your neck," Claire said, "then hid it from Reverend Mother, so she wouldn't take it from you. I guess it served it's purpose. "

"I kept it in a box in a drawer."

Claire nodded. "The medal is how she knew you were you."

We sat in a circle taking up the biggest table in the restaurant. Conversations hummed around us. Smoke filled the room. Little by little, we revealed our own pasts to Finn and Devon. We released parts of our lives that they would have no way of knowing. Claire sat back and beamed, that her namesake had come home.

We drank and laughed. For a while we forgot there had been any distance between us. We forgot, it was a tragedy that brought us together, and we forgot, we didn't know we were family.

The cousins laughed, talked and found they had a great deal in common. Devon the oldest, then Jean, Paddy, Izzy and Marie. The next generation of the Leary family.

We were together.

"I'm afraid I have to be going," Connor broke in. "Early morning, but I must say, Finn and Devon, it has been a delight to meet you. And no worries, the tab is taken care of."

We watched Connor and Jenny leave the restaurant. Then one by one, everyone started saying their good-byes. Marie and Jenny left next, along with Claire. Izzy and Paddy stood to bid their farewells, it was just Francie, Devon, Finn and myself.

"Devon," Izzy said, "you should stay with me tonight. It would give our moms a chance to catch up, and I could get to know my new cousin."

"My stuff is at Grandma's house."

"No problem, we can stop by, it's right on the way. Paddy has room in his car for your luggage and he can drop us off. We can meet up again tomorrow."

"I think that is a great idea, Izzy," I said, looking over at Devon. "I'm sure you both have a lot of stories." I looked at Finn who was taking in all the chaos. "Would that be OK Finn? Francie and I would like to spend some time with you."

"Sure, whatever works for everyone," she said.

I watched Finn brush the hair from her face and wondered what must be going through her mind. Here we were, this Irish clan, who had rejected her for so many years. I wanted to know this woman. I wanted to understand the drive that kept her going. At any point, if she had stopped, she never would have found Mum. There would be no pictures, no texts. She would have remained a secret hidden in a swan garden.

Thirty

It was just past ten when we arrived back at the house. This was the first time Finn had set foot inside, and she stood frozen in the entry. She looked around the room, letting her purse slip to the floor.

"When I was here, I peeked in the window, after eight years it's still the same, the sofa, the afghan, even the dining room table with the flowers."

"She's always loved her flowers. She made it a point to have them in the house. I replace them every few days," I said, "just in case she comes home."

"They're beautiful."

"What would you like to do?" I asked, feeling like a kid on my first sleepover.

"I know I should be tired, but so much has happened. Would it be all right if we just talked for a while. I still have so many questions, especially after tonight."

She continued to look around the room, taking in every detail. "The last time we talked, she said she had a garden. I'd love to see it."

"Of course, I'll take your luggage upstairs. Can I get you something to drink? Wine?" I asked.

"No, I'm afraid I've had too much. Could I have some water?"

"I'll get a bottle from the kitchen," Francie said.

"I'll be back down in a minute." I grabbed her suitcase, along with the carry-on, and took it up to our room.

As I came downstairs, I heard my sisters laughing, chatting as if they had never been separated. It felt real.

I went upstairs into Mum's room and closed the door. I thought one last time couldn't hurt. I could tell myself I tried. I rang her number and waited. After five rings, it went to the message.

"I wish you'd come over. She's here and she's delightful, so much like Mum in so many ways. I think you'd really like her." I clicked off the phone and stared at the black screen. I didn't know what else to say. I went back downstairs to the giggles of my sisters.

"This home is lovely," Finn said, looking up at me as I moved into the dining room.

"You know, I came here four days in a row, looking for her, hoping she'd answer the door, terrified she would."

"Did she know you were coming?" Francie asked.

"Yes. I wrote her before I came and gave her the dates. She had gone to London to visit one of the grandchildren."

"I remember that," Francie said. "It must have been Jean. How ironic."

"I left notes for her to call. She didn't call until the fourth day."

She took a deep breath. "Can I see the garden?"

I flipped on the lights and stood back as she gazed out. I thought I saw tears, she brushed her cheek with her hand. "Can I go out?" She motioned.

"Of course. Our Da did this for her, a little bit each year. It became her sanctuary," Francie said, standing behind her. "It's where she learned about all the different plants. Year-by-year it grew bigger and bigger. I never understood what it meant, until one day I was out here, and it started to rain. I just stood and watched everything. It was magic. After that I came to understand her passion."

We stepped through the French doors and though the evening had long passed, the night was clear. With the patio lights, the garden shimmered.

"This is lovely. I can see why she loved it so." Finn twirled in circles, taking everything in, as she looked around.

"It's been her pride and joy, along with Mittens. Have you seen her yet?"

"No. A cat?" Francie nodded. "She never mentioned her. Hmm, something else we have in common. I love cats."

"She's around here somewhere. Don't worry, she'll show up. Just look for a fat, fluffy-tailed old girl."

"It really is a lovely home."

"Mum took great stock in it, always kept it clean, but allowed it to be livable.

"And the smells—in the winter, her stews and soups filled the house. With spring, came the flowers." I strolled beyond the patio, still talking. "She never went a day without fresh flowers.

"Certain things were very important, her garden...her dinners. Unfortunately, she didn't pass it on to any of us, except Francie loves to cook." I laughed as I nudged her. "I took more to books. And Rose? Well, she fought everything tooth and nail."

"We have more in common than you know. I love flowers—have tons of books—and only cook, when I have to. And I have my cats."

"Let's go in. I don't know about you, but it's getting chilly. We'll have lots of time to be outside," Franice said.

"Sure."

"Do you need more water?" Francie appeared nervous.

"No, I'm good, thanks. I do have a question. Is the bathroom downstairs or upstairs?"

We both laughed, "Sorry right down the hall," I said.

"Francie, I can't believe Mum couldn't tell us about her. She's really something special."

"Let's take advantage of the time we have," Francie said, turning back toward the living room with the wine bottle in one hand and a bottle of water in the other.

"That's better, too much wine," Finn said grinning, as she stepped into the living room.

"So, Catherine, you live in Boston?" she asked.

"Yes. We left Dublin for my husband's business, but when Mum got sick, I came home."

"Do you like it?"

"It's not Dublin. I missed home. I think there's more Irish in Boston than all of County Dublin."

"I've heard that," Francie said.

"I feel the same about Oregon, but I agree, Dublin holds a piece of my heart." Finn took a sip of water.

"Izzy is delightful. Has she always loved art?"

"It's been her passion," I said.

"And what is your passion?" she asked abruptly.

I took a deep breath and looked over at Francie. "The Law, but lately, finding you."

Finn blushed and set her bottle on the table. "I can only imagine what you must have thought. I assume you found my album?"

"Yes, after Mum went to the hospital." I looked away, embarrassed by my disclosure. "Mum cherished everything from you. It was hidden in the closet."

"She told me. When we gave it to her, she said she couldn't have it on the coffee table."

"Well, she can now. Nothing will stop that."

Finn grew silent, her eyes red.

"I'm sorry. I didn't mean to…"

"No, it's just me. It hurt so much when she said that…I felt like an intruder, like I was trying to force myself, where I didn't belong. And then Rose called." Finn looked up. "What could I do?"

"The album is beautiful. It deserves to be out where everyone can see. We should all do that." Francie said.

"I wanted her to see my life, what it was like. I kept thinking, if it had been me, I'd want to know everything." Finn was making an incredible amount of sense.

"Do you know anything of your adoption?" I asked.

"A little, the local church brought over fifteen children. I was one of them. I was five."

"Where were you for those five years?" Francie asked.

"From what I could find, I made the rounds of foster homes and the orphanage."

"My, god."

"They never really gave me an answer."

"Did you live in Oregon your whole life?"

"I never left St. Helens. It's the only town I've ever known. My children all live there with their families, too."

"Have you ever thought about coming back here?" I asked.

"Pretty much every day," she laughed.

"What are your plans?"

"To see Alice every day. I'd like to try to make amends with Rose, if I can. It's important. I kind of understand what she's feeling."

"How?"

"I became the youngest when I was adopted. I had no say. It changed me. I'm sure it changed her, when she found out she wasn't the first."

"I have a question for you," I said, again looking over at Francie.

"Anything."

"What do you want us to call you? We've been calling you Finn, that must feel weird. You've been known as Claire, your whole life."

"It's different,"she laughed. "I didn't even know I had another name until I was grown. My Mother thought my middle name would be easier."

"Do you ever remember being called Finnouala?" Francie asked.

"No, I've only known Claire.

"I wish I'd have known sooner, I'd have given Devon the name. It means a great deal, now that I understand.

"Let's see, it would be confusing with Claire, so I guess

it's OK to call me Finn. At least there won't be any confusion. You'll have to bear with me, if I don't answer right away."

"That will be grand." We giggled like schoolgirls.

"Then Finn, it will be. You must be exhausted," I said as she rubbed her eyes.

"Yes, but I'm afraid if I go to sleep, I'll wake up at home."

"This must be a lot to take in," Francie said, leaning in on the couch.

"To be honest, I didn't know when, or if, I'd ever be here again."

"You have Cate, to thank for that. She wouldn't stop pushing," Francie teased.

Finn wasn't ready to let go of the evening yet. I could see it in every movement. She was right. If she closed her eyes, she might be back in Kansas, but Finn wasn't Dorothy and there was no chance we were going to let Rose be the wicked witch. No matter how hard she tried.

"Can you tell me how she fell?" Finn asked.

"It didn't start with the fall. The doctors found a slow growing tumor. It's been causing memory lapses and severe headaches for almost a year," Francie said.

"What can they do?"

"Nothing. It's inoperable. She's had two falls, and the last one put her in a coma, of sorts."

"What does that mean?"

"She comes in and out. There are days when everything's great, she knows who we are, and then sometimes, she sleeps for days."

"Did she ever ask for me?"

"In a way, yes," I said.

"There were times we would go and see her, she'd be in an episode," Francie began

"She would cry out for you," I interjected."

"What do you mean?" Finn asked?"

"She had episodes where she thought she was back at the Home and they were trying to take you away. She would call out to Claire, or Sara. Do you know who Sara was?"

"Yes. I read about her in the journals."

"That's right. I forgot she gave you her journals," I said. "More and more, she was searching for you. We knew we had to call you."

"And where was Rose in all of this?" She asked.

"Oh, we approached her, repeatedly, but she would have nothing to do with you. That was when we found out she wrote you."

Finn started to cry. "I'm sorry."

"Don't be," I said, reaching my arm around her.

"We are so glad you came. She needs you here before she dies," Francie said.

"You really think she is going to die?"

"Yes, the doctors think it's sooner than later. The tumor has grown rapidly since her first fall.

"She's getting worse every day. I was surprised she was so clear this afternoon. She must have known you were coming," Francie broke in, looking back and forth between us.

"I hope you know I never meant to come between anyone. When I got the letter from Rose, I decided to back off completely, but, to tell the truth, I was a little unsure why Rose was so upset."

"Rose told us about the letter and the call, after. We didn't even know she knew about you."

"How did she find out?"

"She said, Mum told her years ago."

There was a long pause. Finn got up and moved to the dining room table, rubbing her fingers against the vase. She didn't turn back toward us. Francie and I looked at each other confused. Had we said too much?

"I searched for her for over twenty-five years," she said, stroking the petals. "I found her once, but she turned me away, because you—Francie, it must have been you, were still living at home. Your Da was still alive. She didn't want to hurt her family, so...."

"She thought of you every day. You need to know that," I said.

"Thank you.

"I'm sorry. I used to dream about standing here, in this very room.

"I'm here, but I'm on the threshold of losing her."

"You know, she wasn't the only victim, Francie said. "We all were. Each of us in different ways."

She was right. I understood her clearly. We were the ones left behind, all of us. We had all paid a price for the sin committed against our mother. Rose was broken, almost beyond repair, Finn, had somehow found a way to come out whole, but I saw the chips in her armor. Francie and I, well we continued to wear our masks.

"Can I ask you something?" I asked.

"When's your birthday?"

"In November. Why?"

"I knew it," Francie said, getting up and going toward the dining table.

"Every November, Mum baked a lemon cake and put candles on it. She said, 'it was someone's birthday, somewhere.' It was you. Every year, she celebrated you. She'd bring in tons flowers and put them in the window. After everything was cleaned up, she'd sit in the garden. I'd watch her and wonder where she went, what she thought about. It was you."

"I had no idea."

I saw a sadness crawl over her face. It wasn't until that moment, I realized what it really meant.

She was family. She had come home.

"I think everything's catching up with me." Finn said.

"Me, too. Tomorrow is going to be a long day," I said, picking up the glasses and the wine. "We'll be back at the hospital and you'll get to meet Rose. I'm sure she'll come tomorrow.

"That's a lie, you don't know what she'll do. She can be a little stubborn," Francie said. "Ever since Mum took sick, Rose has been acting strange. But Connor is good at settling things. He'll bring her around."

"I really appreciate you letting me stay here."

"Where else would you stay? You're family." Francie said.

"It's time I head home, so I'll see you in the morning." She gave Finn a massive hug, burying her head into Finn's neck.

I took Finn upstairs to the bedroom. "You can take this bed. The bathroom is down the hall. Everything you need should be there"

"Yes, I know you said. Thank you."

"I'm going to go downstairs and shut everything off. We'll see you in the morning"

I closed the door and moved slowly downstairs. I went through each of the rooms, locking the windows, turning off the lights.

I sat at the kitchen table in the dim light, lit a cigarette and poured a glass of wine, I knew I didn't need.

Mittens jumped in my lap, circled around and settled in. I rubbed her behind the ears. She almost squirmed in pleasure, purring and pushing against my fingers. So much had happened in the last few weeks, I couldn't begin to take it all in. One thing I knew, my mother would be dying soon, but having Finn here, having had the chance to meet her would bring us all closer, if Rose could come down off her high horse.

After what seemed like hours and two glasses of wine, I slipped into Mum's room, fell into bed and said a final prayer that Rose would change her mind.

Thirty-One

Before I could even pull myself from under the covers, I heard Finn down stairs, rummaging through the kitchen. I smelled bacon and coffee. She greeted me as I came down the stairs, holding a mug of steaming heaven.

"Thank you. This is perfect."

"I don't know how you like it."

"I add two teaspoons of brown sugar," I said, moving over toward the sink. "How did you sleep?"

Before Finn could answer, Francie stormed through the front door, calling our names as she reached the dining room.

"Good morning. Everyone up?"

"In the kitchen," I called back.

"How's everyone this morning?" she asked, as she slipped out of her coat and threw it over the stool by the door.

"Grand. And you?" I looked over at Finn and gave her a smile

"I just got off the phone with Rose," Francie said, her arms open for a hug. "Oh my, she's in such a tizzy."

"Why?" Because of me?" Finn asked.

"Darlin', you don't get all the credit. Our sister is in a fit most of the time. Usually of her own making, of course," I said, patting Finn on the shoulder.

"Come sit down, Francie. Do you want breakfast?"

"No breakfast, but coffee would be great. How are you doing, Finn?"

"Rested, thank you."

"How was your first night? Did you sleep in our room?" Francie laughed looking over at me.

"Yes, she did," I said, "but she slept in your bed. I wouldn't put her in Rose's."

"I really enjoyed looking at everything. I could see your personalities. I think I even figured out who's who. Rose had the dolls, Francie, you had the posters, and Catherine, the books? Right?"

"That's a little scary," Francie said, with a shy smile.

"I think we know each other better than you might think," I said, adding, "we're sisters. Blood."

For the next hour we chatted as if we had known one another a lifetime. We laughed, shared, and spoke of our beliefs. We had in common, a deep devotion to our children. Francie and Paddy, my Izzy, the artist of the family, and Finn, blessed with Devon and Adam.

As Francie took her last sip, she sat back. "What time should we leave for the hospital?" she asked.

Just then, my cell lit up. "It's Connor." I put it on speaker. "Morning Connor."

"Are you girls together?" he asked.

"We're all here, except for Rose."

"You need to come in now."

"What's wrong?"

"This might be it.

"I'll call Rose," he said.

"What about Claire?"

"She's here. Came early this morning to spend some time with her."

"Claire had stepped out for just a moment, and when she came back, nurses were all over the place.

"OK, we're on our way. I'll call the kids."

Finn began to clear the table, but Francie nudged her upstairs. "Go on, you two, get dressed. I'll clean up and call everyone."

We took to the stairs and were back in the kitchen in record time.

Francie had cleaned up and put everything away; even Mittens had been fed and lay curled in her bed.

I called Dylan, and told him everything that Connor had said. He promised to meet us at the hospital after his staff meeting.

"Did you call the kids?" I asked Francie.

"Yes, Paddy called Izzy and Devon is with her. Izzy is calling Rose's girls. They should be at the hospital long before we are."

Francie took her place behind the wheel as the rain beat against the window. The M-50 motorway, busy with morning traffic, kept Francie's focus on the road. None of us spoke. I flipped on the radio to fill the silence.

We went through the double doors and took the elevator to Mum's room. Connor and Claire stood in the hall, their faces crestfallen.

Suddenly, Rose came around the corner, her purse strap hanging from her shoulder, her eyes like daggers, darting between Francie and me.

"All right, I'm here, but I don't want to meet her. I'm here for Mum, so don't even try."

"A little late for that. She's right here."

Connor stepped forward. "Enough of this, Rose. This is Finn. Whether you like it or not, she's your sister. Grow up."

Finn reached out her hand. Rose kept her gaze on Connor, her eyes full of hatred. She turned and walked down the hall.

"What the hell?" Connor said.

We were shocked. That was completely unexpected.

"Finn, I'm so sorry," Claire said.

"That was awful," I said, looking over at Finn. "Don't worry, it'll be fine." I touched her hand, her fingers trembled.

After a few moments, the nurse came to us. "You can go in, but she may not be responsive."

"Thank you," Francie said.

"Claire and I will wait downstairs with the kids. You go on. Say good-bye to your Mum," Connor said.

We walked in as sisters.

Seeing Mum reminded me of when I first saw her in the hospital, so tiny, fragile. But now…. She was so different from yesterday. Wires came from all directions. We stood silently, I wasn't sure what we were waiting for. The hum of the machines keeping Mum alive.

"Finn, do you want to say good-bye privately? We can step out."

"No, please stay."

Francie and I moved over to the side of the bed, while Finn

remained at the foot, watching all of us. Despite the hum from the machines, a calm encompassed the room.

Unexpectedly, the door opened and Rose slipped in, moving to the farthest corner. She didn't acknowledge anyone. She just stared at Mum.

The silence was overbearing. I looked at Rose and could see the strain etched on her face. Her eyes narrowed, her jaw tightened. Whatever the reason, it didn't matter. She finally looked around, her gaze settling on Finn, her distain apparent. When she noticed me watching her, she turned her attention back to Mum. I stepped closer, and touched her shoulder.

"What? I'm here, aren't I?" Rose snapped.

"Thank you," I whispered.

"You don't need me here. You have her, now."

"You're kidding? Right?"

"I'll do this in my own time." Rose turned and left.

How could she be so selfish? I moved toward the bed, between Finn and Francie. I looked at Mum, she seemed strangely content. Her arms nestled against the blankets, eyes barely open, muscles relaxed, with a faint smile. She was at peace.

"Can I talk with her? Is that OK?" Finn asked.

"Of course, we'll step outside."

"No, no, please stay."

Francie and I stepped back, and Finn moved to the bed rail. She took Mum's hand and lightly stroked her fingers.

"Should we be hearing this?" Francie whispered, looking at me.

"Yes," Finn said.

"Alice, this is Finn. I don't know if you can hear me, but I just want you to know, I'm here." She paused. "I met your beautiful girls, my sisters. I've seen your house and your garden." She bowed her head and gripped tight to Mum's hand.

"Oh, Francie," I whispered, "I can't bear this." She put her arms around me.

"I've wanted to be a family for so long, but..." Finn continued, "Your girls told me how you held on to my memory. I've waited so long..."

Finn bent down and brought Mum's hand to her cheek, kissed it, placed it gently on top of the blanket. I saw the pain in her face, she moved to the window, brushing her tears away.

"I don't know how to say goodbye. I don't want to," Francie said, kissing Mum's hand. "You're my Mum. You're all I've ever known."

Francie didn't say anything more, but laid her head on the bed, still holding tight to Mum's hand.

I moved opposite to Francie and touched Mum's cheek.

We were watching her die.

As hard as it was for Francie and I, there was Finn, trying to reconnect.

I could feel the spirit leave her body.

The machines slowed, the lines fell to horizontal traces.

"Da will be waiting, Mum." Francie raised her hand and kissed it, one last time.

When Francie stepped away, Finn moved in and kissed her forehead, and both stepped out of the room.

I stood alone with her, terrified. I'd never talk to her again, never listen to her stories about Howth, or hear how she fell so desperately in love with Da.

The machines began to blink wildly, and bells and alarms went off. The lines stopped squiggling over the screen and everything went still.

"Ma'am, I need you to step out," one of the nurses said.

"I know, give me just a minute."

Before leaving, I bent down low and whispered.

"We dug up your box. We found the money and used it to bring your daughter home. You no longer have to keep any secrets. I'm sorry you lost so much time." I brushed a wispy strand of hair from her forehead, touched her cheek, and kissed her.

"Ma'am, please step outside." Another nurse took hold of my arm and led me to the door.

Outside, we stood like lost children, not knowing which way to turn. We huddled together, unsure what to do. It seemed like forever before a nurse finally came out and stood in front of us.

"What do we do now?"I asked

"You can go in if you like, if you need more time."

"I prefer not to remember her that way. If either of you want to go..." Francie said.

"Thank you," I said to the nurse. "We'll go downstairs and tell the family."

"If it's OK, I'd like to go back in, just for a minute," Finn said.

"Do you want us to wait?" Francie asked.

"No, I can find my way."

"OK, we'll go downstairs." Once on the elevator, we stood in silence. I gripped Francie's hand, to feel the comfort in her touch. As we stepped out, Claire sat in the corner, flipping through a magazine, the cousins were huddled by the coffee machine. Dylan stood next to Connor, deep in conversation. I felt a sense of relief to see him there. My need to be strong evaporated, and I felt the tears begin. I needed him to hold me.

I wondered how we would tell them she was gone.

From the look on their faces, they knew.

The double doors to the Nurse's station burst open, as we moved toward the family, Michael surged through, in a rage.

"They told me I'd find you here."

"What do you want, Michael?"

He looked around, noticing the family. "I've had papers drawn up. I want a divorce," his voice low, but intense.

"What?" I stared at him, stunned.

"You heard me. I want a divorce."

"Michael, I can't do this now. Mum just died," I said, trying to whisper to keep the kids from hearing.

Michael's outburst drew everyone's attention. Francie moved next to Connor and Claire. The kid's looked up from their conversation. Izzy stared at her father with a look of disgust.

"I don't care. We need to do it now. I have things to do and you're not going to control everything for your convenience." Michael grabbed my arm, trying to force the envelope into my hands.

In an instant, Dylan had hold of his wrist. "Who the hell do you think you are?"

"I'm her husband, so back off, it's none of your business."

"Michael, this is not the time. You need to step back." I pulled my arm away."

"You heard her, step back... now." Dylan said with a force that drew Michael's attention.

As he stared at Dylan, "I see you found someone to protect you. How long have you been fucking him?

"You know what Cathy, it doesn't matter. You're still my wife, at least until you sign these." He threw the envelope in my face, as it fell to the floor, the papers scattered.

"It's time for you to leave," Dylan said in a very quiet, ominous tone.

Michael smirked, shaking his head. "I don't know where you find them, Cathy.

"Sign the papers. The sooner you do, the sooner I can get on with my life and you can fuck whoever you want."

Dylan's fist connected with Michael's face in an instant. A moment later, Michael was on his knees.

"You know this is all your fault, Cathy. If you had done what I told you..."

"I don't have to do anything." I took a deep breath. "You will never tell me what to do again.

"It's time for you to leave, Michael. Enough is enough." I could see the rage in Michael's eyes. Dylan moved to stand between us and crossed his arms.

"Fine. Just sign the Goddamn papers."

Michael went back through the double doors, muttering.

"You OK?"

I couldn't hold back the tears, or the rage. "How could he do that? Especially now. How did he even know?"

"He didn't know," Dylan said.

"I'm so sorry Mom," Izzy said coming up behind me. "I didn't know he would come. When he called, I told him it didn't look good for Grandma and..."

"He actually knew? That son-of-a-bitch. He knew, and he came anyway." Dylan pulled me into his arms. "Get me out of here."

I looked down at the papers, before I could ask, Francie came over and gathered them together. I leaned my head on Dylan's shoulder. "Thanks Francie."

"Connor, we're leaving, call me if you need anything."

"We'll take care of things here. Alice had everything planned out. We'll make the necessary calls. Go ahead."

"Francie... Finn is..."

"No problem. When she comes down, I'll explain. Get out of here before he comes back."

I vaguely remember Dylan guiding me through the double doors. It all seemed a haze. Everything happened too fast. Mum was gone. Michael....

Thirty-Two

We drove through quiet neighborhoods in silence. Dylan kept looking over to make sure I was still there. I laid my head back on the headrest and closed my eyes. I didn't remember him bringing me to the car, or driving down the thoroughfare, away from Dublin Center, away from Mum, away from the chaos of Michael.

"Feeling better?"

"I can't believe he did that."

"Don't worry about him. I don't think he'll bother you."

"Dylan, he threw divorce papers at me. I will never forget that."

"I don't think anyone will."

"Why would he do that at the hospital? He could have called, could have mailed them, but to barge through like that?"

"Cat, there's nothing you can do about it. It's over. Try to forget today."

"What about Mum? I should have stayed."

"No, Connor promised to take care of everything. Francie will call you tomorrow. They won't do any more today that would involve any of you. The hospital has procedures, things they need to take care of, then they'll call the mortuary. I'm sure if there's anything they need, Claire or Connor will take care of it."

"Where are we going?"

"My cottage. Is that all right?"

I nodded. "What about Finn?"

"She's with Francie. She'll be fine. Francie already sent a text that she and Claire took Finn back to the house."

"Good." I watched him as he drove. Determination was etched on his jaw. As was worry. I love this man. The thoughtfulness, the compassion.

We pulled into the driveway and he turned off the motor. We sat for a few minutes, he took a deep breath, and I watched as he rubbed his hands down the knees of his cords.

"And you?" He said, turning, looking into my eyes. "How are you doing?"

"I need you Dylan," I turned toward him and touched his fingers.

"I'm here for you."

"No. You proved you're here for me. I need for you to make love to me."

"As much as I would love to, Cat, it's not right. You need to just rest, pull yourself together. You would—

"You don't want me?"

"Oh God, no...I mean yes, I've wanted you since the day I saw you at the café. I don't want to mess it up."

"You could never mess it up.

"Look I'm going to open the door, so I can take you inside."

"And then you'll make love to me?"

"Come on, Cat, don't torture me. Give it some time. You'll

feel better if you lay down for a while."

I laid my head back on the headrest and I could feel him still staring at me. "When did you start calling me Cat?" I asked, trying to take my mind off everything.

"What are you asking?" He leaned toward me.

"When did you fall in love with me?" I looked at him trying to understand why I felt I needed him to love me.

He pushed his cap back and smiled. "It was a Thursday. We just finished our first court debate and you had kicked my butt. I wanted to get your attention, so I called out Cat, and you turned around. Brushed your wavy curls from your face and smiled. From that day, I never went back." He grinned and stepped out of the car.

As I watched him come around to my side of the car, I realized we weren't young any more. Time was slipping away. Was it too much time? Michael was the past. Dylan—he was right here for the taking. I needed to take him, to make him want me. More importantly, I understood I never stopped loving him.

"I don't remember this place," I said when he opened the door.

I looked around the curved driveway and across to the rock garden

"You should. You've been here before. It's is my cottage."

He took hold of my hand and guided me through the front door. Once inside, I started to cry. Everything was too much, Mum—Finn—mostly Michael.

"What have I done?" I asked him.

"What do you mean?"

"Look at me, I've fucked everything up. I've lost my

mother, Michael made an ass of me in front of everyone. And to top it off, I left my baby sister to take care of a lost sister we never knew we had. What's wrong with me?"

"Come on, why don't you lay down for a while. I'll make some tea. You can sleep. It's been a long day."

"I should be there."

"And what good would you do? You're talking in circles, you can't think straight. Lay down. When you wake, if you feel better, I'll take you home."

He guided me to the edge of the bed and pushed me down. He knelt and pulled off my shoes. Between his touch on my ankles and the closeness of his body, before I knew it I had my arms around his neck, pulling him toward me, kissing him, pressing hard against his lips. His tongue excited me. I needed him more than anything in the world. He leaned in and kissed me again. I pulled him up to join me. I felt the weight of his chest, and smelled a faint scent of sandalwood that lingered in the creases of his neck. I couldn't pull away. I didn't want to.

I kissed him, while his hands caressed my body. I shared in his excitement, enticing him further. He kissed my shoulders and traced his tongue down the hollow of my breasts. I didn't stop him. I needed him so much.

Slowly he rolled to his side, leaned on one elbow. "Are you sure?"

I began to unbutton my blouse and stroked his cheek. I saw laughter in his eyes. I pulled him down to me, lost in the wonder of him. His hand moved down my trembling body, cupping my breast, his fingers smooth and firm.

"Wait."

"What? Did I do something wrong?" He asked.

"I feel like I'm forcing you to...to love me." I pulled myself up, away from him. "You said I should rest. Did you mean that or were you trying to avoid making love? You seem hesitant."

He fell back onto the bed. "You think I don't want you?"

"It did seem like you were trying to avoid it."

"Cat..., I forgot how frustrating you could be."

I quickly pulled my blouse closed. "Well, then..."

"Well nothing. Cat, I love you. I don't know what your husband did, how he made you feel.

"But I saw what he did at the hospital... I saw how he treated you, so yes, I want to take it easy... slow.

"Think about this. Your husband is an ass, your mother died, not more than two hours ago. I am not Michael. You need to realize my passion for you isn't contingent on someone else's definition or actions. Neither is my love."

"Now you're sounding like a lawyer, methodical."

"And you're being obstinate."

I took a deep breath. "Dylan, if you don't want to —"

"What do you want, Cat? Do you want to stop? Do you want me to leave and let you rest?"

"No," I whispered.

"Then what?"

"I want you to need me the way I need you."

He cupped my chin with his hands and pulled me to him. I felt trembling in his lips, as his tongue parted mine. The subtleties of his kiss, melted any obstacles.

"OK."

"OK."

I pulled my blouse closed, feeling foolish.

I fiddled with the buttons of my blouse, looking at my fingers. "You know, I'm not twenty-five anymore." I paused. "I don't look like I did."

"If you haven't noticed, I'm not either. We're both older. More seasoned. You're beautiful."

"It's been a long time since I've let someone see me... with the lights on."

He chuckled. "So, what do we do now?"

"Can one of us go into the bathroom?"

"Only if you promise to come out."

"Don't make fun of me."

"I'm not. I haven't done this for a very long time myself. I want you. I don't much care how either of us look."

"Really?"

"Really."

I got up and moved to the bathroom, holding my blouse closed.

"Remember, you promised to come out," he said chuckling.

I closed the door and started undressing. I watched the reflection in the vanity mirror, as I removed my blouse and slacks.

The woman before me was old. The strain around her eyes, flashed like the beacon of the lighthouse in Howth. Her make-up had been completely erased by her tears.

I removed my camisole and stood in bra and panties. *What was I doing?* I removed my bra and slid my panties off my hips to the floor.

The woman's body stood in contrast. The stretch marks from a past time, had turned from a pale veined pink to more of a stark white, Her breasts lay to the side, not as full nor as firm as he might remember. I folded my clothes and placed them on the vanity. I felt like a teenager at a sleepover.

My God, this is ridiculous. I shook my head. *He must think me a fool.*

I heard a soft tap at the door. "Are you all right?"

"I've been better."

"You know it doesn't matter."

He said it so gently; I wanted to cry.

"Are you coming out?"

"Yes, but get in bed first. I'll be there in a minute."

I took a towel from the shelf, and wrapped it around me. "OK." I took a deep breath. I opened the door to a darkened room. He had read my mind. I pushed the cover back and stood by the bed. I let the towel fall to the floor, and slid beneath the covers.

"I smell jasmine." He nuzzled into my neck.

I moved toward him, brushing back fallen strands of hair. He took my face in his hands and kissed me, under my ear, around my neck, and down my shoulders. I felt a flush over my entire body, like a blush from the sun. I wrapped my arms around him and buried my head in his chest.

He lifted my head, and I lay gently entwined in his arms, wanting to look at him, watch him as he explored my body. I traced his chest, moved my hand across his nipples, down to his stomach and further to the memories I didn't know I had cherished.

He pulled me on top of him. "You don't play fair."

"Why, what do you mean? I asked as I straddled him.

He rolled me over again in the tangled sheets, pulling me close in his embrace.

I gasped as he pushed inside, slow and gentle. I dug my fingers into his back. He slowed, then moved at a steady pace.

Anne Biggs

I lost myself in the rhythm of our lovemaking.

"So you love me?" I whispered, still holding him tight.

"I've loved you from the first day."

"Tell me again."

"Cat, I never stopped loving you. I've loved you forever."

He laid his head on my chest, then slid his body to the side. Still in my arms, I didn't want to move, didn't want to lose what we had.

"Good morning."

I opened my eyes and saw light coming through the window. He sat at the edge of the bed, dressed in sweats, staring, waiting for me to move. I pulled myself up, against the headboard, trying to fluff the pillow.

"I think it's time I feed you at least a little something. I'm going into the kitchen. What would you like for breakfast?"

"It's already morning? I have to go."

"Go where? It's just past seven. It's Sunday. No one will be awake. You don't have to be anywhere."

"I shouldn't have stayed."

"Why not? Come out when you're ready." He closed the door before I could argue with him. I lay looking at the ceiling.

"I've loved you forever."

When I came out, Dylan stood by the table with two cups of coffee,

"My shirt?" he asked, one eyebrow raised.

"It just felt right", I said, taking the mug from him.

"Not shy anymore?"

I set the coffee mug on the counter and opened my shirt. He smiled, "definitely not shy anymore."

I pulled the shirt closed and we sat at the table, toasting our cups.

"I'm so glad I found you, again." His words still took me by surprise. Though we had made love, I blushed at the thought of a commitment. I took a sip of the steaming coffee, then a bite of the toast Dylan had placed in front of me.

Thirty-Three

After breakfast, and a few more kisses, I gathered my things for the drive home. I stashed Dylan's shirt in my purse. Just a little memory. His smell was something I wanted to hold.

He drove me back to Mum's house, keeping his hand on my knee as we drove through the early morning streets, wet from the late-night storm.

He had rescued me. Our history was now our present.

As we sat in Mum's driveway, I leaned over and kissed him on the cheek. He kissed me back, taking my face in both hands.

"We did nothing wrong," he said.

"I know. Thank you."

"For what?"

"For not running away screaming. For not making me feel foolish. For putting up with my reservations about my boobs and stretch marks. For everything."

"Well, just for the record, I kind of like your boobs. And your stretch marks are a work of art. They lead to all sorts of discoveries and insights."

I kissed him again. "I like your body, too," I whispered.

"Good to know, but what's not to like?"

"You're terrible. I'll call you later, after I know more." I pulled him close and hugged him as tight as I could.

I had called Francie from Dylan's. She and Finn were at the house. She would fill me in on the details for Mum's funeral. I waved as he pulled from the driveway and headed back to Dublin Center. He would be at Trinity until seven, when he would come and have dinner.

I found Finn and Francie on the patio. For the first time in two weeks, the sun was out by ten o'clock in the morning.

I dropped into the empty chair and stared back at my sisters. "Are you OK?" Finn asked.

"I shouldn't have left like that."

"Yes, you should have. Michael was crazy. Dylan did the right thing." Francie said.

"I'm so sorry that happened," Finn said.

"I told her about Michael and what had happened. I also told her about Dylan. Do you mind?"

I blushed recalling my evening. It wasn't shame, more a teen-age reaction to an adult situation. I had felt more shame staying with Michael, than being with Dylan.

"I'm fine. You can tell her anything. I am tired of secrets, so think what you like Finn, I am tired of saying what is not real. Do you want details?"

"That's OK, too much information," Francie laughed.

"After what you went through, I'm glad you had Dylan. He seems quite the gentleman."

"I have your papers," Francie added. "When you want them."

"I'm not doing anything about Michael until everything with Mum is settled."

"Well, they are on the table, when you're ready."

"Come on. We have coffee ready. We need to make arrangements," Francie continued, "the hospital called this morning."

"Uncle Connor said that Claire had all the information."

"Is she coming over?" I asked.

"Yes, actually, she's on her way."

"What about Rose?" I asked.

"She won't answer her phone. I don't know."

"This is my fault, isn't it?"

"No. Rose would have found another way to mess things up. You just gave her a new target."

I took the steaming mug from the table and looked around the room. Things were so different, instead of sitting around the table with silly gossip, we were planning Mum's funeral. I hadn't thought about her since Michael stormed into the hospital and then with Dylan I didn't want to think about anything.

"I'm here," Claire called.

She came through the dining room, holding numerous envelopes in her arms. She plopped them on the table and took a seat.

"OK, these are all the things related to your mum's requests. These are the funeral arrangements, and this one is her will."

"What about that one?" Francie asked picking up the smallest of the envelopes.

"Some letters, I think. I never read them, but she asked me to be sure that you girls read them, after she passed."

"Should we wait for Rose?" I asked.

Once again, we had come together, and Rose chose to be an outsider. Besides being ridiculous, her behavior showed a total lack of maturity, even for her.

"I called this morning, but no one answered. I left a message," Claire said.

"I called as well," Francie said.

"I think we just need to at least get her arrangements made at the funeral home," Claire said, pulling out the contents of the largest envelope.

As Claire flipped through the papers I watched and had to smile, thinking how Mum had organized her life. Claire read off the directions. She had the arrangements listed, like one does groceries.

"OK, let's call her one more time, if she doesn't come, we move forward."

I took my cell from my purse and tapped Rose's picture. I set it on the table and put it on speaker. I had nothing to say that no one could hear, even Finn.

"What do you want Catherine?"

"I'm here at Mum's with Francie and Claire...."

"Is Finn there?"

I looked over at Finn and gave her a smile. I would not let her make Finn feel guilty for being with us.

"Yes, of course she is. Claire brought Mum's paperwork, so we were going to make the calls for her arrangements."

"So why are you calling me?"

"You're kidding right? Come on Rose, don't be like this."

"You're acting a little childish," Francie called from across the room.

A hush came over the room. I looked down at my phone to see if she had hung up.

"Rose, don't do this. Not now. If there's ever been a time we needed to come together, it's now."

"You decided who you want to come together with. You don't need me. I'll contact the church to find out when her service is. As long as she is here, you will not be seeing me."

I wanted to throw my phone across the room, drop it in water, anything but to have Finn hear what she said. No one deserved to be talked to like that. I tapped the button and the phone went black. We no longer had any reason to listen.

"OK," I said. "I guess we plan this on our own. I won't reach out to her again.

We spent the rest of the morning making calls and final arrangements. In three days, we would bury Mum next to Da. We would go through her things together, and sort through her valuables like we had done with Da. Finn would find all her letters and pictures that Mum had been so desperate to hide. Francie and I would find lost memories tucked in crevices for safekeeping.

It didn't seem right. We hadn't had enough time. I wanted more time on the bench, or walking in the park, even the late-night calls.

And Finn...I could only begin to imagine. It had taken her so long to find Mum. Now within a week of coming home, Mum died. She only had us, strangers, though our blood said we were sisters. I wondered if we would be enough. If, after time passed and she went home, would she write and text as she had done with Mum. Would she still be part of us?

She sat across from me, dressed in jeans and a simple sweater, her hair tied back, staring and touching the pictures that Francie had brought out for her to see; of Mum and Da, Mum and Claire, and random pictures of Sara and Jonathan. They were her past as well as ours. Without her, Mum would never have met these people. They formed our lives, gave us our foundation.

I found myself being thankful to Finn for every part of my life. Without her, everything would have been different.

Out of nowhere Claire stood up. "We need to go out, a fine lunch, with wine and china, and waiters who wear suits."

"I think that would be grand. We could chat, laugh, and tell Finn about everything she missed not growing up in Dublin." It would be a long time before we would have a chance to laugh, again.

"If I might, since the waiters will be wearing suits, do you think you could gussy yourself up a bit, Catherine? I mean, I know you're comfortable, but..." Claire remarked.

"You mean, I don't look like I'm ready to meet the Queen?" I laughed.

"You look more like a ragamuffin, to be honest."

"Ow!" Francie interjected.

I went upstairs to change.

We grabbed our coats and purses, as we stepped out like schoolgirls ditching a class.

We would deal with Rose and her wrath, another day.

Mum would be buried exactly as she wanted.

Thirty-Four

On the day of the funeral, Finn and I waited at the house for Connor. It would be at the church we all knew so well. Where Mum and Da had married, where we had all been baptized, and where Mum had laid Da to rest. Mum had said her last prayer to Da, and now in an hour, with her guidance, we would say good-bye to her.

While Finn strolled around the yard, I leaned against the French doors and wondered what would happen to Rose. She had been unable to say good-bye to Mum. Could she put her feelings for Finn aside? From talking to her last, she would never make concessions to come together with Finn.

Dylan called, and I stepped onto the patio as we talked. He would meet me at the church and wait until I came for him, but I told him I wanted him standing next to me, holding my hand, being with me as Colin would be with Francie.

Connor arrived at exactly twelve. We greeted him at the door, and without a word, got into the car and drove the mile and a half to the small church. People were already filling the pews. Surprisingly, the skies had cleared. On a day like this, Mum might have skipped church and would have loved spending the day in her garden.

Claire and the girls all came together when they saw us nearing the door. Finn and Devon immediately embraced, even though they had seen each other at the Rosary the night before.

Rose had still not arrived. I couldn't imagine the possibility, but it horrified me to think she would miss her chance to say good-bye out of jealousy. It was something she could never get back.

Mum, obviously loved Finn and had since the day she had been pulled from her arms. *Why couldn't Rose understand that? How could she be so stubborn?*

We had all seen Mum during the Rosary, laid a white rose in her casket, and kissed her cheek. Her directions had been clear—no wake and a closed casket at the funeral.

At her funeral, it was everything she had requested. Francie and I had double-checked, and Claire had confirmed. Her funeral would be the regular Mass she attended each day. Nothing extra, nothing special.

I looked up at the altar, stunned by the beauty of the flowers that filled every inch. They had been sent by life-long friends, and members of her parish who had known her longer than us. Those who knew her through her life, had loved her. This was how they showed it. I waited until Dylan arrived and after we greeted everyone, we took our seats in the front rows of the church. I kept turning around, hoping to see Rose. We were together as a family, except for Rose. No one would have done that to Mum, or so we thought. Francie tapped my leg as Monsignor came up to the altar.

"She's not coming."

"I just don't understand. Why?"

At last, I saw a familiar face. At the far end, stood Rose, separate from her family. Her face sullen, her cheeks pale.

But I could see anger in her eyes, such like never before, and I couldn't understand.

I turned away as the service began. I took hold of Dylan's hand on one side, and Finn's on the other, as we listened to a young voice singing *Amazing Grace,* per her request. I could feel Mum's presence, grasping—in my mind, grasping my shoulder to keep me steady, as she often did.

"Do you understand now?" she whispered. I felt her presence let go of me. I felt the breeze as she left the church.

I understood it all. I understood what she had lost, what she had loved and what she had given up. When the tears came, I was not sure if it was for her or me.

Statues of saints stared down at us, and the candles glowed, splashing images across the wall, people stood and told their stories of the moments they had shared with Mum. I listened as they spoke of Mum's tireless effort to help people, her kindness, sense of humor. Everything that anyone would want to be remembered for. I smiled, thinking to myself the flaws Mum would have acknowledged, but this was her day. She was remembered as everyone had seen her, not how she had seen herself.

The funeral mass came to a close and people began to file out, whispering softly to each other. I saw Rose slip out the side door. We walked out to the last notes of the beloved hymns sung in her honor. Everyone crowded around the front of the church. Finn and Devon remained close to Claire and Connor. I didn't see Rose come up behind us until she was standing directly in front of Finn.

I stood with Dylan hand and hand, ready to face whatever was about to happen. I could have faced it alone, but standing with Dylan gave me power I didn't know I had.

"Perhaps I should go," he whispered, leaning in.

"Don't even think about it," I whispered back. "You won't want to miss this if she steps up."

"Do you really think she would do anything at a funeral?"

"You don't know my sister. Just wait and watch."

"I can't believe this. What right do you have to be at my mother's funeral?" Rose screamed. I moved away from Dylan toward her, to stop her from saying anything she might regret.

Finn reacted first by reaching out her hand. "Hello, I'm Finn." Rose stood stock still, staring straight into Finn's eyes, but not extending her hand.

"Rose, what are you doing?" Francie asked, looking at her older sister, but her response was too late. None of us could have been prepared for Rose's attack.

The slap echoed across the crowd. Finn moved her hand to her mouth, either covering the pain, or the shock.

Rose had only seen Finn in passing. No one had ever said it, but Finn looked exactly like Mum. I didn't know what was worse for Rose, meeting her sister, or realizing the resemblance was so great.

"I had no idea you could be so brazen," Rose mumbled, letting her hand fall to her side.

"Are you OK?" Claire asked wrapping her arm around Finn.

"You have no right." Rose's face had turned ashen.

"She's our sister. We all have the right to be here," Francie said, trying to calm the turmoil that was brewing.

"I will never accept you into this family. I don't care what anyone says, or how you think you fit. I buried my mother today, not yours. You have no idea what she liked, her beliefs, or even her favorite color. You don't know anything about her."

Then she stopped. Her mouth closed and she leaned in

closer to Finn, in an eerie way, almost touching her. For a moment, I thought Rose had seen it, that she understood, then it came, without notice, Rose continued.

"Why did you come here? We were doing fine without you. You had no right to try to claim our mum."

"Rose, you have to stop," Claire asked, moving toward her.

"No, I mean it. Why did she come?" turning toward us and pointing at Finn, as if she were a stranger.

"Rose, you know why she's here. She came because Mum wanted her here. She wanted all of us here. Mum knew she was sick and she wanted all her girls to meet before it was too late, before she forgot everything. You know that."

"I don't believe you," Rose cried.

"I don't really care if you believe it or not," I said.

I looked over at Francie and she looked at Finn, who stood in shock and silence. Though her eyes were red, she held back her tears and stood tall as Rose continued to rage.

Then it stopped. It was over. Rose said nothing more. She turned and crossed the street toward her car. I knew no matter what I did, to Rose it would be taking sides. If I stayed with Finn, I'd betray Rose, and if I went with Rose, I'd betray Mum. No one went after her as she walked away. She drove from the parking lot as everyone watched. I turned away from the chaos she had created and went back to where Dylan and my family stood.

No one said a word.

We moved from the church across the street, to the cemetery in silence. Da's family had been buried at Glassnevin Cemetery, but he had requested the privacy of a small cemetery in the town where he had raised his family. The headstones did not lean so far over, nor were the crosses broken, but the names dated back long before our parents moved to Finglas. Though small, groundkeepers kept the stones cleaned and family members replaced flowers daily. The gate to the small cemetery always remained open and mourners were found at all hours praying for their loved ones.

The sun disappeared, and we waited under the overcast sky while everyone gathered. We remained in small circles, chatting in vague conversations, waiting for the ground beneath our feet to implode.

Monsignor began the services. We all stood motionless, frozen through the process of honoring Mum. I tried to pay attention, but I couldn't erase the memory of Rose assaulting Finn.

Half the people left after witnessing Rose's attack. The family remained together until the last prayer and the official lowering of the casket. It angered me that people considered leaving, but then I wondered if I stood in their shoes, and witnessed the attack, would I feel comfortable staying? I recalled the ritualistic actions of the services, and held on to Dylan, trying to figure out what Mum would have thought of everything that just happened.

My heart ached. I could feel my muscles twist, the physical pain of the shock. My mother deserved better. I watched the remainder of people file out, like going down aisles of a church. A few came and acknowledged my sisters and me, others nodded, and just walked to their cars.

I was so angry at Rose for not being able to understand, for judging so harshly.

I looked at Finn, standing motionless, seemingly empty. Even with Connor and Claire holding her back, Rose had made herself heard, and it would be a long time before her actions would be forgotten. For me, I could never forgive.

"Are you OK?" Dylan asked, wrapping his arms around me.

"Jesus, tell me that didn't happen?" I looked over at him, my jaw tightening, unable to even raise my head.

"Oh no. It happened. I'm pretty sure everyone saw it. Do you think she is OK?"

"I don't know what to think." I shoved my hands deep in my coat pockets and looked up at him. "None of us are OK. I can't believe she did that, not here, not now. What the hell was she thinking?" I whispered, leaning into his shoulder.

"I think your sister is in a great deal of pain."

"You know what?" I continued whispering. "I don't care. Everything about what she did was wrong. I will never forgive her."

"I don't think you mean that," he said, pulling me close.

"Dylan, I know you're trying to be understanding, but this is too much. Nothing can justify what she did. We're all confused and angry and hurt, but none of us acted like that. My mother would never have treated anyone like that, and Da? He's rolling over in his grave right now. I can guarantee that."

"It's worse for her. She feels like she lost everything."

"You're doing a really good job of defending her, and you don't even know her. I'm having a hard time forgiving her for anything."

"She wouldn't expect your forgiveness because she doesn't think she did anything wrong. She doesn't see what is going on. She is just lashing out and she knows Finn can't fight back."

"That makes me even madder."

"So, what happens now?" Dylan asked.

"I don't know." I turned and looked up. "I imagine it will be a long time before she'll come to the house."

"Are you going home?"

"I need to be with my sisters, especially after everything that just happened."

"Can I see you after everyone leaves?"

"Can I call you? I don't know what's going on. I can't believe what a fiasco today turned out to be."

"Of course. Do you want me to take you back?"

"I think I better go back with Finn and Francie."

"OK. I understand. I'll be home all evening."

"You can come to the house if you want," I said, knowing that possibility would be unlikely.

"No, I don't think I belong at your house right now. Call me when you're ready."

I walked away from Dylan, feeling secure in a way I hadn't felt in a very long time. I could get through the rest of the day, if I knew I could be with him later. He was my one piece of sanity. I turned and watched as he got into his car and drove down the narrow road.

I went to where Francie and Colin stood, holding on to our very distraught sister. We had failed to keep her safe from the wrath of Rose. I'd regret that for years to come.

"Is everyone all right?" I asked, looking back and forth between Finn and Francie.

"What the hell was that?" Francie asked, putting her arm around Finn. "Wow. OK, I know Rose can be a little off, but that was bat shit crazy."

Claire couldn't take her eyes off our wounded sister.

There was only family left, so we walked across the street

to the church. I whispered to Francie that I'd ride with Colin
and her. She nodded and opened the door for Finn, who
crawled in next to Devon. I came in behind her.

Colin waited as the other cars pulled out, then fell into
line. He looked into the mirror at me, and I saw confusion
in his face. I nodded and gave a half smile back to him.
There was nothing to say. No words could explain what had
happened.

Thirty-Five

Rose had made her message clear. After the funeral debacle, I wasn't even sure if Finn would stay another day. I couldn't comprehend how Devon must have felt seeing her mother assaulted. I half expected them to grab a cab at the cemetery, but they remained encased in the family.

Rose's outburst destroyed any sense of decorum, for the people who had come to celebrate Mum's life. Hell, half of them left before the graveside service. I think they decided to go home, go shopping, get a drink, anything but come back and watch another confrontation

No one came to the house after the service. By two o'clock, Francie and I had cleaned up the last of the dishes and put the untouched food in the refrigerator. We closed the front door knowing no one would be coming. Finn stayed in the garden, even as the rain began again, petting the few remaining buds that peeked their heads through the winter storms. She bent down, stroked the swan planter, then walked around the garden that had become sacred to us all. Claire went out and stood with her for a while, though we couldn't hear what she said, after a few minutes they both walked back into the house, arm in arm.

Rose slipped through the front door as we had all taken

a seat at the dining table. She had changed from her pearls and black matching pumps into jeans and a sweater, her hair brushed out, her make-up wiped away. She actually looked quite beautiful.

Claire greeted her in the living room, whispering something. The first outburst came as soon as Rose moved away from Claire.

"You can't stop me. I have something to say, and you're all going to listen."

We sat at the dining room table, watching, not sure how to act. Surely wondering what she could have to say that she hadn't already.

"I'm sorry." Her voice was so low, I barely heard the words, like she was struggling more to breathe than to talk. "It was wrong. It was a disgrace and I never meant to do that. I never meant to do that to Mum's memory."

"Sorry? That's what you have to say?" I cried out before anyone could stop me.

"Yes. I said I was sorry."

I guess she thought if she said it louder, it would have more meaning. It didn't. Finn turned away and stared into the garden, unable to even look at her.

"That isn't enough," Francie said, looking more riled than I'd seen her in a long time. "You owe Finn an apology, not just walking through the door saying, I'm sorry. You owe us all an apology after what you did."

"You're right. I was wrong to do that, and I know I'm sorry doesn't make up for any of it."

Claire kept her balance as we listened to Rose, looking back and forth at each other, wondering who had walked in the door. She looked like Rose, but in the last six weeks I had never heard her utter a kind word and now she was apologizing. It was hard to take it all in. Rose walked in to the dining room with bowed head and trembling fingers.

"I can't give you a reason for what I did. I don't think I even know. It was all too much, too soon. I'll say it here and you can all hate me if you want, but I hate that you came back," she said staring straight at Finn. "I hate that she might have loved you and thought of you every single day, while she was with us."

"Why are you blaming her?" Francie asked.

"Because I wanted Mum to myself."

"Mum loved us all, equally," I said.

"Did she, now?"

"How can you say that with a clear conscience? You have your two girls. Do you love one more than the other?" Claire asked.

"Of course not."

"Your Mum was no different. She loved you all. You had no idea what she went through having to give Finn away, the way they treated her."

"I told you I'm sorry. I don't have anything more to say. You can accept it or not."

Rose slumped into the chair, dropping her head to her hands.

In the corner, Claire whispered to the grandkids. They all stood, grabbed their coats and phones and headed toward the door, not saying a word. Izzy looked at me, though she didn't say anything, her silence spoke volumes. I could see the fear in her eyes. She had never seen such rage, not even from her father. She walked out with Devon. Paddy walked out with Marie and Jean.

"The kids are going out," Claire called from the dining room.

Claire followed them to the front door and waited until each crossed the entryway. Claire came back and took the only empty chair. Rose remained in her seat at the head of the table.

"I don't know if this is the time or not, but since we have everyone together, I think we need to talk about something. Rose, we appreciate your apology, but your actions were outrageous, so it's going to take a while to be civil, but you need to hear this."

Rose fumbled with the edge of her ears, scrambling for something to hold on to. The rest of us watched as Claire took control of the room.

"Your mum pretty much took charge of her life, in the years after your Da passed. She wanted things to go certain ways, and she set about to make sure they did. I know you're going to be angry that she didn't include you in her decisions, but that was your mum, and quite simply, it was her right."

Claire spoke in a soft, soothing voice. Francie had a smile on her face, lost in thought. Rose sat tense, waiting for Claire to come out with some disparaging remark. And then there was Finn. I couldn't imagine what might be going through her head, as she sat quietly, her arms clasped together, her eyes intense and unmoving.

I was relieved. This had been a long journey and now with Claire presenting the finale, we could all let it go, and move on.

Maybe what Claire had to show us would reaffirm Finn's rightful place in the family.

"I have four envelopes that were given to me by your mother. I don't know what's inside, but before she died, we were able to talk. She was coherent and very lucid."

"How would we know that?" Rose blurted.

"Because I'm telling you so. I have no reason to lie. I have no hidden agenda, but before I give you these envelopes, I think you all need to know a little something. Some of you know, others have refused to listen, so I'm going to try to present it one more time. Then I'll leave the envelopes with you and I'll go. If you want to tear yourselves apart, it won't be my doing."

"I think we owe it to Mum, to listen to what Claire has to say," Francie said, placing her hands on top of the table.

I looked around the room, knowing what Claire would tell us, and positive that Finn and I were the only ones who knew the whole story.

"OK, here goes. I met your Mum at Castlepollard, on my first nursing job. Her parish priest brought her in after she became pregnant from a rape. Her Da sent her way and her Mum did nothing to stop it. I helped her deliver Finn, when the time came. While in the Home, she experienced tremendous abuse." She stopped and took a drink of tea, then continued. "Beside me, she had Sara. You all remember Sara? The tiny bundle of energy who filled your mum's life with laughter and kindness. After nine days they sent Finn off to an orphanage, she and Sara were sent to a Laundry in Dublin to work. It wasn't the kind of job you're used to, getting paid every week. It was hard labor. While there, the abuse continued in ways you could never imagine."

Claire took a breath and looked around the table. Rose began to tinker with the ends of her hair. Finn, had tears in her eyes. Francie dropped her head into her hands. I looked straight ahead, sitting tall, because I knew if I slouched, even a little, I would crumble.

"While your mother was in the Laundries she met Jonathan. You all know him."

Everyone but Rose nodded.

"I never met Jonathan, but Alice told me about him," Finn said, leaning forward.

"A priest at the Laundries took advantage of your Mum." Claire took a deep breath, then stopped.

"He raped her, repeatedly. He did things to her that she could never speak aloud."

Rose suddenly looked up. "I don't believe you."

"It is not my job to make you believe me. What you do with what I'm telling you, is up to you."

"She would have told us," Rose said.

"You think so?" Francie looked over at her. "You couldn't even tell us that your girls moved out and your husband isn't sleeping in your bed any more. Catherine couldn't tell us her husband beat her. You think Mum could have told what a priest did to her, the way she felt about the church?"

"We were her daughters," Rose said.

"And that's why. Don't you understand Rose?" Claire looked straight at her. "Your mother loved you. She never wanted to hurt you. She never wanted you to think worse of her because of what she had been through."

"Did she ever tell Da any of this?" Francie asked.

"That's the irony of it all. Your mum thought she was protecting him as well, so she kept it from him, or so she thought."

"What do you mean?" Rose asked, truly engaged for the first time.

"Jonathan made sure that your Da knew everything. Jonathan felt responsible to keep her protected because no one ever had. He had to be sure Aidan would love her, in spite of what she had been through. He told him everything. While she was keeping her secret, he was keeping it, as well."

"You're lying," Rose said moving away from the table. Connor grabbed hold of her arm.

"You just sit and listen," Connor said, not letting her go.

"My God girl, why would I lie? Hasn't there been enough lying going on in this family? I would think that you would all be glad that the secrets have come out."

"Rose, you have to stop this. You say you love Mum so much and that you want her protected, yet every time you learn a new truth, you lash out." I tried to keep my voice calm, but now it seemed the only one hurting us was Rose. Finn looked over at Claire, then Connor and took a deep breath.

"I have something to say," Finn said.

"No one cares about what you have to say," Rose shot back, finally looking over at her.

"You have every right to speak," said Claire.

"I have something that I don't think any of you know about. Well...Claire and Catherine know. When I met *my mother* for the first time, I gave her a medal on a string that she had given me at birth. When I met her, I wanted her to have it back. Most of you know about that."

"She has it in her jewelry box, upstairs," I broke in.

"What you don't know, is what she gave me. I can prove I'm not lying, that I do belong here, that I am your sister. Rose, you must know I never intended to hurt you. I kept your mother's secret for almost ten years without calling any of you. I had your phone numbers, I knew where you lived, and I knew your children's names. Catherine, I knew you were in Boston, but I never contacted you because she asked me not to. She didn't want any of you to be hurt, but most of all, she was afraid of what you would think of her."

"I can't listen to this anymore. I'm leaving," Rose said,

getting up from the chair, stepping away from the table, but Connor still held tight to her arm.

"I've had about enough of this," Connor said, pulling Rose down to the empty seat. "You've been making everybody miserable with your attitude, and your half-assed apology. You can't deny it anymore and if you love your mother the way you say you do. You'll stop this nonsense now. You'll listen to Claire and thank God that your mother loved you so much."

At that point Finn stood up and went upstairs without a word. We all watched. Once out of sight, we immediately turned toward Rose.

"Why don't you just wait to see what Finn has to show us?" I said. "If you want to leave after that, then you can go with our blessing."

"We can't keep beating this dead horse. We can't make you do something you are dead-set against," Francie said. "But, Uncle Connor is right. Mum wanted us to know these things, so we could better understand her, not just as our mother, but as a woman. You have to give her that." Francie looked over at Rose, her face tight.

The only thing keeping Rose in her seat was Connor holding tight to her wrist. I had never seen my sister in such a state. The entire family had finally stood up to her, not allowed her to belittle or ridicule what they said. She slumped back in the chair, still holding her purse, but not looking at us. I held my arm across my stomach, worried what would come of this, what her rage would be like.

In a few minutes, Finn came down the stairs carrying three books and Claire came back in to the living room holding another envelope. They were leather bound journals. Finn sat down and placed her treasures on the table.

"I have three volumes of journals your Mum wrote," Finn started. "I learned all about you, and your life here in Finglas. I learned about her life in the Home and the Laundry. She wrote about the abuse, and her fears, and her hatred for what her parents had done, and how she would never let any of you experience what she had gone through."

No one moved. It was as if Finn had placed a sacred text on the table. We stared in awe, as if we were waiting for it to come.

Rose reached for one of the books. "You're lying, Mum never kept a journal. I don't believe these are hers," she said.

"You have to believe me, I'm not lying. They are in her handwriting. Look at them. They're her words," Finn pleaded. "She gave them to me so I would understand why she signed me away, that she didn't want to. Maybe she had to write it down for herself, so when she went back to it, she knew that it really happened. I don't think she ever wanted to forget."

"How do we know they really say what happened?"

"Then read every word, Rose. Learn about your Mum as a young woman. She wrote so much. She had so many feelings about her life, that she had been too afraid to tell anyone. And your Da, he knew about them and he loved her still."

It terrified me to think Rose might tear apart the one thing that connected us all. She didn't. As she flipped through them, she slowed down, everything about her almost came to a screeching halt.

"Please remember they are mine. She gave them to me. I want to take them home. You all have your real memories. I just have the words she wrote on the pages. I don't know if the words were meant for just me, or if she freed herself from her past, but they're enough for me."

Finn handed a journal to each of us, on the cover, *"The Swan Garden."*

Francie held one of the volumes, then looked over at Claire. "You said you had something else. What is it?"

"I have the letter your Da left for your Mum when he died, telling her how he learned about everything and how much he still loved her. I think you should all read it. So you can really understand the relationship your parents had."

"That's private isn't it? I don't think we should be reading that," I said, staring at the yellowed envelope Claire had placed on the table.

"It was your mum's idea. She asked me to be sure to have each of you read it."

"I know what you are all trying to do. You don't fool me. Well I can't do it and I won't. I knew my Mum. I knew what she believed and how she lived her life." Rose pulled her arm out of Connor's grip.

"I will have the letter when you are ready to read it. If you think you need to go, we aren't going to stop you anymore," Claire said.

Rose got up from the table, and looked around at all of us. "You have no idea what it's been like."

"She was our mother as well, Rose. We are all devastated by her death, but you're refusing to accept who she is. She was more than just our mother. She had a life before us. She had secrets, along with hopes and dreams. I believe these journals, and I believe she loved us all. You, me, Catherine, and Finn. Finn, maybe more, because of what she sacrificed," Francie said, still seated at the table.

"She doesn't know her," Rose screamed. "She has no idea what our life was like. She is not her child."

"You are wrong Rose," Claire said, moving over to stand in front of her.

"She was every way her child. It was not your Mum's

choice that Finn was taken from her. How can you be so cruel, pretending that she isn't even here in the same room?"

"I don't have to put up with this." Rose went to the couch, grabbed her keys and went out the door. No one went after her. The conversation didn't stop. It had stopped too many times, because of her.

Thirty-Six

Claire read Da's final letter to Mum, aloud. The words filled in the blanks of my parent's life. Da had loved her with a kindness that Michael would never know. He had listened when she had no words. He had trusted, when all others failed her.

The letter solidified memories that had once been vague. Their undying love had kept our family together. I didn't understand how he could capture her memories between the pages. He gave us a view we could have never imagined, capturing their life in moments of sadness and joy. I had no idea about Da in this way and for the first time I envied my mother for the love she held.

I looked at my sisters, seeing how simple differences separated us, from torn jeans, to diamond studs. And then Finn, she came across the world to claim her family. I didn't know Finn well enough to know our differences, but I came to realize we were the core of the family Da had created from love. Why hadn't we learned from it? Why did we pretend, like children, that we had no clue how to understand any part of it?

I walked around the room, stepped back to take in a view I might never see again. My sisters listened to the *real* stories of their ancestry; the strands that had been woven to form our tapestry. But in this love story, I learned that I had no idea how Mum had loved, what she had endured. It broke me that I had been so selfish.

As she read Da's letter, Francie and I grabbed one of the journals. I couldn't wait to read the memories my mother had written. I knew they were her moments, that alone would help me heal. I could not speak for anyone else, most of all, not Rose. I didn't know if Rose could ever heal.

I knew Finn had read them, again and again. If I had the chance, I'd have done the same, until I had memorized them. After an hour of discussion about a past that needed no debate, Claire left her place at the table and went to the kitchen. We all agreed that enough had been said for one day. We took a break.

Connor and Claire toasted Mum with a glass of whiskey. I followed Francie into the garden and took a seat on the bench while she fingered the lilacs. The garden Mum had cherished with every part of her being, lay in front of us. We had survived her loss. We had not been destroyed. Like her garden, we had weathered another storm.

"Getting away from all the excitement?" I asked.

"I don't know if I'd call it excitement... perhaps foolery," Francie looked over at me, her fingers playing with the vines.

"Why do you think she did it?"

"Rose?" Francie brushed her curls back from her face. "Because she's Rose. She will always be Rose. The one who pushes everyone beyond their limits."

"I'm afraid for her. She's alone. She's helpless and so angry."

"It is all her own doing. She pushed her girls away, and poor Charlie, he doesn't know what to make of her," Francie continued. "He lasted as long as any man could, even longer I suppose. I think he thought he could save her."

"How did you do it?"

"Do what?"

"Keep it all together? Come out unscathed?" I asked.

"You think I'm unscathed? You think our broken family left me untouched? Think again, dear sister."

"Oh, come on Francie, look at you. You've kept it together, in spite of it all."

She got up from the bench and walked across the yard, and took hold of the vines that blew in the breeze. "I had no expectations. Remember," she said, "I was the baby, I had the opportunity to watch my sisters screw up. I watched dress rehearsals my whole life."

"Did we screw up that bad?"

"No," she turned toward me with a smile. "You let love slip through your fingers, now and again. You had huge expectations for yourself."

"And you didn't?" I asked.

"You have to remember, I didn't go into life expecting anything from myself, or anyone else. You and Rose expected so much from everyone. I never understood where you got the drive. Mum and Da were thrilled with every minute of every day to have what they had. I saw it in their eyes. I tried to do the same. It made a difference in how I viewed the world."

"Why didn't we see that?" I asked, perplexed by her perception.

"You were busy wanting more, expecting everything to be better. Rose more than you, though." She took hold of my hand. "It's OK, we just look at the world different."

"But Rose?" I asked, knowing by pure luck that I had

survived my expectations better.

"There's something about Rose that she hides from people. I don't know what it is, but it separates her from everyone who tries to love her."

"What do you think it could be?" I got up from the bench and strolled around the garden.

"She had a time. Remember when she went off to London for a while, just before she and Charlie got married? She told everyone she needed some time. She wrote that she had gotten a job and would be staying for a while. Less than a year later, she came home and they got married."

"Where was I?"

"All caught up in your own life. I think you were at Trinity. I remember a phone conversation Mum had with her."

"What did she say?" I asked.

Francie took a seat on the bench. "I remember her telling Rose that whatever she was planning, was not a good idea. She told her it would backfire and that she'd lose him."

"What else?" I asked, engrossed in an event of Rose's life that I had missed.

"I didn't hear anything else, Mum shushed me out of the room. But I remember thinking she must have lied about something, maybe to Charlie."

"Rose wasn't the only one. I failed as well, maybe not as bad, but my marriage crumbled like ashes," I said.

"You had no idea," Francie came and stood next to me. "He never showed himself to you."

"No, I should have seen it. I should have known," I shook my head.

"And what do you see in Dylan? Is he the one?"

"I'm not making the same mistake with him," I said.

"Do you love him?" Francie asked, as she grabbed a flower from a free-floating vine.

I stopped in my tracks and realized I couldn't answer the question. "I don't know." I took a deep breath and looked at the world around me.

"Then you ARE a foolish girl," Francie said, tipping her head.

"Why do you say that? Sounds a bit arrogant to me."

"I remembered Dylan. He loved you. I saw it in his eyes. Not how he touched you, but how he perceived you in his life. You had him, and you let him go. I thought you were foolish then. I hope you're not so foolish now."

"What are you saying, without saying, may I ask?"

"I'm saying that you need to go to him. There's nothing more to be said. You have plenty of time to unravel Mum's live, I think it is time you unravel yours."

"I've been with him. You know that don't you?"

"Good for you. It's about time."

"Francie, what if I can't unravel my life?"

"Cate, you're a grown woman, it is time you figure it out."

"How did you do it?"

"Do what?" she asked.

"Never mind, I think I know." I reached over and hugged her before she had a chance to pull away.

My smart baby sister had a big heart. She never took herself too seriously, and had found everything she needed in her life to be happy. I should take heed.

Thirty-Seven

The Garden of Nails

Two days after Mum's service, on the day Finn and Devon were to leave for Oregon, Claire arranged a simple brunch at the Alex, a restaurant near Stephen's Green. After two hours of chatter, we stood, each gathering our coats, expecting this to be our formal good-bye to Finn and Devon.

Claire slightly tapped her glass with a spoon. Her age had become more evident over the last couple of weeks.

"I know that everyone is busy, but I'd like you to indulge me." She looked around the table, making sure that we all read her expression. "I'd like you to spend a few more hours with me. I promise to have everyone back by two this afternoon."

"Claire, I don't mean to be rude, but I have work." Claire took hold of Jean's hand as she stood to make the first attempt to leave. I couldn't see the look that Claire gave Jean, but she sat down, pulled out her phone and sent a text.

I looked over at Francie, then at Finn. "I have no problem with that," Finn said, "as long as we are back by three. We need to be at the airport by four. Our flight is at six-thirty."

"I promise, you'll be at the airport in plenty of time." Claire smiled. "Your Mum would have wanted this. There's a place she'd have liked all of you to see together, but time slipped away. Well the time is as right as it will ever be."

"Where are you taking us?" Marie questioned, as she squirmed in her chair.

"It's already been arranged. Paddy will drive the cousins." Claire looked over and gave him a weak smile. He squeezed her veined hand, winked at her with what must have been a shared secret.

"Francie, you'll drive the rest of us to Castlepollard?"

"You know I will."

I had expected the cousins to bring up excuses as Marie had attempted, but they said nothing, just pulled on their coats and lined up behind Paddy.

Looking over at Claire, I saw a resolve in her reddened eyes. We would all go. There was no question. Claire was moving in on her last steps with Mum. She was taking a part of her home by taking us there. We were all so close. We had lived in the vicinity our entire lives, but never took the drive out past Dublin. Today would change all that. I didn't know for sure, but something told me once again that Finn and Devon knew way more than any of us about where we were going.

The sign read Castlepollard, 25 kl. I looked over and watched Finn as she stared out beyond the road. She sat tense. I reached over and held her hand.

"You all right?"

"Just anxious I guess. We've been there before."

"I might have thought as much. You seem to know so much more about our history then we do."

"Don't feel bad," she said. "You had no reason to search. You had your life, your mum, everything was right here. I didn't, so I kept searching. You do that when pieces are missing. I can't explain why you just keep going until all the pieces are together. It just took me longer than usual."

"I'm so glad you did. We all are."

"That is debatable, as we've seen over the last week," Finn said.

"Oh, no. You could have come in with a grocery list and Rose would have questioned its very existence."

Even though she made all the sense in the world, I could see the doubt seeping in to the corner of her eyes. She wanted so much for us to understand what this journey had been like, but we had failed her miserably. I took hold of her hand in the back seat and patted it, as I might have Mum's if we were going on a journey.

"This is where I learned everything about you," she said leaning in, "about what happened. Mum's secret." I sat back at that, thinking about Mum and all those years she held everything in, hid them away like one does a treasure.

"I don't think this is for us. I think Claire needs this to pass Mum's legacy on, so it'll no longer be a secret. So we can all be free of it."

I heard Claire give the last of the directions to Francie when we reached the turnabout in Castlepollard Village.

"You'll see a long gray driveway on the right, take that turn."

Francie slowed. "I got this." I looked up to the mirror and saw Francie smile. Somehow we both knew what was about to unfold.

Before long, massive gray buildings stood before us, towering over the lush lawn in an iconic contrast. Once we were up the hill, both cars stopped in the driveway. Umbrellas protected us from the rain as we stepped from the car.

"This is it? Isn't it?" Marie asked, turning around staring at the gray structures, seemingly for the first time.

The windows were piled in rows, separated by pipes. They looked like boxes, one atop of the other, but connected. Jean pulled her coat tight around her shoulders, holding her umbrella against the wind.

"This place is eerie. I feel like ghosts are looking out through the windows," Izzy said, swirling around in circles as she took everything in.

"It looks like a prison. It's just missing the bars on the windows. I couldn't imagine anyone being here," Jean said, focusing her attention on the two small bunkers standing in front of us.

"Alice, your mother," looking over at Francie and me, "and your grandmother," she continued looking over at each of Alice's grandchildren, "were here for five months and nine days," Claire said with a flat tone. "I was here, as well. I helped the girls, like your mum, deliver their babies." Paddy and Izzy huddled next to Marie and Jean.

"So, this is where everything changed for her?" Jean asked, looking more shocked than saddened.

"I was the first to hold her." Finn brushed tears from her face and took hold of Claire's hand.

"How bad was it?" Paddy asked.

"I looked out for her the best I could, but I couldn't stop the beatings, or the abuse."

"This place is awful," Jean said, walking over to the

chipped door of the closest building. She touched the tarnished handle. Her hand lingered a moment. "The windows are broken." She peered in, then looked back at the rest of us.

"The girls came through those doors when they worked in the garden. Alice was not allowed in the garden. She stayed inside. She cleaned the banisters and floors. Do you remember how she always drenched her hands in lotion? How she wore massive rubber gloves when she cleaned?"

"Because of this place?" Izzy asked, joining Jean at the window as they peered in.

"Yes. They washed the laundry and the floors with pure lye soap. It nearly ate their skin away." Claire tucked herself under Paddy's umbrella to keep from the rain.

Together they walked toward the smaller bunker style building that stood in front of the tall three story empty structure.

Paddy peered into the window. "There's a cot inside and a sink. What was this used for? It's too small to be an infirmary."

"The Sisters called it the "screaming room," Devon broke in. She looked over at Claire who nodded for her to continue. The torch had been passed. "Girls were taken from the infirmary if they made too much noise." She paused and ran her hand along the peeling trim of the black door. "When their contractions came close enough, they were allowed back inside to deliver." She placed her hand on the door to push it open.

The tightness in Marie's face changed. She softened, and touched the wall. "It's cold, and wet."

Claire led us across the lawn to a narrow, tarred path that took us deeper into a forest atmosphere. We swept long branches to the side, and ducked from the clinging grasps of vines.

With Claire and Paddy leading the way, it wasn't long before we arrived at a small wrought-iron gate with a metal cross embedded in the formation.

We unlatched and pushed the gate open, not even a squeak marked its movement. We stepped onto the lawn and sunk into the wet ground. There stood a long narrow plot of lush green grass. A bare rock wall stood to one side, the opposite wall, not as tall, was covered in moss and variegated ivy.

Even in its loveliness there was an unnerving sense about it that seeped into my bones. It was cold and isolated. Where the ivy dangled over the rock wall, my eyes were drawn to the color of ribbons floating in the air.

"Where are we?" Jean asked, stepping over to the wall and running her hand along the rocks.

"It's a cemetery," Claire said, "They call it 'The Angels' Plot.'"

"Where are the gravestones?" Izzy asked.

"There are none, only mass graves," Claire said in a hushed tone.

The questions stopped. The stillness spoke for itself. The rain continued, softened to a mist. Steady, but light, as if frozen in time, back to the moment each infant may have been buried. I bowed my head, feeling that I had violated this sacred ground by even walking on it.

"How many?" I asked.

How did we not know any of this? We lived here. This was our country. I felt this incredible shame, as if I had been the one to lay them in the ground, to perpetuate this terrible secret.

Suddenly Claire stepped out from under Paddy's umbrella, toward Jean, who was running the palm of her hand along the rock wall. "Do you feel anything?"

"There are nails in the stones?"

"Worker's nails. They cover the entire wall," Devon added, touching the stones herself.

"There must be hundreds of them," Jean said in amazement.

"It is said, there are over five hundred in this wall alone." Devon spoke up again. "After the 1930s, when the babies died, the caretaker who buried them, hammered nails into the wall." She paused, "so they would never be forgotten."

"And the ribbons?" Jean asked.

"A few years ago, survivors held a Remembrance. They put ribbons there to honor those who died," Claire said.

I looked over at Finn standing in silence, her hands shoved deep into her pockets. How the hell, did we not know about this? It is a piece of our heritage.

"So, is this the end of the secrets" Francie asked. "Can we let go now?"

"Yes, along with Meadow's Glenn," Claire said.

We walked the full length of the plot. At the back wall, a curved stone was partially buried. It read:

IN MEMORY
OF GOD'S SPECIAL
ANGELS ACCEPTED
IN THIS CEMETARY

"Your Mum wanted you to know this history," Claire said.

Claire tugged at Paddy who leaned down, allowing her to

whisper. He smiled, and patted his jacket pocket. As we stood in the rain, Claire motioned for us to draw closer. In a few moments, we had formed a circle.

The rain rolled off our umbrellas. We didn't pray or sing, just bowed our heads in silence. I dropped Izzy's hand and reached to touch a jagged nail.

Claire reached over to Paddy. He slipped purple ribbons from his pocket and handed them out. "I brought ribbons for everyone," she said. "Choose a nail and tie a ribbon around it, for whatever memory you hold dear." She spoke with such tenderness; tears filled her eyes.

Paddy took his ribbon and reached as high as he could, choosing a twisted rusted nail that protruded. "This is for you, Grandma."

Marie bent down and tied her ribbon, and with a bowed head said. "This is for my mother, that someday she will embrace our past."

Francie knotted her ribbon tight. She looked over at Paddy with tears in her eyes. "This is for my boy, and Mum, who had the strength to spare us."

Izzy moved along and picked a nail at eye level and tied her ribbon. "This is for my grandmother, who found the strength to survive."

With tears streaming, Jean stepped forward, picked a nail covered in moss. She entwined her ribbon. "That some day mum will stop being so angry."

Claire motioned for me to step forward. I took my ribbon and walked a ways down the wall, finding a protruding nail. "My ribbon is for you, Finn," I whispered.

Claire added a final ribbon, moving farther down the wall. "This is for Alice and Sara, who fought so hard to be free."

One by one, each of us touched the nails with newly placed

ribbons. I turned back one last time, knowing I would come back someday with my grandchildren. I would come back to keep her memory alive, to keep the story as more than just a tale of times past. Rain trickled down the walls, the ribbons blurred in the mist.

Acknowledgements

This sequel came about when I wondered what it would be like for my birth-mother's daughters to meet me. I imagined that they would all respond in a very different manner. Each sister was created in the sense of how I saw it unfolding.

I hope someday, I will have the chance to tell it like it really happens.

There is a special place for three ladies who opened their hearts and let me inside. For Gayle, your incredible depth and knowledge. Karen for being able to look past and find a deeper meaning, and Kathy for always knowing no matter what, we had somehow walked in the same shoes.

To Janice Stevens and our writing class, for everyday making me better.

To our "Friday Writers" Gayle, Kara and Susan, we always found the time because it was that important.

My children, Aaryn for your vision and Kyle for never questioning what this journey has meant to me.

My grandchildren, Kyler, Kasen and Madden, so you will know that when I couldn't be there with you, that I really was writing.

HBEPublishing, Dan and Peggy Dunklee, your unwavering support, guidance and love for Alice, Claire, and Finn brings me to my knees.

CPSIA information can be obtained
at www.ICGtesting.com
Printed in the USA
FSOW01n2116260218
45059FS